Fade to Blue

Books by Bill Moody

Solo Hand
Death of a Tenor Man
Sound of the Trumpet
Bird Lives!
Looking for Chet Baker
Shades of Blue
Fade to Blue

Fade to Blue

An Evan Horne Mystery

Bill Moody

Poisoned Pen Press

Poisoned Pen Press
6962 E. First Ave., Ste. 103
Scottsdale, AZ 85251
www.poisonedpenpress.com
info@poisonedpenpress.com

Printed in the United States of America

For Emily, who has made all the difference.

Acknowledgments

Special thanks to three good friends. Captain Tom Mapes retired, Santa Monica Police for his expertise with law enforcement. Composer and arranger Reg Powell for insight into composing music for film, and Fred Caruso for an informed look behind the scenes in moviemaking and the politics of Hollywood.

Four Bar Intro

I'm at Ruth Price's Jazz Bakery in Culver City, California and this time not as a sub for Monty Alexander or anyone else. This is my own gig. Three nights, my old friends Buster Browne on bass and Gene Sherman on drums. The first night has gone all too quickly.

I glance at my watch and turn toward them. One more tune will do it. "Pretty Eyes," I say. Buster nods and wipes down the fret board on his bass with a cloth as Gene pulls out his brushes.

I look down at the keyboard for a moment then lean in toward the microphone. "We're going to close out this evening with a beautiful waltz by Horace Silver called 'Pretty Eyes'." I see Andie in the front row reach over and squeeze Coop's arm and smile as I count off the tempo.

Gene's brushes smooth us in as Buster's bass line sets up the vamp for the theme. We glide through the changes in the concert hall quiet of this no-drinks-served atmosphere, gradually building in intensity through four choruses. Buster takes over for two more, managing some free-like lines but never losing the feel and pulse of the tempo. We ease back into the theme that had once been used as a jingle for the soft drink Tab. That always makes me smile.

The applause is generous as we finish the set. Ruth Price comes up and takes the mike. "Let's hear it once again for the Evan Horne Trio. They'll be back for two more nights."

The *Los Angeles Times* had done a short piece for our opening, which might partially account for the good crowd. But the article once again mentioned that I was not only a jazz pianist, but also a sometime-detective. I'm used to it now so I just accept it. It's publicity and that puts more people in the seats, and that makes Ruth Price happy.

The house lights come up as I gather my music and the guys start packing up. Ruth turns to me and hands me a business card. "This guy wants to see you," she says.

I glance at the card. Grant Robbins Creative Talent, it says. "He's some kind of Hollywood agent," Ruth says. "Maybe he's going to make you a movie star." She laughs. "I'll send him back."

Andie and Coop make their way to the piano. Andie gives me a kiss and Coop pats my shoulder. "Nice, baby," Andie says. "Very nice."

"You done good, sport," Coop says.

"Thanks, Coop. Some agent wants to talk to me, so I'll meet you guys in the lobby."

"Don't be long," Coop says. "I'm hungry."

Ruth is waiting in the small backstage dressing room with a tall wiry man in thick, black-rimmed glasses and a suit that could probably pay for our whole three-night gig.

"Evan, Grant Robbins," Ruth says.

Robbins takes my hand and pumps it with just a little too much enthusiasm. "Wonderful, just wonderful," he says. "Lot of Bill Evans in you, isn't there?"

"Thanks. Well, I hope so." I wonder if he really gets it, or is he just name-dropping. Why is it people in other fields want to impress you with their own limited knowledge? We sit down and Robbins crosses his legs, straightens the crease in his suit pants, and gives me a long appraising look.

"Evan, what I'm about to say I hope you'll keep in complete confidence, at least for now."

I look away and sigh. Here we go. "Look, Mr. Robbins. I'm a jazz pianist. I don't know what else you've heard but—"

Robbins puts up his hand and cuts me off. "Don't worry, I'm not going to try and hire you as a detective, although you're right. I'm very aware of your skills in that department. No, I'm here because of your piano playing. He leans forward and unbuttons his double breasted suit.

"I represent Ryan Stiles." His eyebrows rise when I don't immediately respond. "The actor?"

That throws me. There's Brad Pitt, Tom Cruise, George Clooney, Will Smith, and then there's Ryan Stiles, although "movie star" might be a better fit than "actor." As far as I know, at the moment, he's the hottest thing going. I'm enough of a movie buff to know who he is, and it's hard to miss his face on the covers of those magazines at supermarket checkout counters. I've even seen a couple of his films, the huge box office blockbusters. The ones with car chases, explosions and Stiles saving the world from one disaster or other had made him one of Hollywood's biggest box office draws. I've also seen him in a small independent film on cable television that was, to me, more impressive. He was surprisingly good, playing a down-and-out young lawyer faced with a major ethical choice in a high-profile case.

"I know who he is," I say, "but I really don't understand."

Robbins look relieved. "Good, and I know what you're thinking. What does a big box office star like Ryan Stiles have to do with you?"

"I hope you're going to tell me." I was getting annoyed with Robbins' dramatics. "I have some friends waiting for me outside, and one is my impatient girlfriend."

"Yes, FBI Special Agent Andrea Lawrence and Lieutenant Dan Cooper of the Santa Monica Police," Robbins says, taking in my surprised look. "I've done my research."

I shift in my chair and glance toward the door. "Okay, Mr. Robbins, let's get to it."

Robbins nods. "This is about Ryan's interest in jazz piano."

He lets that hang in the air for a long moment.

I lean back and smile. "Don't tell me. You want me to teach Ryan Stiles how to play piano."

Robbins shrugs and almost rolls his eyes. "No, there aren't enough years for that, and as far as I know, not enough talent either. What I want is for you to teach Ryan how to *look* like he's playing piano and be so convincing, even you'd believe it."

I stare at Robbins for nearly a minute in stunned silence. He waits for my surprise to fade.

"There's a script, a jazz pianist caught up in a murder case. I'm against it, but despite my misgivings, Ryan wants to do it. Not his usual thing. A small indie, low-budget kind of thing, but he holds the cards. He agreed to another big one but only if the studio agreed to let him do this one, and, well, what Ryan Stiles wants..." He doesn't need to finish the sentence.

I take a breath. "Look, I understand all that, but why me? There are a hundred pianists here in L.A. who could do this."

Robbins smiles again. "Yes there are, but none of them is a real detective."

I like the sound of that even less but Robbins goes on before I can say anything.

"There's plenty of precedent for this. You must have seen some of the films. Shelly Manne taught Frank Sinatra to look like a drummer for *Man With the Golden Arm*. Sal Mineo played Gene Krupa, and Forest Whittaker never had a saxophone in his hands before he did *Bird* for Clint Eastwood. I think you'd have to admit, thanks to somebody, he was convincing."

"Yeah he was, but—"

"Look, forget the remark about you being a real detective. Perhaps I spoke out of turn. I know that was all just stuff you got caught up in. Ryan is just fascinated by the concept." Robbins leans back in his chair. "You'd be well compensated of course. We're talking about a few weeks' work, and we can work around your schedule if necessary."

My schedule, such as it is, would not be the problem. "I don't know, Mr. Robbins. It's just not something I think I'd want to do. Stiles and I don't know each other. We might not even get along."

"Grant, please call me Grant. Fair enough. I know what you're thinking. Spoiled young movie star—but Ryan is not like that. Think it over. Can I at least tell Ryan you'll do that?"

I find myself nodding. "Okay, but I have to tell you, I don't think it's going to happen."

"Great," Robbins says, as if I'd agreed. "I'll get back to you real soon." He gets to his feet and shakes my hand again. "Great to meet you." Then he's gone.

I sit for a moment, listening for that little voice in my head, but it's not there. I get up and head for the lobby to find Andie and Coop.

At least Robbins didn't say "let's do lunch" or "his people would call my people."

Chapter One

"Oh my God," Andie says. "You're going to teach Ryan Stiles how to play piano?"

"Settle down, girl. I said I'd think about it."

We're in a late-night deli on Wilshire waiting for pastrami sandwiches and coffee. Coop is drumming his fingers on the table, scanning the room for our waitress. Andie leans back in the booth and gazes at the ceiling. "Ryan Stiles. I mean he's just so…"

"Dreamy?" Coop offers sarcastically, and catches my eye. "How much are they going to pay you for this, ah, service?"

"Yes," Andie says. "Dreamy. All that dirty-blond hair and those piercing blue eyes."

"We didn't talk about money, and anyway I didn't say I'd do it."

"Oh, you have to," Andie says, gripping my arm. "I so want to meet Ryan Stiles. Could we visit the set, maybe have dinner with him?"

I laugh. "Listen to Miss Starstruck FBI Agent. Maybe I can get Coop on as the police consultant, too."

"Hmm. I like that idea," Coop says as the waitress brings our order. "My years of experience could lend a certain authenticity. They always get it wrong in these cop movies."

"They usually get the music wrong, too," I say. "How many times have you watched a scene where a band is playing? The drummer is clearly playing brushes but what you hear is a stick on the cymbal."

Coop and Andie look at each other. "Who notices something like that?" Andie says. Coop nods in agreement.

I shrug and give up. We wolf down the sandwiches and Andie is impatient for the check.

"C'mon, baby, I'm in a mood now."

The second night at The Bakery goes just as well as the first, but there's no sign of either Grant Robbins or Ryan Stiles, and frankly, I'm relieved. On Saturday, however, I spot Robbins in a front-row seat, next to a man with long dark hair and even darker sunglasses. I try to ignore Robbins' presence and not think about how I'm going to tell him I'm going to pass on his proposal.

I'd spent Friday browsing through some movies on the hotel's VCR while Andie was out visiting old friends from the L.A. Bureau. Robbins was right, I thought, as I watched Martin Milner look pretty convincing as a guitarist in *Sweet Smell of Success*, Steve Allen as Benny Goodman, Jimmy Stewart as Glen Miller, and Richard Gere as a trumpet player in *Cotton Club*. Sal Mineo playing Gene Krupa looked good, but then, he actually played drums, so he had all the moves down, and it was Krupa playing on the score.

I was disappointed in Spike Lee's *Mo Better Blues*. Denzel Washington looked like he knew his away around a trumpet, but after being beaten up, he turns up at a jazz club a year later and discovers he can't play. Wouldn't he have tried at home first? Maybe I'm just too picky.

I had to admit Forrest Whittaker was the most impressive as Charlie Parker in *Bird*. Who tutored him, I wondered? Probably saxophonist Lennie Neihaus, who scored most of Clint Eastwood's films.

But now, I lose myself in "My Foolish Heart" as we finish our last set at the Jazz Bakery. When I look up from the keyboard, Robbins is gone. I thank the audience once again, sorry to have the gig over. Nothing until a few days at Yoshi's in San Francisco next month.

I head back to the dressing room and find Grant Robbins and the man I'd seen next to him waiting for me. The long dark hair and the sunglasses are gone. He jumps to his feet and grabs my hand, and I'm shaking hands with Ryan Stiles.

"Oh man, that was so cool," Stiles says. "You're even better in person than on record." He turns to Robbins. "Isn't he?"

Robbins smiles. "I told you, didn't I?"

"Man, I can't wait to get started. Whatta you say, Evan? You going to do this for me?"

I sit down and look at them both. Up close and personal, Stiles is even more impressive. The unruly blond hair, the glimmering blue eyes, the persuasive voice are all part of the package. He's shorter than I thought, but has a compact athlete's body. I imagine few people ever refuse to do anything Ryan Stiles wants. He's like a young Robert Redford, exuding charm—and now he's turning it all on me.

Robbins considers for a moment, taking in my expression, deciding, I think, how best to handle me. "Well, Evan. Have you given our proposal some thought?

I light a cigarette and sit down. "Yeah, I have," I feel Stiles' eyes on me. "Look, I'm very flattered, but I think I'm going to pass on this." I see Stiles slump down in his chair and clasp his hands as he looks at the floor. "There's a couple of great players who've done movie work I can recommend."

"Is it me?" he says quietly. "You don't like me?"

"I don't even know you," I tell Stiles. "I just, I don't know, it just doesn't feel like something I want to do."

"Tell him," Stiles says to Robbins. I look at Robbins.

He nods and takes a slip of paper out of his suit jacket and hands it to me. "I told you you'd be well compensated."

I look at the number. "You've got to be kidding. Five hundred dollars an hour?"

Robbins smiles. "Less than a good attorney gets these days."

"I'm sure, but—"

"Tell him the rest," Stiles says, cutting me off.

"Ryan has optioned this script. We have full control over casting and more importantly, the music." He pauses again for one more look at Stiles. "We—Ryan, wants you to score the movie, and for fun, you'd have a cameo role. You could stay at Ryan's beach house in Malibu while you work with him. Scoring the film would be a separate deal of course, with very generous compensation."

They both watch me as my mind reels. I probably look like I've just been told I won the lottery. Always, somewhere in the back of my mind, has been the desire to score a film and here it is, dropped in my lap. "I don't know what to say."

Stiles looks at me, his megawatt smile on full charge. "Just say yes, man. Do this for me."

"I took the liberty of drawing up a preliminary contract," Robbins says. "I can have it to you first thing tomorrow. In the meantime, we've reserved a suite for you at the Beverly Hills Hotel, while you consider further." Robbins pauses. "If that's necessary," he adds.

I lean back and put my hands up. "Whoa, slow down," I say. "This is all coming too fast."

"Hey, no pressure," Stiles says. "We want you to be comfortable is all. Bring your lady of course."

No pressure? Teaching a major movie star how to look like he's playing piano for five bills an hour, scoring his film, a Beverly Hills Hotel suite while I decide? "I just need a little time to think, and I'd like to talk this over with Andie, my girlfriend."

"Absolutely," Robbins says. "I understand. Take your time." He gets to his feet. Stiles stands and takes my hand, those piercing blue eyes boring into me with all the sincerity he can muster.

"Do this for me, Evan. Your playing is awesome. If I can just *look* enough like you, I'll show these Hollywood assholes I can act." He nudges my shoulder. "Is there a back door out of here?" He dons the dark wig and sunglasses. "Paparazzi." He shrugs, even manages to look a little sheepish.

Robbins shakes my hand. "Thanks for listening, Evan. I'll make arrangements for your hotel. You can check in tomorrow and we'll have a car pick you up."

For several minutes, I sit there in the spartan Jazz Bakery dressing room, wondering what it's going to be like to work with Hollywood royalty.

"What's he like?" Andie wants to know. "Did you talk to him?" She's kneeling on the bed facing me as I lean back against the headboard in our hotel.

"Of course I talked to him. He's seems okay. He likes my playing and—"

"He's okay? How can you be so calm? Do you know how many people would like to meet and talk with Ryan Stiles?"

"I'm guessing a lot." I have to laugh, seeing how excited Andie is. She just stares at me, shaking her head. "Okay, it's pretty heady stuff. Not because it's Ryan Stiles but that they want me to score the movie. I'm not sure what it will be like seeing him on a daily basis for the piano lessons."

"Evan, listen to me. You deserve this. All the years you've spent scuffling for gigs, the setbacks, the disappointments. You have to do this. Just think about us sitting in a darkened theater, the credits rolling and we see: Music by Evan Horne." She looks toward the wall and waves her hand across it dramatically.

She jumps up and straddles me, her hands around my neck. "You're going to do this, Evan Horne."

I lie awake long after Andie falls asleep. Scoring a movie, even a small one, could open a lot of doors. I squeeze my right hand into a fist. Still no pain, but how long is it going to last? Is it time to start thinking about a future without playing the piano? Andie is right. I couldn't get near somebody like Ryan Stiles, and here he is coming after me.

We're just about finished packing when the phone rings. Andie answers, nods, and mumbles a few times. "Yes, that's fine. We're ready." She hangs up and turns to me. "Our car is here.

They're sending somebody up for the bags." She looks at me for a moment. "What car? Where are we going?"

I try to hide my smile as I zip up my bag. "Oh, Ryan sent the car. We're going over to the Beverly Hills Hotel for a couple of days while I think things over." I duck when she throws a pillow at me.

"Oh my God, I've got to go shopping."

We go down to the lobby and are shown outside to a black Lincoln town car. The driver touches the bill of his cap and opens the door for us, as a bellman stores our bags in the trunk. We get in and settle back for the short ride to Beverly Hills.

Andie squeezes my hand and slides against me. "You know what one of my fantasies is?" she whispers in my ear.

"I can guess, but it's ten o'clock in the morning." I glance at the rearview mirror and catch the driver's eyes and we both smile.

At the Beverly Hills Hotel, two bellmen greet us. One takes our bags. The other escorts us to the front desk where the manager, dressed in an expensive suit, smiles and flourishes a pen for me to sign in.

"Your suite is ready, Mr. Horne. Just sign here please. As a guest of Mr. Stiles, please don't hesitate to call on me for anything." He smiles again and we cross the lobby with the bellman just ahead of us. At the elevator, we step aside and several people get out.

Andie nudges me and whispers. "That was Jane Fonda."

Our room overlooks the pool. It's large, airy, and furnished like a condo. On a table is a large basket of fruit, a bottle of wine, and a carton of my brand of cigarettes. There's a card with them. "Enjoy," it says. "RS." I show the card to Andie. She wanders around, taking in the rich furnishings, the canopy bed, and the bathroom that's bigger than some of the apartments I've lived in.

"I feel a long bath coming on." She looks at the array of bath oils and lotions.

When the phone rings, it's Grant Robbins. "Evan. I trust everything is to your liking?"

"Perfect. This is all very generous."

"How about lunch," Robbins says. "One o'clock. Ryan will be joining us so we can talk details a bit more."

"Fine, I'd like that."

"Great," Robbins says. "The patio dining room."

I hang up and turn to Andie. "Better take that bath. We're having lunch with Ryan Stiles."

Just before one, Andie and I arrive at the hotel restaurant. Before we can say a word, the manager appears and escorts us to a plush booth surrounded by palms and flowers. Grant Robbins rises as we approach and holds out his hand to Andie.

"Miss Lawrence, how nice to meet you." Andie has outdone herself with a quick shopping trip for a mid-thigh dress and heels, and her hair fluffed up like she'd combed it with her fingers. Tasteful yet very sexy, as only Andie can be. She looks anything but an FBI agent.

"My pleasure," she says, taking Robbins' hand and sliding into the booth as she looks around.

Robbins catches her. "Don't worry, Ryan will be joining us shortly. He's finishing up a few scenes this morning for a new film."

I slide in next to Andie. Robbins sits on the other side of her. A waiter appears instantly and takes our drink orders. Bloody Marys all around.

"Well," Robbins says. "I hope everything is all right. Room okay?"

"It's lovely," Andie says, sounding almost shy.

"Yes," I say. "Thank you very much, but none of this was really necessary."

"Nonsense," Robbins says. "I admit, we wanted to impress you, give you a taste of what's in store. I trust you've given our little proposal some more thought."

Before I can answer, Robbins looks up. "Ah, here's Ryan." He gets to his feet as Ryan Stiles approaches. He's in jeans, running shoes, and a light pullover sweater, his eyes hidden behind the dark glasses.

He takes off the glasses and zeros in on Andie. "Wow, the most beautiful FBI agent I've ever seen." He offers his hand

and Andie almost knocks over a water glass as she reaches out to shake it.

"Hello," is all she can manage as she stares.

Stiles sprawls in the booth next to Robbins as a waiter appears with a tall glass of orange juice. I can't tell if it's just juice or spiked with vodka.

"So, everything cool? Grant take care of you guys?"

"Yes," Andie and I say in unison.

"Good." Stiles turns to Robbins. "You need to speak to that director," he says. "We had to do three takes for that one dumb scene."

Robbins nods. "I'll handle it." He takes out his cell phone and dials a number. "Excuse me for a minute," he tells us, waiting for his call to go through.

Ryan smiles and shrugs our way. "Sorry," he says. "Just some artistic differences."

Andie and I sip our drinks as Robbins talks softly but firmly to whoever is on the other end. He clicks the phone shut. "All taken care of," he tells Stiles, who just nods as if he knew it would be.

"So, how 'bout some lunch?"

Robbins does most of the talking as we work our way through some melt-in-your-mouth grilled salmon, risotto, and a caesar salad. It's more about how much he and Ryan want me to join the Stiles team in what could be cinematic history, the way he describes it.

By the time we order coffee, I have some questions of my own. "What is the story about in this script?"

Robbins and Stiles exchange glances. "There's a security issue with the script," Robbins says. "As I'm sure you can imagine, the press would love to know what Ryan's next project is. Until we know you're with us, we prefer to keep the content confidential. I'm sure you understand."

I don't but I let it go. "So I would get to see the script if I agree to score the film?"

"Of course," Robbins says. "Absolutely."

"He means when we have you signed," Stiles chimes in with a big smile.

It all seems a bit over the top to me. It is, after all, only a movie, but I guess Robbins has a point. Both men look at me expectantly.

I glance at Andie, who manages to take her eyes off Stiles long enough to give me a searching, you-better-do-this look. Under the table I feel her hand squeeze my leg.

"Okay, here's what I've decided. I'm in for the piano tutoring. I still want to take some more time on the rest of your offer if that's okay with you." I catch a slight frown from Stiles but Robbins touches his shoulder.

"Well, we're halfway there, then, aren't we."

I hear Andie sigh in relief. "I guess we are."

Stiles jumps up and grabs my hand. "Way cool, man, way cool!" He glances at his watch. "I have to get back to the set. Grant will fill you in on the details. I can't wait to get started on this." He waves at Andie and then he's gone.

Robbins has already taken some papers from a slim leather briefcase beside him and slides them across to me. "This is the formal agreement," he says. "Nothing tricky, just the payment terms. If you'll just sign where the arrow is."

I glance at it briefly, see nothing unusual, and take the Mont Blanc pen Robbins offers, aware of Andie's eyes on me as I scribble my signature and hand it back. He pulls off one copy. "This one's for you," he says, and returns the rest to his briefcase. He stands. "Sorry to run off, but I have several pressing matters to handle. Enjoy your stay. I'll call you about the beach house."

Andie and I lean back and look at each other. "What beach house?"

Chapter Two

Andie and I watch as a short, powerfully built man in a torn shirt and faded jeans shoves Ryan Stiles against the bannister of a staircase. Ryan fights him off for a moment, but eventually loses his grip. The short man slams a forearm into Ryan's face and he tumbles backwards, rolling head-over-heels down the staircase where he lies crumpled and still. The short man, breathing hard now, glares, reaches behind his back and pulls a gun from the waistband of his jeans. He starts down the stairs, the gun trained on Ryan.

"Cut!" a voice comes from behind us. A bell rings and suddenly there's a flurry of motion and activity. The man on the stairs grins and twirls the gun on his finger. We watch as Ryan, at the bottom of the stairs, jumps to his feet. But it's not Ryan. He turns and high-fives Ryan, who approaches, dressed identically in jeans, boots, and a black tee shirt. Another man in a baseball cap walks to them and talks briefly with Ryan and his stunt double.

"Okay, let's set it up people," the director says. Ryan nods, reaches down, and checks a gun in an ankle holster under his jeans. As the stuntman walks away, Ryan lies on the floor, positioning himself in exactly the same pose as the fallen stuntman. There are a few more minutes as the camera and lighting are adjusted. Another man steps in front of the camera with the clapboard.

"Don't Die Again, Scene 57, Take one." He moves back and the director's voice again pierces the already quiet set. "Quiet please. Roll sound. And, action."

Ryan stirs on the floor, looking up at the short man coming down the stairs. Ryan pulls the gun from the ankle holster and fires. A splatter of blood erupts from the short man's chest. He staggers and falls forward, rolling down the stairs and landing next to Ryan. I feel Andie flinch at the sound of the gunshots.

"Cut! All right, people, that's a wrap," the director says. "Great, guys. Very nice, Ryan."

Ryan leans over and claps the short man on the shoulder. "You okay, Barney?"

Barney sits up and smiles at Ryan. "Never better." He unbuttons his shirt to reveal the plastic bag of fake blood and pulls it off. "Loved working with you," he says.

Ryan gets to his feet, smiling, and saunters over to Andie and I. "So. How'd I do?"

"You shouldn't turn the gun sideways," Andie says. "They always gets that wrong in movies. It's not nearly so accurate."

Ryan's smile fades. He glances at Andie for a moment, then at me.

"Hey," I say. "She would know."

Ryan gazes at Andie for a long moment. "You ever shoot anybody or been shot?"

"Both," Andie says, matching Ryan's gaze.

Ryan looks away then smiles again. "Well, I guess you would know then."

Andie just nods, turns, and walks away.

"It wasn't that long ago, " I tell Ryan. "Bank robbery shooting in San Francisco."

"Oh shit," Ryan says. "I'm sorry, I didn't know." He looks around. "Look, I'm going to change and then we'll go out to Malibu, show you the house. I'll meet you guys outside."

I find Andie outside the sound stage, leaning against a vintage car. "You okay?"

She nods. "Yeah. I know it's a movie, fake and all that, but…"

"The star shine fading?"

"I don't know. There's something about him."

"Of course there is. He's a good-looking, millionaire movie star."

The ride up the Pacific Coast Highway to Malibu is uneventful. Ryan takes a few phone calls while Andie and I watch the scenery. It's one of those perfect sunny California days. A light breeze blowing off the ocean, the sun, an orange ball starting its decline to the sea. For me, it's a homecoming of sorts. I grew up in Santa Monica, lived a few years in Venice before I went to Europe, and I've driven this road countless times. It was also the road where I had the accident that nearly ended my career as a jazz pianist.

We pass Pepperdine University and go another ten miles or so, past Point Dume, then down the hill to Trancas canyon. At the light, the driver veers to the left down Broad Beach Road, past the rear of a number of large homes that, according to Ryan, are full of television and movie people. We get an occasional glimpse of the ocean between houses. Then finally, the road curves to the left and up a slight incline and stops behind a large white villa. Tall wrought-iron gates block the entrance.

Ryan gets out and, blocking the driver's view, punches in some numbers on the key pad. The gates slowly open on a half-circle driveway. There's a red BMW sports car already parked, as well as a chocolate brown Mercedes sedan. The driver pulls in and opens the rear door.

Before we get out, Ryan leans forward and takes Andie's hand. "I'm really sorry, Andie. I hope you'll forgive me. I was way out of line." He turns on that megawatt smile.

"Nothing to forgive," Andie says. "I'm just still a little tense about guns."

"Yes, I know that now."

Andie and I get out and follow Ryan inside. The door is opened by a tall young blonde. "Hi, baby," she says. She wraps her arms around Ryan then steps back.

She's maybe twenty-five, wearing sandals, a flimsy unbuttoned shirt, and a white bikini that leaves nothing to the imagination. Her eyes flick over Andie and she holds out her hand to me. "You must be Evan Horne," she says. "I'm Melanie Hammond."

"This is my honey," Ryan says, draping his arm around her shoulder. "Isn't she something?"

"Indeed," Andie says. "I'm Andie Lawrence. I'm Evan's honey." Andie smiles sweetly.

"Melanie just wrapped a movie with Adam Sandler," Ryan says. "Not a big part but she was great."

"I bet she was." Andie squeezes my hand so tightly I can feel her nails dig into my palm.

"C'mon, Evan," Ryan says. "Let me show you the guesthouse."

"We'll meet you by the pool," he says to Melanie and Andie.

Andie shoots me a look then goes off with Melanie. I follow Ryan out a side door to a flagstone walk that leads to a small guesthouse. One window faces the ocean and the sound of the surf filters up. "I hope this is okay," Ryan says. He opens the door with a flourish like a bellhop showing me a room in a luxury hotel.

There's a queen-sized bed, two stuffed chairs facing a small fireplace, a flat-screen television mounted on the wall, a small refrigerator. Ryan opens it and shows me it's full of beer, soft drinks, an array of juices. "You need anything special, just let Emillio know. He cooks and runs the house."

I nod. "It's beautiful," I say.

Ryan beams. "C'mon. I haven't shown you the best." We go back in the house to an enormous living room. The wall facing the ocean is almost all glass with a spectacular view of the surf and beach that stretches back as far as I can see. In one corner, black and gleaming in the filtered sunlight, is a baby grand piano. "Try it out," Ryan says.

I sit down and run my hands over the keys. It's in perfect tune, of course, and the action is wonderful. I play a few bars of blues and glance at Ryan. "Very nice," I say. The sound fills the room.

"Use it all you want," Ryan says. "You probably practice a lot, right?"

"When I can."

"You'll have plenty of time," Ryan says. He stands, looking at me as if memorizing the moment. "C'mon, let's get some lunch."

We join Andie and Melanie on the glassed-in patio, where Emillio is serving. Melanie is on her cell phone. Andie is staring at the ocean, a Bloody Mary in front of her.

"Yeah, it was like, whoa," Melanie says into the phone. "Just awesome."

Andie rolls her eyes at me and takes a long pull on her drink. Melanie glances up, sees Ryan. "Gotta go," she says and quickly closes the phone.

"Why don't you put a top on," Ryan says. Melanie gets up and excuses herself. Ryan glances at us. "Body like that, you want to flaunt it."

When Melanie comes back, she's wearing a denim shirt, buttoned halfway over her bikini top. Ryan nods and smiles. "Well, let's eat," he says.

Over a lunch of shrimp salad, rolls, and iced tea, Ryan entertains us with movie stories and a rundown of other celebrities that live along the beach. "Don't be surprised if you run into Ali McGraw walking her dog," he says. "Stallone too. He had a place down here for awhile. He hired a boat to set off fireworks on the fourth of July a couple of years ago. Very nice guy and a major talent, right, honey?" He looks at Melanie.

"One of a kind," she says.

"Well," Ryan says, getting to his feet. "Melanie and I are going to take a siesta." He winks broadly. "You two make yourselves at home, take a walk, whatever. Anything you want, just ask Emillio."

When Ryan and Melanie are gone, Andie looks at me. "Are you kidding me?"

"Okay, okay. He's trying."

"She's afraid of him," Andie says. "Did you see the look on her face when he told her to put something on?"

"Yeah, I did. I was kind of disappointed." Andie just glares. "Okay, just kidding. C'mon, let's take a walk."

Just down from the pool, there's a short, worn path leading down to the beach. We leave our shoes and socks and let our feel sink into the sand and walk along the water's edge, checking out the impressive homes. Lots of wood and glass, decks and balconies, but not many people. We pass a few other beach strollers, but no one gives us a second look.

We find a spot just out of reach of the encroaching surf and sit down in the sand. The ocean air, the breeze, the sun, all feels good as I lean back on my elbows. Andie sits up, hugging her knees, staring out at the water.

"Something on your mind?"

Andie shrugs. "I don't want to rain on your parade, but how long do you think it's going to take to get him to look like a piano player?"

"I don't know. Couple of weeks, maybe three. I think he's probably a quick study. Why?"

"Just don't get all caught up in this celebrity thing, okay."

"C'mon, Andie. You know me better than that. I've been around money before."

"I know you have but this is different. It's not just money. It's limos, beach houses, stars, girls like Melanie. It's a whole other world." She turns and looks at me. "Trust me, there's something not quite right about all this. The way he asked me if I'd ever shot anybody or been shot myself. He already knew."

"Ryan Stiles can't help being a movie star. He likes it."

"He likes the power. Melanie and I are going to have a siesta? Please. That was for our benefit. Sex on demand with Miss Hard Body."

We look up as a woman in shorts and tee shirt runs by with a small dog on a leash. She waves and smiles.

"Hey," Andie says. "I think that was Ali McGraw."

We get up and walk back toward the house. "I know what you're saying but none of it really bothers me except for one thing."

"What?"

"They want me to score the movie, but I still haven't heard a thing about the script."

Back at the house, it's all quiet. I show Andie the guesthouse and we have our own siesta to the sound of waves crashing. I leave Andie asleep and walk back out on the deck by the pool. Emillio is standing, staring out to sea.

"Beautiful, isn't it."

He turns. "Mr. Horne. Can I get you something?"

"A beer would be nice if it's no trouble. And please, it's Evan." Emillio nods and heads for the kitchen and returns with a bottle, a chilled goblet, and an ashtray.

"Try this," he says.

I take the bottle from him and do a double-take. On the label is a picture of Thelonious Monk. Brother Thelonious Belgian-style abbey ale. I take a sip and nod. "Nice. Who makes this?"

Emillio smiles. "A small brewery in Northern California. I found it at Trancas market. It seemed appropriate for your stay."

I take another drink and light a cigarette. "So how do you like working for Ryan?"

Emillio turns and looks out at the ocean again. "It's fine," he says, "not too demanding, and of course this is a great extra benefit." He waves his hand toward the surf, crashing now as the tide comes in. "If you'll excuse me, I have to start preparing dinner."

I finish my beer, wander into the living room, and sit down at the piano. I play some chords, then drift into "What's New." When I look up, Ryan Stiles is standing, leaning against the wall, shirtless in a pair of long shorts.

"You make it look so easy," he says.

"Well, I've been doing it a long time."

He comes closer, watching my hands. "Want to show me a few things, kind of get started?"

"Sure. You'll probably be playing on a mock keyboard, no sound, but to look authentic, your hand movements will have to match the sound track as closely as possible." I show him some left-hand voicings, a blues, and work through the changes with my right hand. "Like this, see?"

Ryan nods and watches. "Man, wish I could do that."

"Well, hopefully, we'll make it look like you can." I get up and have him sit down. I position his left hand and show him the movements. He's awkward at first but gradually begins to get the idea, repeating the left-hand three-note voicings over and over.

"That's good," I say. "Now play against it with your right hand."

He stumbles then and stops. "It's like patting your head and rubbing your stomach."

"Exactly. The natural tendency is both hands want to do the same motion."

He tries again, playing a chord with his left hand, then single notes with his right. He does it several times. It's clumsy but he gradually gets his hands working independently.

"There you go. It'll come eventually."

He nods and stops, rubbing his wrists. "I can feel it already. Muscles I haven't used before. You play again. Let me watch."

We exchange places. I sit down and play a blues solo for a couple of choruses and take it out, feeling Ryan's eyes on my every movement.

"I gotta get that head movement too. The way you lean in or tilt back, your eyes on the keyboard. The camera will catch all that."

"You don't have to look like me," I say. "You can decide. Bill Evan kept his head down a lot of the time. Keith Jarrett rocks back and forth, sometimes even stands up as he plays. Every pianist is different."

Ryan nods. "Lot to learn," he says. "I've going to videotape you while you play and study the tape if that's okay."

"Sure." I begin to realize how hard this is going to be for him to simulate the movement and motion of a jazz pianist in a relatively short time.

"Good. I get into researching a role. I really want this to look right."

Ryan sits down in a nearby chair and I turn sideways on the piano bench. "Don't forget, Forrest Whittaker never had a saxophone in his hand, but he looked pretty good playing Charlie Parker."

"Where's your lady?"

"Taking a nap."

Ryan smiles. "Yeah, Melanie too. Wore her out."

I let that go and get up. "I'm going to check on her."

"Hey," Ryan says. "She's not still mad at me."

"No, she's just a little touchy about guns and shooting."

Over dinner, Ryan announces that he's throwing a party Friday night. "Some of the cast from *Don't Die Again*, few friends, you know, just something casual."

"Sorry I have to miss it," Andie says. "I have to get back to work."

"Catch some bad guys, huh?" Ryan says.

"More like catching up on some reports."

Ryan turns to me. "Hey, invite your cop friend. What's his name again? Cooper?"

"Yeah, Danny Cooper. I'm sure he'd enjoy it. I'll call him."

"Do that," Ryan says.

Emillio begins to clear the table. "We'll have coffee in the screening room," Ryan tells him. He motions us to get up. "C'mon, I've got a surprise for you."

We follow Ryan to another level of the house. There's a huge screen, several soft easy chairs, and a couple of couches. Andie grabs my hand and we curl up on one; Ryan and Melanie sit on the other. Next to Ryan's is a small panel of buttons. He presses one and the movie begins. It's black and white. Burt Lancaster and Tony Curtis in *Sweet Smell of Success*. I've seen it once before. Lancaster as a powerful columnist and Curtis as a sleazy press agent are both fantastic, but I know it's the music scenes that Ryan has chosen it for.

Martin Milner, who later played in *Route 66* and one of the television cop shows, plays a jazz guitarist involved with Lancaster's sister. The band is drummer Chico Hamilton's group. Milner must have had a good tutor as his hands on the guitar match the sound track very well. It really does look like he's playing with Chico Hamilton.

"You going to make me look that good, Evan?"

"I hope so."

"So do I," Ryan says. "So do I."

Chapter Three

Driving down the Pacific Coast Highway toward Santa Monica in a red BMW sports car, courtesy of Ryan Stiles, is an experience I won't soon forget. I glance over at Andie. She leans back against the headrest, her hair blowing in the wind, her eyes hidden behind dark glasses. With the top down it's too noisy to talk, which is probably just as well. But before I drop her at LAX, I know I'm going to get another lecture about Ryan Stiles and Hollywood.

I bypass the California Incline and speed through the tunnel and pick up Lincoln Boulevard. The traffic is light for a late Friday morning, so when I pull into the airport, we make it to departures with plenty of time to spare. I stop the car, turn off the engine, and look at Andie. She takes off her glasses and meets my eyes. Smiling, she pats the dashboard.

"You like this, don't you," she says.

"I like it better that it's Ryan Stiles' car," I say, grinning, knowing I'm pushing her buttons. I glance in the rearview mirror and see a security guy heading for us. Andie sees him too, and takes out her Bureau I.D. and holds it up for him as he nears the car.

"FBI, special assignment," she says without looking back at him.

The guard looks, gives her a mock salute. "Yes, Ma'am."

Andie turns back to me. "How long do you think you'll be here?"

I shrug. "I don't know, two or three weeks maybe for the piano tutoring. If I ever get a look at the script, that will come later. I can't score a movie that hasn't been made yet."

"That's just one of the things that bothers me," Andie says. "Why wouldn't they want you to see it? That can't be normal."

It bothers me too, and I've already decided to push it with Ryan and Grant Robbins the next time I see him. "No, you're right," I say. "What else?"

Andie opens the door and gets out. "Keep an eye on Melanie," she says.

"Hard not to." I grin again and get a glare from Andie. I get out and take her bag out of the BMW's small trunk.

We stand at the curb for a moment, passengers and cars flowing around us. "Maybe I'm just jealous that you get to spend a couple of weeks at a movie star's Malibu beach house while I'm writing reports in San Francisco." She moves closer and hugs me. "Just watch yourself, okay?"

I nod and kiss her. "Maybe you can get back for a weekend."

"Maybe." She turns, smiles, and heads into the terminal. "Call me."

I stand for a minute, watching her disappear into the crowd, then get back in the car and merge with the exiting traffic. At a signal on Lincoln, I call Coop.

"Hey, you busy?"

"Ah, pianist to the stars. Always busy keeping Santa Monica safe," he says. "Am I going to see your picture in *People* magazine anytime soon?"

"How about breakfast? I just dropped Andie at LAX."

"Give me twenty minutes," Coop says. "Norm's?"

"See you there."

It's more like a half hour when Coop slides his bulk into a booth opposite me. He's in jeans, a black tee shirt, and a light, dark blue windbreaker, his gun and badge clipped on his belt. I'm already working on a Denver omelet and coffee. "Sorry, I was hungry."

Coop nods and signals a waitress for coffee. She brings it and a menu which Coop waves away. "Short stack and bacon," he tells her, then turns to me. "So how goes it with the rich and famous?"

I catch him up on the house and the little I know about Ryan Stiles and Melanie, who interests Coop far more. "She's Stiles' girlfriend? She was one of the *Sports Illustrated* models. And you had lunch with her with Andie sitting at the same table?"

I push my plate aside. "Ryan was there too. You can see for yourself tomorrow night if you have a spot in your busy schedule."

"Are you kidding?"

"Ryan is throwing a little party and told me to invite my cop friend."

"I like him already," Coop says as the waitress brings his pancakes. "Tell me more."

"Stiles is okay. He's eager and I think we'll get along."

Coop nods. "I've seen all his movies. I like those action flicks."

"Why does that not surprise me? This one is going to be a small-budget independent type."

Coop wipes some syrup off his lip with a napkin. "Oh, you mean one with a story and dialogue, that slow kind."

"Yeah, maybe a little too deep for you."

"And Stiles will play a piano player who—"

"Gets caught up in a murder or two, and no you don't have to remind me."

"I didn't say a word."

"More coffee, guys?" The waitress has returned.

"Did you know I've been invited to Ryan Stiles' party in Malibu tomorrow night?"

"Give him my regards," she says. "You gonna arrest him?"

"I hope it doesn't come to that." Coop turns back to me. "So what's the catch? My detective skills tell me something is not quite right."

"Just what Andie says. I don't know. He and his agent know an awful lot about me already, and they're being very evasive about showing me the script for some reason."

Coop shrugs. "Security? They like to keep things secret in Hollywood, then make a big splash announcement, don't they?"

We walk outside to the parking lot. "I guess that could be it, but I am now kind of in the loop, so to speak." I grin at Coop and lean on the BMW.

His eyes get big. "Does this belong to…"

"Yep. Sure does."

Coop nods and walks toward his car. "Hey, enjoy the experience and keep your eyes off Melanie."

"Funny, Andie said just the opposite."

"Sure she did. Oh, about the party?"

I get in the car and start the engine. "I'll have my people call your people."

Back at the house, it's all quiet. I find Emillio fussing around in the kitchen but Melanie and Ryan are nowhere to be seen.

"Miss Blake went shopping," Emillio says. "Mr. Stiles is at the gym for his workout."

"Oh, where's that? In Malibu?"

"In the basement." He points to some stairs leading off the kitchen.

I should have known. I go to the guesthouse and change into some swim trunks and a tee shirt, opting on a walk along the beach. I find the stairway to the basement and decide to look in on Stiles. I open the door and I'm suddenly assaulted with earsplitting rock music. Stiles is on a stair master, his tank shirt darkened with sweat.

The room is filled with all kinds of equipment besides the stair master. Free weights line one wall in front of a huge mirror, a life cycle exercise bike next to that, along with several pulley machines. The ultimate home gym.

Ryan senses me or the open door and turns. "Be with you in a minute," he yells. I can barely hear him over the music. He stops finally, turning off the machine, grabs a towel and switches off the stereo.

"Aerosmith," he says. "It pumps me up. Want to have a go?" He takes in my swim trunks.

"No, I'll pass. I was just going to take a walk on the beach."

"Cool, mind if I join you?"

"Hey, it's your beach."

We pass through the kitchen and stop for a couple bottles of water, then down the path to the beach. Ryan jogs every few steps, like a fighter cooling off. I look at the surf. The waves are fairly big and the sun is very bright. It's been a long time. I strip off my tee shirt.

"You do any surfing?" I ask him.

"No. Living here, I guess I should buy a board and take some lessons."

"It's been a while for me, but I have to see if I can still catch a wave or two." I break into a run, splash through the churning surf and dive in, chilled for a moment at the water's coldness. I surface and turn back toward Ryan who's watching me. "Feels good. Come on in."

Ryan stands still for a moment. He looks up and down the beach then takes off his shirt and tentatively walks in, letting the water churn around his legs then his chest as the water gets deeper. I turn and swim out toward the break. Ryan catches up eventually and we bounce up and down at neck level.

"Here we go," I say. A mountain of water rolls toward us, bigger than I would have liked, but what the hell. I turn, facing the beach, and start swimming, feeling the mass of water catch me, start to feather at the top then rise up. Ryan looks a long way down as I start to slide across the face of the wave. He's too close to avoid the rising wave, not far enough back to avoid the break of tons of water.

I catch just a glimpse of his panicked face as I put my arms to my sides and let my body rush down the incline of the wave. It's a good ride. It finally breaks and I'm under water but in control as I dig for the surface. It feels so good I start laughing, then look around for Ryan.

I turn back and see him bobbing in the water, his arms thrashing as another wave looms, his head going under, over and over. On the beach I catch a glimpse of Melanie, pointing, yelling something. I turn and go back toward Ryan, swimming against the undercurrent to reach him. I hook my arm around his chest and start to pull him toward the beach. He fights me off at first then relaxes and lets me pull, swimming with one arm till we reach waist-high water. Ryan collapses against me, then flops on his hands and knees, coughing and spitting up water as Melanie rushes over.

She tries to help him to his feet but he angrily brushes her aside. He staggers a few more feet and lies back on the sand. I reach him and look down as Melanie kneels beside him. "You, okay, baby?"

Ryan sputters, "No I'm not fucking okay," he says.

"What happened?" I move closer.

He gets to his feet and bends over, his hand on his knees, taking in gulps of air.

Finally, he stands upright and stares out at the ocean. "I can't swim."

Back at the house, Ryan has dismissed Melanie, and we sit at one of the poolside tables. He's changed into a white terry cloth robe with a hood, leaning back, staring at the ocean that almost got him.

"My dad was one of those guys who thought it was best to learn by doing," he says. "We were at one of his friends' home. They were drinking, having a good time and decided it was time for me to learn. He just picked me up and threw me in the deep end of the pool. I sank like a rock. It felt like I'd swallowed half the water in the pool. I heard my mother scream and jump in after me and drag me out."

"How old were you?"

"Seven. My dad was just laughing about it, thought it was hilarious. He and my mom had a huge fight all the way home. You couldn't get me near a pool after that. Stupid huh?"

"Not really. That's a pretty scary way to be introduced to water."

"I went to Mexico with some friends when I was in college. I thought I was over it and went in the ocean. I was okay at first but I drifted out too far. Strong current and I couldn't get back. I thought that was it, man. Then some guy on a surfboard saw me, gave me a ride back in. I told my friends I got a leg cramp." He laughs. "They all bought it. Until today, I haven't done anymore than splash around."

"Why didn't you tell me?"

He shrugs. "I don't know. Action movie star can't swim. I didn't want you to think I was a pussy." His voice trails off.

I lean toward him. "Ryan, it doesn't matter what I think."

"Sure. Anyway you know something about me only a couple of people know. I just hope there were none of those paparazzi fuckers around with a telephoto lens." He looks at me. "Can I trust you?"

"What do you mean?"

"The trade press would love to get wind of this."

"Not from me."

He turns and looks at me. I hold his gaze for a long moment. He nods. "I believe you, and thanks for pulling me out." He stands up, slaps me on the shoulder. "I'm going to lie down for awhile."

I go back to the guesthouse, shower, and stretch out on the bed, already missing Andie. She was right. There was a lot not right about things with Ryan Stiles.

I'm still getting dressed when Emillio knocks on the guesthouse door. "There's a policeman here to see you," he says. "A Lieutenant Cooper."

I smile. I thought Coop would be early. "Tell him I'll be right there. No, wait. Send him down here."

I'm pulling on a light sweater when Coop taps on the door and walks in. He looks around, takes in the furnishings. "I'm in the wrong business," he says. "All this just to make him *look* like he's playing piano?" He's dressed in a sports coat, slacks, and loafers. "Hope this is okay. Been awhile since I've been to a Hollywood party."

"Come on, let's find Ryan and I'll introduce you."

"What about Melanie? Do I get to meet her, too?"

"Down, boy. She'll be around."

We go into the main house, dodging catering people headed for the kitchen with trays of hot food, all under Emillio's direction. I take Coop to the living room. He checks out the view, runs a hand over the piano. "Wow, wonder what the payment is on this place?" Coop says.

"Seventy-five thousand a month." We both turn. Ryan and Melanie are standing in the doorway. "Of course I have an option to buy," Ryan adds.

Ryan Stiles is in all white—shirt, pants, shoes, and a thin gold chain around his neck that matches the gold watch on his wrist. Melanie is in all white too, but in much less material. A mid-thigh skirt, scoop-neck top, and three-inch heels. For once Coop is speechless.

Ryan steps forward and holds out his hand. "You must be Dan Cooper."

"Huh? Oh yeah, I am." He can't take his eyes off Melanie. "My friends call me Coop."

"I'd be honored," Ryan says. "And this is Melanie Hammond." She sways over like a model, one foot directly in front of the other. She takes Coop's outstretched hand. The white outfit accents her tan, and when she smiles her teeth are dazzling.

"Can I call you Coop too?"

I try not to laugh as Coop swallows. "You call me whatever you want."

"Well, you guys ready to party?" Ryan says. He grins at the effect Melanie is having on Coop.

Coop looks at me and shrugs. "Yeah, I guess."

"Good," Ryan says. "Bar is in there." He points toward the kitchen. "I have to make sure everything is going okay." He takes Melanie by the arm and starts away, then turns back. "Oh, Evan, can I ask you a favor?"

"Sure."

"Later, maybe, can I get you to play a couple of tunes?"

I glance at Coop and shrug. "Hey, why not."

"Great," Ryan says. "I really appreciate it."

When they're gone, Coop sits down. I can see little beads of sweat on his forehead. "I've never seen a woman like that, up close I mean," he says.

"You mean Melanie? Yeah, she's kinda cute."

"Kinda cute? I would have walked here from Santa Monica to meet her."

"Well, relax cop friend. She's all Ryan's."

"I'm sure she is." He shakes his head and takes a deep breath. "I need a drink."

Within a half hour, the house is full of people laughing, talking, sampling the food and drink, moving from the house out to the pool surrounded by torch lights. Some faces are vaguely familiar from movies, television, or magazines. Ryan introduces me to a few, whose names I don't know, but who I've seen in several pictures. The food is good, the bar flows freely. I drift around feeling, despite the crowd, kind of alone as I overhear snatches of conversations.

"Oh, it's definite, honey. I've got a deal with Universal."

"God, did you see that photo of Carol? She's so over."

"I love the concept. Call me next week."

Whenever I spot Coop, he's talking to somebody different. Later, I find him huddled with a dark-haired woman out by the pool. She's no starlet, more in her mid-thirties, but strikingly beautiful.

"Hey, this is Connie," he says. "I was just telling her about stakeouts."

"Sounds like exciting work," she says, winking at me.

"Coop leads a pretty exciting life," I say.

She looks at Coop. "Maybe you could call me sometime?"

Before Coop can answer I see Ryan shouldering his way through the throng. "Evan, ready to do a little playing now?"

"Sure." I follow Ryan back to the living room. I'm not crazy about this idea but feel like I have to go through with it. I don't like the feeling of being imposed on.

Ryan stands on a chair and everybody quiets down.

"Can I have your attention please," he says. "I have a special surprise for you. Evan Horne is going to play for us." I catch people looking at each other, wondering who I am. "Evan is one of the top pianists in jazz and my good friend. Let's show him some love."

I glance at Coop and roll my eyes. He slips his arm around the dark-haired woman. "Go get 'em, sport."

I sit down at the piano, deciding to just immerse myself in the music, forget the setting, the people, and just enjoy playing this beautiful piano. I start with a ballad, "Moon and Sand," which seems appropriate, slide into "All of You," and end with an up-tempo blues line. When I stop, I'm suddenly aware of the total silence in the room. I turn on the bench and then there's an eruption of applause and whistles.

Ryan steps up. "How about that? Is that fucking jazz piano or what?" He leans in closer to me, Melanie by his side. "Awesome, man, just fucking awesome! I taped the whole thing. This could be a scene in the movie."

Melanie gives me a peck on the cheek. "Yeah, there is a party scene in the script."

Ryan turns on Melanie. "Not now, baby. Get us a drink." He pushes her away. She looks back once then heads for the bar, just as Grant Robbins steps up. I had looked but hadn't seen him all evening.

"That was almost as good as the Jazz Bakery," he says. "How are you, Evan? All settled in?"

"Fine. Quite a party."

"Oh, pretty tame as these things go with Ryan."

"If you've got a few minutes, I'd like to talk with you somewhere quiet."

"How about in the morning. I really have to go. I'll call you." Before I can say more, he's gone.

The party breaks up around midnight. Early for a Hollywood bash I imagine. I catch Coop saying his goodbyes to Ryan, then he comes over to me.

"Thanks for the invite, sport," he says. "Had a little talk with Ryan." He winks and gives me a knowing smile. "I might join the payroll, too. Technical consultant."

I nod and look around. "Where's that woman?"

"Not to worry. We're going to get together. She's working on a TV show." He claps a hand on my shoulder. "Stay in touch."

I head for the guesthouse, wishing Andie could have stayed another day.

Chapter Four

I had cracked the window a few inches when I went to bed, so I awake to the sound of the surf and the smell of cool, fresh, sea air. I splash cold water on my face, throw on some sweat pants and a tee shirt, grab my cell phone and cigarettes, and go in search of coffee. In the house, there's little evidence of the party. It's all quiet and somebody, probably Emillio, has already done some serious cleaning up. No sign of Ryan or Melanie.

In the kitchen, I find a fresh pot of coffee on the warming pad. Sugar, cream, a spoon, and a large mug emblazoned with some studio insignia, are all laid out neatly on the counter. I take the coffee and cigarettes outside and settle into a chair by the pool, soon caught up in the hypnotizing view of the surf and sand. Sunday morning in Malibu.

I go back in the kitchen for a second cup when Emillio comes in from the garage carrying two shopping bags. "Breakfast," he says. He sets the bag on the counter and begins unpacking. "I have bacon, eggs, bagels, fruit, orange juice. Can I make you something?"

"Hey, morning. Nothing right now, thanks." He nods and starts putting everything away. "Do you ever get a day off?"

"Sundays, usually." He glances at his watch. "Mr. Stiles won't be up till noon anyway. Let me know if you need anything."

I nod and go back out to the pool. I'm just starting on the second cup when my phone rings.

"Hi, baby," Andie says. "How's everything in Hollywood land?"

"Very Hollywood. Coop is adapting nicely. He came to the party last night and I think scored with an actress. He also said Ryan tapped him to be technical consultant for the new movie."

"At least you'll have an ally. How was the party?"

"Also very Hollywood. Lots of people I vaguely recognized. Ryan had me play a few tunes."

"That's not part of your duties is it?"

"No, but I didn't see that it hurt anything."

"He wanted to show you off. He loves that power thing," Andie says.

"Got him all figured out, huh?"

"Not entirely, but I'm working on it. How about Melanie?"

"How about her? She looked gorgeous. I thought Coop was going to pass out when Ryan introduced her."

Andie laughs. "I can just imagine him panting and sweating. Any other news?"

"Grant Robbins came late. I tried to corner him but no luck. He's supposed to call this morning, so maybe I'll find out more." There's a pause from Andie. "What?"

"I don't know. Just being my FBI paranoid self I guess. When do you start the actual tutoring?"

"Probably tomorrow. I'll get more of a handle on things then, I think. What are you doing?"

"I'm still in bed, dreading work tomorrow, wishing you were here with me." Her voice drops to a throaty whisper. "Want to fly up for the day?"

"You temptress you."

She laughs. "Always. Well, take care, sweetie."

"You too. I'll call you tomorrow."

"You better. Say hello to Melanie."

I just close the phone when it rings again.

"Evan. Grant Robbins. Not calling too early I hope. How about some breakfast?"

"Sounds good. You coming here to the house? Emillio just brought in some stuff."

"No, I'd prefer someplace we can talk. You know where Point Dume is?"

"Yeah."

"Okay. Turn in the road there. There's a restaurant at the bottom of the hill by the beach. Half hour?"

"See you there."

I park Ryan's BMW and look across the parking lot to a strip of beach, suddenly realizing that's where the trailer James Garner lived in the *Rockford Files* series. Inside, I find Grant Robbins already in a booth by a window, drinking coffee and staring at the ocean. He half rises to shake hands and signals a waitress.

"Thanks for coming. It was just too wild last night." He's dressed casually in slacks and a sweater.

"No problem." I order pancakes and sausage.

"Over easy with bacon and toast for me," Robbins tells the waitress. She pours some coffee for me and leaves us.

"First things first," Robbins says. He looks around, making sure we're out of earshot, although there are only a few people scattered about. "That was really something you did yesterday. Ryan is very grateful and so am I."

I shrug. "No big thing."

"Yes it was. A very big thing, and keeping it quiet is even bigger. You do understand that don't you?"

"I haven't called the *National Enquirer* if that's what you mean."

"I'm sorry," Robbins says. "I just want to make sure we're on the same page."

"Why did he do it?"

"Who knows. He can be careless, reckless even. Trying to impress you. I don't know. Look, Ryan is this young guy, competent actor, who quite suddenly became a big movie star. He makes millions per picture. He's been thrust in the limelight in such a big way, the pressure sometimes gets to be too much.

You've seen these new kids. Money, fame, drugs, arrests, scandals. Ryan has money, power, fame, control, but he can't swim."

Robbins stops as the waitress brings our order and refills our coffee cups. He digs in then looks at me. "Ryan just wanted me to talk to you, kind of reassure him."

I wondered when that had happened. Sometime during the party? "Tell him he has nothing to worry about with me. Is that why we're meeting here?"

"Not entirely. I know you must have some questions you'd probably not discuss in front of Ryan."

"Actually, I do." I take a few bites of my pancakes thinking about it. "I can show Ryan about the piano, but he has to realize that it's up to him to work it out. I can't do it for him."

"No problem there. He's obsessed. He'll put in the time. I guarantee it, and he'll try to become your friend in the process. Believe me, he's very impressed with you, both as a person and a musician."

I look up at Robbins. "Am I missing something?"

Robbins gestures at me with his fork. "You've earned your place. You studied, practiced, nurtured your talent, and overcame a tremendous setback when you had that car accident." He glances at my right wrist. "Still give you any trouble?"

"Sometimes." I flash back to the months of physical therapy, the counseling before I could return to playing full time. "It was a long road to recovery."

"Exactly," Robbins says, "but you did it and also survived some other pretty scary experiences."

He knows it all without going into detail. "I got myself into those situations," I say.

"You also got yourself out. Ryan admires you for that. It wasn't a script made up for a movie. That was real life. You dealt with a real serial killer and helped bring her down."

I push my plate aside. "We don't really have to go into that do we."

"Of course not," Robbins says. "I'm sorry for bringing it up. I'm just trying to tell you where Ryan is coming from in regard to you."

"So what about this new movie. You were serious about me scoring it?"

Robbins looks genuinely surprised. "Absolutely. We just have some contract details to work out."

"To do even some preliminary sketching it would be nice to know what the story is about, maybe even see the script, don't you think?"

"And you will," Robbins says. "All in good time."

"There's something else, isn't there?"

Robbins smiles. "I should have known you'd pick up on that. Let me just give it to you in a nutshell."

"I'm listening."

"This is an independent film. No studio involved until it's done. Then we'll try to get a deal for distributions, get it in one of the festivals—Sundance, maybe even Cannes. The financing comes from a group of investors who think Ryan Stiles stock is first rate, and of course it is. We don't anticipate any real problems, but a couple of them are concerned about various other elements. The costar, the story, the fact that it deals with Ryan as a jazz musician. They want to know why we can't have Quincy Jones or some other hot shot Hollywood composer score the film."

Robbins pauses, glances out the window at the surf rolling in. "I can't tell them you're an experienced film composer can I? Not that I don't think for a minute you can't do it," he adds quickly.

I nod, knowing he's right, and realize how much I don't know about the movie business. "So, how do we get around this?"

"Here's what I want you to do. Get started with the tutoring. Concentrate on getting Ryan up to speed. We're meeting with the investors again soon. It's kind of a dog and pony show. By then we can say how happy Ryan is working with you, and you're the man to score this film. You see where I'm going with this?"

"Yeah, I think so. Will that be enough for the investors?"

Robbins smiles again. "Remember what I told you before. What Ryan Stiles wants, he gets, and these guys not only want to see a return on their money, they want to see themselves attached to a big name movie star and their names in the credits."

"Okay. I figure to get started tomorrow."

"Good," Robbins says. "One other thing. You have any problems, you call me. I'll handle Ryan."

Back at the house, I pull up in front of the gates and realize I don't know the code to get inside. I press a button on the key pad.

"Yes?" It's Emillio's voice coming through the speaker.

"It's Evan. You'll have to let me in." I wait a few seconds for the gates to open, pull in, and park the car. Ryan and Melanie are having breakfast by the pool. "Hey," Ryan says. "You're an early bird." Melanie is thumbing through a magazine. She looks up and smiles. "Sit down, dig in. Emillio makes a great omelet."

I take a chair. "No, thanks. I already got something. Decided to take a drive. Hope it was okay to use the car again."

Ryan nods. "Sweet, isn't it. Where'd you go?"

"Point Dume. I was curious to see where James Garner's trailer was parked." Ryan looks at me blankly. "You know, *The Rockford Files* television series?"

"Must have been before my time." We lapse into silence for a bit, which seems to make Ryan edgy. "Melanie and I are going to drive into Santa Monica later, have some lunch. Why don't you come along?"

Why not? The alternative is hanging around the house all afternoon. "Sure, but isn't it difficult for you in public?"

"Photographers, you mean? Yeah, but I gotta get out sometimes." He grins. "You'll be a diversion. They'll be trying to figure out who you are," he says. He glances at his watch. "I'll make a reservation. About one, okay?"

"Sure. I think I'll get in some practice time."

"Cool." He stands and Melanie follows suit.

I go into the house and sit down at the piano, playing some scales chords then slide into "If You Could See Me Now." I play for a little over an hour and when I look up, I see Emillio, standing in the doorway watching.

"You play beautifully," he says. He hands me a slip of paper with some numbers. "That's the code for the gate."

"Thanks."

"Can you really teach Mr. Stiles to play?"

I take my hands off the keyboard. "I can teach him to *look* like he's playing."

Emillio smiles. "That I have to see."

We drive into Santa Monica in Ryan's other car, the Mercedes. I sit in the back behind him, and watch Melanie flinch occasionally as he drives way too fast, changing lanes, swerving and zipping around other cars. He has a Keith Jarrett CD playing. I recognize it as *Live at the Blue Note*.

"What's with all the moaning?" Ryan says as he turns up the California Incline to Ocean Avenue. He means the way Jarrett sings along with the notes he plays.

"That's just Keith's way."

"I like it," Melanie says, turning her head toward me. "It sounds so...so real."

Ryan glances at her. "Yeah, you like moaning, don't you."

She colors slightly and shakes her head. "God, Ryan."

He grins at her and pats her leg. "Just kidding, baby." She pulls away and gazes out the side window.

Just off Ocean Avenue, we pull into the parking lot of a restaurant called The Bistro. At valet parking, three guys in black pants and white shirts stand ready to take charge of the car. A few feet away are a half-dozen photographers pacing around. How does this work, I wonder. Ryan Stiles makes a reservation. The restaurant tips off the photographers for a kickback?

The valet guys open the doors for us and we all get out.

"Hey, Ryan," one of the photographers yells. "Over here."

Ryan turns, flashes the smile and waves. I hang back to watch the show. They close in, cameras clicking, jockeying for position and then focus on Melanie, who smiles big, but keeps an eye on Ryan. They all ignore me.

"Thanks, guys," he says and waves again, then heads into the restaurant. Melanie and I follow just behind him.

"You ever get tired of this?" I ask her quietly. She looks stunning in a black miniskirt and white top, her blond hair flowing around her face.

She nods. "Yes, but it's all part of the game. Ryan loves it," she says quieter.

Inside, we're seated quickly with little stir. Ryan must be a regular. The service and the food are excellent. Melanie picks at a seafood salad. Ryan and I go for steak sandwiches that are so tender they could be cut with a fork. Nobody talks much and Ryan seems restless, distracted, as if he'd expected someone who didn't show. Maybe he and Melanie had an argument.

We both look up as a man in a Hawaiian shirt stops at the table. "Mr. Stiles, I don't mean to interrupt your lunch, but would you mind?" He holds out a pen and a piece of paper.

I see the manager fast approaching the table but Ryan waves him off. "It's okay." He takes the pen from the man, and signs his name with a flourish. "There you go. Don't go selling it on eBay."

The man nods and smiles. "Oh no, never," he says. "I'm too big a fan for that." He smiles at Melanie and backs away.

Ryan signs the check and throws down two twenties for the tip and we go back outside to wait for valet to bring the car around. The photographers are still hovering for more pictures as the car arrives. Ryan waves again but as we start to get in the car, one of the photographers moves closer. He's a big guy with longish hair and a beard. He kneels in front of the passenger door and points his camera at Melanie's legs.

"How about some thigh, Melanie?"

Ryan is quickly around the car. "Back off," he says, pulling off his sunglasses.

"Hey, come on," the photographer says. "It's hot, we've been out here for over an hour."

"I said back off." Melanie gets in and shuts the door as Ryan puts his hand on the photographer's chest and pushes. The photographer lets go of his camera, letting it dangle around his neck. He backs up, plants his feet, and turns to his comrades.

"You guys see that?" Ryan moves closer. I can see the veins in his neck pulse, his face darken.

I start around the car but the photographer backs up. "Okay, okay." He grins and puts his hands up. "No harm."

Ryan stalks back around to the driver's side. "Get in," he says to me. He shoves some bills in the valet guy's hand, guns the engine and we roar out of the parking lot, tires screeching as the photographers click away.

"Fucking vultures!" Ryan yells. He pounds his fist on the steering wheel and looks over at Melanie, almost cowering in the passenger seat, as far away as she can get. "You okay, baby?" She nods and turns her face to the window again.

Back on the coast highway, Ryan drives fast until we pass Topanga Canyon. He suddenly yanks the wheel and turns in front of oncoming traffic into a parking area on the beach side and brakes to a stop. "I'll be back in a minute," he says, getting out of the car and stomping down a slight incline toward the beach.

I get out of the car and light a cigarette and walk around to the passenger side. Melanie lowers the window and looks at me. "You okay?" I ask her.

She nods, her eyes following Ryan's trek down the beach. We can see him now, standing by the water. "He…he just gets like this sometimes." She glances at the beach then back at me. "Can I have one of those?"

I offer her a cigarette and light her up. She leans out the window, careful to blow the exhaled smoke away from the car.

"Why go out someplace he knows there will be photographers?"

She shrugs. "He likes the rush, being recognized, being photographed, but he hates it too. It's a trap. At first you want the exposure, then when you get too much—and, well you saw. He's very protective of me."

"Do you need protecting?"

She gazes at me for a long moment. "No," she says, "not usually."

I'm not entirely sure what she means, but I don't press it. We both watch Ryan turn and head back toward the car. Melanie hands me her cigarette and I crush both of them into the dirt. She digs in her purse for a mint and pops one in her mouth as

Ryan jogs up the rise, all smiles now. "Sorry, just had to clear my head," he says. "Hey, how about you drive?"

I hesitate for a moment, glance at Melanie. "Sure."

Ryan gets in the back seat. "Back here, baby," he says to Melanie.

I turn the car around, wait for a break in traffic and get back on the highway to head for Trancas. I glance once in the rearview mirror. Ryan is leaning back against the seat, his eyes closed, his arm around Melanie.

Ah, lunch with a movie star.

Chapter Five

"Hold your left hand on the keys," I tell Ryan Stiles. "Spread your fingers wider."

"Yeah, yeah I know," he says. I can hear the irritation in his voice. I know exactly what he's feeling. We've been working for over an hour and he's tiring. I can see beads of perspiration on his forehead. He stops and massages his left forearm. "I can really feel it."

"Good, you should. You're using muscles you didn't know you have." I'd showed him some fingering, how to play a C scale with his right hand. Up and down, all white notes, making it easy. He was getting that but he continually pulled his left hand off the keyboard.

"Let me show you again." He gets up and stands behind me as I sit down. "Like this." I play a three-note chord with my left, and run up and down the keys with my right, alternating the order. "See? Chord left, scale right."

Ryan flops down in a chair next to the piano. "Jesus, fight scenes are easier than this."

I laugh. "You'll get it. Just takes time and practice. I'll write out some exercises for you."

I put my left hand on the keyboard again and play a three-note C chord but with a different kind of voicing. "Now watch my hand." Barely moving my fingers, I change the voicing to a F chord then a G chord then back to the original position for the C chord. "That's a basic blues progression." I do it again and this time play corresponding scales with my right hand each time I change the position of my left hand. "See what I'm doing?"

Ryan leans forward, nodding, watching closely. "I think so."

I get up. "Okay, you try it."

He's awkward at first, fumbling, looking at the keyboard, but gradually the transition and coordination between his hands starts to get better. I watch him for a minute or two, see that he's got it. "Okay, practice that for awhile. I'm going outside for a smoke."

I leave him to it and go out by the pool. There's a strong wind coming off the ocean, churning up the surf, whipping up little clouds of sand. Emillio opens the sliding glass door and comes out with a pitcher of orange juice and two glasses and sets them on the table. I nod my thanks and watch him stare out at the ocean.

"You're being very patient with him," he says. "You must be a good teacher."

"First time for me." We both listen for a moment as Ryan's efforts filter out to the pool. "He's trying. It's all new for him."

"So is a patient teacher." He turns and goes back inside.

I hadn't been sure what to expect with Ryan Stiles. Even a major star has to take direction, suggestions on how to do a scene, timing, shaping the dialogue. But this was different. Ryan was a novice, learning a totally new skill. I'm not a movie director, but I can play the piano and Ryan, at least so far, seems to accept the childlike instructions without reservation.

I finish my cigarette and look up as he joins me. He pours himself a glass of orange juice and drops in a chair next to me. "My arm is so fucking sore," he says. "Does it go away eventually?"

I laugh. "Yeah, in about ten years."

He nods and downs half the juice. "How about your hand. You had some kind of accident, didn't you?"

I look at him and automatically flex the fingers of my right hand. "You know about that too?"

He shrugs. "Grant did a lot of research."

I nod. Sometimes I still wake up in a sweat, remembering the sirens, the lights, the cool asphalt of the Coast Highway under me, and later, the fingerless latex glove, squeezing the rubber ball as daily rehab. "Yeah, car accident on the Coast highway. Cut some tendons in my wrist. Took a lot of rehab. I wasn't sure I'd be able to play again. Took a long time."

"Jesus," Ryan says. "I didn't know it was that bad."

"It's okay now. Hardly bothers me."

We sip the orange juice and gaze out at the surf. "Listen, something I want to talk to you about."

"Sure. What's on your mind?"

"It's about yesterday, at the restaurant. I want to apologize. I was out of line."

"No need," I say.

He puts up his hand. "Yes there is." He takes a deep breath. "I've got a bit of a temper, as you may have heard." He shrugs and looks away. "Sometimes it gets the best of me, especially if it's about Melanie."

"The photographer was out of line too. Melanie was almost in the car."

"Yeah, he was, trying to get a crotch shot. I mean, what would you have done if that had been Andie?"

I shrug and smile. "Don't forget Andie is an FBI agent. She would have probably pulled her gun." I pause, thinking for a moment. "Maybe I would have reacted the same way, but you have to know these guys make their living on photos of people like you and Melanie. That doesn't make it right but that's the way it is, right?"

Ryan nods and grips the glass tighter. "Yeah I know, all too well, but sometimes…" His voice trails off. "There's something else too." He looks at me. "This is just between you and me, okay?"

"Okay."

He takes another deep breath. "Melanie wants a baby."

I don't answer for a moment, not sure what he wants me to say, surprised that he's confiding in me like this. "And that's a problem for you."

"Fuck, I don't know, man. I love Melanie. She's a sweet girl, but I just don't know if I'm ready for that yet. She's always reminding me about all these couples that aren't married and having babies."

"How long have you been together?"

"Little over two years. We met on the set of a movie I was doing. She had a tiny part."

"Well, maybe you just need more time. You should be sure."

I think about Andie and me. She doesn't want kids, and we're still getting used to being together as much as we are. We have our own places. I love my Monte Rio getaway, and Andie keeps her apartment in San Francisco to be close to the bureau office. Moving in together isn't such a remote idea anymore. It's just a question of where. We both know that, but anything beyond sharing living space I haven't thought about.

Ryan finishes off the rest of his juice and stands up. "Well, thanks for listening." He watches me stub out my cigarette. "Dude, you have to give those up."

"Go practice some more. I'll be in soon."

He grins and salutes. "Yes, sir."

We go for the rest of the morning then break for lunch. Ryan goes to his room and I decide to take a long walk on the beach. It almost feels like I'm back in Venice. When I look up, I see I'm near the shopping mall with Trancas Market. I cross the highway and go inside for a cold drink then check out some of the other nearby shops. At a video rental store I browse through some movies and find a few music DVDs.

I take them to the counter. The clerk, a young kid in jeans, tee shirt, and green streaks in his dark hair looks up and asks for my video club card. "This isn't local," he says.

"Right. I'm staying with some friends on Broad Beach." I wonder for a moment if I should tell him where I'm staying, but he'd never believe it if I said Ryan Stiles.

"I'll need a credit card then," he says. "Sorry, store policy."

I hand over my American Express. He puts everything in a bag and returns my card. Outside, I decide to walk back along Broad Beach Road rather than on the beach. About halfway to the house, I notice a dark green van slowly trailing behind me. I turn and look, waiting for it to pass, but it slows. I stop then, waiting as it pulls up alongside me.

"Can I help you?" I lean toward the passenger side window. I see a couple of cameras and a large bag on the floor. The driver is maybe thirty, with longish hair, wearing dark glasses.

He smiles. "Just thought you might want a ride."

"No thanks. I'm fine." I step back and turn away but he doesn't move on.

"You're Evan Horne, the piano player, aren't you? "

"What if I am?"

"Staying with Ryan Stiles? You just friends or are you working on something?"

"Not really your business, is it?"

He takes off the glasses. "C'mon, man. I'm looking for a story. Famous, well not-so-famous jazz pianist staying with Ryan Stiles? Something is up. You working on something with him?"

"Can't help you," I say. "Why don't you ask him?"

He puts his glasses back on. "I would if I could get to him." He leans toward me. "There's some nice money in it for you."

"We're done." I turn and walk away. I listen for the van and hear him throw it in gear. "Thanks," he yells and makes a fast U-turn.

Welcome to Malibu.

I cut through a public access path that leads back to the beach. At the house, Ryan and Melanie are lounging by the pool. Ryan is stretched out on a chaise lounge. Melanie is flipping through a magazine with Angelina Jolie on the cover. When I tell Ryan about the guy in the van, he sits up and takes off his sunglasses and glares. "Sonofabitch. What'd you tell him?"

"That I couldn't help him. Not his business."

"You're sure."

I look at Ryan for a moment.

"Of course he's sure," Melanie says, sitting up straighter.

Ryan glares at Melanie for a moment, then leans back. "I'm sorry, I just get paranoid over this shit."

I feel Melanie's eyes on me as I sit down and light a cigarette. "Look, Ryan, maybe this isn't such a good idea after all. We can just forget the whole thing if you want."

"No, no, it's fine really. I just get spooked with these guys, always trying to get to me."

"I understand, but you have to trust me. I'm working for you."

"I know, I know."

"Well then act like it," Melanie says, her outburst surprising me.

Ryan turns toward her. "If I want your opinion, I'll ask for it."

She throws down the magazine, gets up, and stomps away.

Ryan plops back on the chaise and shakes his head. "Great, now I've pissed her off too."

I watch him for a moment, trying to imagine what it would be like to be him. Stalked wherever he went by photographers, his privacy constantly invaded, unable to go anywhere without exposing himself to scrutiny. The more famous he became, the less free he was. And these days, anybody with a cell phone camera could catch him in an off moment in an unfavorable light.

As Grant Robbins said, Ryan Stiles was young, rich, famous, ambitious, with a beautiful girlfriend, a big expensive home, but he was paying the price. And the fame, being constantly in the public eye, was getting to him. He seemed always on edge, never really relaxed. Who could he trust? Grant Robbins? Melanie? There were probably others I wasn't aware of. As the newest, temporary member of the inner circle, I could understand his paranoia. For Ryan Stiles, anonymity is long gone.

He sits up again and leans forward, his elbows resting on his knees. "What did this guy in the van look like?"

I describe the van and the driver. "I noticed some cameras on the floor."

Ryan nods. "Yeah I think I know the guy. He freelances for some of the trade mags. They all want a story."

I try to kid him out of this dark mood. "Well, you are *the* Ryan Stiles."

He manages a smile. "Yeah, I am aren't I?" He looks at me closely. "It doesn't impress you at, all does it?"

"Oh, I'm impressed. I've even seen a couple of your movies."

"Which ones?"

"The terrorist one. Lots of car chases, explosions, special effects."

"And?"

"It was okay."

"Okay? You know how much that movie grossed? I topped the charts for five weeks."

"Is that what it's all about? Money?"

He nods. "It's how you get to make more movies." He looks away for a moment. "What was the other one?"

"*Too Late to Die.* You played a district attorney."

"And that one?"

"I liked it. You were good."

"It was a flop. Minimal release, almost went straight to video."

"Does that matter?"

"That's what I like about you. Straight ahead, no bullshit, just play the piano."

I shrug. "What can I say? Not many jazz musicians are really famous. Miles, Dave Brubeck, Wynton Marsalis. There aren't many known to the general public."

I pull my chair closer. "Let me tell you a story about Bill Evans. He was famous in the jazz world, but nothing like movie star fame. He was in Los Angeles once for a gig and later stopped by this bar in his hotel. It was noisy and crowded but not a single person recognized him. He sat at the bar, listening to this young solo piano player who was being ignored by everybody. The guy almost fell off the bench when he turned and saw Bill Evans.

"He went over and introduced himself and they talked for a few minutes. Evans was pleased, flattered that the young pianist recognized him, but you know what Evans said?"

"What?" Ryan was hanging on every word now.

"He said sometimes he thought it would be better to be like that pianist. Just do the gig, get your money, go home. No dealing with record companies, interviews, just play the piano. The young pianist was stunned, then he asked Evans if he'd like to play a couple of tunes. To his surprise, Evans said yes. He sat down and still nobody recognized him. Head down like always, playing one of his own songs, 'Waltz for Debby' in that crowded noisy bar, and not a single person said, hey, isn't that Bill Evans?"

Evans finished and came back to the pianist. He looked around the noisy, crowded room and said, 'You know what, maybe not.'"

Ryan looks puzzled for a moment, trying to put it together, then finally does, and smiles big. "No shit." He gets up and slaps me on the shoulder. "Thanks, man." He starts to walk away, then turns back. "You think that story is true?"

"I know it is."

"How do you know?"

"I was the young pianist."

Chapter Six

Another week goes by and Ryan is really starting to get it. I use Red Garland's playing from a Miles Davis recording, *Workin'*. There's a trio cut, "Ahmad's Blues" that features Red's famous two-handed block-chord style. I play his solo over and over, making Ryan try to emulate and synchronize his hands with the rhythm of Garland's playing. By the end of the week, he's getting close, at least on the first two choruses.

"I never even heard of fucking Red Garland," Ryan says, rubbing his left forearm, "and now I'm sick of him."

I have to laugh. "Well, you're starting to look like you play like Red, so don't be too hard on him."

"Really? Are you serious?" He jumps up from the piano bench, excited.

"I'm serious. You're not there yet, but you're getting close."

"Yes!" Ryan says, punching the air.

My cell phone rings. I flip it open but don't recognize the number. "Keep going. I have to take this." I go out on the patio. "Evan Horne."

"Evan, it's Ruth Price."

"Hey, Ruth. Got another gig for me?"

"Well, not quite. I'm organizing a benefit for an old friend. One of the jazz DJs, Herman Cassidy. Remember him? Everybody calls him Hoppy."

Herman Hopalong Cassidy's Jazz Avenue had been a fixture on L.A. radio for decades. I remember listening to him when I was still in high school. "Sure I do. What happened?"

"Old story, medical problems, little or no insurance," Ruth says. "He's in the hospital now. Anyway, I wasn't sure you'd still be in town. The trio I had lined up had to cancel. I was wondering if you could fill in for me."

"Where is it?"

"It's in Malibu. Place called the Anchor, Friday night. I know it's short notice but can you get a trio together? I'll be forever in your debt."

I think for a moment. I'm sure I can get Buster Browne and maybe the same drummer I had at the Jazz Bakery. "Let me call you back, but yeah, I'll do it."

"Oh, you are a sweetheart," Ruth says. "Let me know as soon as you can."

"Will do."

Buster Browne is not big on benefits, but he's free when I track him down, and when he hears it's for Hoppy and Ruth Price, he agrees. "I got a wedding gig in the afternoon, but evening is cool. Where is it?"

"Place called the Anchor in Malibu."

"Yeah, I remember that place. They used to have jazz regularly. I think Art Pepper recorded there once. Do we get dinner?"

I smile. "Yeah, Buster, I'm sure we'll get something to eat."

"Cool. I'm there then. Want me to get a drummer?"

"That would be very helpful."

"Okay, no problem. I know several who would like to play with you."

"Thanks, Buster. You're a prince."

I close the phone as Ryan comes out on the patio. "Everything okay?"

"Yeah, just somebody calling me about a gig."

Ryan's face creases into a frown. "You're not going out of town, are you?"

"No, it's right here in Malibu."

When I tell him the details, he nods, thinks for a moment, then says, "Can I help?"

"How, what do you mean?"

He looks a little sheepish. "Well, maybe if I was there, it might draw more people, raise more money."

"Are you sure? Man, that would be great."

"Consider it done. Is your cop friend Cooper coming? Might be cool to have some low-key security."

"Good idea. I'll call him."

"Just let me know what you want me to do," Ryan says. "Maybe I could comp some movie passes or something." He walks off leaving me astonished.

Ruth Price is no less so when I call her back. "Are you kidding? Ryan Stiles will be there? How did you, I mean, how, oh never mind. That's wonderful."

I laugh. "I'll have his people call your people."

"I don't have any people."

I think to call Andie but before I get a chance, my phone rings. "Hi handsome. Like a guest for the weekend? I can get away 'til Monday."

"Great, I was just going to call you. I've got a gig Friday night. A benefit Ruth Price is putting on right here in Malibu. This is perfect."

"I love it when things work like this. How's it going with the megastar?"

"Better than you would imagine. I've been pushing him pretty hard and he's hanging in there. I'll fill you in when you get here."

"Have they showed you the script yet?"

"No, but soon, they tell me."

There's a brief pause. "Well you can catch me up later. I can hardly wait. I'll call you when I get a flight."

Friday morning, leaning against the BMW, risking a warning from security, I wait for Andie to come out of baggage claim at Southwest. She spots me first and runs over, drops her bag and wraps herself around me. She kisses me, then leans back.

"My, don't you look all tanned and Malibu. I'm jealous," she says as we get in the car. I ease away from the curb, merging with the exiting traffic, and watch her lean back, letting the sun wash over her.

I catch her up on everything as we roll down the California Incline to the Coast Highway. She listens, eyes closed, nodding, but sits up when I tell her about dragging Ryan out of the surf, and my meeting later with Grant Robbins.

"He can't swim?" She shakes her head and leans back again. "Who would have thought."

"Exactly. There was also a little skirmish when we went to lunch. He kind of flipped out when some photographers crossed the line with Melanie. He's got quite a temper."

"She okay?" Andie asks, turning toward me.

"Yeah, but shook her up. She's a bit scared of him."

Andie nods. "I'll have to get with her, have a little girl talk."

We glide through Malibu proper. I slow and look for the Anchor Restaurant. It's wedged between a motel and a surf shop. "That's where we are tonight." I pull over and see a makeshift banner strung across the entrance. TONIGHT ONLY—JAZZ EVAN HORNE & RYAN STILES.

Andie looks then turns toward me. "He's going to be there?"

"He volunteered. Amazing, huh?"

"Very," Andie says as I pull away from the curb and merge with traffic. "I bet it's the first time he didn't get top billing."

We pass Malibu pier and race up the incline past Pepperdine University where the traffic is lighter. Andie is silent. "What?"

"I don't know," she says. "Something just bothers me."

"About Ryan, you mean?"

"Everything."

When we get to the house, we hear loud voices coming from the living room. I peek in and see Ryan and Grant Robbins going at it. Ryan has his back to the doorway and doesn't see me.

"I don't care what it's for," Robbins says. He has his coat off and his tie loosened. "You have to let me know about things like this. There could be security issues." His eyes go to me and Ryan turns around. He smiles at Andie and me.

"Hey, we got Santa Monica Police and now the FBI. Nothing to worry about."

Robbins straightens his tie. "Hello, Evan. Miss Lawrence. Ryan and I were just having a, ah, a discussion about tonight's event."

"Look, if it's going to be a problem, Ruth Price will understand."

Ryan plops down in a chair. "There's no problem. I said I'd be there and I will. So will Melanie."

"Of course you will," Robbins says, calmer now. He smiles, as if he doesn't want a scene in front of me. "I just need some advance warning to make sure everything goes smoothly. The first I heard about it was when I drove by and saw the banner."

That surprises me. I thought Ryan would have called Robbins. Ryan stands up and looks at Robbins. "Are we done?" He turns and walks out without waiting for an answer. "Hey, Andie. Glad you could make it."

Robbins sighs and shakes his head. "God, he can be trying. Can we talk a minute, Evan?"

"Sure." I turn to look at Andie.

She nods. "I'll be in the guesthouse."

"No you won't," Melanie says, as she suddenly appears in shorts and a sweatshirt. "We're going for a walk." She hugs Andie. "I'm so glad you came back."

Andie looks taken by surprise. She waves and lets Melanie lead her away.

Grant Robbins and I sit down. "So tell me about this thing tonight," he says.

I run down the details, or as much as I know. "It's not that big a deal," I say.

"Okay, it's a good cause, but if Ryan is making an appearance, it's always a big deal," Robbins says. "Do me a favor. If something else like this comes up, give me a heads up okay? Ryan forgets how his presence can stir things up."

I doubt that but I don't say anything. "I'll have to be there early to get everything set with the band and see what Ruth Price wants."

"No problem," Robbins says. "I'll have a car to pick up Ryan and Melanie. Andie will go with you?" He considers a moment. "Your policeman friend will be there, too?"

"Yeah. Ryan suggested inviting him."

"Good. Maybe you can tell him to stick kind of close to Ryan."

I study Robbins for a moment. "Are you worried about something happening?"

"No, it's just, well, there'll be fans, photographers. You just never know."

"Ryan sort of jokingly asked Coop—Lieutenant Cooper to help with security on the film. By the way—"

Robbins puts up his hand. "Good. Tell him he's hired, as of tonight."

At the Anchor, I turn over the BMW to a valet parking guy. "Be careful with this. It belongs to Ryan Stiles."

"No way," he says.

"Trust me."

"Dude, it's handled. No problem."

Andie and I push through a growing throng of people gathered near the entrance, I assume, to get a glimpse of Ryan when he arrives. Some temporary barriers have been set up manned by some Malibu sheriffs, but it all looks pretty friendly. I see a couple of photographers leaning on the barrier talking to one of the cops.

Inside, there's already a sizable crowd seated at the tables and hovering around the buffet. Near the stage, a blow-up photo of Hoppy on an easel.

Ruth Price comes up as I look at the photo. It had to be taken years ago and shows Hoppy in his signature beret and smoke glasses. "How's he doing?"

"You know, resting comfortably as they always say. Cancer's a bitch, isn't it? Thanks again for doing this, Evan. And my God, Ryan Stiles to boot. I won't even ask how you pulled that off."

I smile. "Good, it's top secret."

Ruth gives me a look. "You're not kidding, are you?"

"Nope."

"He and his girlfriend can sit with me over there." She points to a table off to the side of the stage, with a "Reserved" placard on it. "You can do a couple of sets, we'll make a presentation, a few speakers, you know how these things go. We'll just fake it."

"No problem. The other guys here yet?"

She points to a buffet set up against one wall. "Buster's over there, of course." I look and see Buster Browne piling a plate full of food. "Try the piano. I got a dealer in Santa Monica to donate it for tonight. I've got to work the room a little." She hurries off.

"I'm going to look for Coop'," Andie says as I head for the stage. The piano is a baby grand. I sit down and try a few chords. The action feels good and will be fine. I'm joined by the drummer as he rolls his cases in. He's a tall thin guy wearing thick glasses.

"Evan, Jack Sears. Looking forward to it." He starts setting up and Buster wanders over, his plate still half-full. Seeing Buster, I feel underdressed in a sports coat and slacks. Buster's in his wedding gig uniform: a white shirt, a tie, and a dark suit that looks a size too small.

"Dude, they have some serious food here," he says, his mouth half-full. "Better try this roast beef." He sits on the edge of the stage and finally takes a breath. "This movie star really coming?"

"So I'm told," I say. The three of us have a brief conference, deciding on what we'll play as Jack finishes setting up his drums. "Ruth will introduce us and then go from there. We'll play a short set, then she'll introduce Ryan Stiles and make a few presentations."

We all turn toward the entrance then as the crowd parts and Ryan and Melanie come in, smiling and waving. I walk over to Andie and Coop as Ruth escorts the couple to their table, Grant Robbins trailing behind them.

Ryan is in black jeans and shirt and a leather jacket. Melanie has opted for a tan pantsuit a shade darker than her skin.

"You want to wipe the drool off your face, Coop," I say.

"She is something," he says, blushing a little.

I pull Coop aside. "Robbins would like you to stick close to Stiles, okay? He says you're hired as of tonight."

Coop nods and takes on his cop look for a moment. "They expecting trouble?"

"No, just being cautious."

"Always a good thing to be," Coop says.

Herman Cassidy has been a fixture on L.A. jazz radio for over three decades, so when Ruth Price makes her opening remarks, there's loud applause. "Let's be generous and remember why we're all here," she says. "We have a very special guest tonight who has graciously agreed to be here. Let's show him some jazz fan appreciation." She pauses and glances at Ryan's table. "Ladies and Gentlemen, Ryan Stiles."

Ryan stands and waves and smiles in true movie star fashion. Coop, I see, is standing just behind the table. Andie is sitting with Melanie.

"We'll hear from Mr. Stiles a bit later, but right now, I'm going to turn things over to Evan Horne and his trio to get things started."

We get a nice welcome. I nod at Buster and Jack and count us into "Love for Sale." The groove is there immediately as Buster bears down and Jack's ride cymbal cuts through sharply. It's relaxed, easy, a no-pressure gig. We play three more tunes. As the applause dies, Ruth heads for the stage.

"I'm going to introduce Ryan now."

I nod as she steps to the microphone. "Once more for the Evan Horne trio," she says. She glances toward Ryan. "We're very privileged, and I must confess, surprised to have as a special guest, who really needs no introduction, Mr. Ryan Stiles."

There's a burst of applause as Ryan makes his way to the stage, all smiles and waving. "Thanks, Ruth. I'm very happy to be here and do whatever I can to help one of jazz radio's finest." I catch Buster's eye as we look at each other, both of us thinking the same thing.

Ryan reaches into his jacket pocket and hands something to Ruth. She takes it, looks, and her eyes fly open.

"This is a check for ten thousand dollars," she says.

The audience jumps to their feet and bursts into an ovation that lasts over a minute. I watch from the piano, as stunned as Ruth obviously is. I'm sure Ryan never heard of Herman Cassidy until I told him about the benefit. It's an amazing gesture but it makes me wonder at his motives.

Ruth then motions to a small woman in her late sixties to come up. "Ryan, this is Hoppy's wife." She hands the check to her and steps aside.

Ryan smiles and hugs her. "Young man, you can't imagine how much this means, how much it will help Hoppy. He loves your movies."

There's more applause as she returns to her seat, clutching the check. Ryan grabs the microphone. "Hey, we're not finished yet. I want to invite everybody here tonight to the premiere of my next movie. And hey, you all better be there."

There's laughter and more applause as Ryan walks off and goes back to his table. Looking shocked, Ruth says, "Well the only way to follow that is I guess with some more jazz from Evan Horne and his trio."

We play for another forty minutes, closing with a blues that lets everybody stretch out. Ruth comes back up to the stage. "Thanks so much, guys. That was great. Get something to eat."

I get a plate from the buffet, join Ryan's table, and sit down next to Andie. "You were good as always," she says.

"Yes," Melanie says. "Hearing you with a group was just wonderful."

"Yeah, he's something isn't he, baby?" Ryan says, and he sounds genuine. I glance at Andie and she shrugs.

We talk some more, sample the buffet until I feel Ryan getting restless. "Would you mind if I got going?" he asks me.

"Ryan, I think at this point you could do anything you want."

"Cool. We'll see you back at the house then." He and Melanie and Grant Robbins say their goodbyes to Ruth Price, and to his credit, Ryan stops at Mrs. Cassidy's table for a moment.

"He's really not a bad guy," I say to Andie.

"Yeah," she says. "I'm ready too, if you are."

Jack and Buster Browne are packing up as we head for the exit. I slip them both fifty bucks.

"Hey, not necessary," Buster says, "but much appreciated."

Outside, there are even more fans waving photos and pens at Ryan to stop and sign. Coop hovers right behind him, his eyes scanning the crowd. Ryan gives a final wave and smile and heads for the car Robbins has had pull up.

One of the photographers climbs over the barrier and, walking backwards, keeps shooting. Coop waves him aside but he pays no attention, the camera almost in Ryan's face. I see it's the same guy from the restaurant at lunch. Robbins has the car door open and ushers Melanie inside, but the photographer blocks Ryan.

"Come on, Flash," Coop says. "Show's over."

He ignores Coop and reaches out with one hand. Coop grabs him, twists his arm behind his back and leans him against the car. Ryan glares, starts to get in, then suddenly yanks on the camera strap, breaking it, and throws the camera on the ground before he jumps in the car.

"Go," he says. The car speeds away, and the crowd is suddenly quiet. Then there's another explosion of yelling and flashes as everybody shoots the car and the photographer, on his hands and knees, picking up the pieces of his camera.

Coop leans down and helps him to his feet. "You should have listened, sport."

"Fuck you," the photographer says, jerking away from Coop's grip. "He's going to pay for this. He broke the lens." The body of the camera looks whole, so the film is probably okay.

"I'll get the car," I say to Andie. I leave her with Coop and look for the valet guy. "The red BMW," I tell him.

"It's gone, man. He jumped out of the limo and took it." He looks panicked. "You said it was his car."

"Yeah, it is. Don't worry about it."

I go back to Coop and Andie. "Ryan took the sports car."

"Was Melanie with him?" Andie asks.

"Doesn't sound like it."

Coop frowns. "Come on. I'll take you guys back with me."

When we get back to the house, there's no BMW and no Ryan Stiles. Melanie and Grant Robbins are standing in the kitchen.

"What happened?"

"He just jumped out of the car," Melanie says.

"He's not answering his cell either," Robbins says. "Is the photographer okay?"

Coop nods. "I think he's going to want a new camera though."

Robbins sighs. "I wish it was going to be that easy." He looks at Melanie. "I have to go. Have him call me as soon as he gets in." Melanie nods and heads for her room.

"Me too," Coop says. "Nothing I can do here. He's probably just blowing off steam."

Andie and I head for the guesthouse. "Isn't Hollywood exciting," she says.

Chapter Seven

I leave Andie still sleeping and go up to the house in search of coffee. Melanie is already there, in baggy sweats, no makeup, sipping orange juice and talking with Emillio. She turns when she sees me. "He just called," she says. "He's at his father's house."

"Is he okay?" I take a cup of coffee from Emillio and nod my thanks.

"Yeah, I guess," Melanie says. She seems both relieved and angry.

"So, is he on the way?"

She pauses. "He wants you to come and get him."

"Me? But he has his car."

"I know, I know, but he says he doesn't feel like driving. Do you mind? I just want him back here." She looks away for a moment. "He asked for you."

"Yeah, sure, I guess."

"Oh, thank you." She moves in and hugs me.

"What's going on?" We turn and see Andie walking in.

"Ryan is at his Dad's. I have to go get him."

"Lucky you," Andie says

Melanie turns to the counter, writes down an address on a pad and hands me a key. "Here, take the Mercedes."

I take the key and note and head back for the guess house to get dressed. When I return, Andie and Melanie are sitting out on the deck. Emillio hands me another coffee in a travel mug. "Have fun, girls."

The address is in the north end of the San Fernando Valley. It's a long haul from Malibu, and even on a Saturday morning, the traffic is heavy. Following Melanie's directions, I exit the Ventura Freeway at Fallbrook, drive east to Calvert, and start checking street numbers. I finally find the house a couple of miles from the freeway, almost hidden by big trees that nearly engulf the circular driveway.

I turn off the engine and consider the house. It's a rambling, ranch style, probably built in the fifties. Pleasant enough but nothing to show it belongs to the parents of a multimillionaire movie star.

As I get out of the car, a small compact man comes out to greet me. He's dressed in jeans, a denim shirt, and boots. His hair is graying and his weathered face breaks into a smile. "You must be Evan," he says, shaking my hand vigorously. "Come in, come in. I'm Ben Stiles. Ryan is having a shower and getting cleaned up."

I follow him into the house, through an expansive living room of well worn furniture dominated by a huge projection screen television. He catches me looking. "Gift from Ryan," he says, as if he needed to justify it's presence. "He wanted to buy us a new house, but his mom and I like it here." He shrugs. "This is where Ryan grew up."

Stiles leads me into the kitchen. "How about some coffee?" Without waiting for an answer, he pours us two mugs from a glass pot, and gets a container of half-and-half from the refrigerator. We sit down at a huge oak table that gives us a view of the large backyard dotted with a few trees and shrubs. I glance at a large glass ashtray on the table with a couple of half-smoked butts.

Stiles shrugs. "Not me, my wife," he says. "Smoke if you want," he says, noticing the bulge in my shirt pocket.

"Thanks." I light up and sip the coffee, waiting for more, but Stiles is quiet for a long moment

"Thanks for coming over," he says, looking into his cup. "Ryan was not in very good shape last night. It was really late. I know Melanie must have been worried when he didn't come home. I told him to call her. Such a sweet girl."

"She was worried. We all were."

Stiles nods. "He told me a little about it this morning." He shakes his head. "That photographer. It's terrible the way those guys are. I know they have to make a living, but, sometimes they go too far." He looks up and stares out the window. "Ryan's under a lot of pressure, as I'm sure you know." He looks up and smiles then, "But hey, he told me you're teaching him to play the piano for his next movie."

"Well, just to make it look like he's playing," I say. "He's catching on pretty well."

"Yeah, once Ryan starts something, he throws himself into it, just like he did with swimming."

"Yeah he told me a little about that." Listening, looking at Ryan's father, it's hard to believe this is the same man who tossed his son in the deep end of a pool and left him to literally sink or swim.

Stiles stands up. "I bet he didn't tell you about this. Come on, I want to show you something."

I follow him back through the living room to a small room just adjacent. It's crowded with bookshelves, a couple of easy chairs, and on one wall, a wooden case with glass doors. The case is filled with several trophies and plaques of all kinds. Stiles opens the door, takes out one of the bigger trophies, and hands it to me.

I look at the figure perched on top, and read the inscription. Ryan's name is prominently displayed in big letters. I stare for a moment, not comprehending at first. Stiles takes my silence for admiration. "Pretty impressive, eh?"

I hand the trophy back and he carefully replaces it in the case. "Yeah, very."

"He made the Olympic trials one year. Kid really had it, then he got involved in this movie stuff, and well, that's turned out pretty well, too."

We go back to the kitchen and finish our coffee. I only half listen to Stiles ramble on about life in the valley and Ryan's childhood, my mind whirling, anger building with each passing minute. Finally, Ryan appears, his hair still wet from the shower, dressed in clothes I've never seen.

"Hey, there he is," Ryan says. "Dad been boring you to death?"

I turn and look into Ryan's eyes. "No, not at all. It's been very interesting. I've learned a lot." Ryan meets my eyes for a moment, trying to read my words. I stand up. "Come on, we better get going," I say. "Melanie is waiting."

I shake hands with Ben Stiles. "Nice to finally meet you," he says. "Sorry you couldn't meet Ryan's mother. She's out shopping."

"Some other time," I say.

"Take care, Dad. Thanks for the bed," Ryan says

We go out to the car and get in as Ben Stiles stands in the driveway and waves. Ryan puts sunglasses on and leans back on the seat. "Man, what a night," he says. "I needed to get away." He turns toward me. "What's the fallout? I have to buy that moron a new camera?"

"I haven't heard." I point to the BMW parked near the garage. "What about the other car?"

"Don't worry. I'll have somebody pick it up."

At the freeway, I start to take the eastbound on-ramp but Ryan waves me off. "Go west and we'll take Malibu Canyon. It's faster."

I merge with traffic and don't say a word as we take the canyon exit. A few miles down Malibu Canyon road, I turn off onto am area that allows other cars to pass. I shut off the engine and look at Ryan.

He pushes the glasses up and looks at me. "What? Why did you stop?"

"Your dad showed me," I say.

"Showed you what?"

"NCAA national title. One hundred meter freestyle champion." I watch Ryan's expression change. "Your fucking swimming trophies."

Ryan drops his head down to his chest and groans. "I forgot how Dad likes to brag about me."

"Oh, you forgot? You forgot you were a champion swimmer when I dragged you out of the surf. Who else knows? Melanie? Robbins? You want to tell me what that was all about?" I get out of the car, slam the door, and walk back a few yards to stand and look down at the canyon below.

Ryan gets out and follows me. "Look, man, it's complicated. I can explain."

I look at him. "I can hardly wait."

Ryan scuffs his foot in the dirt and looks away for a moment, gazing out over the canyon. "It was kind of a spur of the moment thing." He shrugs. "I guess I wanted to see what you'd do, how you'd react. I was going to say, 'hey, I'm kidding, I'm all right,' but then I swallowed a lot of water, and it just got out of hand, kind of took on a life of its own."

He gives me that charming smile the whole world knows that has got him out of a lot of situations. "A life of its own, huh? And what about later when you told me that story about your dad throwing you in the pool. Jesus, you made it sound like child abuse, and having just met your dad, that doesn't work now."

He looks away again. "No, Dad's a good guy."

"You were very convincing."

"I'll take that as a compliment."

I walk away a few steps then turn back. "Anything else you're not telling me?"

Ryan holds up his hands. "No, really that's it, and I am really sorry."

I nod and walk back to the car. We get in and I start the engine. I look over at Ryan. I can see him trying to calculate if he's gone too far. Then he smiles again. "But hey, thanks for saving me."

When we get back to the house, Grant Robbins is waiting, looking very agitated. "We have to talk. Now," he says, before Ryan can say anything. "Do you mind?" he asks me.

"Not in the least."

Melanie comes in and goes to Ryan for the welcome back hug. "You had us so worried," she says.

"I know," Ryan says. "Sorry, baby, I'll tell you about it later." He and Robbins go into the living room and Melanie follows me out to the deck.

"Andie is down at the beach," Melanie says. She's recovered and all smiles now.

"Thanks." I jog down the path and find Andie stretched out on a big towel in a black bikini, her hair still wet. She turns her head toward me, looking from behind big sunglasses.

"Like my suit?"

"Fetching." I sit down next to her and light a cigarette.

"Everything okay with our movie hero?"

"Yeah. Guess he had a bad night. I met his dad. Nice guy." I pause. "He showed me Ryan's swimming trophies."

Andie sits up and takes off her glasses. "His what?"

"Yep, a whole case full of them. NCAA hundred meter free style national champion."

The waves are bigger today, pounding and crashing on the beach, the water line creeping up ever closer. "So the whole almost drowning thing was fake."

"Completely." I tell her what Ryan said about it, being a spur of the moment thing.

"Jesus," Andie says, he's a real piece of work." She thinks for a moment. "He was testing you. Not for whether you'd rescue him, but to see if you'd tell anyone, leak it to the press. But it was a safe test. If you did, he could just deny the whole thing, trot out his trophies, and he'd know he couldn't trust you."

"But why is that so important?"

Andie shrugs. "I haven't figured that out yet. For what it's worth, I don't think Melanie knew."

"I don't either. I saw her face. She was genuinely upset when I got him back up on the beach."

"Why wouldn't you tell your live-in girlfriend? We had a long talk. She's a really nice girl, just kind of caught up in this whole Hollywood star thing, and she's more than a bit scared of him, but she loves him."

"Yeah I got that when I talked to her after the lunch skirmish at the restaurant."

Andie puts her glasses back on and looks out to sea. "So what are you going to do?"

"I'm not sure. I'd really like to score this movie."

She moves closer and kisses me. "I know."

We turn and see Emillio coming down the path. "Sorry to interrupt," he says. "Mr. Robbins would like to see you."

I stand up and brush the sand off. "See you in a bit."

Andie nods and lays back down. "Come get me later."

I find Ryan and Grant Robbins still in the living room. Robbins is on his phone, pacing around while Ryan noodles at the piano.

"All right. I'm meeting with Ryan now. We'll take care of it," Robbins says, before he breaks the connection. He turns to Ryan. "That was Cy Perkoff. It's going to cost you. That photographer is going to file assault charges."

Ryan stops playing and turns around. "He's bluffing. Make him a settlement offer. Buy him a new camera, give him some money. He's a jerk."

"It may not be that easy," Robbins says. "He was doing his job, and that was your second run-in with him."

"So what? I'll file harassment charges against him. That was his second time crossing the line with me." Ryan looks at me. "Besides, Evan was there both times. He saw the whole thing."

"I also saw you rip his camera from around his neck when Coop was holding him."

Ryan just grins. "Yeah, that was cool, wasn't it."

Grant Robbins sighs. "No, it wasn't cool, it was stupid. If you had just gotten in the car, we could have gone for a restraining order, but no judge will grant that now. Dammit, Ryan, you just have to get control of your temper."

"Yeah, whatever," Ryan says, waving his hand at Robbins like he wants him to go away.

Robbins looks at me and rolls his eyes. "Anyway," he says, "we have something more pleasant to talk about. How's he doing with the piano?"

"It's starting to come together," I tell him.

"Good enough to stage a demonstration?"

"When?"

"Early next week," Robbins says. "We have the three principal investors ready to talk, but they want to see how Ryan looks at the piano."

Ryan sits up straight. "I can do it, right, Evan?"

I feel Robbins and Ryan both watching me. We have a few more days and I have an idea how to put things together to make Ryan look convincing. "Yeah, I think you can."

"Great," Robbins says, relief spreading over his face.

Ryan stands up and stretches. "I have some making up to do with Melanie." He waves and walks out. "See you later, Evan."

I sit down opposite Robbins. "God, he can be trying. I really appreciate your patience."

"While you're here, there's a couple of things I want to talk to you about."

Robbins puts up his hand. "I know what you're going to say, and I swear, I didn't know about the swimming either. I can't believe he kept that from me all this time."

"It's not only that," I say. "I didn't sign on for all this, the temper tantrums, the drama, but I'm making a lot of allowances for Ryan, because frankly, I really want to score this film. But I don't like being lied to and I still haven't seen any script. I don't even know what this movie is supposed to be about, if there's really going to be a movie."

Robbins goes quiet, just listening. "I know," he says. "Believe me, I know it can be difficult with Ryan, but you're doing a great job and it's important that he likes and trusts you. He talks about you all the time. It may not seem like it, but you're having a lot of influence on him." Robbins looks up like he's searching for words. "It's like you're an older brother he never had."

He pauses, gathering his thoughts. "I wish I could explain how difficult it is getting a project together, the financing, distribution, casting, all those details, but a lot will be riding on this demonstration for the investors."

"I'm sure. I just don't understand why you won't tell me more about the script. What's the big mystery? Is there a script?"

Robbins smiles. "Yes, there is a script, but there are reasons we haven't showed it to you yet, reasons that will be clear once we have the money lined up. Can you just bear with me until then?"

I think for a moment. I don't want to walk away from an opportunity to score a movie, but there are so many unanswered questions, and I don't like the feeling that I'm being sold a bill of goods. "Okay, but next week, after the demo, we have to talk again. And I'm going to want some answers."

"Absolutely. You have my word." Robbins gets to his feet and straightens his tie. Meeting over. "I have to get going on this photographer mess." He starts out then turns back. "By the way, how are you going to handle this demonstration?"

"I'm going to videotape Ryan."

After Robbins leaves, I change into a tee shirt and swim trunks and go back down to the beach. Andie is lying on her stomach. "I think you could use some lotion on your back."

"I've been waiting for you to do it." She reaches behind her and unties her top. "All over, please." I squirt some lotion on my hands and rub it over her back and legs. "Mmm," she mumbles, "you do have nice hands."

I give her butt a little playful slap and stand up, pulling off my shirt. The waves look a little bigger now. I suddenly feel like I'm back in Santa Monica High School, cutting class for a day at the beach. I sprint down to the water, splash up to my knees, and dive in, feeling the chill instantly. I swim out to the break, wait a moment and catch a good-sized wave.

Sliding down the breaking wave's face, I feel the sun on my shoulders, the cool salt water churning around my face as I pick up speed. I see Andie sit up and watch.

If only everything could be this easy.

Chapter Eight

Late Saturday afternoon, Emillio serves a delicious early dinner on the deck of grilled salmon, salad, rice, and a dessert of fresh strawberries and French vanilla ice cream. Ryan and Melanie are back on track, virtually ignoring Andie and me, gazing into one another's eyes and holding hands under the table. Over coffee, we watch the sun start to set on the horizon.

"God," Andie says, pushing her plate aside. "I want to take Emillio back with me."

"Yeah, Emillio's the man," Ryan says. He looks at me. "What are you two up for tonight?"

Andie squeezes my leg under the table. "Just a quiet evening at home, I guess."

"Cool. How about a little siesta then, we'll meet in the screening room for a movie."

I look at Andie, catch her nod. "Works for us," I say. "But now, if you'll excuse us we're going to have a twilight walk on the beach."

We don sweatshirts, leave Ryan and Melanie, and walk down to the beach. It's chilly but still pleasant as we stroll up the beach. We pass a few people walking dogs but otherwise, the beach is quiet. Lights are coming on at many of the homes as evening begins for the beautiful people of Malibu.

Andie holds my hand and leans against me as we walk. "This part is nice," she says. "I'll be sorry to go back." She stops to dig her toes in the cooling sand.

"I'll be sorry to see you go," I say. We pick a spot and sit down on the sand, watching the orange ball of the sun slip into the horizon, the waves rolling in quietly and calmly now.

"Have you decided what you're going to do?"

I nod. "I talked more with Robbins today. We're putting on a demonstration for the investors next week. They want to see how Ryan looks at the piano. Then, he promises to tell me about the script and what this movie is all about."

"Is our boy up for it?"

"Yeah, I think he's going to do okay. He's been working hard and I'll push him more this week."

"So assuming everything goes well, what happens after the dog and pony show?"

"Once the money is in place, they'll schedule the shooting, cast all the parts, all that stuff, and I can go home for awhile, once I sign a binding contract to score the movie and continue as a consultant. I'll probably be on the set at least part of the time, but I can't really start scoring until I see a rough cut of the film."

Andie looks at me and smiles. "You're really getting into this, aren't you?"

"Yeah, I guess I am. It's like another door opening. Let's face it. I've been close but it hasn't happened for me yet and may not ever. There are a lot of great pianists out there, Andie, and they're all younger"

Andie nods and doesn't argue the point. "How binding is this contract you'll have to sign?"

"Like Ryan, the director, the other actors. I assume I'll be locked in for the duration."

Back at the house, we settle in for the movie Ryan has arranged in the screening room. Emillio has brought in a couple bowls of popcorn and drinks while the four of us relax on two leather couches angled toward the television.

"Nothing like the local cineplex is it?" Andie says as she munches popcorn and sips some chilled white wine.

Ryan and Melanie are on the adjoining couch. The lights dim and the film begins on a huge screen that dominates one wall. It's black and white, and as the opening credits roll—Kirk Douglas, Lauren Bacall, Doris Day—the first thing we hear is Harry James' trumpet.

"You were right," Ryan says. "This is a good one."

Young Man With A Horn is loosely based on Dorothy Baker's novel about legendary trumpeter Bix Beiderbecke. Douglas does a convincing job as a trumpet player, and even more so as a misguided alcoholic bad guy who can't see vocalist Doris Day is the right girl for him over the manipulative Lauren Bacall character. But of course this is Hollywood at its fifties best, and the film strays far from the book. Douglas has a meltdown at a recording session trying to find that elusive right note, and ends up on the street. He's found and saved by Day and his pianist buddy Smoke, played by Hoagy Carmichael. Douglas and Day end up together happily ever after. Not quite the way things ended for Bix. He was dead at twenty-eight.

"You going to make me look as good as Kirk Douglas?" Ryan asks, as the lights come up.

"That's up to you," I say. Andie stirs next to me, having dozed off earlier.

Ryan stands and stretches. "I know," he says nodding and smiling, full of confidence. "Back to work tomorrow, right?"

"Absolutely. We only have a few days."

"Don't worry, I'm ready," Ryan says. He takes Melanie's hand and they leave us as the final credits roll.

"Did I miss anything?" Andie asks.

"I'll let you know."

◇◇◇

By midmorning I have Ryan back at the piano. I'd already said my goodbyes to Andie when Melanie offered to drive her to the airport. "Watch yourself," Andie had said as she got in the car. "Call me."

I'd come up with another idea to showcase Ryan's make-believe piano playing. We continued with the Red Garland trio, making Ryan play and listen to it over and over, and then

I remembered another recording that would work well for this purpose. A Chet Baker recording with Phil Markowitz on piano. On one of the songs, "The Touch of Your Lips," Markowitz plays an almost textbook solo that begins with single notes using only one or two fingers, and builds slowly into a two-handed solo. It's a good one for Ryan to emulate.

"I need a break," Ryan says, massaging his forearm. He looks down. "Hey, it doesn't hurt quite so much.

"You're getting used to it now." I tell Ryan about the Chet Baker recording. "You do have a video camera?"

Ryan nods. "Yeah, why?"

"I'm going to tape you but we need a couple of things. The Chet CD and an electric keyboard."

"Why, when we have this piano?"

"So we have a keyboard that doesn't make any sound."

Ryan looks at me, puzzled for a moment, then a smile spreads over his face. "You tape me as we play the record. Fuck, man, you're a genius."

"Do you remember if the store where you rented this piano has electronic keyboards?"

"Yeah, I think so. I can call, have one delivered."

"Or, we could drive into Santa Monica and pick one out, have lunch." I want to keep him relaxed, but edgy too.

He grins. "I like that idea better."

"Better get your blond wig and baseball cap."

Ryan decides to take his chances without the wig but does wear the Dodgers cap and sunglasses. We find the music store in Santa Monica. It's a full-service, professional store, so there's a minimum of fuss as Ryan is recognized. I explain what I want to the manager and why.

He listens, then says, "Just a minute." He disappears in the back for a couple of minutes, then comes back with a keyboard under his arm. "It's from a school, dummy keyboard, no sound, just used for fingering exercises."

"Perfect." Ryan takes out a credit card but the manager waves it away. "Take it," he says. "Just bring it back when you're finished. I'd never sell this anyway. You can send me a ticket to the movie."

We put the keyboard in the trunk of Ryan's Mercedes and head for Santa Monica Mall in search of a record store. I still can't believe Tower Records went under, but we find a good jazz selection at Borders Books. They have almost all of Chet Baker's recordings, including the one I want. We take it and also a couple of Bill Evans'. "Damn," Ryan says. "Never thought I'd be buying jazz CDs."

"We all grow."

Back in the car, Ryan looks at me. "Okay boss, I'm hungry," he says. "Got any place in mind?"

"As a matter of fact I do, if you feel like a burger."

"Lead on."

I direct him toward West Los Angeles to the Apple Pan on Pico Boulevard. We find a parking place on the street and Ryan regards it haltingly.

"You'll love it," I say. "I used to go here when I was in high school."

Inside, nothing much has changed. Counter-only seating and old-fashioned burgers cooked while you wait. We add fries and cokes and it's like a scene from *Happy Days*. It's crowded but with the dark glasses and baseball cap, nobody seems to recognize Ryan, mainly I think because nobody expects to see a movie star eating a hamburger at the counter. I wonder if Ryan is pleased or disappointed.

"That was awesome," Ryan says as we get back in the car. On the drive back to Malibu, Ryan dozes until I stop for gas at a station near the pier. He sits up, rubs his eyes. He hands me a credit card and watches me pump gas.

"Wake up, we got a lot of work to do."

"I'm ready. Bring it on."

Back at the house, I play the opening track on the Chet Baker CD a couple of times for Ryan, letting him get a feel for the tempo. It's a ballad, but they do a quasi double time feel on the solos. Ryan listens intently as Chet sings the lyrics to "The Touch of Your Lips," then opts to scat sing his solo rather than play it. It's an amazing performance that never fails to strike a deep emotional chord for me. Ryan feels it, too.

"Jesus, how does he do that?" Ryan says, shaking his head. "He sounds like he's not quite going to make it, but then he does. Sounds like he lived a lot."

I nod, surprised and pleased at Ryan's instinctive insight. "Exactly, and notice his voice. No vibrato, just like his trumpet playing." I make him focus on Markowitz's piano solo. I'd thought of this recording because of the way he builds slowly, starting with just one note, one finger of his right hand, slowly expanding the structure until at the end he using two hands in block chord style. A lot of space. The tempo is slow enough I think Ryan can emulate the fingering easily enough if he works at it.

I get the silent keyboard out of the car and let Ryan try it while I repeat the track several times. I show him on the keyboard the keys to start with and watch him listen, tentatively touching the keys, head down, his body swaying slightly, feeling Markowitz's easy loping rhythm. After a dozen times, he's starting to really get it. He stops then and looks at me questioningly.

"Look at me," I say. "You can do this. You're going to look like you're playing with Chet Baker."

Ryan nods. "I know," he says quietly. "Thank you."

By Wednesday, he's got it enough that we're ready to tape. I close the lid over the cover of the keys of the piano and lay the dummy keyboard on top. I shoot the video from several angles, gradually moving in on Ryan's hands, then pulling back, catching his facial expressions. I make three versions of the taping, then we watch the playback on a big screen television. The sound track of the recording is virtually matched by Ryan's hands on the keyboard.

"Look at me," Ryan says, grinning. "I'm a fucking jazz pianist."

"Yes you are." It's not quite note perfect but close enough and it should be more than enough to impress the investors when we play it for them. We do some more fine tuning and I make a final taping and let Grant Robbins know we're ready for show time when he calls.

"That's great, Evan." He sounds pleased, but there's some reluctance in his voice that I catch.

"Something wrong?"

"No, I just hoped to get this photographer thing settled before this investors meeting. I don't like this hanging over us."

"What's the problem? He want more money?"

"No, it's not that," Robbins says. "We've put out a settlement offer but his lawyer can't reach him so far. I just hope he's not trying an end run for more publicity." Robbins pauses. "Anyway, my house Friday night. Ryan knows the way."

We arrive at Robbins' Brentwood home around seven. There are three expensive cars in Robbins' driveway. "The jury is already here," Ryan says.

Robbins greets us and takes us into his den. Ryan turns on the big smile as he's introduced to the three men sipping twenty-year-old scotch and puffing on cigars. They've obviously not met him before, and despite their own obvious success, the trio is in awe to be in the presence of a genuine movie star. You can see it in their eyes.

I take a Scotch rocks myself and sit back, listening to the small talk about Ryan's previous movies, how pleased they are to be involved, and listening to Ryan tell a few behind the scenes stories, making them feel like insiders as Robbins orchestrates it all.

Finally, Robbins introduces me as Ryan's tutor, brilliant jazz pianist, and his choice to score the movie sound track. "My man," Ryan says pulling me forward. They acknowledge me politely but their interest remains on Ryan. There's some small talk, then Robbins tops off drinks, and gets down to business.

"We have a tape we want to show you," he says. "I think you'll agree that Ryan is impressive."

I hand Robbins the videotape and he inserts it in the player. I watch the investors move forward on their seats as the tape starts. It's so close I don't see how anybody could not think Ryan is actually playing Phil Markowitz's solo. I watch Robbins sigh with relief and see smiles and nods all around. They all look at Ryan with new-found respect. They're about to talk money when my cell phone rings.

"Excuse me," I say. I get up and leave the room. It's Coop. "Hey, you're interrupting an important Hollywood meeting."

"Sorry, sport, but I've got some news."

I listen, my mind spinning. "Are you sure?"

"Absolutely," Coop says.

"Okay, let me know if anything breaks." I close the phone and go back to the den, motioning Robbins out. He glances at me, puzzled, excuses himself, and joins me in the hall.

"What's wrong?"

"That was Danny Cooper. He has a friend with the Malibu police."

"Yeah?"

"The photographer is missing."

Chapter Nine

Ryan and I leave Robbins with the money guys, get in the Mercedes, and head back to Malibu. He's so excited he yells out the open window. "Man, we fucking did it! Did you see their eyes as they watched that video? That was such a blast. Robbins will have their tongues hanging out to invest now."

"Yeah, it went down pretty well," I agree.

"Pretty well? Dude, it was awesome, and it's all because of you."

"That was you on the video, not me."

"But it was you who put me there."

Robbins had told me not to mention the photographer being missing as he slipped a check in my hand. I hadn't even looked at it yet. I wonder if I should tell Ryan anyway. I hate to break the mood, but he should know. My mind goes back to the lunch altercation in Santa Monica when the photographer turned to his buddies and shouted, "See that, he pushed me," like he was planning something. I keep flashing on Ryan jerking the camera off his neck at the Anchor as Coop held him, then Ryan, roaring off in the BMW and not turning up until morning at his dad's house.

There was something else about that, when I picked Ryan up, but I couldn't pin it down. Something about the car. I shook my head and looked at Ryan as we eased down the incline to the coast highway. He was still smiling, savoring his performance on video and how the investors had totally bought it.

When we stop for a traffic light at Topanga Canyon Boulevard, I say, "Hey, come down for a minute."

Ryan glances over at me, the smile fading slightly. "What?"

"I got a call from Coop while you were in that meeting. Your photographer friend is missing."

Ryan frowns. "Missing? What do you mean?"

"Robbins said he'd made a settlement offer to him, through his lawyer, but he couldn't make contact. I guess somebody filed a missing persons report. That's what Coop's source said."

"Good," Ryan says. "I hope they never find him. He's scum, man, a parasite feeding off me and other celebrities."

I wonder how it must feel to refer to yourself as a celebrity and think nothing of it. "Okay, he got out of line, but you did break his camera, and it's you celebrities that he makes his living from, whether you approve or not. He was out of line that day at lunch too, but he's just doing his job, and from what I can see, it's a very competitive business."

"Yeah? The other photographers didn't pull that shit. It was just him."

Ryan had a point. They all wanted just the right photo, but this guy did seem obsessed. Over the line or overzealous? It wasn't for me to say. "Well, I just thought you should know."

Ryan nods, keeps his eyes straight ahead on the road. "No problem, but don't expect me to worry about that asshole being missing."

For the next half hour or so, we drive in silence, neither of us saying a word until we get to the Broad Beach turnoff at Trancas. When we turn in the driveway at Ryan's house, the gates are open and two cars block the way. One I recognize as Coop's; the other is a Malibu Sheriff's cruiser.

"What the fuck?" Ryan says. He skids to a stop, jumps out of the car, and jogs up to the house. I follow close behind him. Inside are Coop, Melanie, and the sheriff, who I recognize from the Anchor benefit. He's a short, heavy-set man with short cropped graying hair and steel-framed glasses. They're all seated at the dining table, drinking coffee and talking. They all look up as we come in.

Melanie, her hair pulled back in a pony tail, wearing jeans and a sweat shirt, looks scared and upset as she jumps up and runs over to hug Ryan. The sheriff stands politely, looking slightly intimidated and uncomfortable to be standing in big movie star's kitchen. Coop's eyes lock with mine. He stands and pulls me aside quickly. "Be careful what you say," he whispers.

Ryan and Melanie break their embrace. "So, what's going on?" Ryan asks.

"I'm Sheriff Burns, Mr. Stiles. There's been an accident," he begins. "The photographer who assaulted you the other night has been missing for several days."

I try to catch Ryan's eye but he already knows what to say. "Yeah, so?"

"He was found earlier tonight. He apparently went off the embankment on Malibu Canyon Road. A passing motorist spotted his motorcycle and called us." He looks at Ryan. "He's been dead for a couple of days, we think. It's an ongoing investigation," he adds quickly. "We'll know more later."

Melanie gasps and puts her hand to her mouth. "That's too bad," Ryan says after a moment. I can see he's trying to muster up a sympathetic tone and expression but he doesn't quite make it. I can't tell if the sheriff notices or not. "I'm really sorry to hear about that." He glances at us, trying to measure how he's doing. "He and I obviously didn't get along, but, damn, that's really terrible."

"Yes," the sheriff says. "We'd like you to come down to the office tomorrow and make a statement about the, ah, confrontation at the Anchor. It's just routine. We're trying to retrace his movements that night."

"Sure," Ryan says. "Anything I can do to help. What time?"

"Nine, if that's convenient," Sheriff Burns says. He turns to me. "We'd like you to come down too, Mr. Horne. I understand you witnessed the, ah, confrontation."

Coop gives me an almost imperceptible nod. "No problem," I say.

"Good," Burns says. He smiles in relief and shakes hands all around. "Well, sorry to interrupt your evening. I'll see myself out."

We all stand quietly for a few moments after the sheriff leaves. It's Ryan who breaks the silence.

"Jesus, it's always something, isn't it," Ryan says. He looks at all of us. There's a funny kind of smile on his face. The three of us gaze at him for a long moment. "What? Am I being insensitive?"

"Maybe a tad," Coop says.

"Well I'm sorry, but this was a very good, very important night for me. I had nothing to do with that guy's accident." He looks at Coop and shrugs. "What should I do?"

"Just be at the station in the morning, and you might muster up a little concern. Might make a better impression on the police."

Ryan smiles. "Yeah, I can do that. You're right." He turns to Melanie. "C'mon, baby. I got lots to tell you."

Coop and I watch them go then I walk Coop out to his car. "He can be a real charmer," Coop says.

There's a slight chill in the air as I nod and light a cigarette. "What will they ask him?"

"Like Burns said, routine stuff. He'll ask him to give his version of the incident, whether he saw the photographer anytime since. That kind of thing."

"It was an accident wasn't it?"

"Far as they know now. Burns didn't tell me much. They'll know more later when they check out the motorcycle, whether he was drinking, cause of death. You know the drill. But given that angry confrontation, if there's anything funny, Ryan Stiles becomes a person of interest, as we say in police circles."

"And me?"

Coop shrugs. "Just your version of the incident at the Anchor and when you next saw Stiles."

"He called here and I picked him up the next morning at his dad's house in the Valley. He stayed there apparently."

Coop gets in his car and starts the engine. "Should be nothing to worry about. Just tell it straight. I'll try to be there too."

I stand for a minute, watching the gates close and Coop drive off. Ryan was right. I go in the guesthouse, thinking about calling Andie, when I spot something on my bed. It's a small gift-wrapped box with a card taped on top. The card reads, I didn't think you were a Rolex kind of guy. Thanks for everything—RS.

I unwrap the box and flip it open. Inside is a Swiss Army watch. Black casing and black leather strap with a large face. I reach in my pocket then and look at the check Robbins slipped me earlier. The amount is way more than we agreed.

Coop is right. There is always something.

The Sheriff's Office is in a complex of white buildings that include the courthouse and various other offices comprising the Malibu Civic Center. Ryan cruises the parking lot, on the lookout for photographers, but it seems all clear. He parks the Mercedes in a far corner of the lot.

We go inside, through the electronic security device, and though I know everybody recognizes him, they just nod and smile politely. Plenty of stars have been arrested, booked, questioned, arraigned, and released here, so I guess it's no big deal to see Ryan Stiles.

We spot Grant Robbins farther in the lobby, his briefcase in hand, nervously pacing around. He almost breaks into a jog when he sees us. He pulls us aside for a quick conference. "Okay, nothing to worry about," he says to Ryan. "Just a simple statement. I'll be right there with you."

Ryan smiles. "Who says I'm worried?"

Robbins gives him a look. "Always be worried when the police question you."

"Okay, okay," Ryan says, putting up his hands. "I just want to get this over with."

Sheriff Burns comes down the hall then to greet us. "Mr. Stiles, Mr. Horne, thank you for coming in." He turns to Robbins. "I've cleared it with the investigator for you to be present during Mr. Stiles' statement."

"Thank you," Robbins says. "We appreciate that."

"There are some new circumstances, however," Burns says.

"Oh," Robbins says, raising his eyebrows a touch.

"Yes, we'll get to it inside. If you'll just go down the hall to your right, the investigating officer is waiting."

Robbins and Ryan start to walk away and Ryan turns back over his shoulder and winks at me. "Mr. Horne, if you'll follow me, we'll get this over as soon as possible."

I follow Burns to a small room off the hallway. There's a table, a couple of chairs and a clerk already there, I assume to record my statement. She's a small, slim woman in dark hair and glasses. She sits next to Burns and takes out a pad and pencil.

"All set, Peggy?" She nods and we all get seated. Burns starts with names, date, and purpose of the statement.

"How long have you known Mr. Stiles?" he begins.

"Just a few weeks. I'm tutoring him for an upcoming film."

"Really? Must be kind of exciting, staying with a big star like Mr. Stiles."

I smile at Burns. "It has its moments." I've been in these situations enough to know he's trying to make me relax, then perhaps catch me off guard with a surprise question or two.

"Well, can you just tell us what happened at the Anchor Restaurant last Friday?"

I give Burns a quick rundown of what I witnessed, trying not to leave anything out. He nods, makes some notes as I talk, but says nothing until I finish.

"And you saw Mr. Stiles get in the car with Miss Thomas and Mr. Robbins?"

"Yes. I didn't see it, but apparently he stopped the car and got out before they left and took the BMW I'd driven there from the valet man."

"And Lieutenant Cooper drove you and Miss Lawrence back to Stiles' house?

"Yes."

Burns puts down his pen and looks at me. "When did you next see Mr. Stiles?"

"Not until the following morning when I picked him up at his father's home in the Valley. He called from there and asked me to come get him."

"So as far as you know, he spent the night at his parents' home?"

"Yes, that's what his father said."

"And the BMW was there?"

"Yes." I was beginning to wonder where this was going now.

"And you remained at Mr. Stiles' house all night?"

"Yes, with my girlfriend. She's gone back to San Francisco now."

"Her name?"

"Andrea Lawrence. FBI Special Agent Lawrence."

"Well, can't beat that, can we?" Burns smiles a little, looks at his notes and nods to the clerk. She leaves and shuts the door behind her. "I think that about covers it," Burns says. Peggy will get this typed up for you to sign. It'll only take a few minutes."

"Okay if I wait outside? I'd like to have a cigarette."

"Sure," Burns says. "I'll come get you when it's ready."

I get up and start for the door. "I'm just curious. You mentioned there are some new circumstances."

"Yes, well, I can't go into it, but I can tell you we don't think this was an accident."

I mull that over outside, smoking near a concrete ashtray filled with sand, thinking about the implications of Burns' words. If it wasn't an accident then somebody forced the photographer off the road. With Ryan gone all night, following a major confrontation, he would definitely be a person of interest.

I put my cigarette out in the sand and glance around the parking lot. It's busier now, and to the left I see a small group of photographers looming nearby and a television news truck, a reporter primping, talking with a camera man, keeping an eye on the entrance. No Coop, so something must have come up. How do they find out so quickly?

I go back in the glass doors and see Burns coming toward me, some papers in his hand. "All set, Mr. Horne."

I glance over the statement briefly, and sign and date it, and hand it back. "How long will Stiles be?"

"I think they're just about done."

"The press is already gathering outside. Is there a back exit? I can pull the car around and avoid the rush if it's okay." I point toward the front, where a now-sizable crowd is milling around.

Burns nods as if he's seen it many times before. "Ah, here we go," he says.

"No, wait. Stiles drove. I don't have the key." But I'm too late. We see Ryan and Robbins walking toward us, Ryan, in quick hurried strides looking very angry, Robbins, hand on his elbow, talking to him.

"Bullshit," we hear Ryan say. "I'm a fucking suspect."

"Ryan, calm down," Robbins says. "Let's get home and we'll talk about it there."

Ryan pulls away then stops, sees reporters and photographers approaching the entrance. "Perfect," he says. "Just what I need."

"Ryan, give me the car key. There's a back exit. They don't know me. I'll pull the car around."

"Fuck that, I'm going out the front door." He hands me the Mercedes key.

Robbins sighs and shakes his head. "Get the car."

I brush through the swarm of reporters and jog for the car. By the time I get back to the entrance, Ryan, in dark glasses, keeps saying, "No comment," as Robbins guides him to the car.

The television reporter sticks a microphone in front of him. She's a petite blonde in a dark skirt and blouse. "Can you give us anything, Ryan?"

Ryan looks at her and smiles. "Not here."

I throw open the passenger door and Ryan climbs in and waves to one and all as cameras flash. "Go," he says.

I pull away, leaving Grant Robbins to deal with the reporters.

It's the lead story on the six o'clock news, delivered in typically sensationalist style by a typically styled anchor. "Good evening. I'm Tom Duran and this is news at six. Our top story, actor Ryan Stiles, the star of many blockbuster films was questioned earlier today by Malibu Police in the disappearance and death of paparazzi photographer Darryl McElroy," the anchor says, his eyebrows raising, his head moving side to side. "Our own Kerri Thomas has the story."

They cut away to Thomas on the front steps of the Malibu Civic center. She's the same petite blonde I'd seen primping that morning. "This is where it all happened," Thomas says. "Malibu sheriffs confirm Ryan Stiles was called in to give a statement on McElroy's disappearance and death when his motorcycle apparently went out of control and plunged into Malibu Canyon. Our sources say the investigation is ongoing."

Thomas puts on her pensive, concerned expression. "McElroy and Stiles have had several confrontations, the latest being at the Anchor restaurant, following a benefit appearance by Stiles last Friday night. Also questioned was jazz pianist"—she looks down at a note—"Evan Horne, who has apparently been working with Stiles on a new project, and was also appearing at the Anchor."

There's some footage of Ryan coming out of the Civic Center with Robbins, ducking into the car amidst the swarm of reporters. Then it's back to Thomas live. "Malibu sheriffs say the questioning was just routine, but as we know"—she pauses dramatically—"nothing is routine with Ryan Stiles. Kerri Thomas reporting live from Malibu. Back to you, Tom."

"Ryan Stiles and a jazz pianist? What do you make of that, Kerri?" anchor Tom wants to know in a split-screen shot.

Thomas smiles. "Hard to say at this point, Tom, but I'm sure we'll learn more very soon."

"All right. Thanks, Kerri. We'll be following this story closely. In other news…"

"Here we go," I say to myself as my phone rings.

"I go away for a couple of days and you're on the news," Andie says. "What's going on?"

I give her a quick rundown of my statement. "The sheriff said it wasn't an accident. That's all I know at the moment. I don't know what they asked Ryan but he didn't take well to being questioned and treated like a suspect."

"What did they ask you beyond what you saw?"

"Nothing really, other than how I spent the night."

"Lucky for you, you have am FBI agent as your alibi."

"Isn't it though? Just what the sheriff said. Don't worry, I kept it PG rated."

"Good of you," Andie says. "How did the show for the investors go?"

"Couldn't have been better. Robbins already paid me and Ryan gave me a thank you gift."

"Really?"

"Yeah, a Swiss Army watch."

"Oh that's what that was about."

"What?"

"He asked me what kind of jewelry you like. I said nothing but watches." Andie is quiet for a moment. "You've been paid and gifted. Why don't you come home now. Let Ryan work through this thing on his own."

"Andie, I—"

"I know. I just had to ask."

"And you already know the answer."

Chapter Ten

They say there's no such thing as bad publicity for the Hollywood crowd. The public seems to thrive on seeing their favorite stars embroiled in scandal. But I wonder how the investors will take yesterday's news about Ryan. Are they still going to be enthusiastic about coughing up millions of dollars to finance a film with a star who's a person of interest in a photographer's death? I don't sleep very well, spending most of the night tossing and turning, running things over in my mind.

I give up around six, grab a glass of orange juice, and take a long walk on the beach. There are a few other early risers, walking, taking their dogs for a run, but for the most part, I'm alone. When I get back to the house, I find Emillio busy in the kitchen, and Grant Robbins on the deck drinking coffee. He has a copy of the *Los Angeles Times* on the table.

"Have a look at this," Robbins says, pushing the Calendar section across to me, as Emillio brings more coffee and an omelet for Robbins. I scan over the article with the headline:

MOVIE STAR QUESTIONED IN PAPARAZZI DEATH.

There are photos of Ryan and Darryl McElroy but nothing new except now I have more of an idea who Darryl McElroy was. According to the article, McElroy was thirty-two, a Gulf War vet, and formerly with the *Times* before turning to shooting the stars. An avid motorcyclist, he was one of the most successful and competitive paparazzi in the business. There are a couple of quotes from his colleagues, who confirm McElroy's competitiveness, and his obsession with Ryan Stiles.

I look up at Robbins, watch him dig into his omelet, and decide I'll have the same. I signal to Emillio as the doorbell rings. "Not good, is it?"

"That'll be Cooper," Robbins says. "I asked him to come over. "We need to talk about this," Robbins says, tapping the newspaper. "I'm hoping he can give us an idea of how the police are going to proceed."

Emillio lets Coop in. He's in jeans, a sweatshirt, and some kind of boots. His gun bulges on his belt beneath a light windbreaker jacket, and his badge is clipped to his belt. He takes a cup of coffee from Emillio, smiles his thanks, and joins us.

"Gentlemen," Coop says. "We have been busy, haven't we?" He looks at us both. "Sorry I didn't make the festivities yesterday."

"Not a problem," Robbins says. "All things considered, it went well. Ryan was very cooperative."

"Good," Coop says, "because there's going to be more."

Robbins nods. "I know. That's why I asked you here, to get your, ah, police perspective on things."

◇◇◇

I watch Coop take a drink of coffee and put his cup down. He glances at me quickly, then back to Robbins. "You want it straight?"

"Please," Robbins says.

"Okay. McElroy didn't go off the canyon by accident. We already know that. He has an altercation with Ryan in front of a crowd of people, witnessed by several sheriff's deputies, a cop, me, and a pianist, you"—he points to me—"and then Ryan roars off in his little red sports car, not to be seen until the following morning. Does that about cover it?"

Robbins nods and starts to say something but Coop cuts him off. "Not yet. Speaking strictly as a cop, if I were lead on this,

Ryan would be my number one suspect, depending, of course on what they find on the motorcycle, and when they determine time of death."

"What do you mean, what they find on the motorcycle?" I ask Coop.

He shrugs. "Paint traces that can be matched, damage to a car Ryan might have been driving." Coop looks around. "By the way, where is Mr. Stiles?"

"Right here." We turn and see Ryan leaning on the door jam. His arms are crossed over his chest. He walks over to the table and sits down. "Emillio, some coffee please." He looks right at Coop. "So you think I killed Darryl McElroy?"

"I didn't say that," Coop says. "I said you would be my number one suspect."

"Okay, let's calm down," Robbins says, sensing Ryan's rising anger. He turns to Ryan. "I wanted you to know how the police are going to view this whole thing." I watch Ryan and Coop stare each other down for a few moments.

"You don't really believe I did it, do you? Ruin my career over some paparazzi asshole?"

"I would hope not," Coop says, "but you've had problems with him in the past, your temper is well known. You broke his camera, took off, and nobody saw you until the following morning, so from where the police sit, that doesn't look good."

"This is what they call circumstantial evidence, right?"

"Actually, at this point, it's just speculation," Coop says. "I'm just trying to let you know how the police will be thinking and how further questioning is going to go."

Ryan nods and smiles. "I know, and I appreciate it."

"What about his alibi?" I ask.

"Good, if it holds," Coop says. "They'll be talking to your father for sure, and wondering why you took off like that. Is the car still there at his home?"

"Sure. Where else would it be?" Ryan says.

"A body shop, getting repaired and painted." Coop spreads his hands and shrugs.

"Would I be that stupid?"

"I hope not."

"Evan can verify the car was right where I left it, right, Evan?"

I nod. "When I picked him up, it was in his dad's driveway." But then I suddenly remember what had bothered me about the car when I'd picked up Ryan. I decide to keep that to myself for now.

"See," Ryan says. "No case." He shrugs and smiles at Coop, but he doesn't smile back.

"For God's sake, Ryan," Robbins says. "We've got a real problem here. Pay attention to what he's saying."

"I have been," Ryan answers. He takes a drink of his coffee. "How about this for a scenario. McElroy is pissed at me for breaking his camera. He sees me take off in the BMW, jumps on his motorcycle, and tries to chase me down. He follows me over Malibu Canyon Road. He tries to cut me off, bumps my fender, goes out of control and off the road, down into the canyon." He looks around at all of us.

"Is that what happened?" Robbins says, his face ashen now.

"No. Jesus do you all think I'm responsible?" He gets up and paces around.

"In your scenario, why didn't you stop, go back, and help him?" Coop asks.

Ryan stops pacing and sits down again. "Okay, Malibu Canyon is full of curves. I look in the rearview mirror, don't see him, and think he just gave up." He slaps his hands on the table. "End of story."

Coop leans forward. "Believe me when I tell you," Coop says. "the police will explore all these possibilities. They'll go slow because of who you are, but they will go." He holds Ryan's gaze for a moment then stands up.

Robbins follows. "Well, I certainly appreciate your input," he says.

Coop nods and turns to me. "Walk me out to my car?"

"Sure." I get up and follow Coop outside.

"This could get messy," Coop says. "Watch yourself."

I nod. "Don't worry." Coop gets in his car and starts the engine. I lean in his window. "You think he did it?"

"I think Mr. Stiles could be capable of a lot of things. Let me stress the word could. But deliberately running McElroy off the road, I don't think so."

I step back from the car as Coop starts to back up. "Good. Glad to hear you say that."

Coop smiles. "Doesn't mean he didn't do it accidentally, panicked when he realized what he'd done and just took off."

"Thanks, Coop. I really need to think about that."

"I think you have a lot to think about. Look at it this way. Hit and run is better than murder."

Coop is right. I do have a lot to think about. With the tutoring phase over, the investors satisfied with Ryan's performance, there's nothing to keep me here for now. I've been paid for my time, and very generously at that. I could bail out now, go home, and wait to see if the development of the film continues as planned.

Or, I could stick around, see how this all shakes out as the investigation continues, and maintain my rapport with Ryan Stiles. I know what Andie will say, and I know what Grant Robbins will say. As far as the police are concerned, I'm not sure.

I'm something of a corroborating witness for Ryan's alibi. He called Melanie asking me to pick him up, and when I got there he and the car were there. What had bothered me about the car was simply the way that it was parked when I noticed it in the driveway of the Stiles home. It had been at somewhat of an angle, a little skewed, but that could be easily explained. Maybe I was making too much of it.

Ryan arrives home, still angry, parks funny, and goes into the house for a quick word with his dad. I can certainly testify that his dad told me he'd been there all night, as was the car. It was a little thing but it nagged at me.

I'm still standing outside thinking about all this when Grant Robbins comes out, heading for his car. "Evan, glad I caught you," he says. "Your friend Cooper has given us all a lot to think about."

"He gave it to you straight."

"Yes, I know." He looks away for a moment. "What are your plans now?"

"My plans?"

"Well, you've completed your contract, and did an excellent job. The investors were suitably impressed and they're ready to go. But given what's happened, I wouldn't blame you for leaving now. Ryan would be very disappointed, as would I, but eventually he'd understand." He pauses again, then turns to face me. "I'm going to ask you a very big favor. Would you consider staying around until this, this mess is cleared up and we see where we are on the movie? I know it's a lot to ask but—"

"Did Ryan ask you to talk to me?"

"No."

I nod. "I've been thinking myself. I'm sure the police are going to want to talk to me again as the investigation continues. If I go home now, I'll just have to come back for that. I'll go this far. I'll stay until we see if Ryan is charged or not, if there's a trial. I'll help in any way I can."

Robbins sighs and smiles. "God, I hoped you'd say that."

"Wait, I'm not finished. I assume scoring the film is still an option. I want to see the script. I need to see what this movie is about so I can start thinking about the music."

"Done," Robbins says. "Not a problem."

"But all this negative publicity. Won't that scare the investors off?"

Robbins smiles. "Evan, remember this is L.A. O.J., Robert Blake, Phil Spector. Like it or not, this is publicity we couldn't buy. Once Ryan is cleared he'll be hotter than ever."

I look into Robbins' eyes. "So you have no doubt Ryan has nothing to do with McElroy's death?"

"Not for a minute."

When I go back in the house, Emillio tells me my omelet is being kept warm in the oven. "I'll bring you some fresh coffee," he says.

"Thanks, I need some." I go out on the deck. Ryan is sitting at the table, gazing out at the ocean, looking troubled. He looks up as I sit down.

"Hey," he says. "You taking off?"

"No, I'm sticking around. I want to see how this all comes out."

"Really? Dude, that's great." He breaks into that wide grin. He starts to say something more but stops.

"Ryan, you don't have to ask. I believe you." Emillio brings my omelet then, and I take the first bite. It's full of peppers, onions, and some kind of sausage. "Emillio, you are a master."

He smiles and pours me some more coffee. "My pleasure."

I point my fork at Ryan. "He's the real reason I'm staying around."

Ryan nods. "Keep this guy happy, Emillio."

I take a few more bites, savoring the mix of flavors, then pause to drink some coffee. "There's one thing we need to do," I say to Ryan.

"What? You name it."

"We need to go to your dad's and pick up the BMW. Like Coop said, the Malibu police are going to want to look at it. Better it's here than in the Valley."

Ryan makes no argument. "You're right. Finish eating. I'm going to grab shower, and wake Melanie up. She can go with us."

An hour later, we're heading for Malibu Canyon Road in the Mercedes. Melanie is very quiet. She looks tired, like she hadn't slept much, but when we got in the car she'd squeezed my hand and said, "Thank you for staying."

Ryan has the radio tuned to the jazz station, the volume low as we streak down the Coast Highway. He makes the turn onto Malibu Canyon Road. A few miles in, on a sharp curve, we see evidence of what remains of the crime scene. Ryan slows the car.

There are some forgotten orange traffic cones along the shoulder and fragments of yellow police tape. At the apex of the curve, I can see where the metal guard rail is torn open like it's been cut with shears. I close my eyes for a moment, imagining

McElroy hitting the rail, breaking through, and being thrown off the bike and down the steep embankment.

"Pull over here for a minute," I tell Ryan. Melanie doesn't move. Ryan and I get out of the car. Instinctively, I look for skid marks on the road, but there are none. We walk to the edge and look down the embankment into the canyon. It must be a couple of hundred feet to the bottom.

There's hardly any sign of the accident, other than a lot of footprints and tire tracks on the shoulder of the road, and some crushed shrubs where they probably dragged the motorcycle up from below. I flash on paramedics lowering a basket to bring up Darryl McElroy's body.

I watch Ryan staring down, trying to read his expression, but he seems impassive. "Lucky the fucking bike didn't catch fire," he says.

He's right. Fires are commonplace in Malibu and there have been some bad ones, with the dry underbrush going up and spreading like kindling. We stand looking down for another couple of minutes, then get back in the car.

Ryan doesn't say anything until we hit the Ventura Freeway. "That's kind of spooky," he says, "seeing where he went over."

"Yeah, it is."

We hit only a little traffic before the Fallbrook exit, and when we pull into the Stiles' driveway, Ryan's dad comes out to greet us.

"Did he know we were coming?"

"Yeah," Ryan says. "I called him."

We get out of the car. Ryan's dad gives him a hug and shakes hands with me. "Good to see you again, Evan." He turns to Melanie and hugs her. "You too, honey. It's been too long." Melanie smiles but she seems a little overwhelmed by the attention. "You guys come on in. Mom's made some iced tea and sandwiches."

I glance over at the BMW. It's parked straight now, brilliantly gleaming in the morning sun. Ryan's dad sees me look. "I had it washed and detailed," he says.

"You didn't need to do that, Dad," Ryan says.

"Car like that needs taking care of, son."

Ryan, Melanie, and his dad start into the house. I go over and look at the car, trying not to be obvious as I check for any paint scrapes or fender damage. There are none. When I look up, I see Ryan watching me, smiling.

"Everything okay?"

"Perfect."

In the kitchen, Ryan's dad introduces me to Mrs. Stiles. She's a small, slender woman with graying hair and bright eyes. She takes my hand and smiles big. "So, you're the amazing jazz pianist," she says. "I'm Bonnie. Welcome to our home." She's a tad taller than her husband and still very attractive. She beams at Melanie and I can already envision her as a helpful mother-in-law. "Hello, dear. So good to see you again."

On the table are a platter of roast beef sandwiches and a huge pitcher of iced tea. I'm not that hungry after Emillio's omelet, but the five us make a dent in the sandwiches and the tea hits the spot. Ryan and his dad tell a few stories, with his mother making a correction here and there, but never once does either of them mention the news stories about Ryan.

"Tell it right, Tom," she says, as Tom recounts some family tale about fishing.

Tom Stiles grins. "She won't let me get away with a thing."

Bonnie turns to me. "Evan, let me show you the backyard and we'll have a smoke."

I get up and follow her outside. We sit at a redwood picnic table and light up. "Have you ever tried to quit?" she asks. She lights an extra long menthol with a chrome lighter.

"Haven't we all?"

She smiles. "I quit a couple of times, and of course Tom nags me all the time, but what are you going to do." I watch her take a deep drag and exhale. "Non-smokers just don't get it, do they?"

We sit for a few minutes, smoking in silence. I sense she wants to say something, ask me about Ryan, but she's holding back. We both turn as Ryan sticks his head out the door. "Okay you two. That's enough pollution. We have to get going, Mom."

We both stub out our cigarettes and start back into the house. At the door, Bonnie touches my arm and looks at me, her face full of concern. "Is this bad trouble for Ryan?"

"It's too early to tell," I say. "I think it's going to be okay."

"He's a good boy," she says.

Out front, we head for the cars with Tom and Bonnie trailing us. "You drive the Beamer," Ryan says. "Melanie and I will take the Mercedes."

"Fine with me. It looks great."

Tom nods. "Manny's Car Wash always does a great job. Right down on Ventura."

I lag a little, letting Ryan and Melanie get in the Mercedes and start the engine, then I turn back toward the house.

Ryan sees me start back. "Where you going?"

"Go ahead," I say. "I think I left my lighter in the house." Ryan waves and they pull away. "In the kitchen I think," I say to Tom and Bonnie, leaving them to wave goodbye.

I go back in the house, circle the kitchen, and come back out, the lighter in my hand. "Got it."

I get in the BMW and pull out, waving goodbye, but see Bonnie's smile has faded.

I find Manny's Full Service Car Wash a few blocks down Ventura Boulevard just east of Fallbrook. I pull in and park, watching a crew wiping down cars still dripping water as they emerge from the automated wash. There's a small shop and a waiting room, with several people browsing through magazines waiting for their cars.

Off to the side is small office. I see a man at a desk in dark work pants and a blue denim shirt with Manny stitched over the breast pocket. He's focused on some papers on his desk, a calculator to the side.

"Manny?"

He looks up, pushing glasses up his nose. He has a head of thick black hair and a lined face. "Yeah. What can I do for you?"

I step inside and immediately see a framed, signed publicity photo of Ryan on the wall. I point at the photo. "Did Mr. Stiles bring his car in for a detail the other day?"

"Yeah, his dad did. He's a regular customer. Something wrong?"

"No, no, he just recommended you. I thought I'd check out your place. Ryan let me borrow his car today."

"Uh huh. Kid's in a little trouble I guess from the papers."

"Oh I don't think it's anything to worry about."

Manny studies me for a moment then gets up. "Let's have a look at the car. I didn't do the job myself."

We go outside and Manny walks around the BMW a few times, a practiced eye scanning the car. He opens the door, looks inside, and shrugs. "Looks fine. I had Rick do a full wash, wax, and detail." He looks at me, his eyes narrowing, wary now. "What are you really here for?"

"I'm just wondering. Did you or Rick notice any damage at all, even a little ding, on the fender maybe?"

Manny frowns. "I didn't. I'd have to check with Rick, but if there had been, he would have told me."

I smile. "That's what I thought."

"Are the police going to ask me that?"

"They might. Thanks for your time."

I get in the car and start the engine. I see Manny in the rearview mirror, still standing, still watching me as I pull out of the driveway.

Chapter Eleven

When I get back to the house, Ryan's Mercedes is not there. Neither is Emillio's silver Volkswagen Bug. Newer, but one just like mine, still parked I hope, back at Andie's apartment in San Francisco. I go in the guesthouse, change into shorts and a t-shirt, and head down to the beach for a long walk. I lose track of time and drift past Trancas, almost halfway to Point Dune, before I turn back, just walking on the wet sand, letting the cool water splash over my ankles.

The warm sun, the waves gently lapping on the beach are soothing and help me clear my mind as I review the past few days. I'm surprised at the relief I feel at having seen Ryan's BMW undamaged, and having it confirmed by Manny that he was unaware of any scrapes or nicks when he detailed the car. I realize now how much I want to believe Ryan had nothing to do with Darryl McElroy's death. Driving with total abandon, his temper revved up after the altercation with McElroy at the Anchor, it could have easily been Ryan Stiles going off the road into Malibu Canyon.

When I get back to the house, I see Emillio looking down from the deck. He waves. I wave back and sit down on the sand, leaning back on my elbows letting the warmth of the sun wash over me.

A few minutes later, he comes down the steps with a Brother Thelonious beer and a sandwich on a paper plate. "Thought you might be hungry," he says, squatting down next to me.

"Thanks." I take a long pull on the beer. "Just what I needed." The sandwich is crab meat and avocado with some kind of dressing. I look at Emillio gazing out at the ocean. A strong breeze has come up now, and his black hair blows over his forehead. He sits back and scoops up handfuls of sand, letting it trickle through his fingers, something on his mind.

"Is this going to be bad for Ryan?" he asks.

"How much do you know?"

"I've read the papers, seen the TV news reports."

"Nobody has talked to you?" He shakes his head. "How long have you worked for Ryan?"

"Almost four years."

"You've seen a lot then."

He smiles and nods. "Yes, I have."

"And probably kept quiet about a lot, too."

He nods. "I have, but then I had to sign a confidentially agreement." He looks at me. "You didn't have to sign one?"

"Nope. I signed a contract for the teaching, but I don't remember a confidentially clause." I wonder then if I'd just missed it or hadn't read it carefully.

Emillio seems surprised. "It's pretty common with the stars. Nannies, cooks, bodyguards. No star wants an employee leaking something to one of the tabloid magazines, or writing a tell-all book."

I nod. "I was wondering. Why doesn't Ryan have a bodyguard?'

"He did. Went through a couple but they didn't work out. For big events, the studio usually assigns them."

I finish off the sandwich and take another slug of beer." That was great." I set the plate on the sand and get a cigarette going. "Well, the police are investigating, but I don't think there's anything really to worry about. So far, it's just routine."

Emillio gives me a look. "Nothing is routine with Ryan Stiles."

"Because of his celebrity?"

"That and his"—he searches for the right word—"temper."

"There is that," I say. "I'm guessing you have some first-hand knowledge."

He nods. "Twice. Once with Melanie and once with me. He was furious with her over something, some small imagined slight probably. She's beautiful and he's very jealous. I thought he was going to hit her."

"Would you have tried to stop him?"

He turns and looks at me. "Yes. I heard them arguing when I walked in. Melanie looked so scared. He had her pinned against the wall. Ryan turned to me and started yelling, 'What the fuck are you looking at? This is none of your fucking business.'"

"What happened?"

"Melanie slipped away and ran off down to the beach. Ryan stalked off to his room and slammed the door so hard I thought it would break. Later, he came to me for what I thought would be a lecture or maybe to fire me. Instead, he apologized, all charming again, and gave me a bonus on my next check."

That seemed to be Ryan's pattern. Snapping, going off in a rage, then settling down later. "I've seen him twice, too. At that restaurant in Santa Monica when we had lunch, and at the Anchor when he broke the photographer's camera and took off."

"Is that why they're investigating? Do the police think Ryan had anything to do with the photographer's death."

"They don't know."

"Do you?"

"No I don't. There's no evidence."

"I'm glad to hear you say that."

"Why?"

"Because if he did, even if he got off, I couldn't work for him anymore." Emillio gets up then, takes the beer bottle and plate and starts up the steps to the house.

"Emillio." He stops and turns around. "Neither would I."

I wait another few minutes then check my watch, deciding it's time to call Andie. She answers on the second ring.

"It's about time," she says.

"Nice to hear your voice, too."

"So what's the latest?"

I catch her up on the police questioning, checking out Ryan's car, visiting Manny's car wash, and my talk with Grant Robbins about staying on. She listens without interrupting.

"I guess there's no point in trying to talk you out of this, is there?"

"I want to see this through, Andie, see how things shake out." I hear her sigh audibly.

"How long?"

"Couple of weeks. I can't see the investigation going much longer than that unless the police come up with some hard evidence."

"What if it does take longer?"

"Then I guess I'll have to rethink things."

"I hate to be the one to puncture this balloon, but isn't it quite a coincidence that Ryan and this photographer guy both drive over Malibu Canyon the same night, the same time? One goes over the edge, and one goes home to mom and dad?"

"You have me there."

"I guess the chance to score a Ryan Stiles movie is a big tempting carrot."

"Yeah, it is. It could open some other doors."

"Just don't get caught up in something you'll regret. No, scratch that. You've been there. I don't have to remind you to be careful, do I?"

"No ma'am, you don't." I smile, imagining Andie glaring at the phone. "How's work with you?"

"Pretty boring, but something came up yesterday. I have to go to L.A. to see Wendell Cook. Remember him?"

How could I forget. Wendell was the agent in charge during Gillian Payne's reign of murders when the FBI roped me into helping them. It was also when I met Andie. "What's that about?"

"No idea, but it means I get to join you in Malibu if I can swing a few days after the meeting."

"Great. Let me know when you're coming and I'll meet you."

"The Bureau is flying me down. I'll call you after the meeting."

"Bring that black bikini again."

"It's already packed."

I pocket my phone and lie on the beach for a few more minutes, then climb the steps up to the house. Ryan is in the kitchen, talking on the phone. He looks at me and holds up a finger.

"Yes, I can do that. Glad to help," he says and hangs up. "Malibu Police," he says to me. "They want to look at the car. Can you drive it in for me? I'll follow you in the Mercedes."

"Sure. Give me a few minutes to change." I go in the guesthouse and throw on some jeans and a sweatshirt. Ryan is already outside, waiting, running his hand over the fender of the BMW. "Manny does great work, eh?" He straightens up. "This is such bullshit."

"They could get a warrant, come out and impound the car. Looks much better if you're being cooperative."

"Yeah I know." He gets in the Mercedes. "I know, just routine," he says irritably. "Go ahead. I'll follow you."

At Malibu Civic Center, we're directed around back to some kind of garage facility. There are a few sheriff's cruisers parked nearby, and several mechanics in blue coveralls working on the cars. Some have the hoods open, some are up on racks. They all look up as I park the BMW and get out. Ryan pulls in next to me. I hand the keys over to a deputy with a clipboard, who tells Ryan it could be a couple of days. "You'll be notified, Mr. Stiles."

"I can't wait," Ryan says. We get in the Mercedes and head back to the house. He seems preoccupied as we drive, tapping his fingers on the wheel, his head nodding slightly.

"Mind if I ask you a question?"

"What?"

"Was that normal for your dad to take the car to have it detailed?"

Ryan shrugs. "Why not? He was just being Dad. Something wrong with that?"

"No, I guess not. I was just curious."

Ryan keeps looking straight ahead. "Mind if I ask you a question?"

"Sure."

"Was it normal for you to check on the car with Manny?" Ryan sees the surprise on my face and smiles. "Manny called my dad right after you were there. Dad called me."

"Okay, you got me. I just had to satisfy myself."

"I'm a little disappointed but I understand. Satisfied?"

We ride a few more minutes in silence. "Yes. I guess there was no need to worry about Manny, huh?"

Ryan grins again. "None at all."

I don't see Ryan or Melanie the rest of the day. I get in some practice, taking advantage of the piano, and think about lining up some gigs. Maybe Ruth Price can come up with something while I wait. I stop, look at my watch, and see almost two hours have passed when Emillio appears in the doorway holding a small overnight bag.

"I've been given the night off," he says. "There's a meat loaf and a baked potato warming in the oven for you. A salad in the fridge."

"Great, sounds fine." He's dressed in casual clothes, his jacket already on. "Big date tonight?"

He smiles. "No, I'm going to see my sister. I'll be back in the morning."

"Enjoy."

I go to the guesthouse, have a long shower, and change into sweatpants. Back in the kitchen, I find Emillio has everything laid out. I take the meat loaf out of the oven, cut off a couple of thick slices, add butter and salt and pepper to the potato. I grab the salad and a beer, and take the everything out on the deck.

I eat, enjoying the solitude, watching the sun make its final descent, and feeling the air begin to cool. I light a cigarette and think about a second beer or some coffee when Melanie comes out. Her blond hair is in a pony tail, no make-up, wearing jeans and a short top.

"Mind some company?"

"Hey, no, not at all. You better have some of Emillio's meat loaf."

She smiles, but looks tired, a little drawn. "I think I will." She goes in the kitchen and comes back with a small slice, a smattering of salad, and a bottle of sparkling water. She sits down with me and nibbles on the meat loaf.

"Where's Ryan?"

"He was watching a movie and fell asleep."

I watch her eat and see she wants to talk. "How are you doing?" I ask her. "You were very quiet in the car this morning."

She nods, takes a drink of water. "I'm just worried about Ryan I guess. This…this whole thing is just so awful." She looks up at me. "By the way, I'm really glad you decided to stay."

"For awhile anyway. Grant Robbins is very persuasive, and I want to see how this all comes out. With the movie I mean."

"Is it going to be okay?"

Ryan's mother, Emillio, and now Melanie. "The police are examining the car. There's no damage and we know Ryan spent the night at his folks. I know everybody says the same thing, but it is kind of routine." She nods, tries to smile.

"How well do you know Ryan's parents?"

"Not all that well, really. This morning was only the second time I've been to their home."

"They seem like very nice people." I decide not to tell her about having checked with Manny about the car, or that Ryan knows I did. "Well, his dad can vouch for Ryan being there all night, so I don't think Ryan has anything to worry about."

"I know. I just want all this over."

"Andie is coming down again, maybe in a couple of days."

Melanie instantly brightens. "Great. I look forward to spending some more time with her. She's just so…so together. You're very lucky."

"That I am."

"That you are what?" Melanie and I both turn as we hear Ryan's voice.

He comes out on the deck in shorts and a sweatshirt, rubbing his eyes. He sits down and looks at us both.

"Melanie was telling me how lucky I am to have Andie," I say. "She's coming down in a couple of days."

Ryan frowns. "Nothing to do with my situation, is it?"

"No, the L.A. Bureau ordered her down. She used to work in the office here."

Ryan nods, already losing interest. "What are you guys eating?"

"Emillio made his famous meat loaf," Melanie says. "There's plenty left."

"Cool. Why don't you make me a sandwich, baby. And bring me a beer, too."

Melanie gets up and goes into the kitchen. Ryan leans in closer, talking quietly. "She's pretty upset about all this," he says.

"Yeah, I know. I've been telling her it's all going to be okay."

"Cool," Ryan says. He claps a hand on my shoulder. "You're a good friend, Evan."

I shrug. "Well, there was no apparent damage to the car, and your dad saw you come in, so your alibi, if we have to call it that, is solid." Ryan looks away for a moment. "What?"

He checks to see that Melanie is still in the kitchen. "Dad didn't see me come in." He speaks even quieter now. "He didn't know I was there until he went out to get the paper and saw the car in the driveway."

Andie calls me the next afternoon. "Hey, handsome. Want to pick up your girlfriend?"

"Wow, that was fast. Where are you?"

"The Federal Building on Wilshire. There's a coffee shop just down the street. I'll finish up here and meet you there."

"Okay. About an hour?"

I hear something in her voice. "Everything okay? You're not in trouble with Wendell are you?"

She hesitates a moment. "No, nothing like that. I'll tell you when you get here."

I close my phone and start out, then remember Ryan and Melanie are out, the BMW is in Malibu. I find Emillio in the kitchen. "Andie just called. I have to pick her up in Westwood. Would you mind if I borrowed your car?"

"Of course not," he says. He fishes the key out of his pocket. "I'll make a special dinner."

"Thanks, Emillio."

I make the drive into Westwood in record time, my mind bouncing back and forth from Ryan's disclosure that his dad hadn't seen him until the morning after his drive, and trying to guess what Andie couldn't or wouldn't tell me on the phone. I find the coffee shop easily, remembering now Andie and I had been there a couple of times before during the Gillian Payne case. I find her in a booth, nursing a cup of coffee. I give her a quick kiss and slide in opposite her. She manages a weak smile. I reach across the table and take her hand. "Okay, what is it?"

"It could be nothing, but Wendell thought I should know and he left it to me to tell you."

"What? C'mon, Andie, what is it?"

"You're going to need a cigarette. Let's go outside."

I wave off an approaching waitress, throw some money on the table for her coffee and follow Andie outside. We start to walk up Wilshire. The traffic is heavy, cars streaming by as I look across toward the Veteran's Cemetery.

Andie stops, touches my arm. "We, they, lost Gillian Payne."

Chapter Twelve

I just stare at Andie for a long moment, as if I haven't heard what she'd said. Coming from a meeting with Wendell Cook at the Bureau Office, she was dressed more officially today. Dark blue pantsuit, powder blue blouse, the jacket slung over her shoulder. She was right. I did need a cigarette.

I light one and sit down on a narrow wall surrounding a flower bed outside the coffee shop. "What do you mean they lost Gillian Payne? She was in a state prison for God's sake."

Andie stands in front of me, her arms crossed, looking down. "She was being transferred, temporarily moved to another facility for more psychiatric counseling. I don't know all the details, but somehow she managed to slip away. They think she may have had some inside help."

Gillian Payne had murdered four people and almost killed her brother in Las Vegas during a concert. She'd also seriously injured Coop. I'd been recruited by the FBI to help them decipher clues she'd left at the crime scenes nobody in the FBI could make sense of, but it had become personal, and I was made a conduit between her and the FBI when she discovered I was working with them. There were phone calls, poems, threats, music, all directed at me. It was a nightmare for me, a game for her.

"We've notified her brother as well," Andie says. "We're on it, Evan, really. She won't get far." As far as I knew, Gillian's brother Greg Sims was in the witness protection program.

Except for the concert, the last time I'd seen her was in jail. She'd insisted on seeing me and the FBI agreed, catering to her to ensure her cooperation to help strengthen their case. I would never forget seeing her through the glass in the visitors room just before I left for Europe.

I'd picked up the phone and looked at her. "What do you want, Gillian?" I said.

"I wanted to see you once, under different conditions, thank you for finding Greg, see that you understand."

"I'll never understand what you did Gillian. I don't think you do either."

Her smile was chilling. I saw not a trace of remorse. "No, I guess you don't. But think about it, Evan. Are you so different from me?"

I had no idea what she meant. I put the phone down then and walked out, convinced I'd never see her again. But it wasn't quite over. At LAX, Andie had seen me off, and gave me a slip of paper with one of Gillian's poems. It was like all the others, a modified Haiku.

Dizzy Atmosphere
Miles Smiles in a Silent Way
Bird Lives!

That was over five years ago, and now this psycho was out, on the run somewhere. "Jesus, Andie, she got a life sentence. Don't they take extra precautions with someone like her?" I finish my cigarette and stamp it out.

"Of course they do," Andie says, "but she's apparently been a model prisoner. Sometimes things just…happen." She sits down next to me. "We'll get her, Evan. She'll go right to the top of the FBI's most wanted."

"What does Wendell Cook say?"

"That there's no reason to think she will come after you, or have any idea where you are. Wendell just wanted you to know the status of things."

seems relaxed and not at all snappy with Melanie. I catch Andie studying him all through dinner, profiling him I imagine, based on what she already knows. I can't wait to hear about that later.

We linger over coffee then I get a look from Andie. I stand up. "We're going to hit it, folks. Andie's had a long day."

"Hey, sleep in," Ryan says. "I've got to leave at the crack of dawn for the taping. Check me out when you get up."

"Oh, don't worry," Andie says. We make our way to the guesthouse where Andie immediately begins to strip off her FBI suit. She walks naked into the bathroom, turns on the shower, and looks at me. "Want to wash my hair?"

I awaken to light knocking on our door. When I open it, Emillio has left a tray with coffee, all the fixings, and a plate of warm cinnamon rolls. I get the TV on just in time to hear the anchor say, "When we come back, a conversation with Ryan Stiles."

I give Andie a shake and hand her a cup of coffee. "Time for our boy."

Andie groans and buries her face in the pillow. "You watch and tell me about it."

"No, I want your take on his performance."

She struggles upright, leans back on the headboard, and takes a cup of coffee. I join her and we sit through several commercials, then Matt Lauer's face appears. "Welcome back. Our very special guest this morning is one of the biggest box office stars in the business. Ryan Stiles' face is known throughout the world, but of late, the young star is embroiled in controversy surrounding the death of photographer Darryl McElroy." There's a shot of Ryan facing a camera, then it's split screen as they both talk to monitors.

"Ryan, thanks for getting up so early."

Ryan smiles big. "Always a pleasure, Matt. Nice to be here."

"Ryan, it's no secret that the last few days you've been linked to the death of a paparazzo named Darryl McElroy. I understand you've given a statement to the police. It's also no secret that you've had several run-ins with McElroy in the past."

"That's very comforting."

"C'mon, let's go," Andie says.

We get in the car and start the drive back to Malibu. Reliving some of the horrible moments with Gillian's voice in my ear, I negotiate the rush hour traffic to the Coast

Highway. I can still see her holding a knife to Nicky Drew's throat, backstage at the concert in Las Vegas, her brother Greg lunging at her, hitting her in the face with his saxophone, Coop and the police finally subduing her, pinning her to the floor while she screamed, "I didn't mean it, I didn't mean it!"

I try to shake these and other thoughts off but I know in my heart they'll never go away. And now, Gillian Payne, cold-blooded killer, is free again, at least temporarily.

"Evan? The light's green."

I blink and look at Andie, her voice pulling me back to the present. A horn honks behind me. I wave my hand out the window in apology to the driver and pull away, crossing Topanga Canyon Boulevard.

"Are you okay?" Andie asks. I nod but don't answer. At the next available opportunity, I turn off into a parking area on the beach side and stop the car. I turn off the engine and look at Andie.

"It's all coming back."

"I know, but don't get ahead of things. She won't be free for long and there's no reason to believe she'll be looking for you."

"I helped send her to prison. Why wouldn't she?"

"She's a fugitive on the run. She won't have time to think about you or me or Coop. Anyway, she has no idea where you are now or what you're doing."

"I hope you're right, Andie."

"I am. Believe me, escaped killers are high priority for the FBI. They have some leads." I feel her eyes on me as I light a cigarette and stare out at the ocean. "Before we get back to the house, bring me up to speed on Ryan's situation."

I know she's trying to divert my thoughts from Gillian Payne, and it does help to think in another direction. I recount most of what I'd already told her earlier. She doesn't stop me until I mention Ryan's admission about his dad not knowing he was home until morning.

"Whoa," Andie says. "That kind of changes things, at least the time frame."

"How so?"

"He's only got half an alibi now. He can't prove when he got to his dad's house."

"Does that make a difference?"

"It could. He should have told the police that when he made his statement."

I wanted to ignore it, but I know Andie's right.

"What about this Manny guy at the car wash? You think he'd cover for Ryan if there was damage to the car?"

"I really don't know. My take on him was he was telling the truth."

Andie looks away, out at the ocean. It's turned a dark blue now, the sun shimmering off the waves. "You just never know," she says. "You just never know."

We sit for a few more minutes, both lost in thought, mesmerized by the ocean. I start the car and pull out to the highway, waiting for an opening in the heavy traffic. It's slow going until we get past Malibu Pier. The rest of the trip is easy. At the end of Broad Beach Road I pull up to the gates and punch in the number code on the keypad.

Ryan's Mercedes is back and parked behind it is Grant Robbins car. I park the VW off to the side and we go inside. Emillio greets Andie in the kitchen. "So nice to see you again, Miss Lawrence," he says.

"Thank you. I missed your cooking."

Emillio smiles. "We'll make up for that this evening." He nods toward the deck. I see Ryan and Grant Robbins. "There's some good news."

I hand Emillio his car key with a nod of thanks and Andie and I go out to join them with hellos all around. Robbins seems about to burst. "Great news, Evan. The Malibu Police are releasing the car tomorrow morning. Everything is fine."

I look at Ryan. He meets my gaze with a wink as if to say, 'I told you so.' "Great," I say. Andie says nothing and sits down.

"There's more," Grant continues. "Ryan is going on the *Today Show* tomorrow morning to help clear up everything for his fans."

"I'm sure they'll be relieved," Andie says, trying to keep the sarcasm out of her voice but not very successfully. Ryan gives her a look but says nothing in response.

"Is the *Today Show* a good idea?" I ask Robbins.

"Sure. It gets Ryan out there again in a positive light, takes away that cloud of suspicion. I think it's a good move."

Emillio comes out then with two Bloody Marys for Andie and me. "You are a wonder," Andie says, taking the glass from Emillio.

Robbins finishes his drink and stands up. "Well, I have to run. Lots to do," he says. "Could I see you outside for a moment, Evan?"

"Sure." I get up and follow him out to his car.

He turns toward me. "It's all go on the movie now. I'm having a contract drawn up for you to score the film and lock things in. Once that's done, we'll have a script for you."

I feel a rush at his words. "Great. I'm ready."

"Yes, Evan. It's going to happen now."

Why now, is all I can think as I watch Robbins drive out through the gates.

I go back in the house and find Andie in deep conversation with Melanie at one end of the deck. Melanie is in a white warm-up suit that clings to her body. She's wearing light makeup and looks better than I've seen her for days, much of it I think, due to seeing Andie again. She's like an older sister for Melanie.

"Those girls do get along, don't they?" Ryan says, his eyes on both of them. He turns to me. "What's it like having an FBI agent for a girlfriend?"

"It can be exciting," I say. *If you only knew,* I think.

A half hour later, Emillio serves up another sumptuous dinner on the deck. Ryan talks about doing the *Today Show*. He

Ryan's smile is a tad weaker, but he presses on. "Mr. McElroy and I have had our differences, but I understand he had to make a living, and taking pictures of me and other actors is one of the ways he did." Ryan changes his expression then. "His death was tragic, and I certainly offer my thoughts to his family." He pauses for a moment, takes a breath. "I want to go on record right here that I had nothing to do with Darryl McElroy's death."

"But isn't it true that on the night of McElroy's death you had a violent altercation with him at a restaurant in Malibu?"

"I wouldn't call it violent, Matt. We had words and in my opinion, he overstepped his bounds. I simply reacted."

"By breaking his camera? Some people would call that overreacting."

Ryan looks away for a moment, then back to the camera. "Things got a little heated, Matt, but I simply left and tried to diffuse the incident."

Lauer glances down, consulting notes. "So are the police satisfied with your statement?"

"Absolutely, Matt. They also checked my car for damage and found none. As far as I'm concerned, the incident is closed."

Matt Lauer smiles then. "I'm sure your fans will be pleased to hear that. Before we go, can you tell us what new project is in the works?"

"I wish I could, Matt, but for now all I can say is it's a very different role for me."

Lauer nods. "Thanks for taking time to be with us, Ryan. Best of luck with the new film."

"Thanks, Matt. Always a pleasure." Ryan's face fades from the screen.

"We'll be right back with the weather where you are," Lauer says. "This is Today on NBC."

I turn off the TV and look at Andie. "Well?"

She shrugs. "He went public. I'll give him that. He almost lost it when Lauer pressed. He was clearly annoyed, but he recovered well, not too defensive, and once the talk turned to movies, he was his old self." She drains her coffee and sets the cup on the nightstand.

"Anything else?"

"He never blinked once. In his mind, Ryan is convinced he did nothing wrong"

"Unless you call breaking a camera a way to diffuse an incident."

After breakfast, Andie and I head for the beach. We spend the morning walking, splashing in the water like a couple of kids. While Andie plops down on the sand, I take a quick dip, and surf a couple of waves. The water is cold, invigorating. The sun on my shoulders feels good as I reach the beach and make my way back to Andie, who's talking to Ryan.

"Dude, good news," he says as I wrap a towel around me. "I was just telling Andie the Malibu Police are releasing the car. You guys catch me on TV?"

"We did," Andie says. "Very impressive."

"So what's next?" I ask.

"The movie, dude, the movie. Grant says the investors are satisfied and ready to put the cash in place." He takes a long look at me. "You ready to sign a contract now?"

"You ready to show me the script?"

"Grant has the details. The director wants to make some changes, but we'll get you a copy as soon as possible."

I glance at Andie, then gaze out at the ocean. I know what she's thinking. See the script first, then sign. It's my feeling too. "Look, you have a lot to do. You don't need me around here for awhile. I'd like to go home." I catch Andie nodding approval. "When you get a final copy of the script, send it to me with the contract and we'll go from there."

"Fair enough," Ryan says. "We can do that." He looks down for a moment, dragging his foot through the sand. "I'm counting on you to do the music. You're not going to bail on me are you?"

"I haven't yet."

"Cool. See you guys inside." Ryan turns, jogs up the steps to the house."

"Can we get a flight this evening?" Andie takes my hand. "I want to spend some time in Monte Rio."

"I don't see why not. Had enough of Malibu?"

"Malibu I love. Star power gets old."

I make some calls and we get lucky with an evening flight to San Francisco. Emillio offers to drive us to the airport. When he drops us off, he gets out of the car and shakes hands with both of us.

"It's been nice having some real people around," he says.

"You stay in touch, okay?" I hand him one of my cards. "Call anytime."

We grab out bags and walk into the terminal. I turn around and look back over my shoulder. Emillio is still standing there, watching us go.

Chapter Thirteen

Getting back to Monte Rio and my own place is exactly what I needed. The contrast between the beach in Malibu, and the scent and sight of huge Redwoods and the Russian River acts like a tonic. The absence of movie stars helps a lot too, and makes me begin to rethink everything. All these thoughts run through my mind as I open all the windows to air out the place. I pop the top on a Brother Thelonious beer, and sit out on the deck, to absorb the quiet and solitude.

Our flight had been on time, and as we touched down in Oakland, Andie and I were already talking about Chinese take-out. We had picked up her car from long-term parking, made the quick drive to her place and ordered by phone. We stuffed ourselves on rice and kung pao chicken, then fell into Andie's bed. The next thing I heard was Andie as the alarm went off.

"Oh, not already," she groaned. She pulled herself out of bed and stumbled for the shower. When I opened my eyes again, Andie, clad only black bra and panties, was rummaging in her closet. I sat up a little, thought sometimes it's just as fun to watch a woman dress as it is to see her slowly strip off.

She glanced at me, recognized my look as she pulled on panty hose. "Hold that thought," she said. "I'll be down late this afternoon."

"That won't be hard to do. No pun intended."

"I hope not." She finished with a dark skirt, white blouse, and casual dark blue jacket. She stuffed all those things women

"That's very comforting."

"C'mon, let's go," Andie says.

We get in the car and start the drive back to Malibu. Reliving some of the horrible moments with Gillian's voice in my ear, I negotiate the rush hour traffic to the Coast Highway. I can still see her holding a knife to Nicky Drew's throat, backstage at the concert in Las Vegas, her brother Greg lunging at her, hitting her in the face with his saxophone, Coop and the police finally subduing her, pinning her to the floor while she screamed, "I didn't mean it, I didn't mean it!"

I try to shake these and other thoughts off but I know in my heart they'll never go away. And now, Gillian Payne, cold-blooded killer, is free again, at least temporarily.

"Evan? The light's green."

I blink and look at Andie, her voice pulling me back to the present. A horn honks behind me. I wave my hand out the window in apology to the driver and pull away, crossing Topanga Canyon Boulevard.

"Are you okay?" Andie asks. I nod but don't answer. At the next available opportunity, I turn off into a parking area on the beach side and stop the car. I turn off the engine and look at Andie.

"It's all coming back."

"I know, but don't get ahead of things. She won't be free for long and there's no reason to believe she'll be looking for you."

"I helped send her to prison. Why wouldn't she?"

"She's a fugitive on the run. She won't have time to think about you or me or Coop. Anyway, she has no idea where you are now or what you're doing."

"I hope you're right, Andie."

"I am. Believe me, escaped killers are high priority for the FBI. They have some leads." I feel her eyes on me as I light a cigarette and stare out at the ocean. "Before we get back to the house, bring me up to speed on Ryan's situation."

I know she's trying to divert my thoughts from Gillian Payne, and it does help to think in another direction. I recount most of what I'd already told her earlier. She doesn't stop me until I mention Ryan's admission about his dad not knowing he was home until morning.

"Whoa," Andie says. "That kind of changes things, at least the time frame."

"How so?"

"He's only got half an alibi now. He can't prove when he got to his dad's house."

"Does that make a difference?"

"It could. He should have told the police that when he made his statement."

I wanted to ignore it, but I know Andie's right.

"What about this Manny guy at the car wash? You think he'd cover for Ryan if there was damage to the car?"

"I really don't know. My take on him was he was telling the truth."

Andie looks away, out at the ocean. It's turned a dark blue now, the sun shimmering off the waves. "You just never know," she says. "You just never know."

We sit for a few more minutes, both lost in thought, mesmerized by the ocean. I start the car and pull out to the highway, waiting for an opening in the heavy traffic. It's slow going until we get past Malibu Pier. The rest of the trip is easy. At the end of Broad Beach Road I pull up to the gates and punch in the number code on the keypad.

Ryan's Mercedes is back and parked behind it is Grant Robbins car. I park the VW off to the side and we go inside. Emillio greets Andie in the kitchen. "So nice to see you again, Miss Lawrence," he says.

"Thank you. I missed your cooking."

Emillio smiles. "We'll make up for that this evening." He nods toward the deck. I see Ryan and Grant Robbins. "There's some good news."

I hand Emillio his car key with a nod of thanks and Andie and I go out to join them with hellos all around. Robbins seems about to burst. "Great news, Evan. The Malibu Police are releasing the car tomorrow morning. Everything is fine."

I look at Ryan. He meets my gaze with a wink as if to say, 'I told you so.' "Great," I say. Andie says nothing and sits down.

"There's more," Grant continues. "Ryan is going on the *Today Show* tomorrow morning to help clear up everything for his fans."

"I'm sure they'll be relieved," Andie says, trying to keep the sarcasm out of her voice but not very successfully. Ryan gives her a look but says nothing in response.

"Is the *Today Show* a good idea?" I ask Robbins.

"Sure. It gets Ryan out there again in a positive light, takes away that cloud of suspicion. I think it's a good move."

Emillio comes out then with two Bloody Marys for Andie and me. "You are a wonder," Andie says, taking the glass from Emillio.

Robbins finishes his drink and stands up. "Well, I have to run. Lots to do," he says. "Could I see you outside for a moment, Evan?"

"Sure." I get up and follow him out to his car.

He turns toward me. "It's all go on the movie now. I'm having a contract drawn up for you to score the film and lock things in. Once that's done, we'll have a script for you."

I feel a rush at his words. "Great. I'm ready."

"Yes, Evan. It's going to happen now."

Why now, is all I can think as I watch Robbins drive out through the gates.

I go back in the house and find Andie in deep conversation with Melanie at one end of the deck. Melanie is in a white warm-up suit that clings to her body. She's wearing light makeup and looks better than I've seen her for days, much of it I think, due to seeing Andie again. She's like an older sister for Melanie.

"Those girls do get along, don't they?" Ryan says, his eyes on both of them. He turns to me. "What's it like having an FBI agent for a girlfriend?"

"It can be exciting," I say. *If you only knew,* I think.

A half hour later, Emillio serves up another sumptuous dinner on the deck. Ryan talks about doing the *Today Show*. He seems relaxed and not at all snappy with Melanie. I catch Andie studying him all through dinner, profiling him I imagine, based on what she already knows. I can't wait to hear about that later.

We linger over coffee then I get a look from Andie. I stand up. "We're going to hit it, folks. Andie's had a long day."

"Hey, sleep in," Ryan says. "I've got to leave at the crack of dawn for the taping. Check me out when you get up."

"Oh, don't worry," Andie says. We make our way to the guesthouse where Andie immediately begins to strip off her FBI suit. She walks naked into the bathroom, turns on the shower, and looks at me. "Want to wash my hair?"

I awaken to light knocking on our door. When I open it, Emillio has left a tray with coffee, all the fixings, and a plate of warm cinnamon rolls. I get the TV on just in time to hear the anchor say, "When we come back, a conversation with Ryan Stiles."

I give Andie a shake and hand her a cup of coffee. "Time for our boy."

Andie groans and buries her face in the pillow. "You watch and tell me about it."

"No, I want your take on his performance."

She struggles upright, leans back on the headboard, and takes a cup of coffee. I join her and we sit through several commercials, then Matt Lauer's face appears. "Welcome back. Our very special guest this morning is one of the biggest box office stars in the business. Ryan Stiles' face is known throughout the world, but of late, the young star is embroiled in controversy surrounding the death of photographer Darryl McElroy." There's a shot of Ryan facing a camera, then it's split screen as they both talk to monitors.

"Ryan, thanks for getting up so early."

Ryan smiles big. "Always a pleasure, Matt. Nice to be here."

"Ryan, it's no secret that the last few days you've been linked to the death of a paparazzo named Darryl McElroy. I understand you've given a statement to the police. It's also no secret that you've had several run-ins with McElroy in the past."

Ryan's smile is a tad weaker, but he presses on. "Mr. McElroy and I have had our differences, but I understand he had to make a living, and taking pictures of me and other actors is one of the ways he did." Ryan changes his expression then. "His death was tragic, and I certainly offer my thoughts to his family." He pauses for a moment, takes a breath. "I want to go on record right here that I had nothing to do with Darryl McElroy's death."

"But isn't it true that on the night of McElroy's death you had a violent altercation with him at a restaurant in Malibu?"

"I wouldn't call it violent, Matt. We had words and in my opinion, he overstepped his bounds. I simply reacted."

"By breaking his camera? Some people would call that overreacting."

Ryan looks away for a moment, then back to the camera. "Things got a little heated, Matt, but I simply left and tried to diffuse the incident."

Lauer glances down, consulting notes. "So are the police satisfied with your statement?"

"Absolutely, Matt. They also checked my car for damage and found none. As far as I'm concerned, the incident is closed."

Matt Lauer smiles then. "I'm sure your fans will be pleased to hear that. Before we go, can you tell us what new project is in the works?"

"I wish I could, Matt, but for now all I can say is it's a very different role for me."

Lauer nods. "Thanks for taking time to be with us, Ryan. Best of luck with the new film."

"Thanks, Matt. Always a pleasure." Ryan's face fades from the screen.

"We'll be right back with the weather where you are," Lauer says. "This is Today on NBC."

I turn off the TV and look at Andie. "Well?"

She shrugs. "He went public. I'll give him that. He almost lost it when Lauer pressed. He was clearly annoyed, but he recovered well, not too defensive, and once the talk turned to movies, he was his old self." She drains her coffee and sets the cup on the nightstand.

"Anything else?"

"He never blinked once. In his mind, Ryan is convinced he did nothing wrong"

"Unless you call breaking a camera a way to diffuse an incident."

After breakfast, Andie and I head for the beach. We spend the morning walking, splashing in the water like a couple of kids. While Andie plops down on the sand, I take a quick dip, and surf a couple of waves. The water is cold, invigorating. The sun on my shoulders feels good as I reach the beach and make my way back to Andie, who's talking to Ryan.

"Dude, good news," he says as I wrap a towel around me. "I was just telling Andie the Malibu Police are releasing the car. You guys catch me on TV?"

"We did," Andie says. "Very impressive."

"So what's next?" I ask.

"The movie, dude, the movie. Grant says the investors are satisfied and ready to put the cash in place." He takes a long look at me. "You ready to sign a contract now?"

"You ready to show me the script?"

"Grant has the details. The director wants to make some changes, but we'll get you a copy as soon as possible."

I glance at Andie, then gaze out at the ocean. I know what she's thinking. See the script first, then sign. It's my feeling too. "Look, you have a lot to do. You don't need me around here for awhile. I'd like to go home." I catch Andie nodding approval. "When you get a final copy of the script, send it to me with the contract and we'll go from there."

"Fair enough," Ryan says. "We can do that." He looks down for a moment, dragging his foot through the sand. "I'm counting on you to do the music. You're not going to bail on me are you? "

"I haven't yet."

"Cool. See you guys inside." Ryan turns, jogs up the steps to the house."

"Can we get a flight this evening?" Andie takes my hand. "I want to spend some time in Monte Rio."

"I don't see why not. Had enough of Malibu?"

"Malibu I love. Star power gets old."

I make some calls and we get lucky with an evening flight to San Francisco. Emillio offers to drive us to the airport. When he drops us off, he gets out of the car and shakes hands with both of us.

"It's been nice having some real people around," he says.

"You stay in touch, okay?" I hand him one of my cards. "Call anytime."

We grab out bags and walk into the terminal. I turn around and look back over my shoulder. Emillio is still standing there, watching us go.

Chapter Thirteen

Getting back to Monte Rio and my own place is exactly what I needed. The contrast between the beach in Malibu, and the scent and sight of huge Redwoods and the Russian River acts like a tonic. The absence of movie stars helps a lot too, and makes me begin to rethink everything. All these thoughts run through my mind as I open all the windows to air out the place. I pop the top on a Brother Thelonious beer, and sit out on the deck, to absorb the quiet and solitude.

Our flight had been on time, and as we touched down in Oakland, Andie and I were already talking about Chinese take-out. We had picked up her car from long-term parking, made the quick drive to her place and ordered by phone. We stuffed ourselves on rice and kung pao chicken, then fell into Andie's bed. The next thing I heard was Andie as the alarm went off.

"Oh, not already," she groaned. She pulled herself out of bed and stumbled for the shower. When I opened my eyes again, Andie, clad only black bra and panties, was rummaging in her closet. I sat up a little, thought sometimes it's just as fun to watch a woman dress as it is to see her slowly strip off.

She glanced at me, recognized my look as she pulled on panty hose. "Hold that thought," she said. "I'll be down late this afternoon."

"That won't be hard to do. No pun intended."

"I hope not." She finished with a dark skirt, white blouse, and casual dark blue jacket. She stuffed all those things women stuff in their purses and added one most don't: her gun. "Okay, jazzman, I'm outta here. Just little paperwork to catch up."

"I know." We both had avoided any mention of Gillian Payne, but I knew she was mainly going in for an update on Payne's escape and the search for her.

Now, as I sit on the deck with my second beer, I try to avoid it too. But it's there, lurking in the back of my mind, the memories struggling to come to the surface. How could she have escaped without help? A twenty-five-to-life sentence and here she is out there somewhere, hopefully more concerned with her freedom than looking for me.

In the morning, I straighten up a little, have breakfast at a diner in Guerneville, and stop by the vet's to pick up Milton, the basset hound I'd inherited from my old friend Calvin Hughes, who I'd discovered was my birth father only a couple of years ago, a fact I still find hard to believe at times.

"He's missed you," the assistant says, as she brings him out. Milton lumbers over to me, inspects me with his big dark eyes, and thumps his tail on the floor. I thank the vet and take him out to the car. He sits on the passenger seat next to me, and before I pull away, he gives me a look.

"Okay, pal." I lower the window halfway and he sticks his head out for the drive home. I fill his dishes with fresh food and water and check my messages. Only one from a number and name I don't recognize. When I call back, a man's voice says, "Studios."

"Hi, it's Evan Horne. I just got your message."

"I'm Steve Wolf," the voice says. "Thanks for getting back to me. I have a small studio in Santa Rosa. I know it's short notice, but thought I'd give you a try."

"For what?"

"I'm doing some recording tonight. Nothing big, just some demo tracks, but my pianist canceled on me. Pays two bills, shouldn't take more than a couple of hours if you're interested."

I think for a moment. Why not? It'll be good to get back in the swing, do some real playing after tutoring a movie star.

"Okay, you're on. How do I get there?" I copy down the rather strange directions. "What time?"

"About nine," Wolf says. "Bass player can't get here before then."

"No problem. See you then."

I spend the day doing nothing other than taking Milton for a long walk along the river, and checking for mail at the Monte Rio post office. Nothing but bills and junk. I take a nap on the deck, awakened only by Andie calling and telling me she can't get away after all.

"I'm playing catch up here," she says.

"Just as well." I tell her about the recording gig. "Tomorrow?"

"I think so," she says. "I'll let you know."

"Anything new on—" she cuts me off.

"No, nothing."

I grab a sandwich and coffee at a deli in Guerneville, and head east on River Road, then south on 101. I take the Todd Road exit in Santa Rosa and continue west. Following the directions, one street past the stop sign, I turn right and go slow past a school, looking for a driveway. It's so dark, I almost miss it, but turn in sharply and stop. My headlights illuminate a tall dark fence maybe ten feet high with a solid wood sliding gate. Nailed to the gate are at least a dozen CDs, and a small sign proclaiming Wolf Lair Records. I'm a long way from the plush Avatar Studios in New York where I'd last recorded with Roy Haynes and Ron Carter.

I get out of the car and slide the gate back. There's a small yard with two cars parked near what looks like a barn. A single light burns over the door. I get back in my car, drive in, park off to the side, and as instructed, close the gate. There's another sliding door on the barn that sticks a little as I pull it open.

Inside, in dim light, among cables and power cords strewn on the floor, are a couple of instrument cases, a partial set of drums and stacks of electronic equipment. Along one wall is a low table and what looks like blank discs fanned out over the surface. Farther down to the right, I see a grand piano, mixing board and more equipment, more wires and cables in no particular order. A computer is perched on a large table.

"Hello. Anybody here?"

"Hey, you're early." I turn and see a thin wiry man in thick glasses with black rims walking in from a back room. He has a Styrofoam container of soup in his hand. He stops and spoons some to his mouth with a plastic spoon. "Welcome to Wolf Lair," he says.

He puts the soup down on a scarred Hammond Organ, wipes his hands on his jeans and steps closer, offering me his hand. "Steve Wolf."

"Evan Horne." We shake hands and he picks up the soup container again and looks at me. "Want some soup?"

"No thanks."

"I got some coffee going in the back."

"That I could go for."

He turns and walks to the back. I follow him to a tiny kitchenette with a microwave on the counter next to a small coffee machine with a full pot. Wolf puts down his soup, rummages in a small cupboard for a mug, and pours some coffee. He pushes a half-full bowl of sugar toward me, and digs a pint of half-and-half out of a mini fridge. "Help yourself."

I add cream and sugar and take a sip and lean on the counter. Just beyond the kitchen, I can see a small room and a twin-sized bed piled with clothes.

"Sorry for the mess," Wolf says, following my gaze. "I've been editing all day. I do a lot of crap stuff to pay the bills. Wannabe singers, demos, that kind of thing. You have any trouble finding the place?"

"No, your directions were fine."

"Good. The other guys will be here soon. Why don't you try the piano. I just had it tuned recently, so it should be okay."

I nod and walk back into the studio area, taking my coffee with me, and sit down at the piano. The action is a little stiff, but it is in tune. Wolf comes in and starts setting up microphones, running cables, and turning on the computer. He's all business, working fast, and seems totally at home. He looks up at me only when I take my cigarettes out.

"Have to do that outside," he says.

"No problem." I open the sliding door and step out into the yard just as the outside gate opens and a pickup truck with a camper shell pulls into the yard and parks. A tall slender man gets out, opens the back and drags out a bass in a padded cover. He walks over to me, leaning the bass on his shoulder.

"Hey, Bobby Warren." He sticks out his hand and we shake briefly. "You must be Evan Horne."

I nod and watch him fish cigarettes out of his jacket pocket and light up to join me. "Yeah, I caught you at Yoshi's a few weeks ago." He bobs his head. "Awesome, man. I'm looking forward to this. You haven't been here before, right?"

"No, first time."

Warren smiles. "It's a little weird but Steve gets a good sound. This will be low-key. I think he just wants to lay down some tracks for a future project."

We turn as the studio door slides open and Wolf peers out. "You guys come on in," Wolf says. "I want to get level checks before the drummer gets here. How you doin', Bobby?"

"I'm cool," Warren says.

We go inside. While Warren unpacks his bass, I sit down at the piano again and run through some chords and one-hand runs to warm up. Warren plugs into an amp that has suddenly appeared as Wolf adjusts a microphone then sets down at the mixing board and begins to adjust the slide controls.

"Give me something, Bobby," he says. Warren plucks the strings then begins a walking line for a minute or so. "Okay, sounds good. Evan, play something."

I play a minor blues line and go for a couple of choruses till Wolf stops me. "Got it," he says. "Let's try something." Wolf flips open a case near him and pulls out a tenor saxophone. He adjusts the mouthpiece, blows a few notes, and smiles. "Close enough for jazz, huh?" He gazes up at the ceiling for a moment, the overhead lights catching his glasses. "'Just Friends?'" Warren and I both nod. Wolf counts us in at a good clip.

And just like that I'm back doing what I do best, what I love best, laying down the chords for Wolf, taking in Warren's bass line, which is surprisingly solid. Wolf's sound is kind of rough, a bit like Sonny Rollins. He runs through the changes effortlessly for three choruses, his body rocking, displaying ample technique, but I get the feeling he's holding back. He turns then and nods to me.

During my solo, Wolf makes some adjustments on the mixing board, then listens to Bobby Warren, squinting, bent over the bass as he takes two choruses. Wolf listens, head down, then glances at me, twirls his index finger in the air as a signal to take it out. We close just kind of fading at the end on a long tag, letting the notes and chords just disappear in the air.

"Wow, man, those changes," Bobby Warren says. "You gotta write them out for me." He lays his bass down and comes over to the piano. As I show him, Wolf taps some keys on the computer and we get a playback. All digital now, no tape, and Warren was right. The sound is good even unmixed.

We start to talk about some other tunes when the sliding door opens and a young girl in tattered jeans, a sweatshirt, and long blond hair walks in. Wolf walks over to her and they talk by the open door.

"No drums tonight," Warren says quietly to me. "That's his girlfriend."

Wolf comes back. "Guess we're without drums."

"Your call," I say. Warren nods in agreement.

We talk over several tunes, decide on keys, chord changes, and head arrangements. For the next two hours we get five more tunes done. Wolf plays, works the board and the computer. A little after eleven, he plays everything back. "Okay, guys, that should do it. Thanks for hanging in."

Warren packs up his bass and Wolf walks us to the door. "We can do some more of this if you feel like it. I'll give you a call," he says to me. He slides the door shut, leaving Bobby Warren and me in the yard. We exchange numbers and I follow his truck out. I close the yard gate, glancing again at the CDs nailed to it. I head back for 101 and think about what an unusual session it's been.

When I turn in the driveway, I'm surprised to see Andie's car. I go inside and find her asleep on the couch, a blanket over her, the television on low, playing an old black-and-white film. It's Fred McMurray and Barbara Stanwyck verbally sparring in *Double Indemnity.*

Andie stirs a little as I gently lift her legs and sit down on the end of the couch, her feet across my lap. I reach under the blanket and lightly stroke her calf, then move up higher and feel her bare thigh. Her eyes flutter open and she looks at me.

"That's a nice way to wake up," she says. "I'll give you twenty minutes to stop that."

"I thought you weren't coming down tonight."

"I changed my mind." She sits up a little and stretches. "How was the session?"

"Weird. I've been to the Wolf's lair. I'll tell you about it tomorrow." I slide my hand up higher on her thigh and watch her eyes half close.

"You're not going to stop are you?"

"No. I've still got fifteen minutes."

In the morning, we drive up a twisty back road to Occidental for breakfast at Howard's Landing. Over coffee, I tell Andie about the Wolflair recording session.

She listens, nodding, devouring an omelet and hash browns. "You musicians are a strange lot. What was the deal with nailing CDs on the outside gate?"

"Who knows. I'll ask Wolf if I go back again. Maybe they were recordings that went bad or music he doesn't like. I didn't check the titles."

"Would you go back?" Andie wants to know.

"Sure. The surprising part was he got a good sound, and not only played, he set up the microphones and ran the board all at the same time. You never know where it's going to happen.

Don't forget, Margo Highland and Chet Baker recorded in her basement a mile from my place during a rainstorm. There was water on the floor. They could all have been electrocuted."

"Hot jazz." Andie grins. "Come on, let's pick up your mail."

We drive back to the Monte Rio post office, and along with a couple of bills is a flat express envelope. The clerk hands it to me and I go back out to the car. "Too thin for a script," I tell Andie. "Probably the contract."

"Let's see, let's see," she says, trying to grab it out of my hand.

I pull it back from her grasp. "You know it's a federal offense to tamper with somebody's mail."

"No problem. I'm a federal agent."

We get back to the house. I sit at the dining table and rip the envelope open. The contract is fifteen pages, full of standard legalese and some paragraphs are highlighted in yellow. One is a confidentially clause, binding me to this as yet, unnamed film.

"Ah," Andie says, looking over my shoulder. "You can't kiss and tell."

"Funny." I push the contract aside and light a cigarette.

Another is the fee. One-hundred and fifty-thousand dollars, to be made in three payments. One at signing, one at completion of the score, the third when the film is released. There are three places marked with post-it arrows where I'm to sign and a note from Grant Robbins, reminding me to return it immediately.

"What's the matter?" Andie sits down opposite me.

"I don't know. I just would have liked to see the script first."

Andie taps her fingers on the contract. "Does it really matter? This looks pretty legit to me. I don't think you can complain about the money either. They're going to make this movie whether you like the script or not."

I know she's right, and I've never heard of a composer having any say about the script. But something nags at me I can't quite explain.

"What?"

"I don't know. I guess I don't want to score a movie I don't like."

Andie takes my hand. "Look, this is your first time out. You still get screen credit and it could lead to other things, take you a new direction. You want that, don't you?"

"Yes, yes I do."

Maybe I didn't know how much until now. I think about all the years I'd spent scuffling for gigs, the rare recordings, the accident that set me back and sent me into rehab, all the missed opportunities. How many more would I have? I was getting a bit old to be discovered. Maybe this was it, a way out of the maze of the struggling musician. It didn't mean I had to give up playing. I'd never do that.

I blink as Andie waves her hand in front of my face. "Earth to Evan. Sign it. Let's celebrate. You're going to be a film composer."

By almost return mail, I get a check from Grant Robbins for the initial payment, and a note of thanks, promising me I'd done the right thing. We're busy with casting and preproduction, his note said. The screenplay, however, isn't as fast in arriving.

I'd kept the check around for a week or so, just glancing at it occasionally, a reminder that this was the first time I'd been paid for simply signing some papers. Finally, succumbing to Andie's prompts to put it in the bank, I gave in, smiling as I noted the look on the teller's face as she took in the Ryan Stiles Productions, Inc. logo on the check. She hardly blinked at the amount.

I'd spent my days practicing, doing the occasional gig with new contacts I was making, and taking long walks along the river; my nights, with Andie, whenever she could get away from the Bureau. I'd even begun to play around with writing, thinking whatever character Ryan Stiles played he would need a signature theme.

The one dark spot was still there. Still not a word on the capture of Gillian Payne. Not even a lead. According to Andie, she'd simply gone underground.

"Don't worry," Andie told me repeatedly. "We'll get her."

On the second Saturday after receiving the check, I get an unexpected call. "Evan? It's Bonnie Stiles, Ryan's mother."

I try to keep the surprise out of my voice as I answer. "Hi, Bonnie. What can I do for you?"

"Believe it or not, I'm in San Francisco, visiting an old friend. I wondered if you might be free."

My impression of Bonnie and Tom Stiles was not one of them taking separate trips. "Well, yeah I guess. Something on your mind?"

"Yes," she says, sounding a little tentative. There's a slight pause. "I'd rather not talk about it on the phone. I hoped maybe we could meet, get together."

"When?"

"Today, if possible. I'm going back home this evening. I know I should have called earlier. If you're busy, it's okay." She tells me her friend is in North Beach.

"No, that's fine. There's a coffee place near you called Cafe Greco. It's on Columbus Avenue, near City Lights Bookstore."

"Oh, I know City Lights," she says, almost relieved. "One o'clock?"

"Sounds good." We both pause for a moment. "Bonnie, can you tell me what this is about?"

"It's about Ryan."

Chapter Fourteen

Even a little before noon, The Golden Gate Bridge is crawling with traffic heading into the city. The temperature has already dropped fifteen degrees, and the looking across the bay, I can see the city through hazy white clouds, the water dotted with sailboats. I finally make it to the tollbooths, then merge with the traffic heading toward downtown. I take Bay Street, then turn toward North Beach at Columbus, noticing the huge Tower Records store is now vacant and deserted. Yet another ominous sign of the music scene.

I circle around the jammed North Beach streets a few times before finally finding a parking space I can squeeze the VW into, lock the car, and walk down to City Lights Bookstore. I spend a half hour browsing, getting reacquainted with the store, and pick up a paperback copy of Elmore Leonard's *Be Cool.* I pay for the book and walk back up Columbus. I find a free table in front of Cafe Greco and sit down to wait for Bonnie Stiles with a few minutes to spare, still puzzling over her call.

The street traffic is heavy as usual and the sidewalks are swarming with people rushing about. At five after one, I spot Bonnie in the crowd and stand up as she nears the cafe. She smiles when she sees me and comes over, a little out of breath, carrying a bag with a department store logo. She's dressed smartly in slacks, a dark sweater, and a light jacket. "Hello," she says. "Thanks for coming. Sorry I'm late. I couldn't resist a little shopping."

"No problem. Always fun to come into the city. Sit down. I'll get us coffee."

"One of those big yummy lattes for me, please." She sits down and takes off the jacket.

I go inside, jostling my way through the crowd for our order, then thread my way back outside. "Here you go." I set the bowl-sized cups on the table with a handful of sugar packets, and sit down opposite Bonnie. She already has a cigarette going. I take mine out and join her.

"Ah, coffee in San Francisco with a fellow smoker," she says, "and nobody around to tell us not to."

We sip our drinks for a couple of minutes, just taking in the hustle of Columbus Avenue. I wait her out, letting her get to the purpose of this visit on her own time. I watch her study the traffic and people, then finally, she stubs out her cigarette and turns to me.

"Ryan tells me you're going to do the music for his new movie."

"Yes, already signed on the dotted line. How's it going? Have you heard anything?"

"No, Ryan never talks about business things much with us." She looks away for a moment, then turns back to me. "Well, I guess I owe you an explanation."

"I admit I was a bit surprised to hear from you. It's about Ryan, you said."

She nods, looking down at her coffee. There's the same concern on her face I saw when I was at the house to pick up Ryan's car. "Yes. I don't know if it's important, but I just want to tell you something." She looks up at me. "I can trust you, can't I?"

"With what?"

She shifts in her chair. "First, I need to ask you something. The night after the, whatever it was at that restaurant, when he came and stayed at our place, what did he tell you?"

"The same thing he told the police. He left the Anchor, drove to your place and spent the night."

"That's all?"

I look away for a moment, deciding there's no point in holding back. "No, there was more. He also said his dad didn't see him come in or even know he was there until morning."

Bonnie shakes her head. "That's true. Tom was asleep." A tiny smile curls her lips. "He could sleep through an earthquake." She pauses for another moment and takes a deep breath. "Tom didn't see Ryan, but I did. "I was awake. I got up and went to the kitchen for a drink of water when I saw headlights suddenly flash in the driveway. It was Ryan. He came in so fast I thought he was going to hit the garage. I watched him jump out of the car and come in. The look on his face when he saw me, I didn't know what to think. He looked so upset.

"I asked him what he was doing there, what was wrong. He just brushed past me, and said, not now Mom, I have to get some sleep."

"Do you remember what time it was?"

"Yes, just after one thirty. I remember glancing at the kitchen clock." She rubs her hand across her forehead. "I made him stop and sit down at the kitchen table. He looked so scared, and suddenly he wasn't a movie star anymore, he was my boy and in trouble."

"We sat there in the darkened kitchen and he told me how angry he was at that photographer, how he'd driven away up the coast then parked for awhile along the beach, trying to cool off, get control of himself before he went home. He finally decided he didn't want to face Melanie or you or anybody, and started toward our house. Halfway over Malibu Canyon, he saw a motorcycle behind him, driving close. He said he panicked, then drove faster, but the other driver stayed right with him, chasing him."

Bonnie's eyes glaze over as she remembers Ryan's words. "There was a sharp curve and when he looked in the mirror, the motorcycle was gone. He stopped, turned around and went back, saw the guardrail was broken. He got out of his car and looked over the edge. It was so dark. He thought he could see the motorcycle halfway down the embankment, but he wasn't sure." She looks at me again. Her eyes pool. "He put his hands over his face and just sobbed. I've never seen him like that. I tried to comfort him, told him to go to bed and we'd talk about it in the morning."

"But you didn't."

"No."

I let her go, not sure I wanted to hear more.

She shakes her head, rubs her hands together. "I know I should have, but the next morning, he was fine, like he hadn't even seen me, as if the night before hadn't happened."

"Did you tell Tom?"

"No."

I light a cigarette and watch the traffic for a minute. "Bonnie, do you think he was telling the truth?"

Her eyes widen in surprise. "Yes, of course I do." She looks at me for a moment. "I know what you're not saying. That at the very least Ryan should have called the police and reported the accident."

I don't answer that one. "What is it you want from me, Bonnie?"

"Should I have told the police? They didn't even talk to me, just Tom."

"Bonnie, the incident at the Anchor with the photographer was pretty ugly, and it wasn't the first with McElroy. Ryan was angry and upset. I'm sure I don't have to tell you about his temper. He just had to get away, so he went home. I don't think it means anything else."

"Are you sure?"

"I'm going to be frank with you, Bonnie. You might not like hearing this but…"

"What?"

"When I saw that Tom had had the car detailed, I went to Manny's to see for myself. I talked to Manny. He said as far as he knew there was no damage to the car."

Bonnie is quiet for a minute, digesting this. "Good," she says finally. "I'm glad somebody did." She reaches across the table and pats my hand. "I don't blame you. I thought about doing that myself. Did you tell Ryan you went to Manny's?"

"Yes."

"Was he mad?"

"No. He said there was nothing to worry about as far as Manny goes."

"Thank you," she says. "I do feel better now." She glances at her watch, gathers up her purse and shopping bag, and drapes her jacket over her arm. "I've taken up enough of your time." We both stand up and she gives me a hug. "Ryan is right. You are a good friend, Evan. He doesn't have many."

She turns and walks away. I watch her move slowly, head down until she disappears into the crowd.

I sit for awhile longer at Cafe Greco, finishing my coffee, having another cigarette, thinking about what Bonnie had told me, deciding it didn't really matter one way or the other at this point. Ryan had been cleared and the police had returned his car.

I close my eyes for a moment, trying to imagine Ryan's state of mind as he looked down that embankment. Why didn't he hike down there and see if McElroy was still alive, or at least call the police? But I knew the answer. It would have been Ryan's word only, and given their history there was nothing to say Ryan hadn't forced McElroy off the road to his death.

I surrender my table to a couple looking expectantly at me, coffee mugs in their hands, and hike back to my car, just in time to avoid the glare of a parking meter cop reaching for a pen. I call Andie to tell her I'm in the city. Her phone goes to voice mail, so I leave her a message that I'll meet her at her place.

At Andie's I kick off my shoes and stretch out on the couch. I turn on the TV but in a few minutes I nod off until I blink my eyes open and see Andie peering down at me.

"Nice surprise," she says, kissing me.

"Nice way to wake up." I pull myself upright and look at her.

"So what brought you in? The seductiveness of your FBI-agent girlfriend?"

I smile. "Well, that too, but I got a call from Ryan Stiles' mother wanting me to meet with her."

"She was here in San Francisco? What did she want?"

"Little mini vacation she said, visiting with a friend, but there was more." I recount our conversation to Andie. She listens, gets up, goes to the kitchen and brings a bottle of water back for both of us.

"Mom's guilty conscience," she says.

"You think that's all it is?"

"She wanted to tell someone and you got elected. It doesn't really change anything as far as Ryan's alibi goes. She just wanted to hear it from you that it was okay. What did she say when you told her you'd checked things out at the car wash?"

"She said she didn't blame me and was glad I did it."

Andie nods and takes a swig of water. "You think he was telling her the truth?"

"I think she believes he was."

Andie nods. "If it happened the way Ryan told his mother, there's nothing he could be charged with except poor judgment, at least not making an anonymous 911 call."

"And if it didn't?"

Andie shrugs but I know she doesn't like it. "We'll never know, will we?" She stands, takes my hand and pulls me up. "Come on, let's get some dinner." She turns as we start toward the door. "Must be hard being the mother of a big movie star."

"How so?"

"She probably has no idea what all Ryan is into."

In the morning, I drive back to Monte Rio, thinking about Bonnie's visit. It was a long way to come to tell me what amounted to very little. Maybe Andie was right. A mother's guilty conscience, wanting to protect her son, but worried now that she might have withheld something from the Malibu Police. Now, she simply wanted absolution from an objective source.

But Ryan's actions, if they were as he told his mother, bothered me more than I wanted to admit. Given the same circumstances, it's always easy to say what you would have done in any situation when you hear about it after the fact. I try to imagine Ryan's state of mind that night. Angry, driving fast on a dark dangerous curvy road, then panicking when he sees the motorcycle in his mirror, maybe flashing on the paparazzi that chased Princess Diana into that tunnel in Paris.

Then the relief when it's no longer there, and turning back, looking down that dark embankment, wondering if McElroy was in desperate need of help or dead already. Wondering if it even was McElroy. I visualize him looking at the ripped guardrail, starting down a few steps, risking injury himself, then stopping as Ryan Stiles' movie-star mindset kicks in. Did he stop then, call out? Weigh his options?

If he called 911 to report the accident, he'd have had to stay until the police arrived, or make the call anonymous. Could his cell phone be traced? Scores of witnesses at the Anchor had seen him shove McElroy, rip the camera from around his neck. It would be too big a coincidence that they'd both ended up on Malibu Canyon Road. Nobody would buy that, and he'd have a lot of explaining to do for the police. The press would speculate that Ryan, barely an hour after the angry scene at the Anchor, had chased McElroy and, in a fit of anger, run him off the road.

Ryan did neither. He simply got back in his car and drove to his parents' house.

I shake off these thoughts with a reminder to run it all by Andie again, and maybe Coop as well. I pull into the parking lot of the Monte Rio Post Office. I find a yellow card in my box for a package. I present it to the clerk and she hands me a priority mail envelope bulging at the corners. The return address says Ryan Stiles, Inc.

Outside, I open it and find what I've been waiting for. Bound together with brass fasteners are one-hundred and ten pages. The title page reads:

"SOLO BLUES"
by
Dennis Mills
(First Draft)

There's a note clipped to the title page from Grant Robbins.

Evan, love to have your input. GR.

Back home, I take Milton out for a quick walk, then with coffee and cigarettes, take the script out on the deck, feeling a rush of excitement as I begin reading. An hour later, I lay the script aside and light a cigarette. The excitement gone, replaced more by disappointment than anything. I'm not sure what I was expecting, but the story seems unremarkable.

A struggling jazz pianist's former lover, a singer, comes to him for help. Her brother is missing and the police have given up the search. When he reluctantly agrees to help, she turns up dead, and because of their earlier affair, the pianist must first find her brother, then clear himself of the murder. The police don't believe him. By act two, he's on the run from them and the singer's killer, but in the end justice triumphs. The pianist is vindicated and he goes back to his gig with stardom in his future.

The script reads like a collection of crime story clichés, almost as if it was thrown together hurriedly. It's hardly a vehicle for Ryan Stiles to show what a good actor he is.

Why Grant Robbins couldn't have shown me this sooner is beyond me. Security? Secrecy? Maybe because it's so bad they think I would have turned down their offer? I sigh and read over parts of it again, trying to be objective, even making some mental notes about places for the music. I toss it aside finally and take Milton for a long walk along the river.

When I get back, Andie is on the deck, the script in her hand. She looks up and makes a face. "I've read about half of it," she says.

"I know. Finish it. I'll go get us some Chinese."

Thirty minutes later, I spread out boxes of rice, chicken, and broccoli beef on the dining table with plates and a couple of bottles of beer. Andie comes in to join me, dropping the script on the table.

"Well, it reads fast," she says. "Not exactly *Citizen Kane*. Lots of action, but what do I know about movie scripts? It says first draft. Does that mean there will be lots of changes, with luck, some improvements?"

I don't answer. We eat in silence for a few minutes. "Not what you expected, huh?"

I shrug. "No, this is worse. This is more like a straight-to-video thing, but with Ryan in it, who knows."

"What are you going to do?"

"What they paid me for. I've signed on, collected the money. I don't really have a choice now."

"Maybe you could make some suggestions. Robbins did ask for your input."

"Yeah, like start over. I don't think the director or the writer would readily take suggestions from the guy scoring the music."

I go out on the deck while Andie clears the table and rinses the plates. She comes up behind me, puts her arms around my waist. "How about a walk?"

We head toward the river and cross halfway over the bridge and stop. I lean on the railing, looking down at the Russian River, flowing slowly beneath us. There are some lights coming on now along the front as homes and hotels ease into the evening.

"I've been thinking a lot about what Bonnie Stiles told me. I know Ryan has been cleared with the police, but am I obligated to tell them I know what Ryan did?"

Andie turns to face me. "What you mean is you know what Ryan's mother told you Ryan told her. You didn't know at the time the police questioned you, so you weren't withholding anything. A second-hand confession of a son to his mother after the fact doesn't count for much, especially since he's been cleared."

"I know, but somehow it just doesn't feel right."

"Think ahead. You bring this up now and Bonnie might deny it all."

"You really think she would?"

"Never underestimate a mother's loyalty to her son." She looks at me and shrugs. "Hey, maybe I'm wrong. Run it by Coop. See what he says, but I think I know what he'll tell you."

"What?"

"Leave it alone, it's over. Three people know what happened that night. You, Bonnie, and Ryan. You and Bonnie don't count."

Chapter Fifteen

"Evan? It's Grant Robbins."

"Yes." It's been two weeks since the script arrived. I've had only two gigs since then and spent most of my time walking Milton, spending time with Andie when she can get away. I've also been trying to come up with a main theme for an uninspiring story.

"So what do you think?" Robbins says.

"Well, I—"

Robbins catches my hesitation and laughs. "I can guess. It's terrible. We both know that. But don't worry. Remember that was a first draft. There have been lots of changes and decided improvements."

"Frankly, I'm relieved to hear you say that."

Robbins laughs again. "I bet you are. We'll have another version ready by next week and you'll get a copy then."

"I look forward to it."

"Any chance we could get you to come down for a few days? I'd like to have you meet with the writer and director. Ryan, of course, is anxious to get together again. We need to talk about the music."

"Yeah, sure. How's Ryan doing?"

"Okay. He's antsy to get going on this project." Robbins lets some silence pass for a moment. "He wanted to go to McElroy's funeral but I managed to talk him out of it. I'm trying to get him to keep a low profile."

"That's good. Anything more from the police?"

"Nothing. We're totally clear. It's yesterday's news. Fortunately, there have been some other scandals to take the heat off. Anything new with you?"

I don't mention Bonnie Stiles' visit. I wonder if Ryan knows. "Not much. I'm antsy too."

"I can imagine. I'll get back to you as soon as we have a new draft."

"I'll be waiting."

I close the phone and gaze out from my deck at the towering redwoods. There's a chill in the air and a darkened sky, and rain threatens.

"Who was that?" I hear Andie's voice behind me. Just out of the shower, she's wrapped in a big terry cloth robe.

"Grant Robbins checking in. He says they have a revised script and they want me to come down to meet the director and the writer."

Andie pulls the robe tighter around her as she feels the cool air. "When?"

"A few days. Probably next week." I can see from her expression she's not happy.

She takes my hand and pulls me up. "Come on you, we have things to do." She leads me to the bedroom and falls back on the bed, letting the robe slip open.

"Agent Lawrence, you are a naughty girl." I stand and look at her for a moment, then her phone rings. We both stare at it. "Don't," I say, but I know better.

She picks it up and looks at the screen then sits up and pulls the robe around her. Her eyes go to mine. "It's Wendell Cook."

I nod and watch her open the phone. "Agent Lawrence." She listens, her eyes focused on me. "When? Yes, sir, I understand. I'll get out tonight as soon as I can get a flight. Yes, I'll tell him." She closes the phone and sets it on the nightstand. "They've had a sighting of Gillian. I have to fly out right away."

"Where in L.A.?"

"No, Las Vegas. Can you believe it? She went into a pharmacy to fill a prescription. Wendell is putting together a task force and he wants me down there. The pharmacist recognized her, he thinks." She shrugs. I look at Andie for more. "I can't tell you anymore. That's all he said." She scoots across the bed and throws her arms around me. "This is good news, Evan. We're going to get her."

"Do it fast."

Grant Robbins looks around the conference table. "Well, let's get started shall we?"

Robbins sits at the head of the table. Across from me are Dennis Mills, the writer, director Sandy Simmons, and of course, Ryan Stiles.

Robbins had sent a car to pick me up at LAX, and I was whisked to the studio lot in Culver City. After a flurry of checks that rival airport security, I was admitted to the offices and finally to this wood-paneled conference room, mostly bare except for framed posters of movies that had been produced here. Hallowed ground for movie people, I gather, but so far we've just been chatting. I've seen no script.

"Where are the fucking copies?" the always impatient Ryan wants to know. Our reunion had been brief, but he'd seemed glad to see me, and there'd been no talk about Darryl McElroy.

"They're being made as we speak," Robbins says. "I thought we could take this time to get acquainted while we wait."

This is obviously for my benefit. I'm sure the others already know each other. I'd already met Dennis Mills briefly. He was dressed in jeans and a polo shirt. He had longish hair and modish looking glasses. Soft spoken, he'd greeted me with some interest, confessing he was a big fan of Keith Jarrett, which I took as a good sign.

Sandy Simmons had slipped in last with a flourish and a big smile. He was younger than me and also dressed casually in slacks, loafers, a dark green sport shirt, and a black baseball cap with the title of a movie he'd directed stitched in gold. It was one I didn't recognize.

"So, you're the music guy, eh? We're going to be spending a lot of time together," he says, as if that will be an exciting event. Whether he means for me or him I can't tell. We all turn our attention to Grant Robbins.

"Drinks anybody? Coffee, water, something else?"

Everyone seems to look to me for a decision. "Coffee would be great," I say. Mills and Simmons both nod their agreement. Ryan just shrugs in a "whatever" gesture.

Robbins picks up a phone on the table and places an order. In less than three minutes, an attractive young redhead comes in with a thermal pot and four mugs emblazoned with the studio logo. Cream, sugar, and spoons rest on a small tray. I watch her trying not to stare at Ryan as she sets everything on the table, but he catches her and gives her a big smile. She blushes and rushes out of the room.

Before we can take our first sip of coffee, a young man in cargo pants and a UCLA sweatshirt comes in with a stack of bound scripts. He plops them down on the table in front of Grant Robbins. "Sorry for the delay," he says and quickly beats a retreat.

Robbins flips through the top copy then slides one to each of us. Mills hardly glances at his, but since he wrote it, I'm not surprised. Sandy Simmons glances at the title page and tips his cap on the back of his head.

"Is this the title we're going with?"

I look down at my copy. "Solo Blues" had become "Murder in B Flat". The first two pages are a brief synopsis. Halfway through, I feel my stomach tighten. I look up and find Ryan and Robbins watching me, gauging my reaction. I continue reading then close the script.

Now I understand the mediocre first draft. That was to get me to sign the contract and accept the first payment installment. I didn't need to read the script to know it mirrored probably everything that happened with Gillian Payne. Dennis Mills sees me glare at Grant Robbins.

"What?" he says.

"Where did you get the material for this? I slap the script down on the table. Mills flinches and looks at Robbins.

"Newspaper articles, mostly." He looks genuinely confused. "I thought you were okay with it."

"Well, I'm not." I start to get up, but Robbins stops me.

"Evan," he begins, "there are two ways this can go. You signed a binding contract to score this film. Nowhere in that contract does it give you approval of the script or source material. You can fulfill your obligation, or, you can walk away and deal with a failure to comply lawsuit. Since you've been paid and accepted the first installment. The case is public domain, taken from newspaper accounts, interviews, well, you know that as well as I do. Any objections you have won't really fly in court."

I lean back in my chair, knowing everything Robbins said is true. They had me and everybody at the table knew it. I should have known it, too. I let my mind drift back to our first meeting at the Jazz Bakery. Robbins knew the whole story, everything about me, including the fact that Andie and Coop were waiting for me.

Dennis Mills still looks confused. "Did I do something wrong?"

Robbins smiles. "Not at all, Dennis. You wrote a great script and it's going to be a great movie."

Mills looks at me, finally getting it. "Shit, you're the guy, aren't you?" He shakes his head. "I just didn't put it together. Nobody told me."

Robbins looks at me again. "Evan, before you do anything rash, read the script."

I look across at Ryan. He grins and shrugs.

"Hey man, welcome to Hollywood."

I turn from the window of the Federal Building in Westwood, looking down at Wilshire Boulevard from the seventeenth floor. I can see the Veteran's cemetery, the rows of white gravestones stretching as far as I can see, and the traffic crawling along

Wilshire Boulevard. I turn when the door opens and Andie comes out. She'd had me wait after picking me up from the studio, driving me to the Bureau herself in a black SUV with dark-tinted windows.

"Wendell Cook needs to see you," was all she'd said, and brushed off my questions with a simple, "Just procedure."

She was tense and not very talkative on the drive from Culver City to Westwood. When I'd pressed, she said, "Wendell will explain everything."

I assumed it was about Gillian Payne, thinking they'd caught up with her, but Andie wasn't having it. "I can't talk about it. Please, Evan, just be patient."

Now, as I follow her inside, she has trouble meeting my eyes. We walk back down a long corridor to Cook's office, a place I'm all too familiar with. This was where I'd first met Andie, where I'd begun the nightmare of helping the FBI identify clues left at crime scenes that were entirely related to jazz.

As we enter Cook's office, he gets to his feet, his huge former-NFL-linebacker body coming toward me to shake hands. "Good to see you again, Evan."

"I hope so."

"Have a seat," he says, motioning me to a chair in front of his desk. Sensing someone behind me, I turn and see Coop leaning against the wall.

"Hey, sport," he says, giving me a slight wave and a smile.

I sit down, feeling confused and a bit annoyed.

Wendell settles behind his desk. "Well, here we are again," he says, a slight smile on his face.

"So what's this all about? Have you caught her?"

Wendell answers my question by looking away. "I know Andie told you we had a strong lead in Las Vegas," he begins, "but that didn't pan out. We weren't fast enough. Somehow she slipped through." His eyes lock with mine. "I'll be honest with you, Evan. Right now, we don't know where she is." He lets that sink in for a moment then continues. "Which brings us to the purpose of this meeting."

I put up my hands. "Oh no, I'm not going there again. I've been there, done that—"

Wendell shakes his head and smiles. "You've got it all wrong, Evan. You didn't think we'd ask you to be—"

"Bait?"

"No, exactly the opposite. We want to protect you until Payne is captured, and make no mistake, we will take her down."

I look from Andie to Coop then back to Wendell. "Protect me how? It didn't work very well last time." Coop had been stabbed and seriously injured. I'd been terrorized and forced to go undercover in Las Vegas while they set a trap for her that had almost ended in disaster.

"And that is to my everlasting regret. We're putting you in protective custody until she's caught. We don't even know if she'll come after you, but this time we're not taking any chances."

I shift in my chair and sit forward. "What do you mean, protective custody?"

"I mean you'll be in a safe house, at an undisclosed location known only to a very few people in the Bureau and Detective Cooper."

I look over at Andie. "Did you know about this?"

"Not until I got here, but I agree. I think it's best."

"Wendell, I'm right in the middle of something. I can't just put my life on hold. I'm sure Andie told you I'm about to score a movie. I've got meetings, research to do. I can't just, what, disappear like I'm in the Witness Protection Program."

"I'm afraid that's exactly what it means. For this to work, you won't have any contact with anybody—including Andie, the movie people, even Detective Cooper— until Gillian Payne is safely back in prison."

"For how long?"

"As long as it takes." Wendell leans forward, his huge hands on his desk. "This is for your own good, Evan."

"What do I tell Ryan Stiles, the people connected with the movie?"

"You're not going to tell them anything because you won't see or talk to them. We can't chance slipping any clue to Gillian as to your whereabouts. An agent will be with you at all times. I'm sorry, Evan, I know this is going to be hard, but the alternative is not an option."

"I am with an agent, most of the time." I shoot a look at Andie.

Wendell allows himself a smile. "Nice try, but obviously that won't work."

"Isn't this a bit of overkill? Do we really know she's even interested in finding me?"

Wendell sighs and leans back in his chair. "We do know that much. In the years since her imprisonment, we know she holds you responsible. She talked about it a lot in sessions with a therapist. She blames you for her brother as well."

"She's the one who nearly killed him," I say. I stand up and walk around the room. I hadn't testified, but I had made a detailed statement. Her attempt on her brother in Las Vegas had more than enough witnesses, including Coop.

"You know that, we all do, but Gillian Payne is not stable. She's a twisted killer, Evan. We all know that, too."

I feel them all looking at me as I drop back into the chair. "Okay, okay. What do I have to do?"

"To start, I'll need your cell phone," Wendell says.

I nod and pull it out of my pocket and toss it on Wendell's desk. He takes it and places it in a desk drawer. "Do you have any other questions?"

I shake my head. "I don't know. I can't think of anything now."

Andie and Coop both come closer. "It's the best way, Evan," Andie says.

"Hang in there, sport," Coop says. He claps a hand on my shoulder.

Wendell stands and nods to Coop. "We'll give you a few minutes alone with Andie. You'll be given a full briefing later." They walk out and shut the door.

Andie comes over and hugs me. "I know this is a shock, baby, but we, I, want you safe. There's no other way to guarantee that."

"I know, it's just, I'm going to be like a prisoner, and for how long?"

"I did insist on one thing. We've arranged for you to have an electric piano. It comes with headphones so nobody will hear. You can practice, even work on the movie music if you want. You're going to be as comfortable as possible."

I know she's right but the prospect of isolation for an unknown amount of time is not appealing. Andie wraps her arms around me and kisses me. "It won't be for long. I promise."

The door opens and Wendell sticks his head in. "It's time, Evan. We have to go."

I leave Andie standing by Wendell's desk, her eyes on me, wondering when I'll see her again. I follow Cook out into the corridor, the door clicking shut behind me.

Chapter Sixteen

We take the elevator to the basement parking garage. I stand between Wendell Cook and Coop, my mind swirling with questions now. I want to go back upstairs and say something more to Andie but it's too late. Another black SUV pulls up and two men in dark suits and muted ties get out, but leave the engine running.

The driver is about my size with sandy hair and deep blue eyes. The passenger is short and stocky with close-cropped dark hair. They both look me over as Wendell steps forward.

"Evan, this is Special Agent Kevin Hughes," Cook says, nodding to the driver, "and Ron Ardis." I shake hands with both men. "You're in their care now, Evan. Everything goes through me, so if you have any questions, well…"

He doesn't have to finish the sentence. Hughes and Ardis both nod earnestly, their special agent faces on. Ardis opens the rear door. When I start to get in, I see my bag is already on the seat. I feel Coop's hand on my shoulder. "Hang in there, sport," then he shuts the door and steps away. I sit back and look out through the dark-tinted windows, watching them all confer for a minute, but I can't hear what they're saying. They check their watches, then Cook steps back and nods.

Hughes gets behind the wheel and Ardis joins him in the passenger seat. We pull away and head up the ramp out of the garage into the bright sunshine. Ardis looks back at me over his shoulder. "You okay back there, Mr. Horne?"

"Sure. It's Evan."

"Enjoy the ride."

Hughes merges with the Wilshire traffic, then makes a U-turn at the first light and goes back west toward the 405 Freeway. I catch Hughes' eyes in the rearview mirror as he accelerates up the onramp. Ardis is checking the side mirror. He glances at Hughes. "Clear," he says. Hughes nods and relaxes a little, leaning back, loosening his grip on the wheel as we merge with the freeway traffic.

Ardis turns back toward me. "Agent Cook said it's okay for you to smoke. Just crack the window a bit."

"Thanks." I dig out my cigarettes and light one. I lower the window a few inches. "Do I get to know where we're going?"

Ardis faces forward again now. "You'll know when we get there."

Hughes catches my eye in the mirror again. "Procedure."

I finish my cigarette and lean back, my head against the seat, and wonder at the day's events. I'd hardly had time to work up my anger at the script meeting before Andie carted me off to the Bureau offices. It settles over me now like a blanket tucked around too tightly, wrapping itself around my mind, inescapable, and beyond my control.

Grant Robbins and Ryan Stiles had both known I would never have agreed to being a part of a screenplay that would dredge up memories of one of the worst experiences of my life. But they had been clever, establishing trust, letting me in, then slipping in the binding contract, the payment, and now there was no way out. I wonder now what they'll do when I don't show up for the next meeting, what they'll think when they can't get me on the phone.

Ryan will try Andie. Robbins will use whatever contacts he has, and I'm guessing there are many. I hadn't been able to talk to Andie about it, but she'll either be unavailable or, if pressed, tell him she doesn't know where I am. He and Robbins will both conclude I'm bailing on the whole project and look for an alternative, a way to get me back in the fold. And how long will I be unavailable?

I open my eyes as I feel the car slow when we merge onto the Ventura Freeway heading west. Somewhere in the San Fernando Valley or farther. Palmdale? Barstow? Farther still? Las Vegas? Not if that's where Gillian was spotted. They wouldn't take me closer would they? Unless—I don't want to finish that thought.

The car speeds up again as the traffic thins and we pass though Van Nuys, Encino, Reseda, Woodland Hills. Eventually, we exit just beyond Agoura Hills and come to a collection of gas stations, a strip mall, fast-food restaurants, and finally, a good-sized Business Suite Hotel perched on a hillside overlooking the freeway.

Hughes pulls into the underground parking garage and parks near an elevator. "Here we are," he says. "Let's go."

We all get out and ride up to the top floor. Ardis produces a key card, opens the door, and goes inside. I feel Hughes' hand on my arm. We wait for Ardis to come back. "Clear," he says, then we go in and Hughes shuts and locks the door.

It's well appointed with a sitting room, a flat screen television, small couch, and a couple of chairs and a table. There's a mini-fridge and a coffee machine on a table. A sliding glass door leads to a tiny balcony. Ardis quickly draws the drapes closed. Through connecting shuttered doors, I can see a bed and the bathroom. I stand waiting as they check out everything. They both come back and motion me toward the table.

"Have a seat," Ardis says. "Time for the rules." He takes off his jacket and loosens his tie. Hughes does the same. "Okay, one of us will be with you at all times. We'll do rotating shifts. As per instructions from Director Cook, your needs will be reasonably met. The telephone has been removed so don't bother looking for it. The hotel has a health club if you feel like some exercise, and there's a pool as well, but you don't go to either alone."

He takes out a sheet of paper and glances at it. His checklist. "There's a restaurant here for all meals, or we can order in the room." He looks up at me. "You are not to answer or open the door for any reason. There's a big parking lot out back so you can get some air, take a walk, but again, one of us will be with you." He glances at Hughes then back to me. "Any questions?"

"Sounds like fun. How did you two get so lucky?

"Just our turn," Ardis says.

"Oh, there is one thing. Cook promised me a piano."

"Coming tomorrow. Kevin will bring it back when we change shifts."

I know there are other things I want to know, but for now they can wait.

"Okay, that's it for now," Ardis says. "Hope you enjoy your stay."

I smile at the irony and go in the bedroom. I toss my bag on the bed and take out the copy of the script, the couple of changes of clothes, and put my shaving things in the bathroom. I may have to go shopping. There's a pad and pen on the table near the bed. I start to make a list of things I want. There's a clock radio on the nightstand. I turn it on and get the jazz station going while I write. I can hear Ardis and Hughes talking quietly in the sitting room, then the door closes.

Ardis sticks his head in. "I've got the first shift. Kevin will be back in the morning. You need anything right now?"

"No, just thinking of a few things."

Ardis glances at his watch. "We'll go eat about six. That okay with you?"

"Sure. I'm going to stretch out for awhile."

Ardis goes out and pulls the shutter doors closed. In a couple of minutes, I can hear the television. I finish my list and lie down, thinking how exciting it's going to be to have dinner.

When I open my eyes, I glance at the clock. I've been asleep for almost an hour. I get up and go in the bathroom, splash cold water on my face, and wander into the sitting room. Ardis is lounging in a chair, the TV, sound low, tuned to CNN.

I sit down in another chair and light a cigarette. "I can go out on the balcony if this bothers you," I say.

"No, it's okay. Too much exposure out there."

"Aren't we overdoing it a little?" I can't believe anybody could possibly know where we are.

Ardis shrugs. "Maybe, but we have our orders."

We watch the news for awhile until the stories start repeating. "Hungry?"

"Yeah, I could eat."

Ardis puts on his jacket and adjusts his gun. We ride the elevator down to the lobby and go into the restaurant. A hostess seats us, but not before Ardis chooses a table facing the entrance. The other diners appear to be business types, with a sprinkling of women at some of the tables. Ardis orders a club sandwich and iced tea. I opt for a salad and fish and chips.

I watch Ardis, his eyes all over the room for a couple of minutes till he's satisfied there's no one posing a threat. He relaxes a little and leans back. "So, what's it like living with an agent?"

"Do you know Andie Lawrence?"

"Not really. We've never worked together, but I've heard good things about her. I think she's a favorite of Wendell Cook."

"Anything wrong with that?"

"No, not at all," Ardis says quickly.

I smile. "I'm just messing with you. Look, would it be violating any Bureau rules if you call me Evan and I call you Ron?"

"No, I guess not. It's just kind of weird, this assignment I mean."

"Have you done this before?"

Ardis nods as the waitress brings my salad and refills our water glasses. "Couple of times babysitting a witness for trial, but first time I've been assigned to protect one of the good guys."

I look up. "What do you mean?"

"You have to admit it's different. You were stalked by a serial killer, you went undercover and helped bring her down. Plus, you're not a cop or an agent. You're a jazz pianist."

"Yeah, there's that."

"Can I ask you something?"

"Sure."

"This may be a stupid question, but are you famous?"

I smile. "Hardly."

Ardis seems a bit flustered. "I'm not much of a jazz fan, so you could be and I wouldn't know. My girlfriend is though," he adds quickly. "She took me to a jazz club recently. I kind of liked it."

I finish my salad. "Who was playing?"

Ardis looks a way for a moment, trying to remember. He snaps his fingers. "Jarrett. Keith Jarrett."

"Your girlfriend has good taste. He's one of the best and he is famous, at least in the jazz world."

The waitress brings our order then and we both dig in. "So why are you?"

"What?"

"A jazz pianist."

"Why are you an FBI agent?"

Ardis smiles. "I love it. Can't imagine doing anything else."

"There you go."

We finish dinner and coffee then Ardis calls for the check and signs for it. "You ready?"

"Yeah." We get up and head for the exit. "How about that walk in the parking lot. I'd like to get some air."

We go down a corridor that leads off the lobby to an outside exit door. Ardis opens it and steps outside, scanning the lot, half-filled with parked cars. "Okay," he says.

It's dark now. I can see the lights from the freeway and the surrounding area. I light a cigarette and walk the perimeter a couple of times with Ardis at my side. It feels good to be outside and stretch my legs. Halfway around the second lap, Ardis' cell phone rings. He puts up his hand for me to stop as he answers.

He listens, makes a couple of monosyllabic answers, ending with, "Right, no problems." He closes the phone and looks at me. "Just checking in."

We walk back toward exit the door. I watch Ardis constantly scanning the parking lot. He seems anxious to get back inside, but I'm in no hurry. It's only been one afternoon and evening, but already I'm feeling restless and not at all eager to go back to the room.

Ardis tries the handle but it's locked. There's a small sign that says, locked after 8 p.m. PLEASE USE ROOM CARD. Ardis swipes the key card and we go inside, through the lobby, and take the elevator back up to the room. Just as he did when we arrived, Ardis opens the door and goes in first, leaving me in the hallway, then motions me in. He hangs the DO NOT DISTURB sign on the outside handle, shuts the door, turns the lock, and adds the chain.

"Okay," he says, taking off his coat. "Let's see what's on TV."

◇◇◇

I spend over an hour going over my copy of the screenplay, trying to absorb my apprehension at reliving on paper an experience I've been trying to forget. There are plenty of scenes with Ryan's character, Chase Hunter—is that a name for a jazz pianist?—playing in a club, a recording studio, even a big finale concert. The downside is the emphasis on Chase's suddenly developing detective skills. They even have him carrying a gun by the last act, and involved in a shootout with the bad guy.

I stare at the pages until the type blurs when I hear Ardis call out.

"Hey, come look at this!" I go into the sitting room and find Ardis on his feet, staring at the TV.

It's the entertainment segment of a cable news program. A young blonde with perfect hair, perfect face, and perfect smile looks into the camera.

"...in what's been shrouded in secrecy, our sources have confirmed that Ryan Stiles' new project is a gritty mystery with Stiles portraying a jazz pianist investigating the murder of his singer girlfriend's brother. The role marks a departure for the action hero and promises a new serious side of this young star." She tosses it back to the male anchor. Both of them framed now.

"Sounds exciting," he says, "but can Ryan Stiles really play the piano?"

"Not to worry, Bob. To add to the authenticity, a real jazz pianist, Evan Horne, was hired to tutor Stiles. Horne spent weeks at the star's Malibu estate. Horne will also handle the music score chores. In other news, pop singer Prince will…"

"You are famous," Ardis says. He clicks off the TV and looks at me. "Not good," he says. "Not good. I better check in." He opens his phone and punches in some numbers. "This is Special Agent Ardis. I need Wendell Cook."

I sink down on the couch, listening to Ardis' voice fades as he goes out on the balcony. No, not good at all. This little gem has Grant Robbins prints all over it. He wants me out there publicly, but has no idea what he's done. The news will be picked up by all the media and the internet by morning. All Gillian will have to do is pick up a paper, a magazine, watch the news, or turn on a computer. It doesn't matter where she is.

Gillian Payne now knows how to track me down.

Chapter Seventeen

I wake up when Ardis, looking a little grim, knocks on the door jam. "Director Cook is here," he says.

"Okay, I'll be right out." I glance at the clock, get up, go to the bathroom, and splash water on my face. I pull on a pair of jeans and a sweatshirt, not bothering with socks or shoes. Ardis and Wendell Cook are seated at the table. On reflex, I look for Andie even though I know she won't be there.

Wendell stands up and comes forward to shake hands. He's in a muted gray suit, white shirt, and dark tie. "Evan, how are you doing?" He doesn't wait for or expect an answer, just motions me into another chair. "I guess you know we've got a problem."

"You're the master of understatement, Wendell. Less than twenty-four hours in so-called protective custody and we're compromised." I put extra emphasis on protective and Wendell catches it.

He puts up a hand. "You're compromised—and that's not even the right word— but your location is not. We don't know if Gillian even saw that item on the news."

"Oh, come on, Wendell. If not that one, there will certainly be others. Anything connected with Ryan Stiles is news. All she has to do is go to any internet cafe if she hasn't already. It's just a matter of time."

Cook is quiet for a moment. "There won't be any new press releases," he says. "I'm seeing Stiles' attorney, Grant Robbins, this morning."

"And telling him what?"

"That you're involved in a very sensitive matter and unavailable until further notice. In addition, we're going to ask him to cooperate, and make no attempt to contact you, and issue no new releases to the media concerning your part in the movie."

"You think he will go along with that?"

"We're going to make sure he does." Cook meets my eyes. "I'm sure you know the less complimentary meaning of FBI."

"Federal Bureau of Intimidation?"

"Precisely. Robbins will cooperate. There are a number of avenues to pursue."

"Which are?" I wonder what that means. Taxes? A call to the IRS? A friendly audit? A guy like Robbins I'm sure wouldn't like an unannounced visit from the IRS.

"I'd rather not go into that," Cook says. "Just leave it to us. In the meantime, we feel you're safe staying right here."

"What about Gillian Payne?"

Cook shrugs. "We're pursuing her with all vigor and we have every hope of apprehending her soon."

"Sorry, Wendell, that sounds like a press conference statement."

"Payne's an escaped felon now, not so free to move about as she did before. She'll make a mistake and we'll be ready for her. It's just a matter of time."

"How much time? A week? A month?" I have no doubt about Cook's sincerity but the thought of being holed up in a hotel is already getting to me. As long as I'm stuck here, I'm helpless to do anything and I don't like the feeling.

Cook unbuttons his coat and leans forward, lacing his hands together on the table. "Evan, no one regrets this situation more than I do, but sometimes the system fails, things go wrong, people slip through the cracks. That said, I won't have you unnecessarily endangered while the search is on until we have her back in custody."

"Will I be allowed to see Andie?"

"No, I'm sorry. Too dangerous for both of you. Gillian knows about your involvement with Andie, at least from before. I can't approve that."

I sigh and look up at the ceiling. "This is called protective custody, for my own good, but legally, you can't hold me. Isn't that right?" I glance over and see Ardis' eyes on me.

"Don't go there, Evan," Cook says quickly. "Legally, no, we can't hold you, but you'd make our job even harder. We don't need any distractions from tracking Gillian Payne. Promise me you won't do anything stupid."

I nod. "Just checking."

Cook relaxes a bit and leans back in his chair. "Good. Anything else we can do? Agent Hughes is bringing the piano over later."

"My dog, Milton. He's in a kennel in Monte Rio. I need to get word to the vet that I probably won't be back when I thought. Andie has the number."

"We'll take care of it," Cook says as he gets to his feet. "Okay, I'm going to leave you in Agent Ardis' good hands then." He heads for the door then turns back. "Keep the faith, Evan. We'll wind this up as soon as we can."

Ardis chains the door once Cook leaves. "Some breakfast?"

"Sure. Give me a half hour.

I take a long shower, running everything over in my mind, weighing my options which are few. I dress and, as an after-thought, grab the script before I let Ardis know I'm ready. We go down to the dining room, but have to wait a few minutes for a table. The room is full of business types, some sipping coffee with laptops open on their tables. The hostess seats us next to four guys, carry-on bags next their chairs, in intensive conversa-tion about some kind of new sales policy.

Ardis ignores them, but scans the room until he's satisfied, then finally opens his menu as a waitress brings us coffee. We both order omelets. "We're in kind of a hurry," he tells her.

"So is everybody, sweetie." She hurries off before he can reply.

"Relax, Ron. We have nothing but time."

We're on our second cup of coffee when Ardis asks about the script laying on the table, but before I can answer, his cell phone rings. He takes the call, listens for a few moments. "Right, see you then." He closes his phone. "That's Hughes. He's on the way with your piano."

"Great. I'm going to need some cigarettes, too."

Ardis nods. "There's a convenience store next door. I'll get you some when Hughes gets here."

"Thanks." I tell him the brand. We finish breakfast and Ardis signs the check and starts for the elevator. I stop and look down the corridor.

"How about a walk?"

"Yeah, why not."

We go out the exit to the parking lot. It's full of cars, mostly rentals I'm guessing, and a couple of airport shuttle vans are parked near the entrance, doors open, the drivers standing nearby, smoking, checking their watches. I stand close by, watching as the first one starts to fill up.

"I thought you wanted to walk," Ardis says. He's a few steps ahead of me.

"I do." I make a show of looking beyond Ardis. He turns, follows my gaze.

"What?" he says, turning to look.

"Was that van here last night? Over there in the corner."

"I'm not sure. Stay here, I'll check it out."

As he starts for the van, I turn back to the shuttle bus. It's nearly full now, the driver at the wheel, ready to close the door. I slip on and just make it. "Sorry, missed my wakeup call."

I go to the rear bench seat and scrunch down, blocked by suits and bags. I see Ardis at the van, checking the doors. He turns back. When he sees I'm gone, he breaks into a jog, looking all around. As the bus pulls away toward the street, I sneak a look out the back window. Ardis is checking the second shuttle and grabbing his cell phone.

Two minutes later, the bus is heading up the on-ramp of the Ventura Freeway.

I hear the driver click on the microphone. "First stop is Burbank Airport."

I join half the bus getting off at the Southwest Airlines stop, trying to keep in the group, letting the suits shield me as much as possible. Inside the terminal, I lose myself in the crowd and get to a window, scanning the sidewalk. I'm counting on Ardis not being able to leave the hotel until Hughes arrives to pick him up, but of course he would have phoned in. The shuttle I arrived on has already gone, but more are pulling in every few minutes from a number of different hotels.

I make my way to the Southwest counter, mired in a line for several minutes until it's finally my turn. "I need a one-way ticket to Las Vegas on your next available flight," I tell the harried agent, her dark hair in a ponytail.

She punches some keys on her computer and shakes her head. "Sorry, nothing open until 2:15."

"How about standby?"

"You can try. There are always some no shows."

"Okay, let's do that." I hand over my credit card and scan the area while she prints out a boarding pass. So far, so good.

"Any luggage?"

"No. Just a quick trip."

She nods. "Go to C gates to get on standby. Good luck."

On the way to security, I stop at a gift shop and buy a Dodgers baseball cap and a small blue nylon carry-on bag with two big dice and Las Vegas emblazoned on the side. I stuff the script inside and head for security, donning the cap and my sunglasses. I get through fairly quickly without setting off any alarms and check the departure board. Gate 17 is the next flight, but it's a no go. Passengers are already lining up to board and it looks full.

At Gate 12, the guy on the desk says there's a chance. He takes my name. I take a seat in the most crowed area and keep the cap down over my eyes. When the flight is called, I hover near the desk. I don't want my name broadcast over the PA system. As the plane loads, I catch the agent's eye.

"Any chance?"

"Looks like maybe you're in luck." He checks with another agent collecting boarding passes at the gate, comes back and smiles that friendly Southwest smile. "You're on."

I rush down the jetway and find a seat in the back, willing the plane to depart on time. I breathe a deep sigh as the doors shut and the plane starts to back away from the gate. I hate to think what Wendell Cook's reaction will be once he hears what I've done.

Now Gillian Payne and I are both on the run from the FBI.

At McCarran Airport, I'm one of the last to get off. There's no squadron of FBI agents waiting for me, so I make my way to the tram and take the short ride over to the main terminal. Going down the escalator to the crowded baggage claim area, I'd forgotten how noisy it is with jumbo TV screens blaring, touting the Strip shows, and hundreds of people milling around the baggage carousels. I slip out one of the side doors where hotel shuttles and taxis are loading, and grab the first available taxi.

I give the driver the address and sit back, hoping I'm right about my destination being the last place anybody would think to look for me. Once free of the airport traffic, the driver heads east on Tropicana and crosses the Strip past the massive MGM Hotel, then turns north onto Spring Mountain Road.

"Here you go," he says, pulling to a stop in front of a house I haven't been to in several years. I pay the fare, get out, and walk up to the front door, and ring the bell. From inside I can hear the faint sounds of vintage jazz. When the door opens, the tall bearded man and I stare at each other for a long moment, his jaw dropping open.

"Evan, my God."

"Hello, Ace."

Ace Buffington seems frozen to the spot, unable to believe his eyes.

"Can I come in?"

"Yeah, yeah, sure. Come in. Sorry, it's just, I didn't think I'd ever see you again."

I didn't think so either. The last time I'd seen Ace was after returning from Amsterdam at a hotel in Monte Rio where we'd had a big scene over his selling me out to the drug dealers. Ace had been there in pursuit of research on Chet Baker. When Ace had gone missing, I made my own search and found Ace had given me up when the dealers he thought would help him had instead threatened him. Ace pointed them in my direction and left the country with me holding the bag. By the time I caught up with him, I vowed our friendship was finished. I'd thought a lot about it over the years and finally decided maybe I'd been too hard on him. Ace was a college professor, totally out of his element. He'd simply reacted. Now, seeing his face, I think I was right.

We go into the kitchen and sit down. "Some coffee? I just made some."

"That would be great." I look around and see nothing much has changed. When I'd come out of rehab from the accident that almost ended my playing days, Ace had arranged a solo piano gig through his connections with the music department at UNLV where he taught English. My comeback had been solo piano at a Strip shopping mall adjoining Caesar's Palace. I'd stayed with Ace in the guesthouse in back. That gig got me playing again, but also involved me helping Ace trying to solve the 1955 death of saxophonist Wardell Gray at the Moulin Rouge Hotel Casino.

Ace brings coffee and cream and sugar to the table and sits down. "I still can't believe it," he says. "Seeing you here again, after, well, you know. You don't know how many times I've regretted what I did, how ashamed I was, how—"

"Forget it, Ace. It's history now. I wasn't exactly very understanding either."

"Thanks. Thanks for that, but you were justified." He takes a sip of coffee and manages a small smile of relief. "So, what brings you to Las Vegas, and more importantly, to see me?"

"When I tell you, you may want me to leave."

"Not a chance."

I take out my cigarettes and look at Ace. He nods and gets an ashtray. "I saved it from when you were here before."

I light up, take a deep drag, and exhale a cloud of smoke. "I need a place to hide out for awhile."

Ace frowns. "Hide out? From who?"

"Gillian Payne and the FBI."

I catch Ace up on everything, beginning with Grant Robbins hiring me to tutor Ryan Stiles. As I talk, Ace gets up and paces around the kitchen, nodding, taking it all in, but never interrupting once. When I finish with my account of eluding the FBI and landing on his doorstep, he sits down again.

He looks at me and shakes his head, a smile spreading over his face. "You never do anything halfway do you?"

I shrug. "I just couldn't stand being cooped up in a hotel room, waiting for them to find Gillian Payne. I'm tired of this hanging over my head. I want it over once and for all."

"You're not seriously going to look for her yourself?"

"I don't know what I'm going to do, Ace. Not yet anyway. The one lead the FBI had was here in Las Vegas. Payne tried to fill a prescription someplace here. I wanted to get away. I thought of you, and well, here I am. Just let me stay here awhile till I figure it out.""

"As long as you want," Ace says. "I owe you."

"Thanks, Ace."

"There's just one thing?"

"What?"

"Do you have some plan?"

Ace's question is a good one. Do I have some plan? Eluding the FBI's protective custody is one thing, but searching for Gillian Payne on my own is another thing altogether. Once I saw that shuttle bus idling at the hotel, ready to go, the impulse was just too tempting to pass up. My only regret is Agent Ron Ardis. Wendell Cook would ream the young agent for letting me get away, but I knew I'd never make it waiting for word on Gillian's capture, sitting in a hotel room, cut off from everything. But did I really get away? I would find out soon enough.

Stretched out now on Ace's couch, his huge flat screen television tuned to CNN, I begin to assess my position. I'd had no choice but to use a credit card to buy my ticket, so if the FBI was interested enough, and started checking, they would know I'd flown to Las Vegas. Andie certainly would want to know. It was she who had told me about the lead in Las Vegas.

What was in my favor was that during that whole Gillian Payne case, even her capture in Las Vegas, I'd had almost no contact with Ace Buffington. Andie and Coop both knew of my total falling out with Ace, so I don't think either will immediately conclude I'm here. During the case, I'd gone undercover with a band to draw Payne out, and it had worked all too well. Unfortunately for her brother. She'd almost killed him. But why would she come back to Las Vegas? What was the connection? Did she have a friend here, someone helping her, someone she was forcing to help her?

I drift off, my mind swirling with questions and scenarios until I feel a hand on my shoulder. "How about some dinner?" Ace asks.

I rub my eyes and sit up. "Guess I dozed off. Yeah, I could eat." The TV is off now and the sounds of Bill Evans' piano filters in from the stereo. I recognize the tune, "Detour Ahead." I was certainly on one.

"I've got some potatoes in the oven and a couple of steaks to grill. While I get a salad together, have a look at these." He hands me a few computer printout pages. "I got them off the Internet. Most of it's old news from when she was captured, but there's a couple of things about her escape and the nationwide manhunt."

I look through the stories, but Ace is right. There's not much. Just a recap of her reign of terror and eventual capture. There is one photo, probably a booking mug shot. I'd only seen her once. The long black hair is cut short now, but the face is the same, and those deep dark eyes that seem bottomless. My name is in there plenty, more than I would like. I see now where Grant Robbins and Ryan Stiles got their material for the screenplay.

Over dinner, Ace and I catch up. He had a short stint as department chair, had written some more articles, but sheepishly confessed he had abandoned the book about Chet Baker.

"I'll just enjoy his music. My little adventure in Amsterdam was enough to put me off anymore hands-on research. Besides, there have already been two biographies in the meantime."

"So, you're just teaching, doing a little writing, enjoying life, eh? Now here I come about to disrupt all this blissful existence."

"Please. It's gotten pretty boring. I'm ready for a little excitement." He puts up both hands. "Remember, I said a little."

"I promise I won't ask you to do anything illegal or dangerous."

Chapter Eighteen

I have no idea which pharmacy Gillian Payne had tried to fill her prescription, or for that matter, if she was really seen. I also have no idea what the prescription was for, so I'm starting from scratch. I use the Yellow Pages to compile a list of pharmacies in the area, and fan out from Ace's house, using his old VW Bug as transportation. With supermarkets, drug stores, and discount stores, there are dozens of possibilities. Ace wishes me luck and heads for his classes at UNLV.

Las Vegas is a big city now, over two million people. Somebody thought they might have seen Gillian Payne, but who knows what the FBI decides is a lead. My list is discouragingly long, but at least I'm doing something other than sitting in a hotel room. Between stores, I try to fine-tune my cover story, beyond saying I was there to pick up a prescription for Gillian Payne or Gillian Sims. So far I'd struck out at eleven stores and gotten a few mildly questioning glances from pharmacists when I didn't know what the prescription was for. My guess is Valium or Zanex, but for all I know, Gillian could have some real ailment.

Number twelve goes much better. I join the line of a half-dozen people in front of the pharmacy counter at a Walgreens Drug Store on West Sahara. There's only one clerk on duty, so each transaction takes several minutes as people either pick up a prescription they've called in, ask questions, or are told they'll have to wait while their order is filled.

I glance around the store, checking my watch impatiently, then suddenly catch sight of a man coming toward the pharmacy, a slip of paper in his hand. The resemblance is too strong to ignore. I step out of the line, duck down an aisle for toothpaste, and walk to the end. He's the last in line now as I peek around the end of the aisle. I get a quick look at his face as he looks back over his shoulder. There's no mistake. Even though it's been several years, he's changed very little. The hair is a shade lighter, but I'd know that face anywhere.

I'm looking at Gillian's brother, Greg Sims.

It takes another fifteen minutes for Greg to get served. He hands a slip of paper to the pharmacist, who retrieves a small bag, rings it up, staples the receipt to the bag, and hands it back to Greg. He pays in cash, then turns and heads for the exit. I follow him out to the parking lot and watch him get in a late-model Toyota. I run for the VW, start the engine, and slip in behind Greg's car as he exits and starts down Rainbow heading north.

I stay a few cars behind, keeping his car in sight but not close enough for him to spot me. At the end of Rainbow, he takes I-95 North, past several developments of new homes, and finally exits on Lake Mead. He continues east a few blocks then turns left on a two-lane strip that leads into an underdeveloped area. There's a lot of empty desert, some newer houses with FOR SALE signs that look abandoned, a few older houses, many of them run down. I hang back farther, watching Greg turn onto a dirt road to a small isolated house surrounded by brush and cactus.

I park along the main road. Greg gets out of his car and greets a large black dog that comes around from the back of the house, barking and wagging his tail. Greg stops to pet him, the prescription bag in his hand, then goes into the house without looking back. I watch the house for awhile, deciding what to do next. Is Gillian in there? Have I found her? I check my watch. Almost three o'clock. I light a cigarette and wait, still unsure what to do next.

If Gillian is there, I could call the police. But with no cell phone, I'd have to leave, find a pay phone, and chance Greg leaving, maybe to meet Gillian if she's somewhere else. Twenty minutes later, while I'm still trying to decide, Greg comes out. He's dressed in black pants, a white shirt, and bow tie, carrying a rolled-up black cloth in one hand. He gets in his car, turns around, and heads toward me. I duck down in the seat as he turns and passes me, hardly glancing at my car.

I wait a couple of minutes, start the VW, make a U-turn. I catch up with him at Lake Mead. He turns right, back toward the freeway, then pulls into a 7-Eleven store. It's a busy one with lots of cars. I park in front, but shielded from the door. Greg goes inside then returns, a pack of cigarettes in his hand. As he gets in his car, I get a better look at his shirt. I won't have to follow him now. Mirage Hotel is embroidered over the pocket.

Greg is a dealer and he's going to work.

To avoid a sneer from valet parking guys, I find a spot in the self-parking lot for Ace's old VW. I make my way into the Mirage though a side entrance and shoulder my way through the noisy, crowded casino, scanning the tables for Greg Sims. It takes about twenty minutes for me to finally find him at a five dollar Blackjack table, dealing to three players. From a distance, he handles the cards and payoffs with the cool efficiency and detachment that goes with the job.

Occasionally, his eyes go from the table to scan the casino crowd. I move in closer then take one of the seats as one player gathers up his chips and heads off. I lay down a twenty for buy in. Greg nods then his eyes meet mine and for a second, he freezes. He pushes four chips toward me and deals a bit slower. My first card is a king, the second an ace. I turn them both up and smile.

"Thanks, pal. That would have been mine," a guy in a Hawaiian shirt next to me says.

Greg shoves two chips toward me and finishes the hand, turning up his cards that show nineteen, beating the other two players. He scoops up their chips and cards and deals again. When he comes to me, I tap my watch. I have two tens this time and I win again.

"Twenty wins again," he says, turning his head toward the bar across the casino. I nod my understanding, scoop up my chips, and leave the table. At the bar, I find a stool that gives me a view of Greg's table, order a coke, and wait for the change of dealers coming off a break. A few minutes later, a dozen or so dealers, almost in formation, make their way to the tables. As Greg's relief comes up behind him, he backs off, taps the table and joins a group heading for the break room. As they near the bar, Greg peels off and joins me.

He's nervous, his eyes dart everywhere before he takes a seat facing the casino. "I never thought I'd see you again," he says. "I know why you're here."

"Where is she, Greg? Where is Gillian?"

"I don't know. She's trying to keep me out of it." His eyes won't meet mine. "What about the prescription you picked up for her? I was there. I saw you."

"I left it at the house. She said she would pick it up while I was working."

"What's it for?"

"She has asthma. It's inhalers."

"And then?"

"I don't know. I don't want to know."

"Why is she in Las Vegas?"

"She has a friend here."

"Did she say anything about me, wanting to find me?"

"No, nothing. She just said…"

"What?"

"She said she won't go back to prison."

I mull that over for a moment, wanting to believe what he says is true. He glances at his watch. "I have to go. My break is almost over." He stands up, starts to go as another formation of dealers appear.

"Don't go home tonight."

"What are you going to do?" I see panic spread across his face.

"Stay with a friend or something. Get a motel room. Just don't go home."

He turns away and starts through the crowd toward the tables. "Greg. They're going to catch her."

He turns back toward me. "I hope they do."

I watch for another few minutes as he takes his place at the table, then throw some money on the bar and make for the exit. I push through the glass doors and almost bump into a couple coming in. The light is not good. It takes me a second to recognize them, two people I never expected to see.

"Doing a little gambling, Horne?" Ron Ardis says. Standing next to him, hands on her hips in a dark pantsuit is Andie, her eyes fixed on me with wonder.

"You didn't last as long as we thought."

With Andie riding with me in Ace's VW, Ardis follows in his car. They want a place to talk, so I head for the nearest place I can think of, a coffee-pancake house on Spring Mountain. "Let me get this straight. You knew I'd bolt from the hotel?"

Andie smiles. "It took some convincing, but Wendell finally went for it. When you used your credit card to buy a ticket to Las Vegas, Ardis and I drove up."

"You were all very convincing. But how did you know about—"

"Ace? I didn't know about him but Coop did. We've had you under surveillance since you got here."

I pull into the parking lot at Blueberry Hill and shut off the engine. "So Ardis is not in trouble?"

"No, he was in on it, too." Andie watches me for a moment. I just shake my head and stare out the windshield.

"Come on, baby, we're the FBI. It wasn't hard to discover Greg Sims was a dealer at the Mirage. You have to have a sheriff's card to work in this town. We were on the way to see him when you bumped into us. You just saved us the trouble."

Ardis pulls in to the next parking space and we all get out and go inside. It's brightly lit with red leatherette booths and Formica tables. A waitress takes our order for coffee and Ardis studies the big menu. "I've never seen so many kinds of pancakes," he says. When the waitress brings our coffee, he smiles at her. "I want some of these chocolate chip pancakes. A full stack." Andie and I pass.

"How did you find Sims?" Andie asks.

I recount my journey to pharmacies and drug stores. "I got lucky. Sims came in as I was standing in line. I followed him home and waited. He left but stopped for something at a convenience store and I got a look at his shirt with the Mirage logo. I figured he was on the way to work."

"My, aren't we clever," Andie says.

"You did talk to him, I assume," Ardis says.

"Yeah, I did. She's here but not staying with him. She's supposed to pick up the prescription he got for her sometime tonight while he's at work."

"What's the prescription for?" Ardis wants to know.

"He says inhalers. She has asthma."

Andie and Ardis look at each other. "Okay," Andie says. "Here's the deal. You're going to show us the house, then you will go back to your pal Ace's and wait."

I start to say something but Andie cuts me off. "That's not negotiable."

The waitress comes back with Ardis' order. Three huge pancakes, riddled with chocolate chips and topped with whipped cream fill a large plate. Andie and I watch him dig in.

"So what are you going to do?"

"Wait her out. What time is Sims' shift over?"

"Midnight."

Ardis is halfway through his pancakes. "Yummy." He pauses and leans back. "Should we talk to Sims first?"

"No," Andie says. "I don't want to spook him, and we need time to organize some backup. We'll have to get Las Vegas Metro in on this."

Ardis nods and looks at me. "That was pretty slick, jumping on that airport shuttle."

"Sorry. I didn't mean to get you in trouble."

"You didn't. Wendell told me to give you some leeway. We're just glad you didn't steal a car. We'd have had to arrest you for that."

The check comes and Ardis pays at the cashier desk. Andie and I walk outside to the cars. I light a cigarette as Andie digs in her purse and hands me my cell phone. "You might want this back. It's fully charged."

"Thanks."

"Okay, you lead the way. I'll ride with Ron. I've got some calls to make."

At Sims' house I park along the road where I was earlier. We get out of the cars and Andie and Ardis look things over. I point out the house up the dirt track. We can see one light on. "This is not good," Andie says, scanning the area around the house. "It's so exposed."

"There's a dog, too."

"Great," Ardis says.

Andie paces around, thinking, looking at the house. Finally, she stops. "I've got an idea."

She turns to me. "Okay, you're done here. Go on back to Ace's. I'll let you know how it goes."

"What if she doesn't show?"

"Then we go to plan B."

"Andie, be very careful. Greg is still scared of her and he told me she won't go back to prison."

"We'll see about that." She pushes me toward my car and gives me a brief kiss. "Go."

Driving back to Ace's, I start to have second thoughts. At one long traffic light, the urge to make a U-turn and go back to Greg Sims' house is strong, but I manage to stifle the feeling. I'd just be in the way, and Andie would never forgive me if something went wrong. I pound the steering wheel in frustration.

I find Ace sprawled on the couch, an open book on his chest, his glasses halfway down his nose. I give him a shake. "Hey, Professor."

He blinks and sits up, the book slipping to the floor. "Evan. When did you get back?"

"Just now." I sit down and stretch my legs out, feeling the tension start to drain out. There's nothing more I can do now but wait to hear from Andie.

"How did it go with the pharmacies?"

"I got lucky." I catch Ace up on things. He nods and listens and shakes his head.

"Sounds like they have it under control, providing she comes back for the prescription."

"Yeah, that's the key."

"Want something to eat?" He gets up and heads for the kitchen. "A sandwich, or I've got a frozen pizza I can nuke."

"Pizza sounds good."

"Coming up."

I turn on the TV to CNN. Ace comes back with a couple of beers we start on while we wait for the pizza. Ace and I catch up on music, the movie deal, my move to Monte Rio, and Andie as we eat.

We both lose track of time then Ace flips through the channels to a local station for the Eleven O'clock News. A wave of dramatic music and a red banner fills the screen proclaiming BREAKING NEWS!

"I'm Keith Harris and this is happening now," the anchor says as the screen becomes a remote report. A young Asian woman holding a microphone stands about where my car was parked earlier near Greg Sims' house.

"As you can see behind me, Keith, this remote house in the northwest Las Vegas is surrounded by Metro police, and we're told also, agents of the FBI. Police suspect escaped serial killer Gillian Payne may be in the house."

Greg's house and the surrounding area is lit up like a football stadium for a night game. There are a dozen or more Metro police cruisers, lights flashing, and police in SWAT gear around the perimeter. A helicopter circles overhead. The reporter turns her head toward the house. The camera follows and zooms in closer.

"Do we know whose house that is, Kimberly?"

"Not yet, Keith, but we'll keep you abreast of developments. Kimberly Fong, Action News. Back to you, Keith."

"Thanks, Kimberly. You be careful out there." The anchor smiles. "In other news…"

"She's not there," I say to Ace. "Or maybe she's already gone."

"Maybe her brother tipped her off."

"I don't think so. He's too scared of her."

"I hope she doesn't know where I live."

"No reason she would—"

We both stop then as the doorbell rings. Ace starts for the door then stops, looks back at me. I shake my head. We wait for another long moment.

"Mr. Buffington? FBI Special Agent Andrea Lawrence."

I let out a breath and nod at Ace. He opens the door. Andie flips open her credentials. She looks past Ace, sees me, and steps inside. Ron Ardis is right behind her. Ardis nods to Ace and follows Andie in.

Andie meets my gaze and shakes her head. "She got away. We found an abandoned car on the freeway up behind the house we think was hers, but no prescription. We searched the house. There was nothing."

Ace seems a little dazed. He shakes hands with Andie and Ron Ardis. "Can I get you anything? Coffee? A drink?"

"Coffee sounds good," Andie says.

We all sit around the dining table while Ace busies himself in the kitchen and gets coffee going.

"So what now?"

Andie shrugs. "We've got roadblocks set up. We'll get her, Evan." She puts a hand on mine and squeezes.

"Sure," I say, unable to hide my disappointment.

We sit in silence for a couple of minutes until Ace brings the coffee and four mugs. Ace pours, then Andie's cell phone breaks the quiet. She digs in her purse for her phone.

"Lawrence." I watch her nod then stand up and walk away to take the call. We all watch her as she listens. "She's where?" She listens again, longer this time. "I'll be right there. Make sure that room is under guard." She closes her phone and looks at us.

"Gillian is at Sunrise Hospital.

I'm already on my feet. "I'm going too." Andie doesn't even try to stop me. She just looks at Ace.

"It's on Maryland Parkway, near Sahara," he says.

We leave Ace bewildered, standing in the doorway, holding the coffee pot and the three of us pile into Ardis' car and take off. I give Ardis directions to Sahara where he turns east toward Maryland Parkway.

"So what happened?" I sit in back, leaning forward toward Andie.

"I'm not sure," she says. "A motorist found her walking along the freeway and picked her up. She was almost passed out with one of the inhalers in her hand. He called 911, and paramedics rushed her the hospital."

Ardis makes the turn at Maryland and a couple of minutes later, he parks near the emergency entrance. There are cops on the door. Andie and Ardis flash their I.D.'s.

"Third floor," the uniform says.

"He's with us," Andie says, indicating me.

We get in the elevator and punch the button for three. The corridor is swarming with Metro cops as we get off, three of them huddled around a room. Andie pushes through as a young doctor comes out. Before the door closes, I catch a quick glimpse of Gillian lying inert, attached to a monitor.

We walk away from the room with the doctor. "She's stable," he says. "I'm not sure what happened, but the inhaler she had was empty." He looks at the three of us. "You say she's an escaped prisoner?"

"Yes," Andie says. "I don't want anybody in there but you. We'll have a police guard on the room. When can she travel?"

"We'll keep her overnight at least," the doctor says.

Andie nods. "Fine. We'll have some Marshals here to transport her in the morning. Thank you, doctor."

"I think it was Greg," I say, once the doctor is out of earshot.

"What do you mean?"

"I think Greg switched the inhalers and put the empty ones back in the bag.

Andie smiles. "Bless his heart."

The following morning, I awake feeling more rested and relaxed than I have in days. With Gillian back in custody, my mind starts to drift back toward Ryan Stiles and the movie project. Andie and I share coffee in Ace's kitchen. Ace had left earlier, pleading an early class and papers to correct.

"I hope it's not so long till next time," he'd said.

"It won't be, Ace," I promised, but not sure he believed me. It was something I'd have to work on.

Andie has already been on the phone with Wendell Cook, reporting the previous night's activities. All that remains is for word that the U.S. Marshals have arrived to transport Gillian back to prison. Andie and Ron Ardis are to oversee that transfer.

"You okay?" Andie asks. She studies my face and squeezes my hand. "It's all over now."

I nod. "Yeah, I'm fine. It's just going to take awhile for all this to sink in."

Andie's phone rings. "Lawrence." She listens, nods, and says, "I'll be right there." She looks at me. "Marshals are here. You want to come watch?"

We drive to the hospital. Again there are several uniformed Metro cops and two men in blue windbreakers with U.S. Marshals stenciled in yellow letters on the back. I watch out the window as Andie and Ron Ardis shake hands with the marshals.

Minutes later, Gillian is wheeled through the glass doors outside. With the marshals and Andie and Ron Ardis looking on, two Metro cops help her out of the wheelchair. She keeps her eyes down as the marshals handcuff and shackle her, then walk her the few brief steps to a dark station wagon where she's placed in the back seat.

I get one brief look at her face as she turns toward the hospital. Was she looking for me? She's pale and drawn and doesn't look scary at all now. Across the street in his car, I catch sight of Greg Sims. My eyes return to the marshal's car. When I look back, Sims is gone.

Andie signs some forms, hands them back to one of the Marshals and the car pulls away. Only then do I step outside.

Andie turns to me. "See? I told you."

"Yes you did."

We drop Ron Ardis at the airport. We all get out of the car. Ardis and I shake hands. "I probably won't see you again," he says.

"I hope not. Nothing personal."

Ardis grins. "I know. Hey, maybe I'll come hear you play sometime."

"Do that." And just like that, it's over.

Andie and I get back in the car. She drives up Tropicana and crosses the Strip after a long wait at a traffic light. I watch the hundreds of people out already and wonder what they'd think if they knew a serial killer had been recaptured and carted off back to prison.

We pick up I-15 headed for Los Angeles. I lean back in the seat and feel the morning sun on my face. I close my eyes and doze off. When I wake up, we're cruising up the Baker grade, the Las Vegas valley disappearing in the side mirror. I glance over at Andie. I can't see her eyes behind the dark sunglasses. She feels my eyes on her, lifts up the glasses for a moment, looks over, and smiles.

"Go back to your nap. We'll stop in Barstow and have breakfast."

When I wake up again, she's pumping gas at a busy truck stop. Cars and big rig trucks are everywhere. I'm suddenly famished. We pull over and park at the adjacent coffee shop. We find a booth and order coffee. Andie opts for orange juice, scrambled eggs, and toast. I go for the trucker's breakfast— eggs, sausage, hash browns, and a side order of pancakes.

Andie watches me wolf it all down as she pushes aside her still-half-full plate.

"Not worried about your figure, are you?"

"Should I be?"

"I don't think so. I caught Ron Ardis looking at your ass a few times."

"And?"

"I can hardly blame him." She smiles big, but her expression changes quickly. "What?"

"Nothing. I'm just glad we're driving back. We have to talk."

"Oh, those are the four words men don't like to hear." I study her for a moment.

"It's about Ryan Stiles."

Back on the road, Andie is quiet at first. I crack the window open a few inches and light a cigarette. "So, what about Ryan Stiles?"

"What you told me about the meeting with his mother, the story she told you about the night Darryl McElroy died. It got me thinking, made me curious about why she would confide in you."

"You said you thought she was just being a protective mother with a guilty conscience. She needed to tell someone."

"I still think that's true, but I think there's more." Just after Victorville, Andie signals and exits the freeway, taking the Pearblossom Highway. It's a two-lane strip, full of dips and curves, but less traveled, a shortcut to the north end of the San Fernando Valley.

"I got a look at the police report. I wanted to see if there was something more, you know, reading between the lines."

"And?"

"It's just too perfect, like it was sanitized and all in Ryan's favor."

I run that over in my mind for a few moments. "You think Ryan, Manny's Car Wash, the Malibu police are all involved in keeping Ryan clean."

"I don't know what I'm saying. I'm just not satisfied, no matter what he told his mother. It's just too pat."

I look out at the desert whirling by as Andie negotiates the curves and dips of the highway. "What is it you want me to do, Andie? I'm committed to scoring the movie. I signed a contract. They paid me part of the fee already, remember?"

"I know," she says. "My preference would be you pay back the fee and walk away from the whole thing, but I know you won't do that." She lifts up her glasses and looks over at me. "Will you?"

"No. I want to see it through to the end. I want to do this, Andie."

She nods. "I know, and I want you to do it too, but…"

"What?"

"Just promise me you'll be very careful working with Ryan."

"And?" I know there's more.

"And keep your ears open. Ryan trusts you. He might feel in a confessional mode himself. If he's totally clean, if what he told his mother is the real story, it will never come up."

"And if not?"

"He might slip up."

"How?"

"I think his mother told him she talked to you."

At the end of the Pearblossom Highway, Andie merges onto 14 and eventually the Ventura Freeway. Despite my protests to Andie, I have my own reservations about Ryan Stiles and his mother, and Andie has fueled my curiosity.

As we head into the valley, I'm surprised when she exits and stops in front of the hotel I'd escaped from. I look at her in surprise.

"The room is still good. I have to go into the office, catch Wendell up on everything, and write up my report. I'll meet you back here later." She leans across and kisses me. "Go," she says. "Don't be mad, okay?"

I get out of the car and watch her drive away.

Chapter Nineteen

In the days following Gillian Payne's capture, I go back to Monte Rio for some welcome downtime. It takes Andie a few days to finish up her report before she resumes her regular assignment back at the Bureau's San Francisco office. I relish the solitude, immersing myself in long walks along the river with Milton—who I'd bailed out of the kennel—listening to music, and getting back to the piano.

I contacted Grant Robbins and told him I needed a little time. "I understand," he'd said. "I can imagine." Then he completely changed the subject, and brought me up to date on the movie project. "We have a new script. I think you'll find it much improved. Ryan is excited about it and we both look forward to seeing you again."

"That's good. I look forward to seeing the script." He made no mention of my abrupt exit and absence since our last meeting. I don't know how much Wendell Cook told Robbins or for that matter, if he even talked to him, but I detect a decidedly different tone to Grant's voice.

"We'll be ready to start shooting very soon. We'd like to have another meeting with you before principal photography begins, if it's convenient."

Principal photography. The magic words. "No problem. I'll make it."

My first order of business is to find a home for Milton. I'd thought about it a lot. He was Cal's dog. I'd grown attached to him, but he was never really my dog, and I was going to be gone even more now the movie was underway. But when I stop by the kennel to broach the subject with the vet, Carrie, it's easier than I expected.

"I was almost hoping you'd say that, " Carrie says. "I'll take him."

"Really?"

"Yes. I've gotten kind of attached to him myself, and you can visit him anytime you want."

"Are you sure?"

"Absolutely. Milton is no trouble at all. He's just a sweetheart." She reaches down and pats his head.

I shrug and hand over the leash to Carrie, kneel down, and look into Millton's big sad eyes. "Okay, pal, you're in good hands. Thanks, Carrie."

When I get back to the house, Andie is already there, puttering around the kitchen. She's in her big white terry cloth robe, fresh from the shower. "You're not cooking are you?"

"Hey, I can make a salad and heat things up with the best of them." She opens the oven door and looks inside. "I got one of those bake-at-home pizzas. About ten more minutes."

"Sounds good." I sit down at the table and watch her toss the salad.

She stops for a moment and looks around. "Where's the puppy?"

I tell her about leaving Milton with the vet.

"Oh, I'm sorry. I'm going miss him, too." She brings the salad and two beers to the table. She stands in front of me, her hands on her hips. "So, did you talk to the Hollywood brain trust?"

"I did, but first tell me about Gillian."

"Hang on." She goes back to the stove, retrieves the pizza, and brings it to the table. I cut it up into slices and we dig in. "Not bad, eh?"

We both finish our first slice and lean back for a moment. "Okay," Andie begins. "Gillian is back in maximum security and isolation, where she will stay. No privileges, no special favors, nothing, and that's how it's going to stay. We've heard the last of her."

"Good to know," I say, feeling the relief surge through my body. "What about Wendell Cook?"

Andie grabs another slice. "He's happy. He'd like to give you some credit for her capture publicly, but I told him you probably don't want it."

"I don't. In fact, after this conversation, I don't want to talk about Gillian again."

Andie nods. "Wendell knows that, but he'll probably give you a call."

"What about her brother?"

"Nothing. We figure he's been through enough with a sister like Gillian."

"Good. He deserves some peace."

Andie finishes her second slice and takes a long pull of beer. "Now, let's hear about Hollywood."

I bring her up to date about my conversation with Grant Robbins. "They want me to see the new script, and shooting starts very soon. I'll have to go back to L.A., probably next week."

Andie studies me for a moment. "You okay with this?"

"I'll know better when I meet with them, but yes, I'm okay. Kind of anxious to get working on it."

"Just remember what I said about Ryan. I'm still looking into that."

"I won't forget."

"There's one other thing."

I look up at her. "What?"

"I don't know what the arrangements will be while the movie is shooting. I'll visit the set if I'm invited, I'll visit with you, but I won't stay at Ryan's house again."

I nod. "I didn't think you would. I'm not sure I want to, either."

When I arrive at LAX, I scan a group of waiting drivers in dark suits holding name placards, expecting to see one for me. Instead, I see Coop, dressed in jeans and a jacket holding a card with my name on it.

"What's this?" I say, grinning at him.

"Just trying to blend in."

"Your limo is outside?"

"No, but my car is parked at the curb on police business."

"Works for me."

Outside, Coop leads me to a late-model silver Audi. He grins and shrugs when I look at him. "One of the perks for my position as security consultant. Mr. Robbins is a generous man. I thought a BMW or Mercedes would be too pretentious."

"Wouldn't want that would we?" We throw my bags in the trunk, leave the airport, and head into Santa Monica. "Where are we going first?"

"You have a reservation at the Marriott. Soon as you're checked in, they want you at a meeting."

"You taking me there, too?"

"No, they're sending a car for you." Coop looks over and grins. "You're getting star treatment, pal."

I wonder why they're laying it on so thick. When I start to ask Coop, he reaches behind him on the back seat and plops a magazine on my lap. "Guess you haven't seen this."

It's a copy of *People* and smiling on the cover is Ryan Stiles. Inside is a story and more pictures of Ryan. I scan over the article. It's about Ryan's movie that includes a few sentences about Darryl McElroy's death and Ryan's brief involvement.

When I turn to the next page, I see a photo of myself. It's from a CD cover taken a few years ago, and a second photo of Ryan and me at a piano in Ryan's living room in Malibu. The caption reads: Ryan and jazz pianist Evan Horne. I don't remember anybody taking it, unless it was Melanie.

"That might get you some gigs," Coop says. "Hey, maybe you can autograph it for me."

When we pull up to the entrance of the hotel, a bellman takes my bags inside. "Let's catch up later," I tell Coop. "Maybe have some dinner."

"You got it. Give me a call."

At the front desk, I get checked in with more than the usual greetings from the manager. "Mr. Stiles' company made your reservation. Anything we can do during your stay, Mr. Horne, just let us know." He hands me a key card and a message slip. I'm to be picked up in thirty minutes.

The room is a seventh-floor mini-suite on the ocean side of the hotel. I open the drapes and look down on Santa Monica Bay and the path along Ocean Avenue, usually busy with joggers and people walking their dogs. The mini bar is well stocked, and there's a carton of my brand of cigarettes on a side table. They seem to have thought of everything.

I hang up a few things, grab a bottle of water, and go back down to the lobby to wait for my ride. While there, I call and leave a message for Andie, telling her where I am. Outside, I have a smoke and take in the breeze from off the Bay. Just as I finish, a Lincoln Town car arrives. The driver, a young blond guy in a dark suit and tie, waves off a bellman and walks over.

"Mr. Horne?"

"Yes."

"I'm Jerry. If you're ready." He opens the door for me and I get into the backseat.

"I'm Evan. So what do you do, Jerry? Besides drive, I mean."

He smiles at me in the mirror. "Like everyone else in L.A., this is temporary. I'm an actor. You?"

"Musician. I'm here to score a film."

"No shit. Oh, wait a minute. For Ryan Stiles' new pic, right?"

"Right, but don't tell anyone, Jerry."

"Too late for that," he says. "It's been on TV."

At the studio in Culver City, Jerry stops at a security gate while a guard checks my name off a list he has on a clipboard. He waves Jerry through and we stop at the Sidney Poitier building.

"Here you go."

I get out. "Is this where I tip you?"

Jerry smiles. "All taken care of, but you can put in a word for me with Mr. Stiles if you want."

"I'll try but I don't think it would carry much weight."

"You never know." He waves and drives off.

I go inside and give my name at the desk to a gorgeous dark-haired girl who directs me to meeting room twelve with a big smile.

Ryan, Grant Robbins, and two other men are seated at a conference table. They all stand when I walk in. Ryan comes over and gives me a hug. "Welcome back, dude."

"How you doing, Ryan?"

"Much better now," he says, clapping me on the back.

Robbins shakes hands. "Really good to see you," he says. Dennis Mills and Sandy Simmons are already seated. I shake hands with both of them.

"Looking forward to working with you," Simmons says. He has dark curly hair and a beard and a slender lean body that makes me think he's a runner. Clark is shorter, more compact. Both are dressed casually in jeans and sport shirts.

We all sit down then and Grant Robbins looks around. "Well, gentlemen, let's begin."

We all open our copies of the screenplay. I'd read it through quickly on the flight to L.A. after Robbins had overnighted a copy to me. It was greatly changed. There was no specific mention of my previous adventures, but they had kind of used parts from all of them, and made up the rest. It wasn't enough for me to really mount a major protest.

In fact, I found myself detached now. Maybe it was being pushed back into things when Gillian resurfaced. Words on paper didn't come close to reliving the experience until her recapture, and Robbins' words did even more to make me feel removed.

"We're going to rely on you to help with the music scenes, Evan. We want those absolutely as authentic as possible." He glances at both Simmons and Mills. They both nod their agreement. "We'd like you on the set for those scenes, and of course, more if you want."

I look around the table, see them all looking at me expectantly, as if I'm the one they have to please. It's not like I'm Quincy Jones or some other well-known film composer. I don't quite get it, but I nod. "That's what I'm here for, and of course the music," I add.

There's almost a collective sigh of relief, then smiles and nods from everyone.

"I told you, man. Evan is cool," Ryan says. He gets up. I see he's about to leave. "Well, you don't need me for anything else." He points a finger at me. "Thanks for being here, dude." Then he's gone.

Robbins smiles and takes Ryan's exit with ease. "So let's look at the opening, page one."

I'd read this scene on the plane a couple of times and I liked it.

FADE IN
INT. CLUB. NIGHT
　　Fingers on a keyboard. The SOUND of a jazz piano trio. We pull back, gradually revealing the small club with photos of jazz greats on the wall, the small stage and grand piano, then face of CHASE Hunter, his face in concentration as he nears the end of a set. Eventually we see the whole trio and the AUDIENCE, listening in rapt attention. The song ends to applause. Chase announces the trio and stands.
　　　　CUT TO:

"Tell Evan your idea," Robbins says to the director.

"All this is happening over the opening credits," Simmons says. "What I'd like is for you to be playing until Ryan's face comes into view, then we digitally cut in from your hands to Ryan. We stop there, Ryan takes your place at the piano and the scene continues as outlined. It's easier than you might think. You won't be seen, just your hands on the keyboard."

"What do you think, Evan?" Robbins wants to know. "Can't be more authentic than actually having you playing, can it?"

"No, I guess not." It takes me by surprise but I don't see any reason not to go along. I have no doubt the technical side of it can be easily handled. I shrug. "Yeah, sure. Fine with me."

"Great," Robbins says. "The transition will be seamless. You'll see."

Again there are more smiles and nods, as if they were uncertain I would agree. Simmons and Mills close their scripts and get to their feet, clearly by plan. They both shake hands with me again.

"Look forward to working with you," Simmons says.

"Likewise," Mills chimes in.

Then they both leave. I look at Robbins. He smiles at my obvious surprise.

"Little overwhelming, eh? We're not shooting in sequence, so you have plenty of time to come up with that opening music." He studies me for a moment. "Maybe you've already been working on it a little?"

"Yeah, actually I have." I'd been listening to a lot of music. I wanted something specific, something striking that would be playing whenever Ryan was on screen. I remember Quincy Jones using two bassists for the two killers in *In Cold Blood*. So far I was leaning toward something between Benny Golson's tune "Killer Joe" and Herbie Hancock's "Dolphin Dance."

"I'm working up a theme for Ryan and variations, motifs of it when he's in the scene."

"Excellent," Robbins says. He glances at his watch. "I'd like to show you the jazz club set. It's almost complete, then I'd like to talk with you about a few things."

"Lead the way."

Robbins and I ride over to one of the sound stages in a golf cart. In one corner half a jazz club is being finished. It's open on one side but the rest is all there. The stage, a grand piano, two walls with photos and posters, and about ten or fifteen round tables and chairs. There are some workmen still busy with final touches. On a tall ladder, a technician perches, adjusting spotlights facing the stage.

"It'll look bigger on film," Robbins says as we wander around. Yes, Hollywood. The great illusion. "Go ahead, try the piano."

I sit down and play a few chords on the Yamaha grand, surprised at the volume. "Wish all the pianos were like this." I stop when I hear one of the workmen hammering. Robbins watches me taking in the set.

"It's going to be great. Come on, let's get some dinner."

We go to an Italian place on Ocean Avenue in Santa Monica, not far from my hotel. Robbins is greeted like a regular. We're given a table by the window. Robbins orders a bottle of wine to go with salads and seafood pasta that he recommends. Over dinner, he asks about the hotel and Andie. Just small talk until we both order coffee and I await the real purpose of this dinner.

"I know you've been through a lot recently, the recapture of that woman—it must have been hard to relive that again, but I understand she's safely back in prison where she belongs."

"Look," I start, but Robbins puts up a hand and cuts me off.

"No, please, let me finish. There's something I have to tell you." He starts again but his phone rings. He listens for a moment. "Sorry, I have to take this."

I get up, mime smoking, and go outside to have a cigarette. Robbins nods and listens to his phone. The cool night air washes over me as I look at the lights of Santa Monica Pier and watch people strolling up and down Ocean Avenue. I want to keep this separate, but Robbins seems determined, and my mind goes back to Andie's words about being alert, being careful.

Back inside, Robbins has ordered us both a cognac. "Hope you like this." He holds up his glass. To *Murder in Blue*. He sees my surprise and smiles. "I know, another change, but that's the movie business." We tap glasses and sip. I welcome the warm glow of the liquor.

Robbins sets his glass down. "I have a confession to make. You were right from the beginning, that first night we met at The Jazz Bakery when you said 'why me?' Of course there are scores of pianists here who could have tutored Ryan, but we wanted you specifically. For your playing of course, but also because of your background.

"Ryan wanted to do a film like this, but when we didn't really have a clear story idea. When we came across your name and looked into your background, we thought we had the ideal person. You've had quite a life these past few years and undergone some pretty unusual experiences. It just seemed like fate to choose you. We did a lot of research and reading between the lines. Frankly, I didn't think you'd go for it and would be suspicious of our choice."

"You know I was."

Robbins nods. "That's exactly why we downplayed it from the start and cautioned Ryan not to push. It's also why we didn't want to talk about or show you any script till we had you under contract." He shrugs then and looks away. "We almost blew it, didn't we?"

"You did. You had to know I would hate the first script."

"Yes, that was a mistake. I underestimated your desire to not want a film using your life, both the good and bad experiences, and I am truly sorry for trying that."

"I almost sent your check back with a note saying 'no thanks.'"

Robbins smiles. "I bet you did. I'm curious. What changed your mind?"

"It was Andie partly, the chance to score a movie, and strangely enough, Gillian Payne's escape and recapture." I think for a moment, trying to explain how my thoughts had changed. "It was a chapter of my life that finally feels really over now, and it didn't hurt when I saw the new script, how you'd made it kind of a compilation, rather than specific incidents I lived through."

"You don't know how happy that makes me feel to hear you say that." He finishes his drink. "Another?"

"No, I'm fine."

He nods to the waiter and calls for the check. "I guess I need to apologize for the *People* magazine spread too, but I hope you understand. Publicity is important and that went out before your FBI friends contacted me."

I smile. "Hope they weren't too rough on you."

"Wendell Cook can be very persuasive. He said he'd shut down production."

I have to laugh then. "Wendell can play hardball."

"I promise to clear anything further with you first if you promise to put in a good word for me with Mr. Cook."

The check arrives. Robbins signs and we get up. "Come on, let's get you to your hotel."

When Robbins drops me off, I open the door, then turn to him. "There's one thing I need to ask you."

"Of course," Robbins says.

"Is Ryan really completely free and clear on Darryl McElroy's death?" I look for some change in his expression but there is none.

"Absolutely. This film will be very important to Ryan's career. We can't afford any loose ends. Trust me, Evan. If there were any lingering doubts, I wouldn't go ahead with this project."

I nod. "Thanks for dinner."

I go inside and find Coop lounging in the lobby, talking with a bellman. "Sorry, I forgot to call you."

"No sweat," he says. "Thought I might catch you."

"Want to come up or shall we go to the bar?"

"Bar is fine."

It's nearly empty so we get a couple of club sodas and a corner table.

"So how was the meeting?"

"Fine, and so was dinner with Grant Robbins."

Coop frowns. "I had pizza."

"Hardly fitting for security chief."

"It's the little people who make a movie successful." Coop gives me a look. "So, you pick up on anything from Robbins or our boy Stiles?"

"Like what? Sounds like you've been talking to Andie."

"I have, and also a friend with the Malibu Police."

"And?"

"It's just a gut feeling, but I still think there's something hinky about the McElroy thing."

"Such as?" I watch him scan the room as we talk. I'm used to it now, the automatic cop reflex.

"I don't know. I got a look at the report. There's nothing I can really pin down. Like I say, it's just a hunch, you know, a hunch. Cops are naturally suspicious."

I laugh. "This is starting to sound like dialogue from *Dragnet.*"

"I wish."

"Come on, Coop. The guy was cleared, wasn't he?"

"So were O.J. and Robert Blake."

"Meaning?"

Coop heaves a big sigh. "Look, this is high-powered Hollywood. Millions of dollars at stake, every time somebody like Ryan Stiles sneezes. They can't afford even a shadow of doubt hovering over a new project that would affect the box office. No offense, but don't you find it just a tad strange the way they're treating you, pulling out all the stops, making sure you're happy? Andie told me about your conversation with Stiles' mother, and I bet everybody involved knows about it except the police. You're in the fold, and they want to make sure you stay there, a loyal subject."

I shift around in my chair. "It's nice, but yeah I do. But what's that got to do with Ryan? You think they're worried about me knowing what Ryan actually did that night, and that I might say something about it?"

Coop doesn't answer for a moment. "I just think there's something more."

"That's what Andie says. She told me to listen, be alert, be careful."

Coop sets his glass down and leans in closer, making sure I see how serious he is.

"Listen to her."

Chapter Twenty

For the next two weeks, I immerse myself in the music for the opening sequence. It's a process of experimenting, trying something, starting over, watching the notes gradually fill up the pages. I work in a small room on a back part of the studio lot, away from the hustle of activity that kept things as busy as a small city. Just me, a piano, and a table and chair. In between sessions, I visit the set, watching some of the later scenes of *Murder in Blue* begin to take shape and come together.

I've seen enough movies about making movies. I've always been fascinated by the process, and now I get to see it up close as an invited guest. I know there is a lot of waiting, standing around while lighting is adjusted, makeup is touched up, and sound is checked. It's a long list. Growing up in Santa Monica, I'd seen countless movies and television shows working on location.

I remember one hot July afternoon watching an episode of a hit police television series being filmed. The scene called for the actor to jump out of a car, run across the street, and tackle an escaping suspect. They must have done it fifteen or twenty times from several angles. When the episode aired, the whole thing only took up less than a minute of screen time.

Actual time in front of the camera seems minimal, but watching Ryan, it's easy to see he's in his element, basking in the attention whether waiting in his trailer or listening for the three magic words from Sandy Simmons: action, cut, print.

I stand behind the army of technicians watching the director guide the young star through his scenes. It's like watching a conductor coach a soloist with an orchestra. The two had their share of discussions, some heated. Ryan railed, Simmons listened patiently but usually won out. Ryan seemed to trust Simmons and listened to his suggestions for this or that gesture or movement. It is interesting, but eventually gets boring for me. I want to go home.

I wait for a break in the shooting, and finally get Simmons' attention. He nods and turns back to the set. "Okay, people. One hour." Lights go down, cameras are abandoned, and everybody is suddenly scurrying about headed for lunch. Simmons takes me aside, trailed by a young girl in jeans and a sweatshirt, her haired pulled back in a ponytail. She has a stopwatch around her neck, a headset, and carries a clipboard with the shooting schedule.

"You have about ten days," Simmons says, consulting some pages on the clipboard the girl hands him. "It's going well so I think we can bring it in on time."

"Good, I want to go home to work on the music."

"Okay, just stay in close touch and plan on being here on the fifteenth for the first jazz club scenes."

"You got it. I'll let Grant know."

"One more thing. I want to get you with Skip Porter. He's done a lot of music editing for me. He can walk you through the technical side of things with the music. It's a new game now, all digital when you sync the music with the frames of film."

"Yeah, I was going to ask about that." I knew I could do the music, but the technical part of things would be new to me.

"That's not a problem. I'll set up a meeting for you two. It's much easier these days. You used to have to use a stopwatch, splice tape, all that." He turns to the girl again. "Call Skip and give him Evan's number."

"Thanks, Sandy. I appreciate it. How's it going with Ryan?"

"Great. He's doing a good job. He's very serious about this one. He gets a little distracted at times, but he'll be all right. I think he's going to surprise a lot of people." He looks at me then waves to the girl who has walked away but is now motioning to him. "Be right there. I gotta scoot. Anything else?"

"No, I guess not."

He starts away then turns back. "Hey, why don't you look in on Ryan before you take off? He's been asking about you. He's in his trailer."

Ryan's trailer is not hard to find, just a few minutes walk from the set. There's a security guard standing by the door, talking to an actor in a torn shirt with bloodstains on it, and some purplish bruises on his face. All fake I trust.

The bloody, bruised actor steps aside as I announce myself to the guard. He taps on the door. It opens and Ryan sticks his head out. "Evan Horne," the guard says.

Ryan looks at me, breaks into a big grin, and drags me inside. "Hey baby, look who's here."

Melanie, looking gorgeous as ever, gets up and comes over and gives me a hug. "Evan, so good to see you," she says. It's been awhile since I last saw her.

"You too."

Inside, the trailer is plush and well-appointed with, I assume, as many of the comforts of Ryan's Malibu home as possible. "We were just going over some pages to shoot after lunch." We all sit down and Ryan offers me a drink from the mini-fridge.

"Water would be fine." He hands me a bottle and grabs one for himself. There's a moment or two of silence between the three of us, then Ryan drops into a chair. "Melanie, why don't you grab us a sandwich or something. I need to talk to Evan, okay?"

"Sure." She stands up, gives Ryan a mock salute and me a smile as she goes out.

"Haven't seen much of you," Ryan says. "Everything going okay?"

"Yeah, fine. Just been working on the music."

"Cool. You being taken care of?"

I smile. "Probably better than I ever have been."

"You saw the *People* magazine, right?"

"I did. Caught me a little by surprise."

Ryan shrugs. "Publicity, man, publicity." He grabs a remote and points it a small flat-screen television. "Did you see this?"

It's a brief interview with Ryan on one of the E Channels. Ryan looks relaxed and happy. "Did that a few days ago."

I nod. "I don't keep up much with those entertainment shows." I watch Ryan, trying to get a read on him, but there's nothing in his expression, so I take a shot. "Anymore paparazzi trouble?"

"What do you mean?"

There's an almost imperceptible change in his expression, but he quickly chases it with his signature grin. "Well, they were kind of getting out of hand."

"No, everything is cool. With a picture in progress, I'm giving them what they want."

"No fallout from the McElroy thing?"

"No, why should there be? I was totally cleared. You know that." He takes a big swig of water and avoids my eyes.

"No reason I guess. Just curious."

He sits the water bottle down and looks at me. "Something on your mind?"

"No, not really. I just—" Before I can go on the door flies open and Melanie comes in carrying two paper plates.

"Here you go, boys. Pastrami on rye." She hands us both a plate, napkins, and little packets of mustard.

Until then, I didn't realize how hungry I was. Over the sandwiches, we make small talk. Ryan talking about the shooting, Melanie asking about Andie, and me bringing them up to date on the music.

"Hope you've got some cool theme for my character," Ryan says.

"It's all I've been working on. I think you'll like it. Have you been practicing your piano playing?"

Ryan grins. "Tell him, baby."

"Religiously," Melanie says. "Every night when we go home. I feel like I'm living with a jazz piano player."

"I'll be ready for the nightclub scenes. Don't worry."

There's a knock on the door then it cracks open. "Five minutes, Mr. Stiles," the guard says.

Ryan stands up, checks himself in a full-length mirror, and heads for the door. "Stay and visit with Melanie. She gets bored hanging out here, and I don't like her on the set." He waves and starts out, then turns and points a finger at me. "To be continued," he says.

Melanie looks at me. "What was that about?"

"My fault. I think I struck a nerve. I just asked if there was any more fallout from the photographer's death."

For a moment, Melanie's face goes ashen. "Has something happened?"

"No, nothing, Melanie. Everything is fine."

It takes her a few moments but she finally relaxes and manages a smile. "Sorry, that was just such a stressful time."

"I know. It was for all of us." I finish my sandwich. "Well, I should get going. I'm going home for a few days."

She walks me to the door. "Please say hi to Andie. I'd love to see her again."

"I'll see what I can do. Maybe she'll come back down with me."

"I'd really like that."

"You take care, Melanie."

I manage to book a late-afternoon flight back to Oakland, and then give Coop a call.

"You on duty?"

"Always here to protect and serve. What's going on?"

"I'm flying back later this afternoon. Want to take me to the airport?"

"Not part of my security duties, but I'll make an exception for you."

"Duly noted. I want to run something by you. I'll wait for you at the hotel. I'm just going to pick up my bags."

By the time I check out, Coop is pulling up at the entrance. I get in his car and we head for LAX. On the way, I tell him about my conversation with Ryan and Melanie, and their reactions to my questions.

"I think your hunch might be right."

Coop smiles. "Was there ever any doubt?"

"I wasn't exactly probing, but Melanie especially acted like I'd accused Ryan of something."

"She'll crack before he does if she knows something."

"You think he's told her something?"

We pull up at the departure entrance. "Let's see what happens," Coop says. "See if your questions trigger anything."

"What do you mean?"

"My guess is you're going to get a call from Mama."

I call Andie from the airport. "Want to give a struggling piano player a ride to Monte Rio?"

"No, but I might for an up-and-coming film composer. Where are you?"

"Oakland Airport. I just got in."

"Give me an hour. I'm almost done here."

I get some coffee and spend twenty minutes browsing through movie magazines looking for any further photos or mention of Ryan and the film, but there is nothing. Outside, I find a bench by the baggage claim exit, and watch the parade of people rushing for flights or looking for friends and relatives to pick them up. Andie is right on time.

She pops the trunk and I throw my bags in and get in the car.

"What a nice surprise." She gives me a hug and a lingering kiss before pulling away. "No trouble in Hollywood land, I hope?"

"No, I just needed to get away for a few days to work on the music. They don't need me till the fifteenth."

"How's it going?"

"According to the director, great. I watched some of the shooting and I'd have to agree."

Andie looks over as we merge onto 880. "But?"

I shrug. "Nothing I can really pin down. I spoke with Ryan and Melanie earlier today while they broke for lunch." I pause for a moment, gazing out the windshield at the traffic. "Okay,

I think you and Coop are both right. I kind of edged around with Ryan. He was defensive, little wary maybe, but covered it well. But when he left, Melanie was like a deer in the headlights when I asked her if everything was okay."

"Did you talk to Coop?"

"Yeah, the other night, and he took me to the airport today. His theory is Ryan will probably mention to his mother that I was asking leading questions. She might give me a call."

Andie nods. "What I think too."

"What do you think it is? Officially he's in the clear on the whole thing."

"Cases can always be reopened. If something is dangling out there, they want to know who knows. They're walking on eggshells while the movie is shooting. There's a lot of money at stake now. You know Ryan's story, and you know what his mother told you. You're the only weak link."

"And that would explain why they're treating me so well?'

"Not entirely." She pats my leg and smiles. "They want you for the beautiful music and the credibility you bring as the consultant. But they want to make sure you're on their team if anything goes wrong, or if something comes up unexpectedly. All you can do is wait and see if anything happens."

We make good time to Andie's apartment, where we stop for a few minutes while she grabs some things, then continue on to Monte Rio. "If you're really nice to me, I'll stay till Monday morning. Think you can manage that?"

We stop for dinner in Santa Rosa, then press on to Monte Rio. Andie is tired and turns in early. I'm too pumped so I stay up working on the main theme and some of the shorter cues, music that will last only a few seconds linking scenes but are still motifs of the main theme.

It's after two when I crawl into bed, but I still wake up early. I let Andie sleep in late. It's almost ten when I finally hear her coming up to the loft in her robe, carrying two mugs of coffee.

"Want to hear this?" I gulp the coffee and look at the music I've sketched out.

She nods and sits down beside me.

I play the opening sequence, kind of a slow blues to begin that will feature the piano. I watch Andie close her eyes listening. I finish with one of the short motif lines that echoes the opening.

"Well?"

Andie opens her eyes and looks at me. "It's beautiful, Evan, really beautiful."

"I like it, too. Not bad for a first try."

"So what happens now?"

"I can't do much else until I see the uncut film. That's the tricky part, matching the action with music. I'll have to add some standards in there someplace, and write something for the closing credits." I squeeze my hand into a fist and stretch my fingers. Maybe it was the all-nighter, but I'd felt a twinge several times while playing.

Andie notices right away. "Your hand okay?"

"Yeah, just a little stiff. Nothing to worry about."

She takes my right hand in hers and massages gently. I flinch a little when she squeezes harder. Her eyes meet mine. "Promise me you'll have it checked out."

Saturday night after dinner, we walk across the bridge to the Monte Rio theater and see an action thriller. It's not my kind of film, but I play particular attention to the music, the way the composer links scenes, how the music intensifies the action or sets a mood for the quieter scenes. Leaning back in my seat in the darkened theater, my mind runs through a dozen standards that might work for the end credits of *Murder in Blue,* and the cost of permissions.

Sunday, we sleep late, have breakfast in Guerneville, and lounge around the rest of the day, finally ending up with a long walk along the Russian River. I'm ever alert for another twinge in my hand but even when I squeeze it into a fist, I feel nothing. Still, when Andie leaves for the long trek back to the City Monday morning, I call the doctor in Santa Monica who got me through the surgery from my accident.

"Evan, great to hear from you," Dr. Martin says. We spend a couple of minutes catching up, then I run out of questions. "This is not entirely a social call, is it?"

"No." I tell him about the soreness in my wrist. "Probably nothing, but my girlfriend insists I get it checked out."

"She's probably right." He pauses for a minute. "There's a doctor in San Francisco who's doing some good work in performing arts medicine. I know he's worked with some musicians in the symphony. I met him at a medical conference last year, and we compared notes. He's pretty busy, but let me give him a call. Maybe he can squeeze you in. I'll fax him your records." He gives me the doctor's name and number. "I'll have him call you."

Dr. Mark Hanna calls back in two hours. "Dr. Martin sent me your file. If you can get into the city, I can see you this afternoon. Otherwise it'll have to be sometime next week."

"Great. I appreciate it."

He gives me his address. "Three o'clock. I want to see you play."

◇◇◇

Driving into San Francisco, I think about something I'd once read about Bill Evans years ago in the liner notes of one of his recordings. Something about how the discipline of knowing how to make his mind, hands, and feet respond can allow, and at times, even cause the flow of musical ideas. In other words, his whole body contributed to his playing. I hadn't paid a lot of attention to that at the time, but it made sense.

I find Hanna's office in a small building near the University of California Medical Center a few blocks off 19th Avenue. I even luck out with a parking space, and walk in a couple of minutes after three.

"Go right in," the receptionist tells me when I give her my name. "Just down the hall. First door on your left."

I knock and open the door. Dr. Hanna is behind a large desk, his feet propped up, a file folder open on his lap. He looks up and smiles. He's a big man with a bushy beard and ice-blue eyes behind tortoiseshell glasses. No jacket and his tie is loosened, and his sleeves are rolled up. He reaches across the desk to shake hands and envelops my hand in his, but his touch is very gentle.

"Mark Hanna," he says. "Okay if I call you Evan?"

"Sure. Thanks for seeing me."

His eyes go back to the file as I look around his small office. The walls have the usual bookcases, filing cabinets, diplomas, and a few framed photos. He closes the file and sets it on his desk. "That was quite an accident you had. Lucky you can play at all. Martin's surgery was spot on."

"I was lucky to have him."

"Yes, you were." He stands up and comes around his desk. "Come with me."

We go into another room, not much bigger than a walk-in closet, taken up almost entirely by a spinet piano, a bench, and a stool on rollers. Hanna slides the stool over to the piano and sits down. "Okay, play something for me."

I sit down at the piano. "Anything?"

"Yeah, doesn't matter what. Try a ballad."

I start on "What's New," very conscious of Hanna's eyes on me. I play for about a minute and he stops me.

"Feel anything?" He reaches across and presses his finger on top of my right hand. "There?"

"Yeah, a little."

"Okay, play something up-tempo."

I play on a blues for a couple of minutes before he stops me again.

"Good," he says. "You don't stomp your foot."

I look down at my feet. My right foot is sticking out a little to the right, near to the sustain pedal. My left is almost straight.

"Now bring both feet back under the bench, as if you were going to stand up and play again."

I do as he asks and he lets me go on longer this time before he stops me. "How about now? Feel any twinge, any pain?"

I look at him, surprised. "No I don't."

He nods and smiles. "Moving your feet under you more creates a better alignment of the body, and supports the skeletal structure. It takes pressure off the hands. Forcing part of the body to absorb downward shocks can cause, and over time even create hand, forearm, or shoulder pain. Having your feet under you enables your skeletal arch to be reconnected to the floor and the keyboard."

I sit in total shock for a long moment, then begin to play again, conscious of my feet under me even more. I stop and look at Hanna. "You're kidding. That's all it takes?"

"Well, not quite, but it will help a lot. Yours was not a minor injury. You had severe tendon damage, and long rehabilitation, which I'm guessing you probably pushed to the limit." He takes my right hand and runs his fingers all over from the wrist down to the individual fingers before he lets go.

"Surgically, there's nothing more that can be done, but there are some exercises you can do, and if you pay close attention to body alignment, those twinges should go away." He slaps his hands on his knees and gets up. "Okay, we're done."

I get up from the piano and move aside. "Oh, one more thing." Hanna sits down at the piano and plays a short version of a Thelonious Monk tune. He looks up at me and grins. "Not bad, eh?"

"Not bad at all."

He laughs. "That's why I'm a doctor and not a pianist."

"What do I owe you?"

He waves his hand in a "forget it" gesture. "I might use you in a future paper. Just let me know the next time you play at Yoshi's."

Chapter Twenty-one

I'm sitting at Andie's kitchen table when she comes in, studying some photocopies of skeletal hand drawings in front of me. There are also a few pages of exercises Dr. Hanna had given me. Andie peers over my shoulder, studying the drawings.

"So that's what your hand looks like."

"Well, anybody's hand." I point to a place near the wrist marked "carpo-metacarpal joint." "If that was my hand, an x-ray, it would look different, and show the damage from the accident."

I place my hands flat on the table and move each finger up and down, then independently in small circles. "The good doctor promises me if I do these exercises religiously, and keep my feet under the piano bench, except when I use the sustain pedal, I should be okay and those nasty twinges will go away."

Andie drapes her hands around my shoulders. "I'm so proud of you for going to the doctor. Aren't you glad you did?"

I lean back against her. "I am. Thanks for pushing."

Andie comes around and sits on my lap. "We should celebrate."

"We're going to. Dinner and some jazz. I already made reservations."

"What's the occasion?"

"Christian Jacob is at Yoshi's."

There are two Yoshi's. I'd played the one in Oakland twice, but another one, a little bigger, a little more plush, had opened in San Francisco. The theme was the same. Good food, great jazz, and often marquee names on tour.

After an early, sumptuous Japanese meal in the restaurant, we make our way into the main room. I'd managed to get a table near the stage with a good view of the keyboard. We order drinks, and in minutes, the lights dim and Christian Jacob is announced over the state-of-the-art sound system.

As the trio takes their places, a silence falls over the club. I don't recognize the bassist or drummer, but I suspect they are regulars with Jacob. They exude confidence as they await the first tune. I'd first heard Christian Jacob with trumpeter Maynard Ferguson's nine-piece Bebop Noveau Band from a few years back. He'd gone on to lead his own trio and had several CDs to his name.

He begins rubato on one of the most gorgeous-sounding pianos I've ever heard. The word was that it was over $100,000 and shipped in from Germany. Head down, Jacob plays the first few notes of "Sweet and Lovely." I can't help but notice both his feet are back under the piano bench. I glance over at the bassist. He stands, head down, his left hand around the bass, listening, thinking about his first note. The drummer, holding brushes in his right hand, scans the audience, but he's no less engaged. He turns toward the bassist as Jacob nears the end of the first chorus. A brush in each hand now, he strikes the cymbal in unison with bassist's first ringing note as Jacob goes into a medium tempo.

The trio plays with the song for three choruses, loping along with a two-beat feel, floating on the pulse of the rhythm, teasing, establishing more and more tension, building to a point that strains. Long buzzing lines by the bassist, and intricate patterns of brush strokes by the drummer. I can almost feel the anticipation of the bass and drums, then finally, at the beginning of the fourth chorus, they bear down and pull out all the stops.

The bassist pulls the strings into a solid, singing, walking four. The drummer switches to sticks, and the tension is released as they push through two more choruses before Jacob, who barely looks up, turns things over to the bassist for his solo and much applause. Jacob then turns to exchange eight measure solos with the drummer, who plays so closely to the tune, you can almost hear the melody. They close out the tune, and before the applause fades, Jacob slips into "Nardis," a beautiful Bill Evans song. The rest of the set is a mix of ballads, two originals, and finally a rousing version of the old warhorse, "I Got Rhythm" to close out the set that belies any doubt that this trio can swing. The lights come up, the trio stands, exits the stage, and the spell is broken.

"Wow," is all Andie can manage.

I nod, still feeling the chill on the back of my neck as we make our way out to the car. I sit for a minute, lighting a cigarette before I start the car.

"What is it?" Andie says.

"Nothing, I just…"

"What?"

"In there. That's what I should be doing more of."

Friday, after a phone call from Sandy Simmons, I leave for L.A. to meet with Skip Porter, the music editor. "He works out of his house in the Valley," Simmons says. "Let him know when you're coming and he'll pick you up."

I fly into Burbank and find Porter waiting for me. He's early thirties, a scruffy beard, in jeans, t-shirt, a Dodgers baseball cap on backwards, and a friendly smile. "Got any other bags?"

"No, just the carry-on."

"Cool. Wait here. I'll get the car." He disappears into the throng of arriving passengers, and returns in a few minutes in a black Mercedes coupe. I get in and he takes off almost before I can close the door and fasten my seat belt, the radio blasting hard rock. In minutes we're roaring down the Ventura Freeway toward the West Valley. Trying to talk over the radio is impossible, so I just sit back and hope for the best.

We exit in Woodland Hills. Porter careens around a corner onto a side street, then pulls into a circular driveway in front of a rambling ranch-style house. He shuts off the engine and looks at me. "Fun, huh? Man, I love to drive."

"I can tell."

Inside, there's little furniture other than a long couch and low coffee table in front of a large flat-screen television.

"You just move in here?"

"About a year ago," Porter says. "Come on, I'll show you the goodies."

I follow him to a back bedroom. Inside it looks like a recording studio. There's a mixing board, television monitor, two large monitor speakers mounted on the wall, three computers amid a tangle of wires and cables, and an electric piano with a full keyboard.

Porter sits down in front of the mixing board in a plush office chair and gestures toward the equipment. "This is where we do it."

To me, it looks like the command center of a spaceship, and Porter is Captain Kirk. He looks at me and smiles. "It's not as intimidating as it looks. Everything is connected. Let me walk you through something." He motions me to the piano. "Play something, doesn't matter what."

Porter clicks on one of the computers, opens a new file, and names it "E. Horne test." I play a few choruses of blues, varying the tempo a couple of times, then stop.

"Cool." He saves the file then runs it back and plays it over the speakers for a minute. On another computer, he opens a file and hits play, and a film begins with no sound. A man in a car, driving along a beach road in moonlight. After a couple of minutes, the man pulls the car to the side of the road, gets out of the car and gazes over the edge at the surf below.

Somehow, Porter synchs my piano choruses with the film, using the two computers. I watch the computer screen dance with vertical slashes, not unlike a heart monitor, moving across on a solid bar line. At the bottom of the screen numbers flash by. "Okay, let's add something." He opens another file marked "sampler" and selects "walking bass." He plays bits of two or three. "Which one?"

I shrug. They all sound good. Porter selects one, then opens another sample file for drums. "Sticks or brushes?"

"Sticks."

He saves both files then merges them with my piano, and like magic, it's a trio. He listens for a moment, nodding his head. "How about a sax? Coltrane, Stan Getz, Phil Woods?"

"I'll let you do the honors."

He selects Getz sound and links it to the trio, then backs everything up, including the piece of film. He leans back in his chair and hits play. Now the man in the car races down the highway with a quartet. This time, as he gets out of the car, Porter moves one of the slide controls on the mixing board and fades the music entirely.

I stare at the monitor for a few moments, amazed at how quickly and smoothly it was all done. "See, man, we can do anything." He smiles, pleased with my amazed expression. "Digital magic. In the old days you'd have to use a stopwatch, count frames, and match the music to the action of the film."

"Where do all those sampler files come from?"

"Huge database. Every musical sound you can think of. Jazz, classical, rock, you name it, it's recorded and stored somewhere. Remember the show *Miami Vice?* Jan Hammer did the whole thing like this"

"What if you had really used Stan Getz?"

Porter laughs. "He'd get paid."

For another hour, Porter demonstrates the equipment and answers my questions until my mind is reeling with the possibilities before me.

"Don't worry about all this," he says. "You do the music. I'll do the rest."

Skip drops me off back at my hotel in Santa Monica, where I'm greeted once again by the very solicitous manager. "Mr. Horne. Your room is ready and we have a car reserved for you as per instructions from Mr. Robbins." He hands me several slips of paper. "There are also these."

I glance through messages from Grant Robbins, Ryan, and Coop. "Thanks. I won't need the car this evening. I'm just going to stay in my room."

"Very good. And you are accepting calls?"

"You bet."

I try Grant Robbins and Ryan but both go directly to voice mail. I leave them both messages that I'm back. Coop answers his phone. "Where are you?"

"Back at the hotel in Santa Monica. Want to get some dinner?"

"Yeah, give me an hour or so. I got some things to finish up here."

I unpack and take a long hot shower, my mind still swirling from Skip Porter's demonstration. I change clothes, and go back down to the hotel bar to wait for Coop. I'm still on my first drink when he walks in.

"Know anybody with a green van?" He takes a stool next to me at the bar.

I look at him blankly. "I don't think so."

He takes out a grainy black-and-white photo and lays it on the bar. I look at it and shrug. "Guess I have to take your word that it's green. Where was this taken?"

"Near Ryan's beach house in Malibu. Surveillance photo."

"Why?"

Coop orders a club soda and takes a long drink. "Ryan's had some strange phone calls and a couple of e-mails. We put a couple of guys on the beach road."

"Saying what?" I keep looking at the photo.

"Probably nothing. Couple of hang-up calls. The two e-mails can't be traced."

"Wait a minute. I tap my finger on the photo. There was a van but I can't remember if it was green. When I was first at Ryan's house. I was walking back from the shopping center on Broad Beach Road. A guy in a van stopped me, knew who I was and that I was staying at Ryan's."

"You remember anything about him?"

"I do remember a lot of camera equipment on the floor when I got close to the passenger-side door, but the guy, no, not really. It's been awhile."

Coop nods and puts the photo back in his pocket. "What did he want?"

"Photos, information. He knew who I was. He said he'd make it worth my while if I got him to Ryan."

"What did you tell him?"

"That it was none of his business. I told Ryan about it when I got back to the house. He freaked out, practically accused me of giving him up. I remember thinking at the time that maybe it was a setup, a kind of test. Melanie got mad at him for accusing me. He apologized and that was the end of it."

"Maybe not," Coop says.

"What did the e-mails say?"

"I know everything."

At Coop's insistence, we opt for dinner at a small family-owned Mexican restaurant a few blocks from the hotel. Over enchiladas and a large margarita on the back patio, we once again go over the possibility of Ryan's deeper involvement in the death of photographer Darryl McElroy.

"Somebody knows more, or wants Ryan to think he knows more," Coop says.

We both turn down a second margarita and order coffee. I lean back and light a cigarette. "But why wait so long to bring it up now?"

Coop shrugs. "Does more damage now that the film is underway. If this e-mailer thinks he can disrupt the filming, so much the better. Even if it's what Hollywood calls a small-budget movie, there's millions of dollars tied up now, and the last thing Ryan Stiles needs is more scandal and bad press, whether for this film or future projects."

I know Coop is right, but I just can't get my mind around it. "You know, just once, I'd like to do something without getting involved in somebody else's mess." I take a deep drag on my cigarette and exhale a cloud of smoke. "All I was going to do was teach a movie star how to look like he could play piano."

Coop smiles and nods. "I know, but you're in it, too. Ryan's mother made sure of that when she confided in you." Coop gets up. "Be right back." He heads for the men's room just as my phone rings.

"This is Evan."

"Evan, Grant Robbins. Glad to hear you're back. Simmons wants to block the opening scene as soon as possible. How's the music coming?"

"The opening is written, and I met with Skip Porter, the music editor. We just have to record the music and show Ryan the sequence."

"Good, he's ready. Let's get together tomorrow. We can record right on the set, get a feel for the scene."

"Sounds good. What about a bass player and drummer? This is a trio scene."

"I've tentatively scheduled a couple of actors that can go through the motions. You have a better idea?"

"I do." Coop slips back into his chair, watching me. I tell Robbins my idea and he agrees.

"Great. Makes it all the more authentic. Tomorrow then. Ten o'clock."

I close my phone and look at Coop. "On the set tomorrow morning. You'll be there, too?"

"I wouldn't miss it."

Except for the harsh lights, and the camera pointed at the keyboard, it almost feels like I'm in a jazz club. Looking up at Buster Browne and Gene Sherman, both in dark sweaters and jeans on bass and drums, makes it even more real. Buster had been shocked to receive Robbins' call but once on the set, he had warmed to the idea.

"This is very cool, man. I always thought I'd be good in a movie." Gene Sherman is his usual calm self as we take our places. I glance at Ryan just off to the side, next to Sandy Simmons, seated in a tall canvas-back chair. Ryan and I are dressed identically. I'd gone over the sequence with him several times and he seemed fine although, I thought, a little more nervous than usual.

"All right, quiet everybody. Let's try it," Simmons says. "Roll sound. Action."

I play the first chord and try to forget the crew watching and listening. After only a few bars, Simmons yells cut and is out of his chair. "Bass player, don't look at Evan. Just play your bass."

Buster holds up his hand. "Sorry."

"No problem. Let's try again."

We go through it four times before finally getting a complete take, and I hit the ending chord. "Okay, that's it. Good. We got it," Simmons says. He motions Ryan and me to the monitor. We both watch my hands on the piano, occasionally with a glimpse of Buster and Gene in the background. "Looks good. Now we'll cut in Ryan."

With Ryan seated at the piano, the camera rolls, focusing on Ryan's face. His head bent slightly, his eyes half-closed in concentration, he looks for all the world as if he's playing. "Cut," Simmons says again. He turns to me. "Look okay to you?"

"Yeah, perfect."

"Good. Okay, to start the end of the scene, we need your bass player to say a line. It's not in the script. Think he can handle it?"

Buster and Gene are talking quietly as Simmons, Ryan, and I go to the piano. Simmons explains what he wants from Buster. The heavy bassist looks panic-stricken for a moment, then nods. "You'll be fine," Simmons says. "Let's try it. This is just a rehearsal, so no pressure."

Ryan sits at the piano as Simmons backs up. "Do your closing set lines, Ryan. Buster, I'll cue you."

Ryan turns slightly so he's facing the now-empty tables and chairs. "Thanks for coming. We'll be right back after a short break." He stands and starts off. Simmons points at Buster who leans forward and says, "Ryan, I need to talk to you."

"Chance," Simmons says. "His character's name is Chance. Let's do it again."

They go through it again several times until everybody is comfortable. Only Ryan seems irritated and short with everyone. "Come on Sandy, let's not make it a big deal." The two men look at each other for a long moment, then it's Ryan who shrugs as the crew waits and watches. "Whatever."

"Okay, that's it. Break for lunch. Back here at one o'clock."

Buster comes over to me. "How was I?" His voice is just above a whisper.

I smile. "An Oscar performance."

"Cool. Did he say lunch?"

"Yeah, just go with the crew."

Ryan stops me. "How about lunch in my trailer? I need to talk to you."

"Sure." We walk out of the studio to Ryan's trailer. Inside, a table is already set with sandwiches, potato salad, and two large bottles of mineral water. Ryan drops in one of the chairs and looks at me.

"I need you to be straight with me."

"About what?" I can already tell I'm not going to enjoy this lunch.

"Your guy Cooper tell you about the calls, the e-mails?"

"Yeah, he did. We talked last night." I sit down and take a bite of my sandwich, trying to keep it casual.

"Any ideas?"

"About who it is? Why would I know?"

Ryan doesn't touch his lunch. "Let's get real. The only person who knows the whole story is my mother, and I know she talked to you, so that just leaves you as a potential source."

I put my sandwich down and take a drink of water. "And you think I leaked information to this anonymous caller, that I know who he is?" I look right into Ryan's eyes.

He holds my look for a moment then turns away. "Oh fuck, I don't know. This thing just won't go away. It's got me crazy."

"Why would I do that, Ryan? What's in it for me? I don't want the movie disrupted anymore than you do. I'm being well paid, I'm getting to score the film." I see the tension in his face as he watches me.

"But you still have doubts, don't you? You checked out the car at Manny's. You talked to my mother, and I bet Cooper and Andie both checked out the police reports, did a little sleuthing on their own, right?"

"That's what they do. Don't forget, your mother called me. I didn't call her."

Ryan slumps back in his chair and heaves a big sigh. "I know. I'm just paranoid I guess. I just don't want anything to go wrong."

"Is there anything to go wrong? Something else you want to tell me?"

He slams his fist down on the table, shaking the water bottles. "No, nothing. My mother should never have come to see you."

"Get mad at her then, not me."

He gets to his feet and paces around. He stops, facing me. "Look, I'm sorry, I really am. You've been a good friend to me, and you're right. I'm way out of line."

"Okay, forget it. Sit down, eat your lunch, and stop acting like a movie star."

Ryan stops, stares at me, then breaks into a huge laugh. "Sometimes I don't know how to do that."

Chapter Twenty-two

When we get back to the sound stage, there's a CLOSED SET sign hung on the door and two security guards, who nod and let us in. Inside, on the set, the tables and chairs are fully occupied by extras in various modes of dress listening intently to Sandy Simmons giving them final instructions. "You're all jazz fans so look like you're into it." He points to one couple near the front. "Lose the shades," he says to the man. "We don't want to go over the top."

They all turn as Ryan walks in, oozing charm and waving with that megawatt smile. He seems more calm now and ready to work. "Okay everybody. Make me look good. Ready when you are," he tells Sandy.

Sandy nods and motions me to stand with him at the monitor. Ryan takes his place at the piano with Buster and Gene. The lighting dims to nightclub level, a soft glow, heightened only by the spotlights centered on the piano. A technician steps forward and holds the electronic board with the scene and take number in front of the camera. Sandy scans everything once more until he's satisfied. "Quiet everybody. Roll sound. Action."

I watch as the camera, on a dolly, gradually pulls back until the trio and most of the audience of extras is on full view. On the monitor, it's a real jazz club. As the opening music ends, Simmons cues to the audience for applause and the camera moves in closer on Ryan for his set closing lines. He stands, and Buster leans over and says his line without a hitch.

"Cut," Simmons says. "That was fine everybody, but let's do it again."

The entire sequence is repeated and Simmons cuts again. He looks at me. "Look okay to you?"

"Fine. Looks like the Village Vanguard."

The extras get up and mill about until they're released by Simmons, as are Gene Sherman and Buster Browne. Buster stops by me, carrying his bass. "Tell Mr. Simmons I'm ready for my close-up."

"I'll call you," I say. "Thanks for doing this."

Simmons gathers me and Ryan around the monitor, and we watch the sequence one more time. Halfway through, Ryan's cell phone rings. He looks at the screen and frowns.

"Who is this?" He listens for a moment, his face contorting in anger. "Fuck you!" He closes the phone and whirls around to look at me.

"What?"

"It's the asshole again. He said, 'I know what you did.'"

I signal Coop, who's been hovering nearby. He comes over and takes the phone from Ryan. "Don't bother looking," Ryan says. "There's no number."

"Any idea what he's talking about?" Coop asks.

Ryan doesn't answer. He just stomps off, headed, I assume, for his trailer.

Coop shrugs. "Nothing much we can do. The caller is probably using a disposable cell phone. No way to trace it."

Simmons looks concerned. "What's this all about, anyway? That paparazzo guy's death again?"

Coop looks at me, then back to Simmons. "That's my guess."

Simmons pulls off his headset in frustration. "I don't need this shit on my set. Somebody get Ryan back here and let's talk about it." He points to one of his many assistants and sends him off, but he's back in a couple of minutes.

"He's not in his trailer, Mr. Simmons. The security guard at the trailer said he saw him get in his car and leave the lot."

"Great. Now we've got a missing star. He grabs a clipboard from the script girl, and shuffles through some pages. We've got two more scenes to shoot today. How the fuck are we going to stay on schedule with phone calls, e-mails, and missing stars?"

Nobody has an answer for him. Everybody still on the set tries to look busy, but they're all listening. Finally, Simmons points to Coop.

"You're head of security aren't you? Will you please try to find him?" He turns and walks away and out of the sound stage.

I feel Coop tense, but he lets it go. "Let's get out of here," he says. "I've had enough Hollywood for today." We walk outside to Coop's car. "Any ideas?"

"Maybe he went to the Malibu house, or his folks. Let's start there." I call the Malibu house and get Emillio and tell him to call me the minute he hears anything from Ryan.

"Anything wrong?"

"No, just one of Ryan's moods. He left the set. Would you call his mother for me?"

"Of course. What should I say?"

"Keep it low key. I don't want to alarm her."

"I understand."

I close my phone and look at Coop. He seems preoccupied, distracted. "What now?"

"Let's get some coffee and brainstorm a bit."

We leave the lot and drive west, stopping at the first coffee shop, a Denny's on Washington Boulevard. We take a booth in the back and both order coffee.

"I'll have some pie, too," Coop says to the waitress. "Apple if you have it."

"You bet," she says, and hurries off.

"Okay," Coop says. "Any ideas on who the anonymous caller is?"

"None, except..."

"What?"

"I may be reading this wrong, but I think Ryan knows who it is. He was extra nervous at lunch. It was just something about the way he handled the call, like it wasn't supposed to happen."

Coop nods. "I thought so, too. The only remote lead is the guy in the green van we talked about. Everything else has been covered. The police reports, his mother, the car. It's all been covered and Stiles was cleared. But there's a string hanging out there somehow. Something we're missing."

I think about that for a moment, trying to remember Ryan's reaction when I told him about the guy stopping me on Broad Beach Road. "This may sound far-fetched, but what if that was a setup, a test Ryan was running on me? He was so paranoid. What if he promised that guy a payment of some kind and then reneged on it?"

"What kind of payment?"

"I don't know. Money, an exclusive story, photos."

"I like it. You think this guy is a paparazzo too?"

"He had all the equipment in that van. What if he was a friend of McElroy's? What if he knew what happened in Malibu Canyon and now is coming to collect?"

"Slow down. How would he know—"

"Unless he was there."

"Exactly."

The waitress brings our coffee and Coop's pie. He digs in, takes a big bite, then points his fork at me. "Okay, first we need to track this guy down. I'll have to check around and see if any of these paparazzi know of a freelancer with a van. That at least is a place to start."

"Anything else?"

"Yeah, I wish that photo of the van was more tightly focused."

Ryan turns up the next morning after spending the night with Melanie at the Malibu house. Emillio had called Grant Robbins, who said to let it go, but apparently gave Ryan a good talking to and ordered him back to the set.

"Simmons is ready to walk if there are any more of these disruptions," Robbins tells me. "I can't say I blame him. He's a good director and is trying to stay on schedule. Has Cooper come up with anything?"

"He has one possible lead."

"What?" Robbins says. I can hear the urgency in his voice.

"I'd rather not say for now."

There's nothing but silence from Robbins for a few moments. "All right, but we have to get this settled. Whoever it is, if it's money he wants, God knows there's plenty of that."

"But if there's nothing for him to know, if he's just bluffing, won't offering money just complicate things further?"

"Let me worry about that, Evan."

"Gladly."

"How's the music coming?"

"It's coming. I'm going to spend the next few days with Skip Porter working on it."

"Good. I've seen the dailies. If we can keep on schedule, the whole thing should wrap in ten days."

At Skip Porter's we work off the film already completed. There's not as much to do as I originally thought. Some mood cues, short motifs of music to underscore some dialogue, and one obligatory chase scene. Ryan's character tailing a suspect and trying to keep up. I use an up-tempo bebop line, and with sampling, make it sound like a quintet of rhythm section and two horns, reminiscent of Horace Silver. For a scene in a dark, deserted warehouse, I use a kind of avant-garde effect to make it even more spooky and suspenseful.

"Yeah, man, you're cookin' now," Skip Porter says. He runs the cassette back to the opening sequence. "This is really beautiful. You got the essence of his character. You need something sweet and dreamy for the girl."

"I know. I was thinking about a ballad based on the original theme, a kind of variation on it."

"Excellent." He shuts off the equipment and leans back. "How about a break and a pizza?"

"Great idea."

Skip calls in our order and leaves to pick it up. Five minutes later, my phone rings. It's Coop.

"Got him."

"Who?"

"Jerry Fuller. Freelance photographer, does some paparazzi work, and most important, he owns a late-model van. Want to guess the color?

"Do I need to?

"I'm going to pay him a visit, and I need you to go with me."

"Why?"

"Because you can identify him, see if it's the same guy you talked to by Stiles' house. Where are you?" I give him Skip's address. "That's close to where we're going. Pick you up in ten minutes."

I leave a note for Skip and wait outside for Coop.

Jerry Fuller's address is a trailer in Reseda. It looks well kept up. We turn in the entrance, past a white stone fountain weakly trickling water, and a sign that reads SHADY REST MOBILE HOME PARK. Coop consults a piece of paper and negotiates the small streets lined with all size and manners of single- and double-wide trailers. Some are on wheels, some are more permanent-looking. At the end of Avenue C, Coop pulls over and parks.

"Bingo." Parked across the street under a makeshift carport in front of a small trailer is a green Dodge van. "You think that's it?"

"Could be."

"Let's have a look."

We get out of the car and walk across to the van. I look in the passenger-side window but don't see anything. "Probably doesn't leave his gear in the car."

Coop nods and walks up the few steps to the front door, motioning for me to stay where I am. He knocks several times but there's no response from inside.

"Maybe he's out for a walk."

"Trust me. People who live in trailer parks don't go for walks." He knocks again, louder this time. Still no response. He tries the door and finds it open but off-kilter. Coop turns to me. "It's been forced." He pushes the door open. "Jerry Fuller? Police. We need to talk to you."

Coop steps back and draws his gun. "Stay there." I watch him go inside. A light goes on. It seems longer but in only half a minute or so, Coop comes back out, holstering his gun. "I have to call this in."

"What?"

"Back bedroom. Just a quick look. See if it's the same guy." Coop says as he takes out his phone.

I go past him and walk through the tiny kitchen area, past tripods, light reflectors, and other camera equipment stacked against the wall. There are dishes in the sink, a couple of pizza boxes on the counter.

I walk down a short passageway, past a small bathroom into the tiny bedroom. There's nothing there but a twin bed and a tall metal filing cabinet. It's definitely the right guy, the right van, but not the way I expected to find Jerry Fuller.

He's sprawled on the bed, his shirt torn open, a wide Nikon camera strap tightly wrapped around his neck. There's a look of surprise on his face. Coop comes up behind me. "This is a crime scene now. Don't touch anything."

"I wasn't planning on it."

Fifteen minutes later, three police cruisers arrive. I watch from across the street, leaning against Coop's car, and light a cigarette. A group of curious neighbors, roused from their TVs, venture out gradually as a yellow police tape is wrapped across the driveway and trailer. *Law and Order* right in their neighborhood. Two of the uniform cops shoo the curious back while Coop talks with the other uniforms.

Five minutes later an unmarked car arrives with two guys in suits. Coop meets them. They shake hands and I catch snatches of conversation as Coop explains what he's doing there and why he was looking for Jerry Fuller.

"No shit. Ryan Stiles," one of them says. As Coop talks, they glance my way a couple of times, then go inside the trailer with Coop.

Ten minutes later, Coop comes out of the trailer and over to me. "New ball game now."

I'd been so focused on Jerry Fuller, I hadn't noticed what Coop tells me about inside the trailer. "There are clippings all over the walls of McElroy's death, photos of Ryan, Melanie, even a couple of you."

"Me?"

"Yep, two on the beach, you talking with Ryan, and two of Ryan posing friendly, like they knew each other pretty well." He nods toward the trailer. "They're going to want a statement from you. I'll go in with you if I can. I know one of them. Just tell them about your encounter with Fuller at the beach road."

"Nothing else to tell. How was he killed?

"Strangled with the camera strap after he was hit on the head. The killer was probably waiting for him, knocked him unconscious, then used the camera strap to finish him off. Probably happened sometime last night."

"You think he made the phone calls, sent the e-mails?"

"They'll know after they check his computer and phone records. They'll turn the trailer upside down."

We both turn as a black station wagon with Los Angeles County Medical Examiner pulls up. Coop points to the trailer. "Come on, I'll drop you back at your hotel."

The story of Jerry Fuller's murder is all over local TV news when I get to my room. Fuller is described as a freelance photographer, and as usual, the reporter is careful to say "police suspect foul play. Fuller's body was discovered by Lieutenant Dan Cooper of the Santa Monica Police, who is also a security consultant for Ryan Stiles' new film. The star actor is also mentioned as a person of interest."

There are a couple of shots of the trailer park, Fuller's trailer, and a photo of Ryan that fills the screen. "Also present at the scene was pianist-composer Evan Horne, who is scoring the Stiles' new film, *Murder in Blue,* now in production."

Ten seconds later, my room phone and cell ring simultaneously. I answer the cell first. It's Grant Robbins. "Hang on a second," I tell him. On the room phone, it's a reporter from the *Los Angeles Times.* "I'm sorry, I have no comment," I tell him, and hang up.

On my cell, Robbins sounds panicked. "What's going on, Evan?"

I catch Robbins up and he listens without interrupting. "The police are going to interview Ryan."

"Why? Why is Ryan a person of interest? We both know that's just another way of saying he's a suspect."

"Fuller had a lot of pictures and clippings of Ryan and stories about McElroy's death. Did Ryan know Fuller?"

Robbins hesitates just a fraction but I catch it. "I don't know," he says. "I haven't talked to him yet."

"I'm sure I don't have to tell you to prepare him. They're going to ask him a lot of questions about Fuller, and where he was last night."

"I'd be surprised if they didn't, but last night is easy. Ryan and Melanie had dinner with me. Is that when it happened? How was Fuller killed?"

"Strangled with a camera strap."

"Jesus. And you were there?"

"Yeah, Fuller was Coop's lead I told you about. I went along to see if he was the same guy who stopped me near Ryan's house in Malibu."

"When was that?" Robbins sounds genuinely surprised.

"Way back, when I first started tutoring Ryan. When you're done with the police, tell Ryan I want to talk to him too."

"I'll do that." He pauses again. "Do they know if it was Fuller who made the calls?"

"I don't think they know anything yet."

"Evan, I'm sorry you had to be involved in this."

"I'm not involved."

"No, of course you're not. I just meant—"

"I know what you meant."

"I have to go," Robbins says. "I've got Sandy Simmons on the other line. He's going to go ballistic over this. If you hear anything more, please let me know."

I close my phone then call the front desk and tell them not to put through any calls.

I stretch out on the bed, thinking about Robbins' phone call. A man had died, been murdered. Someone had crushed his skull, then wrapped a camera strap around his neck and pulled and twisted it tightly until all the air had been cut off.

Yet Grant Robbins, except for the one brief utterance as I'd told him about finding Jerry Fuller, had been more concerned about Ryan Stiles, and Sandy Simmons going ballistic, and ultimately, the movie.

I didn't know Jerry Fuller. I knew nothing about him. I'd only talked to him once on Broad Beach Road, but he was somebody's son, maybe the boyfriend of a woman who was yet to discover he was gone. The investigation would lead to his background, survivors, family, financial records, his whole life revealed in his death.

Who wanted or needed Jerry Fuller dead? If Fuller was responsible for the e-mails and phone calls, then Ryan Stiles became a primary suspect. But what if he wasn't? Robbery wasn't the motive. All his camera equipment was still there in the trailer, and the police would go through all his belongings in search of a direction to follow. The only thing I know for sure is that it had to be somebody pretty strong.

My cell phone jolts me out of these thoughts. I look at the screen and see it's Andie.

"What's going on? I just saw a scroll on CNN about somebody named Jerry Fuller. Your name and Ryan's were there, too. Who is Jerry Fuller?"

"The guy who stopped me on the road near Ryan's house. I'm not sure I told you about it at the time."

"I don't remember. Are you all right?"

"Yeah, I'm okay." I catch her up on everything, which I realize is not much even though I was at the scene. She hadn't heard about the threatening calls.

"If he is, Ryan will be in the hot seat again."

"Since I was with Coop when we found him, I have to make a statement to the police."

"Should be just routine, right?"

"No other way it could be. I don't know anything about Fuller and only talked to him that one time. There was something odd, though."

"What?"

"Coop says there were a lot of clippings about Darryl McElroy and photos of Ryan, even a couple of me and Ryan together near the beach house."

"Another of those paparazzi guys."

"I think he did some of that."

"I'm swamped here, but I think I can get away this weekend. Want me to come down?"

"I'd like that a lot."

"Where are you staying?"

"Marriott in Santa Monica."

"Okay, baby. You hang in there."

"Nothing much else I can do."

"Evan, you think Ryan knew Fuller?"

"I think they were friends."

Chapter Twenty-three

"Mister Horne, did you know Jerry Fuller?"

"No. I only talked to him that one time in Malibu."

"When you were staying at Ryan Stiles' home?"

"Yes."

In one of the interview rooms at the West Valley Police Station, I'm sitting across from Detective Charlie Farrell, who had been at the trailer park, and was an old friend of Coop's. As a courtesy, and because I'd been in the trailer, Farrell had allowed him to be with me, but he'd cautioned Coop not to comment unless he was asked. We were going over some of the questions he'd already asked, but in a slightly different way.

"Did you ever see Fuller with Ryan Stiles?"

"No, but I told Stiles about—I guess you'd call it an encounter—Fuller when I got back to the house."

"And what was Stiles' reaction."

"He got very angry."

"At you?"

"At first it was at me, then just a general rant on paparazzi. He acted like I was not telling him everything."

"And you hadn't left anything out."

"No." I glance at Coop for a moment. "Ryan eventually calmed down and apologized."

Farrell nods and makes some notes on a yellow pad in front of him. He looks up at me. "How would you describe your relationship with Ryan Stiles?"

"I wouldn't exactly call it a relationship. I was hired to teach him how to look like he could play piano, and later to score the music for his new film."

Farrell frowns. "I'm sorry. Look like he could play the piano?"

"Yeah, it's been done before. Most actors don't play musical instruments."

He smiles then. "You mean like Jimmy Stewart looking like he was playing trombone in *The Glenn Miller Story?*"

"Exactly, but his teacher was going to quit."

"Why?"

"According to the story I've heard, he said he couldn't stand the noise Stewart made on the horn."

"So what did they do, get a new teacher?"

"No, they plugged up the trombone so it wouldn't make any sound."

"Amazing," Farrell says. He leans back and grins and looks at Coop, who just shrugs. "Gotta love Glenn Miller." He looks at his notes again. "I guess that about does it. I'll have this typed up for you to sign." He stands up and offers his hand. "Thanks for coming in Mr. Horne." He turns to Coop. "Good to see you again."

"You too, Charlie," Coop says. "Hope you catch this guy."

Farrell starts out then turn back to us at the door. "If you think of anything else, well, Coop knows the drill. He'll tell you."

"He already has."

We stop in the parking lot at Coop's car. It's a busy station. Black-and-white cruisers slip in and out of the lot, visitors heading in to visit or get their relatives or friends released.

"So how'd I do?"

"Fine. Nothing for you to worry about."

The Valley heat is oppressive. I watch a motorcycle glide by, the rider in boots, black uniform, gloves, helmet, and the obligatory aviator sunglasses. I knew Coop had done a stint on motorcycles. "Must be hot in all that gear."

"It's kind of comforting at sixty miles an hour on the Ventura Freeway.

"When is Ryan coming in for his statement?"

"He's not," Coop says. "Hadn't you heard? Celebrities are interviewed in their lawyer's office by appointment only, and at their convenience."

"I should have known."

"Farrell said he's meeting them later this afternoon."

I take out my phone and dial.

"Who are you calling?"

"Robbins." He answers on the third ring. "It's Evan. I need to talk to Ryan before the police do." I see Coop frowning at me. "Why?"

"It's about Jerry Fuller. I just gave my statement. I need to clear up something with Ryan. I think he knows what it is."

"Hang on," Robbins says. I picture him pressing the hold button, talking to Ryan. Two minutes later, he's back. "Ryan's not sure what you mean. The police are coming at three so get here before then."

"On the way." I hang up before Robbins can change his mind.

We get to Robbins' Century City office in record time. His secretary shows us right in. Robbins is at his desk. Ryan is sprawled on a couch nearby. He jumps up and gives me a hearty greeting, and a brief hug, as if we're in on something together. "Bad scene, man, fucking cops hassling us again." He glances at Coop. "No offense."

"None taken." Coop sits down on one of the chairs facing the couch. The late afternoon sun streams in the windows and casts slender shadows across Ryan's face.

Robbins gets up and comes around his desk. "What's this about, Evan?" He sits down on the couch next to Ryan, and points to a sideboard. "That's fresh coffee if you want."

I pour myself a mug and sit down opposite Ryan and Robbins. "Detective Farrell asked me a lot of questions about Jerry Fuller."

"Yeah, tragic thing," Ryan says, but he's not very convincing and he doesn't meet my eyes. "Do they have any leads?"

"I didn't know how to answer some of his questions, so you need to know what I told him."

"I don't understand. What do you mean?"

"You did know Jerry Fuller, right?"

Ryan shrugs. "I knew of him. He was kind on the fringe but another of those paparazzi freaks."

"You knew more than that. I think you hired him to test me, that day on the beach road, just like you did with the swimming stunt."

Ryan laughs but it's a hollow, nervous sound. His eyes flick to Robbins and Coop, who are both watching him now. He finally wilts under Coop's gaze. He sits up and heaves a great sigh. "Okay, you got me."

Robbins looks away and shakes his head. "Oh, for God's sake."

"You knew him for some time. You were friends."

Ryan just nods. "Yeah I knew him. We were in high school together, then we lost track of each other."

"Pretty hard for him to lose track of you," Coop says. "All he had to do was pick up a copy of *People Magazine*."

Ryan shrugs. "Is it my fault I got famous?" He leans forward on the couch, his eyes on the floor. "I saw him once, taking pictures. I said hello, how you doing. That kind of thing. I told him to call me sometime and we'd get together."

"Like one of those, let's-do-lunch, Hollywood kind of things," Coop says.

Ryan ignores that. "He was hard up for cash. I was doing him a favor, so I asked him to check you out. You know how I am about security. But he wanted more. He kept coming back."

Robbins stands and begins pacing, agitated, trying to control his anger. "Why would you hire him to test Evan? Hadn't you already done that enough?"

"I don't care about it now. It's history, but the cops are going to ask you about Fuller and check it against my statement." I nod to Coop, who takes over.

"There were a lot of photos of you and Fuller in his trailer, and some are not just done with telephoto lenses. Some make the two of you look pretty friendly. Think about your answers carefully. I know it's a hard concept to wrap your mind around, but when Farrell questions you, tell the truth."

Ryan jumps to his feet. "Okay, Grant. That's enough. I want him fired. I don't need this shit from a cop who works for me." He points at Coop. "You're done."

"Sit down, Ryan," Robbins says. "For starters, Lieutenant Cooper works for me. He's making sense and so is Evan. You're lucky they came by with this information. You have a solid alibi, but don't try to finesse things with the police when you're interviewed."

"They will turn Jerry Fuller's life inside-out trying to solve this," Coop adds. "You leave something out now, they'll come back on you later and it won't be good. Don't volunteer anything, but don't withhold anything either. And don't underestimate Farrell. He's an old pro."

Ryan falls silent while Robbins has me recount the essence of my statement and cautions Ryan to pay attention.

"I couldn't tell Farrell you knew Fuller because I didn't know for sure. I only suspected you hired him to check me out, but you had to know him to do that. That probably won't even come up, right?" I turn to Coop for confirmation.

"No reason it should."

Robbins makes some notes on a pad at his desk, then turns to Coop. "I hope you'll accept my apology and Ryan's."

Ryan looks up. "Sorry," he chimes in, but with little enthusiasm.

Robbins says, "The strain of the movie, and now this, has made us all a little tense."

"Forget it," Coop says. "A murder of someone you knew will do that."

Robbins gives a little shudder. "God, a Nikon camera strap. It's too horrible to think about."

"Is that really how it happened?" Ryan asks. His eyes flick from mine to Coop's.

"Looks like it," Coop says.

Robbins checks his watch. "You two better get out of here. It won't look good if Farrell sees us all together." He grips my hand. "Again, Evan, thanks so much for clueing us in."

He walks us to the door and Coop and I head for the elevator. "First time I've ever been fired by a movie star," Coop says.

"Yeah, and rehired by a producer."

"Ain't show business grand," Coop says.

When Coop drops me back at the hotel, the manager catches my eye as I head for the elevator. "A Miss Lawrence has arrived. As per your instructions, I allowed her a key." He gives a discreet wink.

I'd told him earlier that Andie might take a cab from the airport. I lean in closer. "Thanks. It's okay. She's with the FBI."

In my room, I see Andie's bag and some clothes strewn on the bed. I hear water splashing and follow the sound to the bathroom. Andie looks up and smiles, all but submerged in a bubble bath. One tiny bubble is stuck to her nose. "Hey, cowboy."

"Hey yourself."

"I'll be out soon." She slides down deeper in the bath.

"I'll be waiting." I kick off my shoes, stretch out on the bed, and turn on CNN to see if there are any new updates on Jerry Fuller's murder, but I can't keep my eyes open. I doze off for a few minutes and when I open my eyes again, Andie is standing at the foot of the bed, a thick, white terry cloth hotel robe wrapped around her body. Her face is flushed from the bath and her skin glows.

She crawls up on the bed till she's right over me, and presses her lips on mine. "Miss me?" The robe falls open. I inhale her scent from the bath. She runs her hand down my leg. "Mmm, I can see you did." She feels me through my jeans. "You know I've never made love to a film composer."

"Maybe it's time you did."

Later, we lie together, her head on my chest. I catch her up on everything. How the music is going, my statement to the police, the meeting with Ryan and Grant Robbins.

"And?" She raises up on one elbow and looks at me.

"I don't know. There's something I'm missing, something somebody said but I can't remember what it is."

"You don't think Ryan did it, do you?"

"No. He has a solid alibi. He and Melanie were having dinner with Robbins when it happened."

She slides off the bed and slips on the robe. She brings us both a bottle of water from the mini-bar. "Take a little nap while I change. I need to pick up a few things. Want to go down the mall?"

"Sure, take your time."

A half hour later, she's shaking me. "Come on, sleepy. Let's go for a walk."

We leave the hotel and walk over to Third Street to the Santa Monica Mall. The street has long been closed to traffic, but as we pass the Criterion Theater, memories of cruising here on Friday nights when I was in high school fill my mind.

At the mall, we split up and decide to meet at the food court in an hour. I wander around, my mind still trying for that elusive thought. I beat Andie to the busy food court and grab a coffee, strolling around the adjacent shops. I stop in front of a camera store. A huge display of cameras and video recorders fill the window. Everything from tiny digital cameras to expensive ones with telephoto lenses.

"Thinking of buying a camera?" I turn as I hear Andie's voice behind me. She has a large shopping bag in her hand. "How about an expensive Nikon? You have a birthday coming up."

"Me? I can barely operate a little point-and-shoot digital. Get everything you need?"

"Yep, all set. How about a snack? I'm in the mood for a burrito."

I find us a table and wait for Andie. She comes back with a burrito, fries, and a coke. "I feel so decadent." She sits down, takes a big bite of the burrito, and sprinkles salt over the fries. "Mmmm, sex and food. Can't beat it."

When I don't answer, she looks at me. "Something still bothering you?"

I gaze across at the camera store. "What did you say when we were over there?"

Her eyes follow my gaze, then back to her burrito as she slathers it with hot sauce. "I don't know. Something about an expensive Nikon? Why?"

I set my coffee cup down. "Camera strap."

"What?"

"Jerry Fuller was strangled with a camera strap."

"Yeah, you told me already."

"I told Grant Robbins, too."

"So?"

"In his office today, he made some comment."

Andie sets her burrito down and looks at me. "What are you getting at? What did he say?"

"Robbins said, 'God, a Nikon camera strap. It's too horrible to think about.'" I look at Andie. "I never told him it was Nikon."

"Are you sure?"

"Of course I'm sure."

Andie puts her hand on my arm. "Maybe it was in one of the news stories. You know how fast things get out now."

"No, I'm sure it wasn't. At least not on any report I've seen. The first was just that photographer Jerry Fuller was found dead. The police suspect foul play. There were no details, nothing about him being strangled, much less with one of his own camera straps. The brand name would be irrelevant."

"But didn't you say Robbins was having dinner with Ryan and Melanie?"

"Yeah he did."

"There have been other reports. Maybe some enterprising reporter found out and added the name."

"I hope that's true."

"Anyway, why would Grant Robbins kill Jerry Fuller?"

"I don't know. To protect Ryan maybe. Or himself." I stand up. "Come on, I want to run this by Coop."

"Okay, tell me again." Coop is sprawled on one of the easy chairs, sipping a sparkling water from the mini-bar, his feet propped up on the edge of the bed.

I'd called him and got him to come by the hotel. I remind him of Robbins' comment about the Nikon camera strap.

"I remember," he says, "but I wasn't really paying attention. What do you want me to do?"

"Check with Farrell, see if the police released that information to the press."

He drags his feet off the bed and leans forward, running his hands through his short-cropped hair. "That could be tricky."

"Why?"

"I have a certain amount of leeway with Charlie Farrell because we're old friends, and I was first on the scene and discovered the body, but he's a serious cop. He'll get suspicious if I ask him that. He'll want to know why I'm asking, and be all over Grant Robbins in a minute. We don't want to spook him until we know something for sure. If you're right—we don't know that you are yet—we don't want to give him time to cover his tracks."

I sigh and look away, glancing over at Andie lying on her side on the bed, her head propped in her hand.

"Coop's right. There's got to be another way. Besides, what motive does Robbins have to kill Jerry Fuller?"

"Precisely," Coop says. "If anybody has motive it's our movie star friend."

I shake my head. "No, Ryan can be an arrogant, insensitive, self-centered prick, but he's not a killer. Maybe Robbins was protecting Ryan. He has a huge investment there."

"Maybe," Coop says, "but protect him from what? Robbins doesn't strike me as capable either. He's got too much at stake with Ryan to risk something like this."

"What if Fuller knew something more about Darryl McElroy's death, something that never came out?" Andie asks.

"Stiles was fully cleared on that," Coop says.

Andie sits up and swings her feet on the floor. "There's something else you're forgetting. If you point Farrell to Robbins, he'll know it was you who gave him up."

Coop watches me for a moment. "I didn't want to go there, but what she means is you could put yourself in danger, too." He and Andie exchange glances. "Look, as of now, if Stiles and Robbins' alibi holds, neither had opportunity. Show me a motive that makes sense."

"So we just forget it? Do nothing."

"I didn't say that. You raise a legitimate point. We need to check all the news stories, TV reports that have come out since Fuller's murder to see if anybody mentioned that the camera strap was Nikon."

I know they're both making sense, and their combined experience far exceeds mine, but I can't let go of the thought. I know what I heard Robbins say. It was either a slip of the tongue or he heard it somewhere. Or, he was there.

"I can do that," Andie says. "It's all on the internet by now."

Coop nods. "Good. I'll see what I can do with Charlie Farrell. He'll at least expect me to ask about the progress of the case. I'll just have to be careful about what and how I ask. I can't just say, 'hey, Charlie, did you tell anybody the camera strap was a Nikon?'"

"What if he didn't and I'm right?"

"I'll be the first to point Farrell at Grant Robbins."

Chapter Twenty-four

I finish my call and toss the phone on the bed.

"Who was that?" Andie calls over the sound of the hairdryer.

I walk to the bathroom. "Ryan. He wants us to have lunch with him and Melanie in Malibu?" I stand in the doorway, watching her in the mirror.

She turns off the dryer and frowns. She's just out of the shower, running her fingers through her hair. "I'm not sure I want to do that."

"C'mon, it'll be a chance for you and Melanie to catch up, and what could be better than a meal cooked by Emillio?"

She stops drying her hair and looks at me. "Lunch by Emillio without Ryan." She turns away from the mirror. "Why are you so anxious?"

Good question, but I'd been thinking about it. Spending a little time with Ryan away from film sets, directors, lawyers, maybe I could get him to talk. It was worth a try. "Just a feeling that he wants to tell me something with nobody around."

Andie sighs. "Okay, but just lunch. No being talked into staying the rest of the weekend."

"Absolutely not. Couple of hours and we're out of there. They're shooting some night scenes later anyway."

Andie smiles and kisses my cheek. "I hope you appreciate all the things I do for you."

"Should I make a list?"

◇◇◇

Emillio answers the door and breaks into a big grin when he sees Andie. "My favorite FBI agent." He hugs her. "So good to see you again."

"You too, Emillio. What's cooking today?" She sniffs the air. "I smell something good."

"Something very special. Come in, come in."

He leads us to the dining room where Ryan and Melanie are waiting. Ryan immediately stands and puts his hands up. "Honest, Special Agent Lawrence, I didn't do it." He laughs and gives Andie a peck on the cheek.

Andie rolls her eyes and turns to Melanie. She seems genuinely pleased to see Andie. The two women hug and greet each other warmly, and we all sit down. "I'm so glad you could come," Melanie says. "It's been so long."

We talk about the movie's progress and everybody pointedly avoids any talk about Jerry Fuller. Emillio appears with a bottle of chilled white wine, then returns after a quick trip to the kitchen with four bowls, the steam still rising from them.

"Lobster bisque," he says, placing a bowl in front of each of us with an exaggerated flourish.

"Oh, my God," Andie says. She leans over to inhale the aroma. "Emillio, you are a wonder."

We get through the bisque, which is followed by marinated chicken fillets, wild rice, and asparagus, lightly coated in olive oil. If that isn't enough, coffee comes with crème brulee. Ryan is strangely quiet when we all ooh and ahh over the meal. I catch him watching me a few times and know there's something else on his mind.

Melanie and Andie are deep in conversation when I get up. "I'm going out for a smoke. Want to leave the girls to it?"

Ryan nods eagerly. We go out and down the steps to the beach. There's a light wind and the sky is overcast. The ocean is flat, a dull gray out to the horizon.

"No surfing today," Ryan says as we walk up the beach toward an outcropping of rocks that extend out to the water's edge. We sit on one of the biggest rocks and watch the waves gently lap against the shore.

I light a cigarette and wait for Ryan. He stares out at the ocean, then finally turns to me.

"There's something I have to tell you."

"I thought there was something on your mind. Go ahead."

"It's about Jerry Fuller. I didn't want to bring it up around Melanie and Andie." His head drops a little, his eyes on the sand. "You're not going to like this."

"Try me. What about Jerry Fuller?"

"I haven't told you everything. I haven't told anybody everything, even my mother. It's about McElroy too."

"What about McElroy?"

Ryan looks at me. "Give me a break, man. This is hard to say."

I just nod, watching his obvious discomfort. A famous, multimillionaire movie star who has everything. A face known throughout the world now contorted in obvious conflict with himself.

"I totally panicked that night. It was like I told the police, what I told my mother—almost."

"What do you mean, almost?"

"I know it was stupid, but when McElroy chased me on that damn motorcycle, I was really scared. It was dark and he had on a helmet. I couldn't see his face, but I knew he was laughing."

He sighs and looks up at the darkening sky. "As we came around a curve, he pulled in front of me, trying to cut me off. I thought he was going to run me off the road, but he lost control of the bike and bam, just like that he was gone." He pounds his fist into the palm of his hand. "Over the embankment. I stopped and went back and looked over the side. It was too dark to really see anything."

"That's pretty much what you told your mother."

"Yeah it is, but I left out something."

"What? This isn't new."

"I told you I panicked. I didn't know what to do. Call the police, report an accident. I wasn't thinking about anything except how it would look after the scene with him at the Anchor." He turns to look at me now. "I pulled my car off the road and called Jerry Fuller."

"Why?"

"I needed help, someone I could trust. I've known—knew— Jerry a long time. Luckily, I caught him at home and he came right out. He was there in twenty minutes. He got in my car and I told him what had happened. He listened then got out of the car and looked over the embankment where McElroy went over. I sat in my car, terrified somebody would come along, wondering what I would do if the Highway Patrol came by."

I watch him, seeing him almost relive that night, and knew what was coming.

"Jerry got back in my car and told me to go home. He said he'd call 911 and report the accident, and stay around until the police got there. It was an accident," Ryan emphasizes. "Jerry said he would take care of everything."

"Did he?"

"What?"

"Stay around until police arrived."

"Yeah, I guess so. He wasn't worried. Nobody could connect him with me. He was just a good citizen reporting an accident."

I feel a surge of anger. "Like you should have done."

Ryan nods. "Yeah, yeah, like I should have done. I promised him anything he wanted and all he said was, 'don't worry, we'll work it out.' I got out of there fast and went to my folks and, well, you know the rest."

"Let me guess. Fuller wanted more than you wanted to give." I wonder then if Fuller welcomed the opportunity to have Ryan in his debt.

Ryan nods. "He wanted money, which I was happy to give him, but he wanted more, an exclusive interview, photos, the whole nine yards. I realized then, it would never be over."

Ryan gets up and paces around a bit then stands, his foot on the rock, and shoves his hands in the pockets of his jeans. "I couldn't do that. Too many people would wonder why I was giving Jerry Fuller, an unknown, total access,. Especially Grant, who handles all the requests for interviews. He didn't know I knew Jerry from way back."

"So what happened?"

"When I refused, offered him more money, he just laughed and said it was going to take more than that and someday I would pay. I just blew him off. I didn't hear anymore from him until we started the movie. When the e-mails and phone calls started, I knew it was Jerry, and I panicked again."

"And then, Jerry Fuller is conveniently found dead."

His head snaps around. "Jesus, man, I didn't have anything to do with that. I could never kill anyone. You think I could strangle someone with a camera strap?"

"What kind of camera strap?"

Ryan looks at me, incredulous. "What kind of strap? How the fuck would I know? What kind of question is that? What difference does it make?"

Inwardly, I breathe a sigh of relief. "None I guess. Anything else?"

"Christ, isn't that enough?"

I let him settle down a bit. "You know if this ever comes out you'll be a prime suspect."

"You think I don't worry about that every day?" He sits down again and puts his head in his hands. He looks drained.

We all make choices. Sometimes those choices change our lives. Ryan made his that night on Malibu Canyon, as did Darryl McElroy by chasing after Ryan. And it cost him his life. If Ryan's choice had been to face the consequences instead of calling an old acquaintance, he might have seen his name in the tabloids for a couple of weeks, and Jerry Fuller might still be alive.

"Ryan, why tell me about this? What is it you want me to do?"

"Just one thing. If this ever comes up, just tell the police exactly what I told you."

"You know I can't withhold anything if I'm questioned."

"I know that. I wouldn't ask you to."

We sit for a few more minutes. I run over everything Ryan told me. What he had done was not right, but I didn't believe he'd killed Jerry Fuller. "Come on, let's go back up to the house."

Andie and Melanie are still talking, but they stop and look up when we come into the house.

"We thought you got lost," Melanie says. I can see she's trying to gauge Ryan's mood.

Andie signals me with her eyes. I glance at my watch. "We need to get going," I say. "Andie has to check in with her office, and I've got some more music to get to."

We say our goodbyes to Emillio, and Ryan and Melanie walk us out to the car.

Ryan gives me one final look and touches my shoulder. "Thanks, man. I mean it." He turns and goes back in the house. I wonder if he's going to tell Melanie or if he already has.

We get in the car and Melanie waves her goodbye. "Not so long till next time."

We get back on the Coast Highway and head back to Santa Monica. "You first," Andie says.

I briefly sketch over what Ryan told me. "Not good, not good at all. Do you believe him?"

"Yeah I do. How'd you do?"

"We had a nice girl talk. I worked my way around to the dinner with Grant Robbins."

"I won't even ask how you managed to bring that up."

"They did have an early dinner with Robbins the night Fuller was killed, some Italian place in the Valley. But Robbins made some excuse about something he forgot and left early."

I turn to look at Andie. "When did he come back?"

"He didn't."

◇◇◇

Back at the hotel, Andie fires up her laptop and starts searching for stories about Fuller's murder. I go out on the balcony to think things over again. A lot now depends on what, if any-thing, Andie finds, and what time the dinner was, what time Robbins left the restaurant, and most importantly, the time of Fuller's death. That's probably something Coop could coax out of Charlie Farrell, as well as if there were any fingerprints in the trailer other than Fuller's.

As I'm thinking about all this, my phone rings. It's Grant Robbins.

"Evan, how's it going?"

"Fine. Andie and I had lunch with Ryan at Melanie in Malibu."

"Oh? Some special occasion?"

"No, not really. Just nice to get away from the movie I guess, and Melanie was anxious to see Andie again. They've gotten pretty friendly."

"Of course, I forgot." He seems relieved at my explanation, and quickly changes the subject. "I just spoke with Skip Porter. He says everything is coming along fine with the music. He's pretty impressed with you."

"He's been a great help with the technical things. I wouldn't be able to finish without Skip's help."

"That's good to hear. We're shooting some scenes later tonight. If all goes well Sandy Simmons says we should have a full rough cut by early next week. Skip sent over a CD of what you've done so far, and he's very pleased."

"That's even better to hear."

"Ever seen a film without music? It's pretty amazing the impact the music has. You'll see when you sit down with Sandy and go through the whole film."

"I'm really looking forward to that."

"I know you are. Okay, then, just thought I'd check in with you. Let me know if you need anything."

"I will. Oh there is one thing. Melanie was raving about the restaurant you took them to the other night. She said the food was great. I thought Andie and I might try it. She couldn't remember the name, just that it was in the Valley somewhere."

The words are barely out of my mouth when I think this could backfire if Robbins mentions it to Melanie.

"Mario's Pasta House. Best Italian in the West Valley. It's in Woodland Hills, just off Ventura."

"Great. Thanks."

"Let me know if you decide to go. I have a little pull with the manager."

"I'm sure you do."

I hang up and go back inside. Andie is still hard at it.

"Nothing yet, but it's all over the internet. I checked CNN and MSNBC clips. Nobody mentions the camera strap so far."

"Well, keep at it."

"All night if I have to."

I put in a call to Coop. It goes to voice mail but he calls back in fifteen minutes. "What's on your mind?"

"We had lunch in Malibu with Ryan and Melanie."

"Is she still beautiful as ever?"

"You had to ask?"

"You could have invited me."

"Not for this one. Ryan did a little confessing. I'll tell you about it over dinner. Can you get away?"

"I can't wait. I have some interesting tidbits from Charlie Farrell, too. Where?"

"Mario's Pasta House in Woodland Hills. You know it?"

"I'll find it. Why there?"

"That's where Ryan and Melanie and Robbins had dinner."

"See you in an hour."

I tell Andie to order room service if she gets hungry, but she's in the zone and barely looks up from her computer.

I beat Coop to Mario's by ten minutes. I get a booth, menus, water, and order a Scotch rocks. It's one of those places that doesn't look like much from the outside, but the interior is warm and homey. Even at this early hour it's fairly crowded. Waiters buzz about with large plates of pasta on trays, and everybody seems happy.

Halfway through my drink, I spot Coop and wave. He comes over and slides into the booth and looks around. "How un-L.A.," he says. "Not even valet parking. Little downscale for a movie star and a producer."

A waiter comes over and hovers impatiently as Coop scans the menu. "Can I interest you gentlemen in a nice bottle of house red?"

"Just coffee for me," Coop says.

"I'll stick with this," I say, holding up my glass. "I'm not eating."

Coop smiles. "I am. Small Caesar salad and sausage and peppers over angel hair."

"Very good."

"Oh, one other thing. Could you send the manager to our table?"

The waiter hesitates for just a moment. "Of course," he rushes off.

"Might as well get this over first," Coop says. He sips his water and looks around. "Popular place."

"Here we go." A short stocky man with graying hair, wearing an expensive-looking sports jacket approaches our booth and gives us a well-practiced smile.

"I trust everything is okay?" He looks from me to Coop, his hands clasped in front of him. "Anthony Torino at your service."

"Just fine," Coop says. "I just need a word with you. Say, I like your jacket. Is that Armani? Why don't you sit down for a minute."

Torino almost smirks. "Hardly. It's a knockoff. I hope you're not the fashion police." He makes a show of buttoning the jacket.

Coop takes out his badge. "No, we're the real police. Lieutenant Cooper, Santa Monica Division. I'm hoping you can help me out."

Coop slides around to make room. Torino's expression quickly changes. He glances over his shoulder and sits down, eyeing Coop warily. "I hope there's nothing wrong."

"No, nothing to worry about, just routine. Do you know Ryan Stiles and Grant Robbins?"

"Yes, of course. Mr. Robbins is one of our regular customers. Why?"

"They had dinner here the other night, with a tall stunning blonde."

Torino smiles. "Yes, the lovely Miss Hammond." His eyes flick to me then back to Coop.

"I bet you attended to them personally."

"Yes, I did. As I always do. Mr. Robbins is an old friend."

"Do you remember what time their reservation was for?"

"I believe it was seven o'clock. I could check to make sure."

"I'd appreciate that," Coop says. "While you're at it, any chance you have a record of their visit, who paid, a credit card slip, maybe?"

"Yes, certainly, just give me a minute." He gets up and scurries off just as Coop's salad and a small plate of bread sticks arrives.

"I like it when people are cooperative." He starts on the salad.

Five minutes later, Torino returns with a stack of credit card slips. He sits down and flips through them quickly, then pulls one out and hands it to Coop, who glances at it quickly, then lays it on the table next to his plate.

"I'll need to take this with me. Thanks so much. That's all I need."

Torino gets up, a little puzzled. "Please enjoy your dinner. If you need anything else, please let me know."

Coop continues with his salad and slides the slip across to me. It's for a Visa card with a date and time stamp showing 8:20 pm in the amount of $138.72. Coop doesn't even look up.

"He didn't stay long, did he?" Coop takes the last bite of salad and pushes his plate away. "Charlie Farrell says the Medical Examiner estimates time of death sometime between nine and midnight, give or take."

"Plenty of time for Robbins to take care of things. Fuller's trailer is not far from here."

"I did note that. When we leave here, we can drive over and see how long it takes."

While Coop wolfs down the sausage and pasta, I give him a shortened version of Ryan's confession to me. He listens, nods at the appropriate places, then pushes his plate aside, pats his stomach, and signals a waiter for more coffee.

"How's Andie doing on the internet search?"

"She's working on it now. She hadn't found anything when I left."

"If she does, with this credit card slip, Robbins will have some explaining to do."

"I've been thinking. Even with this, it just seems too pat, too easy."

"Don't complain. Sometimes that's how it works. There are plenty of tough ones."

As we leave the restaurant, I spot Torino on the phone at the reservations desk. When he see us he gives a little wave, then turns away and cups his hand over the mouthpiece.

"I wonder who he's talking to," Coop says.

"Probably some big Hollywood player."

Coop drops me off at the hotel after we drive from Mario's to Jerry Fuller's trailer. It takes all of seventeen minutes.

"So what's next?"

"I'm going to take another run at Charlie Farrell, and see if he'll let me have another look in Fuller's trailer. Want to join me?"

"What are you looking for?"

"I'm not sure yet. I'll know when I find it."

I get out of the car. "I'll let you know if Andie finds anything."

"Do that," Coop says. He smiles.

"What?"

"I was just thinking. It'll be kind of strange if my employer is arrested for murder."

"Even stranger if you make the arrest."

"No, that'll be Charlie Farrell's collar."

I go up to my room. There's a tray with a plate and the remnants of a hamburger and fries on the floor by the door. Inside,

I find Andie sprawled on the bed in her robe, watching *China Town*. I slip off my shoes and stretch out alongside her.

She yawns and curls up against me. "How was Mario's?"

"Very Italian. Robbins' reservation was for seven, and the time stamp on the credit card slip was eight twenty. It takes seventeen minutes to drive from Mario's to Fuller's trailer park. We timed it. Time of death was between nine and midnight according to the Medical Examiner."

"So Robbins is looking better all the time."

"Yeah, but like I told Coop, it just seems all too perfect, too pat. Robbins is a lawyer, a smart guy, a major Hollywood player. Unless there's something else about him we don't know, I'm just not sure."

Andie sits up and throws one leg over me and straddles my waist. "Maybe we should look into Robbins' background, see if there's something that would explain a motive." Her robe has fallen open a bit. I reach up and pull it closed. "I need to concentrate. Find anything?"

"In a word, no. I've been through every story and there's no mention of a camera strap, much less a brand name."

I'm not that surprised. I can't remember a single news story or television report about a murder with that kind of detail. They never say the victim was shot with a Glock 9 mm or stabbed with a Shinzu knife. Later maybe, if the victim was famous, or a long magazine article is done months or years after the death.

"We could check local TV news but I don't think there's anything," Andie says. "The window on this is closing fast. Fuller was not famous. The interest is already waning. Another week and it'll be, 'who was Jerry Fuller?'"

"I think you're right. I'm tired of thinking about it."

"Good. You've still got some music to compose." She leans down and lightly kisses me. "All through concentrating?" She sits up and pulls her robe open.

"I am now."

Chapter Twenty-five

Monday morning, I drop Andie at Burbank Airport. "I'll try to do a little digging on Grant Robbins," she says, getting out of the car. She drags her carry-on bag around to the driver's side, and leans in to kiss me. "Good luck on the music. I don't know how you do it with all this other stuff going on." She studies me for a moment as people rush past the car. "Even more, I don't know why you're doing it."

I don't have an answer for that, and Andie doesn't expect one. She turns, waves once, and then slips into the terminal.

I head out of the airport, back to the Ventura Freeway and on to Skip Porter's. He had called earlier to confirm we were going to spend most of the day looking at new film. Traffic is still heavy so I have a lot of time to think as I remember Andie's comment. It is getting increasingly difficult to shift gears from a murder investigation that clearly might involve the very people I'm working for, and composing music and learning the ins and out of scoring a film. I've all but eliminated Ryan Stiles from the mix, but Grant Robbins is another story.

I can't reconcile his money, position, and status with a pre-meditated murder of someone I doubt he even knew. What could have been his motive? If it was to protect Ryan and the progress of the film, then he had to know about Jerry Fuller, and the only way he could know was if Ryan told him the whole story.

I have to remind myself that Ryan's the actor, not Robbins. In his office, when I'd got Ryan to admit he'd hired Fuller to check on me, Robbins had been genuinely surprised and angry at Ryan for doing it. Ryan's confession on the beach also seemed genuine. I knew him well enough to know the pain on his face as he unburdened himself was real, so that left Robbins who, maybe even more than Ryan, needed the film to go well. He had to answer to those investors who'd put up millions, and I'd bet Robbins had some of his own money in this project. Is that enough motive? That's one I don't have to answer. People had killed for far less.

But my mind keeps going back to Robbins' remark about the Nikon camera strap. Where had that come from? That's what I had to find out. If not Robbins, then who else? Melanie? No way. Somebody I hadn't thought of at all?

I'm still lost in thought when the car behind me honks. The heavy traffic is finally breaking up. I pull ahead and exit at the next off-ramp and wind my way to Skip Porter's. I park in the driveway and light a cigarette, trying to get focused on music, not Grant Robbins or Jerry Fuller's murder, but it only lasts for as long as it takes me to walk into Skip's house.

"Hey," he says. "Ready to go to work?"

"Very. Let's get to it."

"We'll have a visitor later. Grant Robbins called. He's coming by to see how it's going."

Perfect, I think as we start to work by going over the list of music cues. Some are brief motifs that last only a few seconds, some are more complete and last a few minutes, depending on the length of the scene. Skip plays them all and we watch as they match the on-screen action.

"Looks and sounds good to me," Skip says. "Got something in mind for the closing credits?"

I'd thought about that a lot. These days, nearly every movie ends with a complete song, while all the credits from the star to the catering truck driver scrolls by slowly on a black screen. I thought I had the perfect way to close out *Murder in Blue.*

"I'm thinking of a Chet Baker recording of 'My Foolish Heart.' Kind of fits with the story."

Skip grins. "Yeah, that would be perfect." He scrolls through a music database and pulls up several versions of the song. "Got a preference for year?"

"Yes, a later recording, something in his later years."

Skip nods, punches in the title, and downloads the track and then hits the "play" button. Chet Baker's airy tone fills the speakers and we both listen in silence to the emotional version that still gives me chills. I don't have to wonder about the choice. I just add it to the cue sheet.

"We'll have to get permissions, of course, but that shouldn't be a problem with this budget," Skip says. He saves the track and adds it to the master recording when my phone rings. I don't recognize the number. "Hello."

"Evan? It's Melanie. I'm so glad I caught you."

"What is it? Something wrong?"

"I'm not sure. Grant mentioned that you asked me about Mario's, you know, the restaurant where Ryan and I had dinner with him."

"Yeah. Melanie I didn't mean to put you in the middle of this."

"I didn't know what he meant at first. I tried to cover but I don't think I was very convincing."

"It's all right, Melanie. Don't worry about it."

She pauses. "That was the night Jerry Fuller was killed. Are you checking on Grant? Did he—"

"No, Melanie. It's just routine. I'm kind of helping out my friend Danny Cooper to establish where everyone was that night. Did Ryan talk to you about it?"

"No, I mean, very little. He said he knew Fuller, but he didn't say much. Do the police suspect Ryan?"

"No, not at all. I'm sure Ryan had nothing to do with it. He was with you, right?"

"Well, yeah. We stayed around after Grant left."

"When Grant left, what did he say?"

"He got a phone call and went outside to take it. When he came back, he apologized, said something had come up and he had to go."

"That was all?"

"Yes. God, Evan, is Grant a suspect?"

"I really don't know."

"I'm scared, Evan."

"Don't be. I'm sure Ryan had nothing to do with it. On an investigation like this the police routinely check out anybody the victim might have known, that's all."

I know she's not convinced. "Okay, but would you do me a favor? Let me know if you find out anything I should know about."

"Sure, no problem."

"All right. Well thanks. I should go. Ryan will be back soon. Goodbye."

"Bye, Melanie." I close my eyes and sigh, then notice Skip has taken off the phones and is looking at me.

"You okay, man?"

"Yeah, I'm fine." We both look up then as the doorbell rings.

"That's probably our guest." He gets up and goes to the door. He returns in a minute with Grant Robbins in tow.

"Hello, Evan. Hope I'm not interrupting the flow. Just thought I'd stop by and see how things are going." He looks at the monitor and the array of equipment. "Quite a setup you have here, Skip."

"Yeah, we do it all here. Want to see a few of the scenes? Evan's written some killer stuff."

Robbins looks at me and smiles. "I'm sure he has. That's why we hired him. Can we go outside for a minute, Evan? There's a couple of contract details I need to go over with you."

"Sure, I could use a smoke." I follow Robbins outside, leaving Skip a little confused.

Outside, Robbins gets right to it. "I mentioned to Melanie you had asked her about Mario's. I really don't think she knew what I was talking about."

I light a cigarette, trying to gather my thoughts. Robbins unbuttons his suit coat and fixes his gaze on me. "Maybe she forgot," is the best I can come up with.

"Evan, let's not play games. You and Cooper went there to check on me. Tony Torino already called me and said Cooper took the credit card slip with the time and date stamp. I told you I had pull with the manager."

"Look, Grant. I was with Coop, but as far as I know, it was just routine. Coop is helping out the investigating detective."

"Why? Be straight with me. Am I a suspect?"

"I don't know. Suspect is a little strong. Person of interest is more like it. You'd have to ask the police. If you were, they would already have questioned you."

"Detective Farrell did and I told him I was having dinner with Ryan and Melanie. Wasn't that enough?"

I shrug. "It must have been. He hasn't contacted you again, has he?"

"No, but I just want to know where I stand. I think I'm entitled to that."

"I'm not the one to tell you that. Detective Farrell hasn't shared his thoughts with me."

Robbins looks away, clearly annoyed. "We're almost finished with this film. I don't need anything hanging over us now. We're too close. I don't know anything about Jerry Fuller."

It takes all my will power to not ask him about the camera strap right then. "Well then, you have nothing to worry about."

"Okay, we'll leave it at that for now," he says. He glances at his watch. "I have to go. Tell Skip I think you're both doing a great job." He puts on sunglasses that probably cost more than the clothes I'm wearing. He turns then, walks to his car, gets in, and drives away.

Before I can go back inside, my phone rings. It's Coop.

"Hey, I've got some big news."

"So do I. Grant Robbins was just here, asking me if he was a suspect."

"Shit. What did he say?"

"I'll tell you later. We need to talk."

"Yes, we do. I have to be in court in Santa Monica at two but I can meet you some place at, say, four."

"Okay, I can get away by then. Working on the music here. Let's make it my hotel then. Andie's gone back to San Francisco."

Back inside, Skip is confused when I tell him Robbins has gone. "He said something came up and to tell you he trusts your judgment."

"Nice if he could tell me himself." Skip sits down and pops open a beer.

"How well do you know Robbins?"

Skip shrugs. "Not well. Limited contact on a couple of movies. Why?"

"Just curious." Skip looks like he's going to say more.

"Maybe just rumor, but the word on the street is he's having money troubles. Bad investments, taxes, that kind of thing."

I nod, making a mental note to have Andie or Coop to look into the producer's financial background if they can.

We work a couple of more hours, and despite all the distractions of the past few days, we have things under control. More importantly, I like what I've written. I have to admit, seeing, hearing how the music fits with the film is a very satisfying feeling.

"I'll get this to Sandy Simmons," Skip says. "As director he has final say, but I think he's going to like every note."

Coop is still in a coat and tie from his court appearance. He takes them both off and heads for the mini-bar, grabs a beer, and settles in one of the easy chairs. He pulls out a small, spiral bound notebook, and flips through the pages.

"You're going to love this," he begins. "Charlie Farrell let me see the ME's report on Fuller. Guess what cause of death was."

"We already know, don't we? He was strangled with a camera strap."

Coop studies me for a moment. "You were only in the trailer briefly. Besides Fuller's body, do you remember what was in the bedroom?"

I think for a minute, trying to picture the cramped bedroom. "The bed of course, small dresser, a chair, and a filing cabinet."

"Exactly. A tall, four-drawer, metal file cabinet."

"So what are you saying?"

"The crime techies found blood on a corner of the file cabinet. Pretty sharp corner, but that's not all. They determined the cause of death was the head wound."

"What? I don't understand. That means—"

"What the ME calls postmortem. When that camera strap was wrapped around Jerry Fuller's neck, he was already dead."

I stare at Coop for a moment, and sit down on the bed, trying to take this in. "Are they sure?"

"Oh yeah, there's no question. Charlie Farrell thinks there was a struggle, Fuller was pushed, fell back against the file cabinet, hit his head, and that was it. Most likely an accident. Certainly not premeditation. Then, the body was moved to the bed and made to look like he was strangled."

"But why? That makes no sense."

"That, my friend, is the big question. Maybe to complicate the crime scene. If you plan to kill somebody, you don't push them into something with a sharp corner and hope for the best. No, I think it was accidental, too, a argument, a struggle that got out of hand. The killer panics when he realizes Fuller is dead, but it was an accident. Depending on who it was, natural instinct would be to call 911, wait for the police to arrive, and accept the consequences. Lots of questions, like what was he doing there. There'd be an investigation, a trial, the whole process, which could mean going to jail."

Coop gets up and paces around. "Or, if it were a different kind of person, one who wants to avoid publicity and has a multi-million dollar project going, get out of there as fast as he can."

"Or he could have said, he came to see Fuller and found him dead."

Coop shakes his head. "But he didn't. Even if he had, there would still be a lot of questions to answer, and a headline like 'Hollywood producer found at death scene.' The press would start digging into Fuller's background and eventually make the connection to Stiles."

"Okay, so why didn't he just run?"

Coop presses on as if he hasn't heard me. "Instead, he moves the body to the bed, looks around, grabs the first thing he sees—a camera strap—tries to make it look planned, something nobody would think this person, whoever he is, would be capable of."

"Making him the least likely suspect."

"Exactly."

I pace around the room trying to digest Coop's theory, the ME's report. "I don't know, Coop, that's a big stretch isn't it?"

"For now, a big stretch is all there is."

"So where does that leave Robbins?" He might have killed Fuller accidentally, but there was still the mention of the camera strap. "By the way he knows we were at Mario's. Torino told him. Robbins came out to see me today, to let me know that he knows you got the time stamp on the credit card slip from their dinner."

"Doesn't really matter," Coop says.

"Why not?"

"When Robbins left Mario's, he had some kind of alleged car trouble, and of course he didn't want to get his hands dirty or muss his expensive suit, so he called Torino, who called a garage. It's all documented by the tow truck driver."

"Farrell verified all this?" Coop looks up at me and raises his eyebrows. "Okay, of course he did. It's just that—"

"It's too well-covered?"

"Yes." I sit down again. "I can see Robbins confronting Fuller, pushing him, cracking his head on the file cabinet. But moving the body, trying to make it look like Fuller had been murdered? I don't buy it."

"Neither does Charlie Farrell. Neither do I, but we both like Robbins for this. But there's no physical evidence at the scene to link Robbins. I've told Farrell as much as I know about Robbins, but you know him better than either of us. You've been working with him, spending time, since that first night at the Jazz Bakery when he offered you this job."

I nod, thinking I know where Coop is going. "You're looking for a way to pressure him, get him to break down and confess."

"Yes. Any ideas you can think of."

"Robbins is big on control, that's his thing. The press, the media, Ryan, all aspects of the movie."

"Don't forget yourself."

"I haven't." Like it or not, Robbins had manipulated and, to an extent, controlled me.

"I know this is a big thing to ask, but Farrell and I agree this could do it."

"What?"

"Push his buttons, get him shaken, off guard. Stiles caved and told you everything. We think Robbins might too under certain circumstances." Coop takes a deep breath. "We want you to threaten to quit, pull out. Tell Grant Robbins you're not comfortable continuing, it's just gotten too complicated for you."

Coop sits down again. "Tell him you're not going to finish doing the music."

For a long time after Coop leaves, I sit out on the balcony, smoking, sipping a beer, gazing at the lights of Santa Monica Pier, and running everything through my mind until I'm dizzy. So much has happened since that night months ago at the Jazz Bakery when Grant Robbins offered me a job.

And now, given all the information Coop and Charlie Farrell have gathered, everything seems to point to Grant Robbins. As Coop said, it's a very strong circumstantial case but not enough to get an arrest. The District Attorney would want more, and more meant one thing: Robbins' confession. It suddenly strikes me as ironic. Even if Robbins had killed Fuller accidentally, as it most certainly seemed, he had done almost the same thing Ryan had done about Darryl McElroy's death.

Instead of calling 911, Ryan had panicked, got Jerry Fuller to cover for him, and left the scene as soon as he could. Robbins had done the same. But he didn't have a Jerry Fuller to call to cover for him. Or did he? I try to visualize the scene. He confronts Fuller, they get into a shoving match, and suddenly the photographer is on the floor dead. Horrified, who does Robbins know who could and would come out to Fuller's trailer and make it look like a murder? Suddenly, I think I know—and how Robbins knew about the camera strap as well.

I go back in the room and dial Coop's number. "All right, I'll do it."

"As long as you're sure," Coop says.

"I am. I just figured out something else, too."

"What?"

"I'll tell you after I talk to Robbins."

Chapter Twenty-six

I wake up early, no less sure of my decision. I get things underway by calling Skip Porter. "Hey, Skip, it's Evan. I'm not going to be able to make it today. Something has come up."

"Whoa, man, we still have a lot to do. I have to edit the last bit of music and Simmons called. He's going to wrap this week. He wants to see everything you've done."

"I know, but this can't wait. Put it all on me, Skip, especially if Robbins calls. I'll be in touch." I hang up before he can argue about it anymore.

I drop one of the coffee pouches into the room machine and check my watch. Robbins calls before I can pour the first cup. "Evan? It's Grant. Skip Porter just called and said you weren't working today. What's wrong?"

I take a deep breath. "It's just getting too much, Grant. There are too many distractions."

"What are you talking about? What distractions?"

"Ryan, Darryl McElroy, and Jerry Fuller to start with."

There's a long pause before Robbins continues. "I think we need to get together and talk, Evan."

"Yes, I think so, too. Let's meet somewhere this morning."

"I can do that. Where?"

"Venice Beach. There's a café along the boardwalk. Cleo's."

"I'll find it. When?"

"Ten o'clock."

Before I leave, I call Coop and tell him where I'm meeting Robbins.

"I'll be nearby. And remember, you're not a cop. You don't have to read him his rights. Just get him talking. Watch yourself."

I get to Cleo's a half hour early, take one of the outside tables, and order some breakfast. It's a bit cool this morning, but hazy sunshine is starting to break through the clouds, and the smell of the ocean is very strong.

A minute after ten, I spot Robbins coming up the boardwalk, dodging tourists and locals already out in droves. It's only the second time I've seen Robbins not in a suit and tie. He's wearing gray slacks and a dark sweater, looking annoyed at being bumped by people in all manner of dress. When he sees me, he looks around and takes a seat opposite me.

"Some breakfast? The food is good here. I used to live nearby."

Robbins shakes his head and signals the waiter for coffee. He waits for it to arrive then looks at me. "All right, what's this all about, Evan?"

I'd rehearsed what I was going to say. Once I get started it comes easily. "I'm dropping out, Grant. I'm not going to finish the music."

Robbins, about to take his first taste of coffee, stops the cup in midair. "You're what?" He sits the cup down hard in the saucer and some coffee splashes out. "Do I have to remind you you're under contract? You've been paid, and very well, I might add, for someone who has never scored a movie. You can't just walk away."

"Not enough to cover babysitting a spoiled brat movie star and being questioned by the police on two different occasions concerning two deaths."

"Is that what this is about? You want more money?" Robbins shakes his head and smiles, thinking he's on safe ground. For Robbins, money can solve anything. "I know it hasn't been easy. Nobody could have anticipated what happened with Ryan and the McElroy thing, but that's all in the past. It was all cleared up."

I look right at Robbins. "The McElroy thing, as you put it, was an accident. Jerry Fuller's death has not been cleared up, and that wasn't an accident. That was a homicide, and I decided I don't like working for somebody who may be the prime suspect."

"What are you talking about?" Robbins shifts in his chair and colors slightly. I see the first crack in his armor. "I've already been questioned by the police, and I have a solid alibi for the night of Fuller's death."

"Yes, I know. Dinner with Ryan and Melanie at Mario's, but I know some other things, too. I know you had a little car trouble when you left Mario's after that phone call, and I know it's only seventeen minutes' drive to Fuller's trailer."

Robbins face goes white. "Car trouble, phone call? How did you—"

"The police know all about it. Anyway, that's your business, not mine. I don't want to be involved in a homicide investigation. I've been there, done that. Get somebody else to finish the music. As of right now, I'm out." I light a cigarette and watch Robbins squirm.

Robbins stares at me for a moment, then slams his fist down on the table. "You can't do that. There's no time to get somebody else. The movie is almost done. Simmons is ready to do a final cut. He loves the music you've done. If you go, he might bail out, too. That would mean bringing in another director and…"

"Is this where you tell me I'll never work in this town again? I don't care about the contract or the money. Sue me, I don't need a contract to play piano." I watch him suddenly contemplating the numerous problems my quitting would bring. He changes tactics and leans forward, resting his elbows on the table, his head in his hands. "Evan, there's a lot of money tied up in this project, a lot of money. Some of it my own. I could be ruined if this picture isn't finished on schedule."

I gaze across the beach toward the ocean. I can hear the light sound of the surf even from here. "I know that, Grant, but I'm tired of being lied to."

He doesn't look at me for a couple of minutes. Then, as if deciding something, he leans forward and meets my eyes. "How much do you know?"

"More than enough to make me want to quit and go home."

"It wasn't a homicide."

"How do you know that?"

He looks around and lowers his voice. "I was there." He shrugs. "I thought, well, I don't know what I thought. Fuller's e-mails and phone calls were getting to Ryan, starting to affect his performance. I thought I could fix things. Please try to understand the pressure I was under."

"I can only imagine."

"No, I don't think you can." He looks around. Tables are filling up around us. "Can we get out of here?"

"Sure. Let's take a walk." I signal the waiter for the check, and leave money on the table. We get up and start to walk along the asphalt path that cuts through the sand and runs all the way to Santa Monica Pier. There are more people now, some walking, some on roller skates, bicycles, even a skateboard or two.

"I knew Fuller had tried to get more money out of Ryan. Ryan just told me to fix it. That's what he always says. 'Fix it, Grant,' like I'm some kind lackey. He finally told me about the night on Malibu Canyon and getting Fuller to cover for him. That was the first I'd heard of it, believe me. He told you too, didn't he?"

"I'm sure you were astonished as I was." As I listen and walk, I glance around behind me a couple of times to see if Coop is nearby. If he is, I don't see him. Robbins stops, seemingly lost in thought for a moment. He turns to face me.

"Are you recording this? Are you working with the police?"

"No, why would you think that?"

"Because you've worked with the police before. For God's sake, your friend is a cop, and your girlfriend is an FBI agent." His voice rises in frustration to the point that several people stop and stare at us. Robbins glares back then loses it entirely. "What are you looking at? Fuck off."

I take his arm and guide him off the path, onto the sand. We walk toward one of the lifeguard stands. He takes a breath and stares out at the surf. "What do the police know for sure?"

"They know everything. They know Fuller wasn't strangled. He was already dead." I watch him closely. His reaction confirms everything. He just silently nods.

"I'd talked to him several times, but he wouldn't listen. He threatened to go to the police, open up that whole McElroy mess again. Don't you see? I couldn't afford for that to happen. The picture was well underway. No matter what I offered Fuller, it wasn't enough. He kept making more demands. Then the night I had dinner with Ryan and Melanie, he called and said he wanted to see me or he was going to the press with everything, including the tape."

"What tape?"

Robbins smiles slightly. "You didn't know about that? Fuller wasn't dumb. The night he covered for Ryan on Malibu Canyon, he recorded their whole conversation. That was his insurance to get anything he wanted. That tape would have ruined Ryan and the picture."

That I hadn't seen coming. That tape would be on the internet an hour after Fuller released it, and would show Ryan to be connected to McElroy's death.

"I left Mario's and went right to Fuller's. He was waiting for me, all smug and smirking, convinced he was going to get anything he wanted."

"More money?"

"No, he wanted an exclusive interview and photos with Ryan. I couldn't allow that."

"So what happened?"

"He turned his back and just walked away into his bedroom. You can't imagine how angry and frustrated I was. This arrogant prick in a trailer, smirking, dictating to me how he was going to bring down the whole production. I got angrier. I grabbed him by the shoulders, shook him, and shoved him back against the file cabinet." Robbins squeezes his eyes shut as he remembers. "I pushed him harder than I thought. He hit his head and just slid down to the floor, like it was in slow motion."

"Are you sure he was dead?"

"Oh, God yes, he was dead. There was no pulse. Nothing. I panicked. I didn't know what to do."

"You could have called the police."

"How could I explain being there? Would they have believed it was an accident? Because, Evan, I swear, it was an accident. I had parked outside the trailer park. I wanted to just run for my car and get out of there as fast as I could. Your mind does funny things sometimes. Fuller was dead. There was nothing I could do about that, but I could confuse things, throw the police off."

"That's when you called Anthony Torino."

Robbins stops and stares at me. "How did you know that?"

"When Coop and I were in your office, you made a comment about how horrible it was, Fuller being strangled with a camera strap. But you made one slip, when you said it was Nikon. The only way you could have known that was if you had been there, or Torino told you."

He nods. "I thought about it later. I didn't think anyone had caught it."

"So Torino came out, moved the body to make it look like a homicide."

"I guess he did. I didn't stay around. He told me later about using the camera strap."

"Why Torino?"

"We go back a long way, and I financed Mario's."

Neither of us says anything for awhile. We listen to the sound of the surf and feel the warmth of the sun as it breaks through more. I look back across the beach and see Coop coming toward us.

"What happens now?" Robbins asks.

"I think you know. I'm betting the police are already questioning Torino. You're going to have to tell the whole story, and I'll have to give a statement after what you've told me."

Robbins nods. He looks up and sees Coop nearing us. "I see you weren't taking any chances."

"Give me one reason why I should."

Robbins glances as Coop as he gets closer. "I can deny this whole conversation. Even if you give the police a statement, it's all hearsay. I have a good lawyer."

"I'm sure you do, but do you think Torino isn't going to give you up?"

Coop stops in front of us. "You gentlemen have an interesting talk?"

The three of us walk back to Coop's car. There's a black-and-white parked next to Coop's with two uniform cops waiting. Robbins is totally subdued now. One of the uniforms opens the back door. He starts to pull Robbins' hands behind him, but Coop shakes his head.

"No cuffs?"

"No, I don't think he'll give you any trouble." He shuts the door and we watch them start to pull away. Robbins gives me one last look, then turns to face forward.

Coop turns to me. "So, he tell you everything?"

"Pretty much. The only thing I didn't know about was the tape Fuller had."

"What tape?"

I tell Coop about what I think of now as the Malibu Canyon tape.

"Interesting. I wonder about Fuller being that smart."

"So do I. For all we know there was no tape. Ryan didn't know about it at all. Robbins never saw it or heard it. Maybe just the threat was enough to push Robbins over the edge."

Coop shrugs. "Could be. Farrell says they found nothing on Fuller's computer other than the e-mails. No tape. They went over every inch of the trailer. It does raise an interesting point."

"Ryan?"

"Without it, there's no reason to dredge up things with our movie star again. He didn't do the right thing. He let Fuller do it for him."

"That's it, then."

"Farrell will want you to make a statement at your convenience." He claps a hand on my shoulder. "You done good, sport. I'll let you know how this comes out. Go finish the music. You've earned it."

Two days later, Coop calls and we meet at his favorite Mexican restaurant, where he recaps Robbins' questioning with the District Attorney.

"He gave a full statement, with his lawyer present of course, and was released, pending charges. The D.A. is satisfied Fuller's death was an accident. It looks like Robbins could be charged with leaving the scene, and maybe involuntary manslaughter, but they have everything to work out a plea deal, and this is L.A., after all."

"What about Torino?"

"He's been arrested and charged with contaminating a crime scene, withholding information, obstructing justice. He's out on bail."

"That's all?"

"He didn't kill anybody. Fuller was already dead." Coop pauses for a minute, letting me digest everything. "Charlie Farrell agreed to keep you out of it." Coop sees I'm not convinced. He leans forward. "Sometimes we just have to work with what we have. Like I said, you done good."

"Somehow it doesn't feel like it."

What does it feel like? Later, back in my room I think about everything. Jerry Fuller's death was accounted for, and the two people responsible would suffer at least some consequences for their involvement. It wasn't perfect justice, but as Coop says, that was all they had. Grant Robbins would probably make a favorable deal, but there would be repercussions for him on the Hollywood scene. He would no doubt recover, but I wonder if his association with Ryan Stiles would survive. Given the way things are, box office receipts for *Murder in Blue* would probably determine things.

I spend the next ten days locked away with Skip Porter and Sandy Simmons for the final cut of the film, going through it scene by scene. There were a few more short cues to write, mostly solo piano themes, or a chord here and there, but in the end, Simmons is more than satisfied.

Skip grins and gives me a hug. "This was cool, man. Hope we do it again."

"Couldn't have done it without you."

Simmons says, "I'll be in touch. As soon as we get a distribution deal and a release date, I'll let you know." He gathers up his things, then pulls a padded envelope out of his bag. "This is for you. It's a little souvenir, a baseball cap for the film. Wear it with pride."

None of us refers to or mentions Grant Robbins once, pretending we haven't read the flurry of news stories, or seen the television coverage citing Robbins' arraignment and Anthony Torino's arrest. Most of them end with Grant Robbins being unavailable for comment.

◇◇◇

When I get to Burbank Airport, I return the rental car and go inside for my flight. I check one bag, and head for security with my carry-on. It's surprisingly quiet this afternoon, but they pull me aside and take my bag off the conveyer. I had forgotten about the envelope Simmons had given me, which I'd stuffed in my carry-on.

The TSA guy asks me to open the bag. He looks inside and pulls out the envelope. It's sealed and has my name scribbled on the front. "Will you open this, please?"

I pull the flap open and take out the blue cap. It's folded flat, and *Murder in Blue* is stitched on the front in gold lettering. The guard looks at the stitching then raises his eyes to mine.

"I just finished scoring the music for a movie. That's the title."

He nods and pushes my bag to me. "Have a nice flight."

I shove the envelope back in my bag and head for the gate.

The flight to Oakland is on time, and for once, so are the bags. In a little over an hour, I make it to baggage claim and walk outside. Andie is already waiting. She jumps out of her car when she sees me and rushes over for a hug and welcome home kiss.

"I see your escape from Hollywood was successful. Everything go okay?"

"Yep, all done, and they liked the music just fine."

I throw the larger bag in the trunk, and keep the carry-on with me. We get in the car and, as Andie pulls away and heads for the exit, I open my carry-on, and take out the envelope, and don the cap.

I grin at Andie. "I just scored a movie and all I got was this baseball cap."

Andie glances over. "Wow, I'm impressed. You can wear that all over town and let people ask what it means."

I take the cap off and start to put it back when I feel something rattle at the bottom of the envelope. I reach in take out a microcassette tape in a tiny plastic box. I stare at it for a moment.

Andie looks over. "What's that? Some of the music?"

"I don't know. I didn't know it was here or how it got in the envelope."

"I've got one of those micro recorders somewhere. You can play it when we to my place."

"I'm not sure I want to."

At Andie's, I grab a bottle of water out of the fridge while she digs around in her desk drawers. "Here we go," she says, holding up a pocket recorder. "I used it to tape some lectures."

I take the recorder from her and sit down on the couch. I put the tape in and press "play."

The first sound is a car door slamming, then a voice.

"Thanks for coming."

Andie looks at me. "That's Ryan, isn't it?"

I nod, hold up my hand, and turn up the volume.

"No problem. Tell me what happened." I'd never heard this voice before, but I know it's Jerry Fuller, and I know they're in Ryan's car on Malibu Canyon.

"It was that crazy photographer, McElroy. He started chasing me." I can hear the anxiety in Ryan's voice clearly. "We came around this curve. He was like, trying to cut me off. He pulled in front of me and went over the embankment. You gotta believe me, Jerry, it was an accident. I didn't know who else to call."

Andie looks at me. "You gotta be kidding."

"Okay, just calm down," Fuller continues. "Where did he go over?"

"Back there, about a hundred feet."

"Show me." We can hear doors opening and shutting, then the faint sound of them walking, their feet crunching on the shoulder of the road.

"Right here I think," Ryan says.

"Too dark to see anything down there," Fuller says. There's no sound for a few moments. I imagine them standing, looking down the embankment.

"You gotta help me, Jerry. I can't afford to be involved in this. You know how the press is."

Again there are a few moments of silence, then Fuller says, "Okay, you go home. I'll call the police and wait for them. I'll just say he passed me and I saw him lose control and go over the side. That's what happened, right? You didn't hit him, did you?"

"No." Ryan's answer is almost a wail. "I thought he was trying to run me off the road."

"Okay, I believe you. Go home. I'll take care of this."

"Thanks, Jerry. I owe you big time."

There's more silence, then the sound of a car starting and driving off.

"Yes you do." Then there's a click as Fuller turns off the recorder. I fast forward a ways, but there's nothing else.

I stop the tape and lean back, thinking this totally proves Ryan had been telling the truth all along. But how did the tape get in the envelope?

Andie says. "Any idea when it was sent?"

"None. Sandy Simmons, the director, gave it to me. I don't doubt if he knew the tape was in the envelope."

"What are you going to do with it?"

"I wish I knew."

Coda

When I get a call from Sandy Simmons two months later, I still don't know. "Evan, great news. It's not an A-list movie, but Ryan is an A-list star. We're opening in several key cities, and a premiere in Hollywood, red carpet and all."

"That's pretty fast, isn't it?"

"You bet it is. You'll get a formal invitation soon. Hope you can make it."

"Thanks for letting me know, Sandy."

A few days later, the invitation arrives and is followed up with a phone call from Ryan.

"How you doing, Piano Man?"

"Pretty good, Ryan. Just trying to keep busy."

"You going to make the premiere?"

"Probably not."

"I didn't think so." There's a moment of silence then, "Listen, sorry I didn't say goodbye. I just got, well you know, kind of busy."

"I understand."

"Look, I appreciate everything you did. I don't mean just teaching me about the piano or scoring the movie. You were a good friend when I needed one. I won't forget it."

"Neither will I."

"There's one more thing," Ryan says.

"What's that?"

"Melanie and I are getting married."

"Well, congratulations."

"Surprised, eh? That's what I'm calling about. We need a band for the reception at the Malibu house. You want the gig?"

I can't help but smile. "I don't know. I'm pretty expensive now, having scored a film."

Ryan laughs. "I think I can afford you. Get those other two guys from the movie, and bring Andie."

"Let me think about it."

A few days later, Andie comes back from the store, carrying two bags of groceries. She pulls a magazine out of one of the bags and drops it on my lap. "Have a look at this. I saw it at the checkout counter."

It's the latest copy of *People.* Ryan and Melanie are cheek to cheek, smiling on the cover. Inside, there's a brief story about their upcoming wedding and the release of *Murder in Blue.*

"You want to go?"

"Why not," Andie says. "I've never been to a Hollywood wedding. I was just thinking though."

"About?"

"What do you give a rich, famous, movie star as a wedding present?"

"I think I have just the thing."

A few days later, Coop calls. "I got some news about our friend Mr. Robbins. As I expected, there was a plea deal. No trial. Involuntary manslaughter. He got six months in county jail, a thousand hours of community service, and three years probation."

"So Robbins will be in orange overalls, picking up trash along the freeway?"

"Not likely. It'll probably be some kind of teaching gig, but we can always hope."

"What about Torino?"

"He got a year for tampering with evidence, contaminating a crime scene, and obstruction of justice."

"So that's it then."

"Looks like it. Have you decided what to do about the tape?"

I had told Coop about it and played it for him over the phone. "Yeah I have."

"Want to share?"

"Not yet. I'll let you know."

By Hollywood standards, the wedding is small. The date and time was a closely guarded secret. When Andie and I arrive, Broad Beach road is crawling with a private security force augmenting a dozen police cruisers. Andie and I have to show our invitation three times to get to Ryan's beach house. We're almost late.

The deck is festooned with streamers and pink and white balloons. Emillio bustles us down the steps to the beach where about a hundred people are gathered for the brief ceremony. Helicopters drone and circle overhead. I briefly think about Darryl McElroy, as I imagine what the photos will go for. This was one he wouldn't have missed.

Ryan and Melanie are both in white. Ryan in a suit, Melanie, looking gorgeous in a designer mini-length dress. When they kiss, there's some light applause over the sound of the waves and a toast, then everybody drifts back up to the house.

Gene Sherman and Buster Browne are both set up on the deck next to the electric piano. When Ryan and Melanie reach the top of the steps, I go into the Charlie Parker blues, "Now's The Time." Ryan looks over and gives me the thumbs up sign and that megawatt grin.

I see Ryan's parents mingling with the crowd. Bonnie Stiles looks over once and catches my eye, but doesn't come over or say anything. We play for an hour, then join the crowd for the catered buffet set up and overseen by Emillio.

"Damn," Buster says. "That's Tom Cruise and Katie Holmes over there talking to George Clooney." He looks at me. "This is the most far-out gig I've ever done."

"Buster, you have no idea."

Later, as things start to settle down, Ryan pulls me aside. "Thanks for coming, Piano Man, and especially for playing." He slips an envelope in my hand. "Everything cool?"

"Perfect. You made my bass player's day. Where's the honeymoon?"

Ryan leans in closer. "Top secret. One of the Caribbean Islands. We're going straight to the airport from here."

I take out the tape, still in it's little plastic box, and drop it in Ryan's coat pocket. "Little something for you. Open it later."

Andie and I pick a theater in downtown San Francisco that features independent films. Despite Ryan Stiles being the star of *Murder in Blue*, there are no long lines at the box office. I buy the tickets and we go inside where I spot a sign at the snack bar: REAL BUTTER ON OUR POPCORN.

I get us a large tub and two drinks, and we make our way into the theater. We take seats near the back. There are only a few patrons already there ahead of us.

"Small crowd," Andie says.

"Don't worry. Eat some popcorn."

Even though I'd seen the film scores of times and was familiar with every frame, I wanted to see it in a darkened theater with other people. The lights go down and we sit through trailers for coming attractions, then the screen goes black and I hear myself playing, see my hands in close-up on the keyboard as the opening credits start to roll.

Andie grips my arm. "I'm excited," she whispers.

As the camera pulls back we see Gene Sherman, Buster Browne, and Ryan at the piano.

"It's not fair," Andie says. "We should be seeing your face."

Finally, in about a minute we see the words that should have made it all worth it.

Original Music Composed and Arranged
by Evan Horne

To receive a free catalog of Poisoned Pen Press titles, please contact us in one of the following ways:

Phone: 1-800-421-3976
Facsimile: 1-480-949-1707
Email: info@poisonedpenpress.com
Website: www.poisonedpenpress.com

Poisoned Pen Press
6962 E. First Ave. Ste. 103
Scottsdale, AZ 85251